NOT MADE TO LAST

JAY McLEAN

Cover Art: Books and Moods

Formatting: Jay McLean

Editing: Tricia Harden

For Tricia Harden
The Jordan to my Pippen

AUTHOR NOTE

Not Made to Last contains sensitive subject matters that may be
triggering to some individuals.
A list of content and trigger warnings can be found on my website.
www.jaymcleanauthor.com/nmtl

PART I

1

Olivia

Standing over the lifeless body, I nudge it with my toe and watch it shift an inch.

I'm being dramatic.

Obviously.

So is the person I just hit with my car. *Hit* would be a slight exaggeration. I tapped it.

Him.

Not *it*.

But, going by how he's lying on his side in the middle of the road, completely silent and unmoving, you'd think I ran him over with a semi at full speed. I was rolling to a stop when he came out of nowhere—dressed in all black, in the middle of the night—and now that I think about it... I'm pretty sure he hit me.

"Are you okay?" I ask, waiting a few seconds for a response that never comes. "I'm sorry." I hunch down with my hands on my knees for a closer inspection. The headlights on my still-running truck illuminate the space around him, but I can't see much of anything with his hood over his head the way it is. He's tall, built, and that's all I can make out from his fetal position.

I take a moment to calm my thoughts, stand to full height, and look around. We're in a part of town that I often frequent, not because I'm invited, but because my second job brings me here. I'd just delivered a pizza to a house a block away—the most lavish home I've ever come across. I'm sure if I looked up the address online, it would be described as an estate, whatever that means. Either way, it's pretty clear that my beat-up old Toyota Tacoma and I—we don't belong.

Here, I'm surrounded by the rich.

Not rich.

Wealthy.

Big difference.

Not that any of it matters. If my eighteen years on this earth have taught me one thing, it's that at our cores, we're all the same. We're nothing but flesh and bones and organs; entire bodies that are over-worked, minds that overthink, and hearts that have the potential to break.

We wake up every day with goals set, hoping for that tiny piece of joy we obtain when we achieve them—all the while knowing in the back of our minds that we have absolutely zero control over this shit-show of a thing called life.

Pessimistic? Maybe. But it's also the truth. And it's not as if I share these thoughts with anyone, because that would be horrible. Life is crappy enough—there's really no need for the reminder. Besides, people my age are made to believe they have the world at their feet. We can achieve anything, so we've been told, and I'm sure as hell not going to be the one to break it to anyone.

I heave out a sigh and blink back the fog, forgetting momentarily about the possible dead body by my feet.

He still hasn't moved.

I feel like I've been standing here for an eternity. In reality, it's likely been less than a minute.

Squatting down, I gently settle my hand on his arm. "Where are you hurt?" I ask.

Nothing.

"Can I do anything?"

Still nothing.

"Do you need me to call an ambulance... or take you to the emergency room? I..." I don't know what to do here, and now I'm starting to panic because maybe I did hit him.

The body moves.

Groans.

Progress.

I release the breath I'd unknowingly been holding and attempt to refocus.

"Ohana?" Max calls from the back seat of the car. "What's happening?"

Shit.

Shit shit shit.

At the sound of Max's voice, the figure moves again, and when his face comes into view, my panic doubles.

Triples.

"Ohana?" Max again.

I keep my gaze on the confused gray eyes in front of me and, not knowing if I'm lying, say over my shoulder, my words aimed for Max, "It's okay, buddy. Everything's fine."

It takes a moment for my victim to roll to his back, tilt his head up, then speak. "Drive much?" he croaks.

All the air rushes from my lungs at the sound of his voice. I used to spend hours imagining it, then, later, re-watching whatever clips I could find of him online. But I'd never heard it in person.

Until now.

Rhys.

Thank fuck I don't whisper his name out loud like I do in my head.

Rhys. Rhys. Rhys.

As in Rhys Garrett—co-captain of the St. Luke's basketball team and, of course, the most popular and powerful guy roaming that school. Or at least he was. From my understanding, he graduated a few weeks ago, and I... I know way more about him than I should. Especially considering he has absolutely no idea who I am.

Nervous energy crawls through my veins, and thoughts fly through my mind faster than I can catch them. It sucks that the one thought I latch on to is: please don't sue me. "Are you okay?" I extend my hand, praying he's well enough to take it. "I'm sorry." Sorry that he came out of nowhere and got in my way.

Rhys accepts my offer, his large hand dwarfing mine as he slowly comes to a stand. I try my best to help him up, but with his towering height and nothing but muscle, I doubt I'm having much effect. Finally, he lets go of my hand and twists slightly at the waist, soothing his palm along his right hip. His low wince slices through the summer night air, and he states, "Yes."

I look from his hip to his hand, hanging lazily at his side, then up the length of his body until my eyes meet his. "Yes?"

"Yes," he repeats.

"Yes... you're okay?"

"Ohana?" Max calls out again.

I glance over my shoulder, through my car's windshield, and to the back seat, where Max's face is lit up by his iPad. "One second," I call out, then look back up at Rhys, my neck straining from our height difference—my 5'4" to his 6'3", and... I catch myself there, at the absolute peak of pathetic.

Look.

It's not as if I stalk the guy, but his height is listed on most websites that include his name, and it's right there beside his weight and a line above his birthday. Which, if I'm not mistaken, was only a few days ago. He just turned nineteen. All information which is completely irrelevant to our current circumstance. "So, you're good?" I ask.

"No, I'm not good." He shakes his head, eyes unfocused as he looks down his nose at me. "So, yes, take me to the emergency room." Without another word, he moves slowly to my car, a noticeable limp in his swagger, and all I can do is watch, frozen, wondering how the hell I got into this situation.

Because I offered to take him?

I didn't mean it. Not really.

Rhys opens the front passenger door, illuminating the interior. Illuminating Max.

I rush to get in the driver's seat, my pulse racing, and glance from Rhys to Max and back again. My supposed "injured victim" sits care-free, legs kicked out, hands resting on his thighs. A slow smirk forms on his lips as his gaze switches between Max and me. Eyes the color of slate, he homes in on mine, his head tilting slightly. "You're not from around here, are you?" he murmurs.

I'm in denim shorts and a plain white tank, no makeup, my hair in a messy knot. My brow bunches as I glare at him. "I didn't realize my attire screamed 'lacking financial wealth.'" I should've hit the gas the moment I saw him.

He sighs, rolling his eyes dramatically. "That's not what I meant."

I don't care what you meant, I say. Not out loud. Just to myself. Because fuck him and his judgmental ass. I face forward, put the truck in gear, and begin the drive, waiting until I've rounded a corner to glance up at the rearview, at Max in the back seat, headphones on, eyes focused on his iPad. I'll be sure to check in on him later.

Rhys must sense my concern because he turns his entire body around, his injury seemingly forgotten. "You okay, kid?"

Through the rearview, I see Max look up and nod once.

Rhys extends his arm, his hand a fist, ready for knuckles. "I'm—"

"Timothy!" I cut in. *Timothy?* It was the first name I could think of, and I blurted it out before I could stop myself. Max doesn't need to know who he is. In fact, I'd highly prefer it that way.

"Right." Rhys draws out the single word. "Timothy." The humorous lilt in his tone has me cringing. He's still facing Max when he asks, "And you are?"

Without thinking, I reach out, place my hand on the side of his head and force him to face forward. "He's... off limits."

2

Rhys

Off limits?

The fuck does that mean?

If this girl has a kid, then... it's whatever—no big deal.

Maybe she's ashamed of having a kid young, out of wedlock or whatever. I don't know. The things people are self-conscious about these days blow my mind.

Ignoring the dull ache pulsating from my hip, I glance behind me again. The boy's around five or six, dark-skinned, with thick glasses sitting crooked on his nose. Then, I focus on the girl behind the wheel. If I had to guess, I'd say she's my age, give or take a year. Dark hair piled high on her head, perfectly straight nose, and rounded cheeks—stained pink from her blush.

She's cute; there's no doubting it, but considering what's transpired the past few minutes, she might also be insane.

Just my type.

I peek over at the kid again. Maybe he's not hers, at least biologically. Not unless his dad's genetics are far stronger than hers. It's possible. Or perhaps she's just babysitting. But then why not just say that?

Why attempt to shield us from each other? Also, why the fuck am I Timothy?

Hmm... now I'm intrigued.

And my intrigue never ends well.

"So..." I start, unsure where to go from here. "How are you?" Odd thing to ask considering what got us here, but what else is there to say?

"You mean besides hitting you with my truck hard enough that I have to take you to emergency?" Her eyes flick to mine, muddy brown beneath long, dark lashes. "I'm doing... fine..." The last word comes out as a question, and she focuses on the road again.

I focus on her.

On her teeth as they clamp down on her full bottom lip—worrying. On her eyebrows as they lower with each passing second. On her eyes as they continuously shift from me to the road and back again.

I bite back a smile, because she looks like a modern-day Snow White, only, unlike the fairy tale, this little princess wasn't wandering through a forest and stumbling across a cottage. No. Tonight, she was driving around in an old truck... and slamming straight into me.

Some might call it fate.

Kismet.

A series of unfortunate events.

"Everything okay?" she asks quietly, glancing at me quickly with her eyebrows raised. She just caught me watching her. Staring at her. Scrutinizing every damn inch of her.

Do I care?

Not even a little bit.

I've already decided that her cheeks are her best feature. At least on her face. I'll be sure to study the rest of her later.

"How bad are you hurt?" she adds, the softness in her voice conveying her concern.

"I'm all right." I shrug, trying to play it cool, but my eyes drop to her legs, all smooth skin and thick thighs, and sure, maybe an illicit thought crosses my mind, but now's not really the time to voice them.

Besides, she seems too nice for that.

Too pure.

Too... sweet.

Like a perfect little porcelain doll.

Breakable.

All assumptions, of course, because I don't know shit about the girl.

I know enough, based on her clothes and the car she drives, that she doesn't come from money, and I have no idea what she was doing in my neighborhood, and the more I think about it, the more the whole babysitting theory makes sense.

Am I being judgmental? Absolutely. But am I lying? Nah.

My phone rings, pulling me from my thoughts, and I quickly shove my hand into my hoodie pocket to retrieve it. I silence the call without ever fully comprehending who's calling.

"Was that your parents?"

I scoff at the thought. "No."

"Is someone looking for you?" she asks, the panic in her voice palpable. And now I'm starting to feel guilty for using her like this.

"Maybe," I murmur. Unlikely, though. I doubt anyone partying at my house even realizes I'm gone. At that thought, I'm reminded of why I left in the first place. Quickly shoving my phone back where it belongs, I stare out the window and re-evaluate my life choices.

The party had barely reached its peak when I determined I needed to get the fuck out of there. Granted, I was the one to invite them, but still...

Here's the thing: I live in an obnoxiously large house, and for the most part, I'm there alone.

Alone and lonely.

So, I throw these mini ragers on the fly, and people turn up. Lots of them. Most are nameless, sometimes even faceless, and it's only once they pack the place with bodies that my sense kicks in.

Somehow, amid the awareness of being lonely, I forget the not-so-insignificant fact that I hate people. Can't stand them, to be honest.

So, I leave.

Which is what I did tonight. I changed out of my jeans and T-shirt and got into sweats—black, to mix in with the night. I escaped through one of the guest bedroom balconies, jumping onto the roof of the first level, then leaped onto the ground like a stealthy fucking ninja. Then, I crept into the darkness of the woods surrounding my property and ran.

I had no real clue where to go, not that I ever do. I simply wanted to get as far away as possible, as soon as possible.

I wasn't looking where I was going or what was around me. I didn't even see the headlights. Just felt the impact. And I thought, as strange as it is, that getting hit by a car may be the best thing that could've happened to me tonight.

It was almost comical.

Until I felt the pain.

So, I lay on the ground, and I didn't move. Didn't even lift my head.

I didn't get up.

Couldn't.

Not because I was being a pussy, or because I hurt, or even because I didn't want to face the person standing above me.

I didn't get up because... sometimes, I feel as if this life, this world, isn't worth getting up for at all.

3

Rhys

I wait by the nurse's station at the emergency room while Little Miss Lead-Foot stands just outside the entrance, phone held to her ear in one hand and the "off-limits" boy in the other. Carrying his backpack on both shoulders, he looks up at her, his blinks slow. It's probably way past his bedtime, and that guilt from earlier returns, weighs heavier on my chest.

"Can I help you?" a female voice pulls my attention away, and I turn to the nurse behind the desk—a middle-aged woman with tired eyes and a forced smile. Her shoulders are hunched, her tone weary, and with a job such as hers, I don't blame her.

"Hi." I give her my most genuine smile and say, "I got hit by a car earlier."

The look she gives me shows her skepticism. After making her way around the desk, she stands in front of me and quickly examines me from head to toe. From the outside, I look perfectly normal. "It wasn't too bad," I mutter. "I'm just a little..." A little what? "Banged up."

The nurse—Marion—going by her name tag, hesitates. "Where exactly?"

"Uh... my hip. Thigh..."

Marion heaves out a sigh and makes her way back behind the desk. "Okay, so a banged-up body?" she questions, looking around the waiting area. There are at least twenty people here; a group of girls in one corner, but mainly guys scattered around, a few with obvious injuries. There's a kid with a clearly broken arm, and one dude has a blood-stained rag held to his temple. And here I am, able to walk, talk, and give Marion my details when she asks for them. At the mention of my last name, her eyes widen. Just a tad. "Garrett?"

I nod.

"As in—"

My second nod cuts her off, and she smiles the biggest, *fakest* smile, her weariness from earlier completely diminished.

A few years back, my parents donated an entire wing in the children's ward at this very hospital and named it after my sister. The Isabel Garrett Wing provides temporary housing for kids undergoing treatment, with enough room for parents and guardians to stay with them.

My sister has never spent a day here. Ever.

I'm not saying it's a bad thing. I'd much rather their money go here than, say, my old high school—which they've done in the past—to bury whatever minor mishap or predicament I found myself in. It's just... it's hard to be a Garrett in this town.

Poor little rich boy, right?

Even without my last name sprawled on the walls of this hospital, I'm almost positive Marion would have the same reaction. We're known around here, or at least my parents are. They're business owners. Venture capitalists. Philanthropists. Millionaires.

And they're not the only ones. Most of the people in my neighborhood have similar titles. The difference between them and us is that they come from old money—generational wealth.

My parents made theirs after Izzy and I were born.

"I'm sure we can have someone check you out right away," Marion says, typing away on her keyboard.

I glance around the room again, at the other people in far worse condition than myself, and then to the entrance as my forced companions make their way inside. "You know what?" I tell Marion. "Just add me to the end of the list." Seriously? What the fuck kind of asshole would I be if I expected preferential treatment on a medical issue just because my parents have money? Besides, the longer the wait, the longer it is until I'm forced to go home and face my living hell.

Marion glances at her colleagues working beside her, uncertain.

My smile is almost pleading. "Please?"

"If you say so..." She taps a few buttons on the keyboard before looking up at me. "We have all your details in the system." Then she motions to the waiting area. "Please take a seat, Mr. Garrett."

I inwardly cringe at her words.

Mr. Garrett is my father.

I'm merely his disappointment.

4

Olivia

"I hope you don't have any plans tonight," Rhys says as we approach him standing by the nurse's station. "We're going to be here a while." Without waiting for a response, he leads us to a row of seats where Max plops down on a chair, his eyelids heavy. I take the seat beside him.

Luckily, our minor incident didn't affect Max as much as I thought it would. But he's tired now. Beyond it. And honestly, so am I. I didn't expect my hit-and-stay victim to actually accept my offer to drive him here, and I definitely didn't expect to have to wait. Rhys is a *Garrett*, and that means something.

Rhys is still standing, hands at his sides as he looks around the space. With his eyes busy elsewhere, I allow myself a moment to take him in.

To really, *truly* look at him.

I'd only ever seen pictures of him clean-shaven. Now, he's got the later stages of what I would call scruff. It's the same dirty blond as the short, almost crew-cut style that's on his head.

He looks older than his nineteen years.

Tougher.

And all the above is only magnified by the harsh overhead lights that create shadows across his features, highlighting the multiple tiny, almost inconspicuous, scars on his face.

The first time Rhys was brought to my attention, I assumed he was "troubled." The kind of problematic over-privileged kid who spent his free time getting off on using random people as punching bags for shits and gigs. Or, more than likely, to see if it would get his parents' attention.

I was wrong on all accounts.

As far as I know, he's never been disciplined for fighting at school, or outside of it, for that matter. In fact, the only time I'm aware of any reprimands handed to him by St. Luke's was for some bullshit prank that involved a child-sized dildo and some heavy-duty superglue on the front doors of the most prestigious high school in all of North Carolina —his own.

Unfortunately for him, his urge to pull such stupid antics hit right before the regional semifinals. It cost him a game and his beloved team a possible championship.

The day after the loss, a video of him being interviewed by a local news station circulated like wildfire, went viral on most social media. When asked if he regretted his actions, Rhys took a moment to respond, looking pensive, before asking the interviewer if he thought a hundred unarmed men could take on an adult-size gorilla.

To anyone else watching it, he came off as aloof, almost unsympathetic. It showed Rhys as just another rich, entitled, fuckboy idiot who gave very little shits about his life, especially his team. But I knew better. I knew *him* better. His team was everything to him, though he'd never admit it to anyone.

Suddenly, Rhys's eyes flick down to mine, and I quickly look away, try to refocus on the present. On Max. He's holding on to my arm, his eyes half-hooded, fighting to stay awake. "Lie down, bud," I tell him, helping him kick off his flip-flops. He does as I say, while I grab his iPad and headphones from his backpack for him. When I look up again, Rhys is gone... back to the nurse's station. It's clear he asks something of them, because they nod enthusiastically at whatever he says, and one disappears through the large double doors, returning a moment later with a hospital-issued blanket. Without a word, Rhys approaches and —wordlessly—covers Max with the blanket, making sure it surrounds his entire body. He stands to full height again before reaching behind him and grasping the back of his hoodie. He lifts the hem higher, higher, exposing the tanned skin covering his flat, toned stomach and the smattering of hairs that lead to—

I look away.

Ignore the way my heart flies to my throat.

It's nothing, I convince myself.

This reaction?

Completely normal.

Rhys's hoodie feels warm on my bare legs when he unceremoniously drops it on my lap. Then he sits down beside me, his arm touching mine.

"Umm..." I look from the hoodie to him.

"You're cold." It's not a question.

"I'm fine," I lie. Truth is, the moment we walked into the building, the harsh air-conditioning pricked at my skin and turned my flesh to ice.

Rhys half turns to me, his gray Nike shirt shifting, pulling tight across his muscled chest. The heat of his hand circles my wrist, spreading through my bloodline. He's gentle when he lifts my arm, and I hold my breath, watching those cool gray eyes of his as they lock on mine. Then, slowly, he runs a finger across the length of my arm, exposing my lies as more goosebumps rise, crawl across my skin. "Wear the damn hoodie."

I glare at him.

He glares back.

And... I wear the damn hoodie.

It's way too big, or I'm way too small, but either way, it's nice. Warm. Smells *delicious*. "What is this?" I murmur, sniffing the neckline.

"A hoodie," he deadpans.

I contain my eye roll. "The smell, you idiot."

He chuckles. "I don't know. Body wash?"

I sniff it again. "Man, you must have some bougie-ass body wash."

He doesn't reply.

Minutes of silence pass.

Max sighs in his sleep.

Finally, Rhys leans forward to look at him, his lips ticked up on one side. "Do you just have the one?" he asks, settling back in his seat.

"One what?"

"Kid," he replies. "Is he your only one?"

I shift my eyes up to his and raise my eyebrows.

"Right." He nods once. "I forgot... *off limits.*" He taps at his temple. "Timothy will keep that in mind." After a heavy exhale, he asks, "Is your name really Honor?"

Confused, I keep my head down and ask, "Honor?"

"Your kid or whatever—that's what he called you, right?"

"Ohana," I provide, shaking my head. "And no, it's a nickname. It's um..." I clear my throat, suddenly anxious. "...it's from *Lilo and Stitch.*"

He shrugs, seemingly uninterested. "Never seen it." More silence passes, and he slumps lower in his seat, kicking out his legs and crossing them at the ankles. "So... are you going to offer your name, or should I just keep referring to you as my attempted murderer?"

"Shut up," I whisper, looking around the room to see if anyone heard him. "And it's Olivia."

"Olivia..." He seems to turn over each syllable in his mind—all while his gaze skims each of my features. "Suits you."

What am I supposed to say to that? *Thank you?*

"I'm Rhys, by the way," he offers, getting more comfortable. "You know... just in case you cared about the guy you almost killed." He smirks, and my stomach does this weird thing I haven't felt in years. "But you already know who I am, don't you?" It's not so much a question as it is a statement, and he says it in a way that's almost... teasing.

I admit the truth, however cringeworthy it is. "I know *of* you."

"Yeah, most people around here do," he mumbles, nodding slowly, before looking away and glancing around the room.

I stay quiet, but inside, my mind is racing, trying to come up with excuses to get the hell out of here.

"Hey, thanks for hanging around," he says, tilting his head toward me.

I lower my gaze, murmur, "Yeah, well, I'm kind of the reason you're here, right?"

"Not kind of," he's quick to respond. "You *are* the reason."

Ouch. And also: *fuck off.* "What the hell were you doing dressed in all black creeping around at night, anyway?" I'm defensive, and so I should be. He can't place all the blame on me.

He lifts his head, nose up in the air like he owns the air we breathe. "I fail to see why that matters."

Dick. "Oh, I'm sorry." My sarcasm is palpable. "Did I ruin your night of breaking and entering, burglary and debauchery?"

"Debauchery?" He laughs once. "And breaking and entering and burglary are the same thing."

Of course he's trying to outsmart me. "No, they're not."

"Yes, they are!" He pulls out his phone, taps it a few times, then reads aloud. "Burglary offenses are often referred to as breaking and entering or unlawful entry."

I roll my eyes. "You were practically asking for this to happen."

"You realize you hit me with your giant truck, right?" he almost yells.

I match his tone. "You realize I was going, like, two miles an hour. Right?"

He shakes his head, shouting, "You're unbelievable!"

"Right back at ya!"

"What's going on over here?" a man calls out, approaching us quickly. He's in navy scrubs and a white coat, his credentials visible by the hospital-issued ID clipped to his breast pocket. Gripping the stethoscope around his neck, he stops only feet in front of us, his gaze shifting from me to Rhys, and back again. "You're Mr. Garrett?" The doctor, a man close to retirement, asks.

Rhys slowly gets to his feet. "Rhys is fine, sir," he states.

Doc heaves out a sigh, saying, "Well, I was told I had to come out and see you immediately." Ah, so the Garrett name does work like magic, just as I thought it would. "Besides feeling the need to have a shouting match in the middle of the waiting room, what seems—"

"We weren't—" I attempt to interrupt, but Rhys cuts me off.

"I got hit by a car."

I grimace.

"Did they stop?" the doctor asks.

Rhys is *too* quick to respond. "Nah, they bailed before I could get any info."

The doctor looks Rhys up and down for any obvious signs of injury. "Where are you hurt?"

Rhys looks around the waiting room before a slow smirk creeps across his features. It's so slight that I may be the only one to notice. Then, without warning or a second's hesitation, he grasps the band of his sweats *and* boxer shorts and pushes them down one side, past his hip, only stopping once he reaches the middle of his thigh. Clouds of red, green, and purple form over his skin, and I outwardly wince in response. And then I notice the other parts of him exposed: that smattering of hair again, the deep V that leads to the base of his—

Girls behind me break out in giggles, and I force my eyes away.

Jesus. I said that out loud. *Ah, shit.*

"You like that, huh?" Rhys murmurs, and when I flick my gaze to his, his eyebrows are raised, his teeth showing with his cocky smile.

Flames of embarrassment lick across my flesh, up my neck, to the tips of my ears. And, of course, it's not enough that I'm practically at eye level with forbidden dick, but now the doctor is inspecting his injuries and asking questions.

Lots of them.

For minutes that feel like hours, I sit ramrod straight, my heart racing, my blood simmering just beneath the surface. I stare at the ceiling as if Michaelangelo himself painted it. I don't think I take a breath. Not one.

Completely normal reaction, I try to remind myself, again, only it's getting harder and harder to believe.

Speaking of hard...

"You can pull your pants up now," the doctor says.

Thank God.

Swear, the girls in the corner audibly groan in disappointment.

"Aw, do I have to?" Rhys smirks over at them. "I think my audience likes the show."

Smug.

It's the only way to describe him.

Rhys Garrett is a smug motherfucker.

And I'm only just realizing it now.

5

Olivia

After getting advice from the doctor to ice his wounds, Rhys lifts Max into his arms and carries him all the way to my truck. Max never wakes. It's a thoughtful move—one I wasn't expecting.

I buckle Max into his car seat, making sure he's safe, and then get behind the wheel. Already in the passenger's seat, Rhys watches me, his arms crossed as if contemplating my next move. I start the car, and then... I just sit there because I have no idea where to go from here.

Literally and figuratively.

I have so many thoughts racing through my mind, and I push away all the forbidden ones first. "I'm sorry," I blurt out. "I honestly didn't think I hit you that hard, but it looks—"

"Worse than it feels," Rhys finishes for me. "I've had more serious injuries playing ball."

I nod, assuming as much. Though, I doubt he would've gone to the hospital for those, so why now? "Hey, why did you tell the doctor it was a hit-and-run?"

He seems distracted when he answers, "I wasn't sure if they had to report it to the cops. I didn't want to get you in trouble."

I never even thought of that.

He adds, "I'm not going to sue you if that's what you're worried about."

A giggle forms in my chest, but never escapes. "Not gonna lie, the thought did cross my mind."

He stares ahead as he shifts in his seat. "Of course it did," he mumbles. But the way he says it—as if it's all he expects from the world —it's kind of... sad.

"I mean... if I recall correctly, I offered to take you even before I knew who you were, so..." I'm trying to console him, and I don't know why. "I would've done it, either way."

"Yeah, but would you have stayed?" he asks, his focus on me again.

Honestly? "Probably not."

"That's what I thought."

Silence stretches between us, and I don't know what else to do. What else to say. I put the car in gear. "I should probably take you home."

He releases a long, drawn-out sigh, his head rolling against the headrest. "What if..." he starts, then shakes his head.

"What if... what?"

Another sigh. "I want to ask you something, but I don't want you to take it the wrong way."

This can't be good. My hands grip the steering wheel tighter as I tell him, "Ask me anyway."

"You guys gotta be somewhere?" He pauses a moment. "I mean, do you have to get your kid home?" I don't get a chance to respond before he adds, "Because I'm thinking we drive somewhere and... hang out. We can sit in your car and just... talk."

"Um..."

"Or not talk. Just, you know, stare blankly at the space in front of us..."

"I don't—"

"I'll give you all the cash in my wallet."

"As if you carry cash." That was not what I meant to say.

What I meant to say was *no*.

As in... *hell* no.

"I do." His smile is almost wicked—as if he can somehow sense my temptation. "A lot of it."

"How much?" *Ugh.* I could do with "a lot" of cash, and I'm sure his standards of measurement are far greater than mine.

"You'll have to wait and see."

I can't believe I'm even entertaining this. "For how long?"

He pulls out his phone and, at lightning speed, sends out a text. Almost immediately, there's a response. "One thirty."

I check the time: 11:45.

I check my tank: empty.

"I'm low on gas."

"So go fill up. I'll cover that, too."

I take in a sharp breath, then rest my back against the door, eyeing him. He stares right back. But the flicker of light in his eyes is gone, and he's no longer the cocky boy who brazenly dropped trou in the middle of the waiting room. Now, he seems smaller somehow, less... confident, maybe? "You're really desperate not to go home, huh?"

His voice is quiet, almost a whisper when he says, "You could say that."

"Want to tell me why?"

He shakes his head, eyebrows lowering. "It's not anything that would warrant your concern."

I stare into his eyes and try to seek the answers there. He watches me back, his gaze moving from my eyes to my nose. My mouth.

"What do you say, *Cheeks*?"

"Cheeks?"

"I like your cheeks," he replies. "They're... pinchable."

Heat rushes to said cheeks, and I attempt to hide it with a scoff that sounds more like a snort. "You want to pinch my cheeks?"

"Why?" That cocky smirk is back. "You going to let me?"

Circles. That's what we seem to do every time we talk. Go around and around and around in circles. "No, I will not let you pinch my cheeks." I sound like an indignant snob.

"Fair call," he says, so nonchalant—and I don't know why it's getting under my skin. "So... what do you say? Feel like getting paid to spend the night with me?" He shakes his head, chuckling. "I didn't realize that would come out so creepy."

Surprisingly, I find myself laughing with him. "Until one thirty," I confirm. "And then I take you home."

"So that's a yes?"

I suck in all the air my lungs can handle, release it slowly. "I'll do it on one condition."

He blinks.

"You have to tell me why you don't want to go home."

"Deal," he's quick to say. "I'll tell you once we get there."

"Get where?"

"I know a place."

6

Rhys

Apart from some small chatter at the gas station and me giving Olivia directions, we don't speak. Besides, I was too busy on my phone searching up Lilo and Stitch.

Lilo and Stitch is a movie about a lonely little Hawaiian girl who, along with her much older sister, loses her parents, thus making the sister her guardian. In order to bring some form of order into their lives, Nani (the sister) allows Lilo (the little girl) to adopt a dog (Stitch), who ends up being an extraterrestrial being from outer space. Spoiler alert: shit happens. A lot of it. But, through all of the absolute mayhem that occurs (which includes visits from a social worker), Nani never once stops fighting for Lilo. And through their love, faith, and a little Elvis, the trio never falters in their unwavering belief in Ohana, the Hawaiian concept of family. It's repeated throughout the movie that "Ohana means family, and that means nobody is left behind"... or something like that.

Anyway...

I can tell Olivia's wary of where we are and who she's with, but she doesn't voice her concerns.

I'd be wary, too, I guess.

It's not every day a random stranger leads you to a rooftop parking lot of an unoccupied building in the dead of night, but here we are.

Had it not been for the security gates on the ground floor and me having to lean over her to enter the passcode, I'm sure she would have physically kicked me out of her car by now.

As soon as Olivia parks, I open the door and hop out. The cool night air hits my lungs, and I head right for the edge of the parking lot. The cement half-wall is low enough for me to lean my forearms on, and so I do and look down over the edge of the building. Where we stand is only four floors high, and at an average of 15.5 feet per floor, that would make us 62 feet from the ground. At 200 pounds myself, it would mean I'd hit the ground at forty-three miles per hour. The fall itself would take less than two seconds.

Give or take.

Thanks, fifth-period physics.

It's not that I've actually considered jumping. I just get curious about these things.

About death.

Not the finality of death or even the act of dying. More like... what would happen if?

At only four floors up, death wouldn't be instant, if at all. Unless you land directly on your head, you'll likely have a few minutes of pure agony before you suffocate on your own blood and bleed out through the holes made from all the broken bones you created.

Pretty damn interesting if you ask me.

Footsteps near, and for a moment, I'd forgotten I wasn't alone. "So... you come here often?" Olivia quips.

I don't turn to her when I say, "I do, actually." At least once a week. Twice if I feel like I need it.

Stopping next to me, she mimics my position and looks down at the alley between the two buildings. There's really nothing to see besides dumpsters and drainpipes. "Well, I can see why..." She pauses a beat. "This is some view...." The girl's got jokes, and usually, I'd be all about it. Right now, though, I can't bring myself to feel much of anything.

"Yeah," I murmur. "I don't really come here for the view." I come here for the escape.

Or maybe it's the opposite.

I haven't figured it out yet.

Olivia's quiet a moment, and I can only imagine the thoughts bouncing around that pretty little head of hers. "Are we currently committing what one would call burglary..." she says, and I finally turn to her, my head tilted, watching her profile as she takes in our surroundings. I wonder what it would be like to see this place from her eyes. To see it for the first time.

"Would that be a problem?"

"Well, yeah." She offers a smile, and I wish I knew what it meant. "I'm not, like, poor, but I don't have fuck-you money to throw around, and neither does my family, so bail money? Kind of out of the question."

I've already decided that I like the girl. I like that she doesn't bow down to bullshit or worship whatever version of me she's admitted to knowing. I like that she pushes back, that she doesn't take shit she doesn't deserve.

Most of all, though, I like that she's present.

That she's here.

With me.

"I'd bail you out," I murmur, glancing over at her truck. It's only a few yards away with the parking lights on. Usually, when I come here, I sit in the darkness, the moon and stars my only source of light. Of life. I try to peer inside her truck to make sure her kid's okay. "Is he good in there?" I ask, stepping toward it.

Olivia follows me, saying, "The windows are open, and once he's out, he's out. Plus, I left the lights on so if he wakes, he can see us."

"Are you sure, because—"

She tugs on my arm, forcing me to stop, and I do, momentarily dazed by her touch. And not in a creepy Edward loves Bella way, but I don't know. It's surprising, is all.

I spin to face her, my lips instantly forming a smile when I see her standing there, hands on her hips, nose in the air, like an adorably annoying little brat. "I haven't forgotten," she says, and I have no fucking clue what she's talking about.

I tilt my head, confused. "Forgotten what?"

"That you owe me a truth."

My shoulders drop.

"Why don't you want to go home, Rhys?"

I shrug. "There's a party at my house tonight."

"Oh, yeah?" she asks, distracted by her phone. She taps it a few times, and when I peek over at the screen, I see that she's setting an alarm. Great. She can't wait to get the hell away from me. And me? I can't seem to get enough of her. Shoving her phone into her back pocket, she asks, "What's the occasion?"

"There is none."

"So... who's hosting it?"

I move toward the basketball hoop I keep in the corner of the parking lot, and with my back turned, answer, "Me, apparently."

"Rhys!" she gasps. "How does that even happen?"

I shrug, shifting the weights off the base of the hoop before dragging it toward the middle of the lot. The entire time I keep my eyes on the kid in the truck, make sure he doesn't wake from all the noise I'm making. Olivia was right—he's out.

She waits in silence as I grab a ball from the same corner and dribble lazily to position. I take a shot. Sink it. Then finally answer, glancing her direction, "I was bored at home. Lonely. Big house, just me, you know? And so, I invited a bunch of people over. They invited a ton of other people, and the next thing you know..." I run a hand over my head as I jog toward the barely bouncing ball to retrieve it. "I was all right for a bit until I remembered that I hate most people there, and I wanted out, so I left."

"You left?" she almost scoffs, moving beneath the hoop.

She catches the next shot that goes through the net and passes the ball effortlessly back to me.

"Yep," I tell her after catching her pass. I hold the ball to my hip, adding, "And that's when you impaled me with that beast of a vehicle."

Her shoulders sag. "*Impaled* now?"

I crack a smile. "I'm milking this shit, Cheeks."

She rolls her eyes, and it's only slightly cute. "Where are your parents?"

"Colorado," I'm quick to answer. "My sister goes to college in Boulder. She's one of those people who is crazy smart but socially awkward, so she needs them more than I do right now." It's only half the truth, but it's all the information I'm willing to give. Anything more might literally send me over the edge.

Of this building.

And in under two seconds, I'd be nothing but mangled flesh and shattered bones, bleeding out onto the concrete.

"Can I ask you a question?" she asks.

I switch positions and score again, then wait for her to catch the rebound and return the ball to me. "Another truth?"

Her smile warms parts of me I keep hidden from the world. "Is college in your future?"

I give her what she wants and hope it leads nowhere. "I'd be the worst kind of jerk if I took a spot on a team when someone else could use it as a stepping-stone to better their lives. Their futures." Plus, I was never sure if the colleges that threw offers my way wanted me or if it was the money my parents could provide the program. "Besides," I continue, "I'm not passionate about the game so much as the discipline it provides me."

"What do you mean?" She's cute when she's inquisitive—all scrunchy nose and squinty eyes.

I take a moment to come up with a simplified explanation. "It's easy to push aside all other thoughts and everything going on around you when you obsess over something. Basketball's been my obsession for a long time, and with it came discipline. Self-discipline." And God knows how badly I needed that. Without waiting for her response, I throw the ball toward her, completely unsurprised when she catches it flawlessly. I step to the side, offering her my position. "Take your shot."

Olivia does as suggested, and I can tell the moment the ball leaves her hands that it's in.

"Nice form," I say, jogging to retrieve the ball. I face her, holding the ball at my side. "Now it's your turn."

Head tilted slightly, she replies, "I just had my turn."

I shake my head, stopping a few feet in front of her. "It's your turn to give me a truth."

She chews her lip, looking everywhere but at me.

"Did Dominic teach you to shoot like that?"

Her intake of breath is audible, and her eyes drop. *Busted.*

I hold my ground, stay silent.

Finally, she looks up, eyes right on mine. "I taught him."

I nod, slowly, watching every single emotion pass through her features. Fear, shame, something else I can't quite put my finger on.

Dominic Delgado: soon-to-be senior at Philips Academy—my school's rival. Like me, he, too, is the captain of the basketball team. Unlike me, he's a complete and utter dickbag. And I can't fucking believe he's Olivia's brother. Though, just like she and the kid in her car —they look nothing alike. Dominic is half black, half Iranian, earning him the nicknames: The Dominator, The Prince of Persia, and my personal favorite only because I know how much he hates it—The Persian Persuasion. I know girls at St. Luke's who'd be more than willing to jump ship for the guy... too bad he'd always had his girl, Dani, by his side. Until I came along. But, that's a story for another time.

"How did you know?" Olivia asks, her voice quiet, words trembling with each syllable.

I dribble leisurely around her. "You went into the gas station after I did and got a call from him. Your phone was still connected to the Blue-tooth in your car, and I saw *'lil bro'* show up on the screen."

"And you know it was Dom, how?"

I shrug, lazy. "I typed the number into my phone to see if I knew him, and wouldn't you know it..."

"Of course, you have his number."

Another shrug. "Keep your enemies close..."

Her eye roll is so dramatic, she must be seeing stars.

"I didn't even know Dom had a sister."

She steps forward so fast; I don't have time to get rid of the ball before she swoops it out of my grasp. "Yeah, that's kind of the point."

"Why?"

Her lay-up is fucking perfect, and I don't think I've ever been so turned on. Neither of us makes a move to retrieve the ball, and after a few seconds, she turns to me, her smile soft, eyes warm, and something switches in that moment. Something rare. Something... easy. "No more truths tonight, okay, Timothy?"

I laugh.

Because what else can I do?

7

Rhys

After a good hour of playing ball and talking shit, none of which has to do with two specific boys in her life, we give up for the night and sit on the bed of her truck, my phone softly playing music she seems to enjoy.

"What a wild night," she says through a sigh. She'd taken my hoodie off while we were playing, and now she puts it back on, releasing her hair from its knot so she can slip the hood over her head.

For a long moment, we sit in silence, staring ahead, and surprisingly, it's not awkward or unbearable. I've always disliked people who need to speak just to fill the dead air with even deader words. So, this? Sitting quietly with her, it's almost... comforting.

She's the first to speak, saying, "So, I was thinking about what you said earlier, about the loneliness thing..." Swear, I hope she doesn't ruin the fucking moment. "I don't know if it's normal. If it's an unconscious choice not to let people in or whatever... but, I don't know..." She pauses, inhaling deeply, before adding, "You said you live alone in a big house, and I... I live with people in a small house, and I still get lonely."

For a full minute, the only sound that forms between us is the single, quiet clearing of her throat. She doesn't look at me, and I'm too damn afraid of what I'll feel when I look at her.

Maybe getting hit by a car wasn't the best thing that could've happened to me tonight.

But getting hit by a car driven by Olivia definitely was.

I release my breath, slowly, slowly, and I wish I could say something. Something to show that her words have meaning, that they're not dead like the air around us. Like the soul that wonders what it would be like to jump off the edge. Instead, I tell her, "Is that an invitation to come over?" I'm an idiot, but I don't stop there. "Because I could cure your loneliness real quick, Cheeks."

Olivia scoffs, but it's clear she wasn't expecting anything else out of me. Smart girl. "Oh yeah. Dominic would love that."

Right. Dominic The Dominator. Stupid name. So stupid, I almost forgot about his existence. "So, I take it you're not going to tell him about tonight... about me?"

"No," she laughs—as if the idea itself is ludicrous.

"Why not?" I ask. "It's not as if we planned it."

"Because if he knew it was you I hit, he'd tell me to one: hit you harder. Two: reverse and hit you again. Three: all of the above, then leave you there."

"Holy shit." It's my turn to laugh. "He hates me that much?"

She nudges my side with hers. "You stole his girlfriend, Rhys!"

My eyes widen, because just like his existence, I'd forgotten about that, too. But... hold up. "Is that where his story ends?"

"What's that supposed to mean?" she accuses.

"Look," I say, hands up in mock surrender, "I'm just saying, whatever history your brother and I have, it's got nothing to do with us—you and me."

"There is no us," she says, defiant, and nah.

Fuck that.

I grab my phone from between us, tap it a few times. "So... he wouldn't be too happy if I tagged him in a pic of us together?"

"You wouldn't!" She tries to grab the phone from my hand, but I hold it away from her.

"I wonder if he'd recognize you with your eyes covered," I murmur through a chuckle, trying to handle my phone with one hand while I tug down on her hood. It only covers half her face, so her mouth is still visible, and I shove down the urge to kiss her.

Just once.

Just to curb my curiosity.

I keep hold of the hood while I snap shot after shot of nothing, laughing at her panic every time the fake shutter of my phone sounds. "Don't you dare," she practically squeals. And then she's on me, trying to get the phone from my grasp, and I can't stop laughing. Neither can she. I fall onto my back and release the hood when she climbs over me, and I stretch out my arm, keeping it from her reach. The hood still covers her eyes, because she's too busy using both her hands to blindly search for my phone.

She's practically feeling me up—warm hands gliding over my stomach, my chest. She finds my shoulder and follows my arm up, up, up, and I'm shaking from withheld laughter because she's got the wrong fucking arm.

"Give it to me!" she almost growls, right in my ear, and I swear to God, I'm rock fucking hard.

How can I not be?

Those words? From her mouth? Not to mention that she's practically spread out on top of me, her breasts brushing against my face as she continues to reach up, her heated fingertips making their way up my arm.

I can feel the fire—their flames flicking through my bloodline, pulsating throughout my entire body, right down to my cock.

Her hand searches my empty one, and she groans in frustration.

I'm no longer laughing.

No longer breathing.

Her hands move again, searching for my other arm, and I grip the phone tighter because no fucking way am I letting her have it. Her hand's on my wrist now—so close to her end goal—and without thinking, I brace my arm around her waist and pull her away.

Pull her down.

Right onto my erection.

We freeze, our entire bodies locked.

Surrendered.

In the few seconds since she came for me, I hadn't realized that she'd practically straddled my hips, her knees on either side. That dull ache from the impact earlier? Completely gone, it seems. Now her pussy's pressed against my hardened cock, and I'm sure she can feel it because she—

She moans.

I exhale. Slowly. Silently. And I can feel the heat emitting from her center, can feel her short breaths against my chin. She attempts to lift herself up, but I tighten my grip, push her back down. This time, she shifts on me. Not a lot. Just enough to let me know she feels me too. My pulse pounds, vibrating across my flesh, and I can't seem to inhale enough air to satisfy my need for life. The hoodie still covers her eyes, but her mouth...

Her mouth is so close to mine, lips wet, parted. All it would take is a slight lift of my head... but, I wouldn't do that to her. I can't. Instead, I release my phone, let it drop on the metal beneath us, and then grasp the back of the hood, clearing her vision.

Her eyes are closed when they're first revealed, and they land right on mine when she opens them.

And those cheeks... stained pink from exertion, from lust.

She wants this as much as I do.

I lick my lips, and she does the same.

Gently, I thrust up, wanting to see her reaction.

Her breaths falter, her eyes widening just slightly.

And then she responds to my action with one of her own—a slight circling of her hips. I almost lose all control at the sudden pleasure that spreads through me—like a series of waves about to create a tsunami.

My hand is on her thigh—thick fucking thighs made for grabbing —and I don't know how it got there. I move up slowly, watching her every breath, her every reaction, until I find the bottom of her denim shorts, and I can't look away. I don't even want to blink. I go higher, higher, until my palm settles on the curve of her ass. I squeeze, pushing her onto me firmer, harder. I want her to know what she's done to me, how my body's reacted to her. How she so easily controlled me, possessed me. Every single inch of me.

Her head falls, lands on my shoulder, but she doesn't move.

Doesn't speak.

I keep one hand on her ass as the other bunches the fabric of the hoodie until I find the end, and then I reach beneath it. Her skin is flaming hot against mine, and I trace down her spine to her waist, memorizing the shape of her.

Her grinds are short, tiny circles, and I can feel the warmth of her scattered breaths through my T-shirt, spreading onto my chest.

Fuck, I'd give anything to be inside her.

"Liv," I croak, my throat aching with the single word that could possibly end this.

She lifts her head just enough to meet my eyes, and I don't know who kisses who first.

I don't care.

Her lips are soft, her movements slow, and I can't fucking get enough of it. The first swipe of our tongues has us both moaning into each other, and I don't know where to put my hands. I want to touch her, feel her everywhere, all at once.

Kiss her everywhere.

Everywhere.

I reach up and grasp a handful of her hair. Tug. The sound that escapes her is pure fucking pleasure, and I kiss down her jaw, her neck, sucking hard. Biting. I pull her hair again. Teasing. Testing. She turns languid in my arms, and I crack a smile against her flesh.

Liv likes it a little rough...

...and I'm all fucking for it.

She dips her mouth to mine, catching my bottom lip between her teeth and pulling it away before running her tongue along the length of it. I groan, my dick throbbing, pulsing, warning me of what's to come. "Fuck," I spit, holding her ass in place. The way she moves... the sounds she makes... it's too fucking much. "You're too fucking good. I can't—"

I don't get a chance to finish the sentence because her phone goes off—her alarm—and before I can stop her, she's off of me. Completely. The sound of the alarm shrills through the air and rings in my ears louder than the blood rushing through my body.

She jumps off the truck, and I stay on my back, looking up at the stars as I try to catch my breath. "I'm so sorry, Rhys," she rushes out.

Sorry?

"Please don't tell anyone about this," she cries. Actually cries. And I sit up just to witness her pain. To make it mine. She swipes at a single tear on her cheek. "I'm sorry," she repeats. "This was a mistake."

I push away the sudden sharpness of anger that flickers inside me.

Flick.

Flick.

Flick.

A *mistake?*

Me?

I might as well sound the buzzer and call this a loss.

A failure.

The problem is... I *don't* fail.

I did it once, and fuck if I'll ever let it happen again.

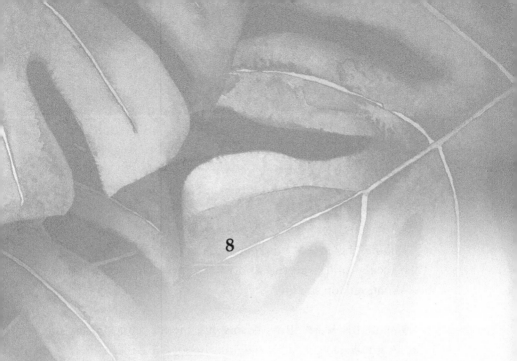

8

Olivia

I can't speak to Rhys.

Can't look at him.

I can't even breathe around him.

Which is a problem, it seems, considering he's sitting right next to me, and I'm driving him home.

As if it wasn't bad enough that we did what we did with a sleeping Max only feet away or that he's... Rhys fricken Garrett, but now we're here, in the cab of my truck, and there's no means of escape.

I should've left him on that rooftop and fled, crashed through the closed security gate if I needed to.

"You're overthinking it," Rhys says out of nowhere, and I white-knuckle the steering wheel to stop myself from climbing over the center console and choking the life out of him. Overthinking it? No. That's not the problem here. The problem is that I wasn't thinking at all. "It's really not that big a deal," he continues.

Of course it's not... to him.

"It's just biology, right?"

"Biology..." I suck in air through my nose and try to keep my composure. "Sure."

"If you think about it, we're just two consenting adults attracted to each—"

"Can you—" I cut myself off when I realize the loudness of my voice. After a long exhale, I roll back my shoulders and try again. "Can you just... stop?"

"Stop what?"

"Talking." I glance at him quickly. "Please."

His cocky smirk returns, and I force myself to ignore its effect on me. "Whatever you say, Liv."

True to his word, Rhys keeps his mouth shut during the few minutes it takes to get to his neighborhood. Once there, he tells me to turn into the same street where this entire shit-show of a night started. "Don't park under a streetlight, and kill your headlights," he says, just as his phone goes off with a text.

I do as he says, not bothering to ask questions because what would be the point? Rhys seems to live in his own world where he makes up his own rules, like, it's totally fine to do what we did because "biology."

Fuck biology.

And fuck Rhys Garrett.

And fuck me for being so unjustifiably irate toward him. It's not entirely his fault, obviously. I was there, too, grinding on that forbidden dick like an undersexed, overpaid stripper. Or is it exotic dancer? Sex worker? Whatever.

After replying to the text, he sets the phone on his lap and turns to me. I look away. "He's around the corner," he states, as if I'm supposed to know who "he" is. "Want to make out while we wait?"

I drop my forehead on the steering wheel and let out my frustrations in a groan.

"You're so dramatic." Rhys laughs. Because, of course, he does. "Chill the fuck out."

"I can't," I tell him honestly. He has no idea how bad this situation is. Not for him, but for me. I lift my head, turning my entire body toward him. I try not to look in his eyes... or at his mouth...

"You want to kiss me again, don't you?"

"Oh my God," I murmur, lifting my gaze in search of a god who clearly doesn't exist.

"We kissed, Liv. That's it."

"No one calls me Liv!" I rush out, as if that's the topic at hand. It's not. I'm heated, clearly, and I don't know how to fix it. "No one can know about this, Rhys. I mean it."

"Why do you care so much about what Dominic—"

"That's not—" I cut myself off before I reveal too much. If this gets out, Dom will be the least of my problems. "Just swear you won't—"

"Relax," he says, stretching out the single word. "I won't say dick to anyone, and as long as you can keep your shit together, no one has to find out."

I look at him, right into his eyes, and I search for any hint of a lie. "You swear you won't tell anyone?"

"You want me to pinky promise?" He doesn't even try to hide his irritation. "Write it out in a fucking contract, and I'll sign it with my blood if that's what you need."

I exhale, wishing I were anywhere but here. "Now you're just being mean."

"Me?" he scoffs. "You're the one treating me like a child, demanding shit from me—as if you didn't just rub up against my cock less than ten minutes ago."

A gasp catches in my throat, my attention flicking to the back seat. Max is still fast asleep. "Stop talking about it!"

Rhys drops his gaze, his shoulders slumping as if he just realized we're not alone.

"Let's just never speak of this again, okay?"

His gaze roams my features, his dark eyes thinning to slits as he assesses me. "You got it... *Olivia*."

I hate the way he says my name now. I jerk my head toward his door. "You can leave."

"I could..." His shoulders lift with his shrug. "... But I won't." He stares out his window, and I stare at him. Just when I'm about to ask him to leave again, a brief flash of police sirens has me momentarily frozen. He slides down his seat, murmurs, "You better duck down if you don't want people to see us together."

"What?"

"Three... two..."

I duck down, matching his position, my heart hammering against my rib cage. "What's going on?" I whisper, just as the sound of cars screeching and people yelling fills my ears.

Rhys is... smiling.

Great. I'm stuck in a car with a sociopath.

We're on our sides, our legs bent in the floor space with our upper bodies resting on the back of the seats, and thank God I have a big truck because I can't imagine this being possible any other way.

We're facing each other now, his slate-gray eyes barely visible in the darkness.

My exhale comes out shaky as I try to breathe through the fear racing inside me. "Relax, Olivia," he murmurs, his voice somehow deeper, richer. He reaches across the console, his fingertips running a line across my forehead, pushing my hair aside.

I can no longer breathe. No longer think. It's almost surreal—the way my eyes close as he trails one finger down my temple, under my eye, back again. And then he...

He pinches my cheek.

I swat his hand away.

His low chuckle fills the cab and replaces the fear in my chest with another emotion. "I had fun tonight," he says. "Even if you take away the last few minutes on that rooftop... I had a good time with you."

This boy may be bipolar.

Either that, or he's just as confused as I am. "So did I," I whisper, and as soon as the words come out of my mouth, I know them to be true.

Outside, cars whip by us, their intermittent headlights creating a light show in the cab and across Rhys's face. It takes a few minutes for silence to surround us again, and not once has he taken his eyes off me, and I...

...I can't seem to look away.

"I don't want you to worry," he says finally. "I swear on my sister's life, I won't say a word."

"Thank you," I whisper. He doesn't make a move to leave, and for some reason, I don't feel compelled to ask him to. Headlights shine into my truck again, and I assume it's just passing. It's not. The car stops right behind us, and the lights cut off completely. A car door opens. Closes. Footsteps approach, and then I hear something that has my heart jumping to my throat, clogging my airways: a police radio.

"Rhys..."

Rhys sits up, and I follow his lead. His fingers search for the window button on the door, but it won't go down because the car's not on. I turn the key to the first click, illuminating the dash. Rhys winds down the window all the way and puts his fist out for a bump. "Thanks, man. I appreciate it."

The cop, whose features I can't make out until he dips his head and looks farther into the truck—responds, "Anytime, bro. You know this." He's shorter than Rhys, but has a similar build, and he's around his mid-to-late twenties. He smiles at me, and I attempt to smile back.

"This is my friend, Olivia," Rhys tells him. "Olivia, this is Curtis."

We exchange brief, generic pleasantries, as if this is all completely normal. Until Curtis looks into the truck, notices Max in the back seat. His eyes narrow, just enough to notice but not enough to fear. "Who's this?" he asks, looking from a sleeping Max to me.

I swallow, nervous. "He's my brother."

Rhys turns to me, his eyebrows raised. "Another one?" He looks from Max to me, again and again, as if he'll suddenly find a similarity between us. He won't. "How?"

I face forward, don't bother responding. Really, it's none of his business, and unless this cop is going to take it further, I have nothing more to say.

"I have to get back to work," Curtis tells Rhys, finally breaking the silence. "But you're still coming to Layla's party this weekend, right?"

"Like I would miss my goddaughter's birthday," Rhys answers, tearing his eyes from mine to his friend. "You know I'll be there."

"Do me a favor?" Curtis says. "Don't outshine us with whatever present you plan on getting her."

Rhys chuckles. "So cancel that VIP tour of Disney? Got it."

"Bruh."

"I'm kidding." Rhys laughs. "The 'Uncle Rhys is my hero' tattoo should be enough, right?'"

Curtis laughs at this.

"What did you guys get her?" Rhys asks.

Curtis sighs. "Belinda got her a dollhouse. It's in pieces, of course, and she sure as hell isn't the one to put it all together. Guess what I'll be doing the night before?"

"I'll come by Friday night and give you a hand," Rhys offers.

"Yeah?"

"Of course."

"I'll supply the beers."

Rhys's hand goes to his chest in mock horror. "To a nineteen-year-old? How dare you, Officer Murphy."

Curtis reaches into the truck, shoves Rhys's head playfully. "I fucking forget how old you are sometimes." Then he ducks his head again, focusing on me. "It was nice to meet you, Olivia. Thanks for taking care of my boy tonight."

I nod but stay quiet.

"Later, Garrett," Curtis says, and then he's gone.

I have questions. So many of them. A goddaughter? Cute. But also: Who the hell is this version of Rhys I just witnessed? "Did you call the cops on your own party?"

Rhys nods as he winds up his window, then faces me. "Turn left up there," he says, motioning to the T intersection in front of us. "I'm the third house on the left, just after the bend."

I start the car and follow his directions, realizing quickly that his house is familiar. I pull over at the curb, just before the open security gates. "I'll drop you here if that's okay?"

"I don't know," Rhys mumbles. "It's a long-ass driveway."

"I know," I tell him. "I delivered a pizza here tonight right before—"

"You slammed into me with your truck and dragged my bloody and beaten body four blocks?"

I crack a smile. "You're really milking it now." I look toward his house, though it's so set back from the road that it's impossible to see. "I'd drive you to your door, but I'm sure you have security cameras..." And the idea of him having physical proof that I was here, with him, makes my stomach turn.

His eyes narrow as I speak, head tilting to the side when he assesses me. And then he laughs. Just once. "You're so fucking paranoid, Cheeks." Shaking his head, he doesn't make a move to leave. Instead, he seems to get more comfortable. "That's what you were doing tonight? Delivering food?"

"Yeah."

Rhys turns, looking to the back seat. "You guys don't have a long drive, do you? Because you can crash here if you're tired. I have the space." He pauses a beat. "I can disconnect all the cameras just for you."

"No, we're good," I'm quick to answer.

"You sure?" There's that smirk again. "I'll even let you share my bed."

I jerk my head toward his gate. "Get out."

He chuckles as he opens the door. "Goodbye, Liv."

"Goodnight, Rhys."

9

Olivia

It's almost 2 a.m. by the time I pull into my driveway, and it's only then that I notice the wad of cash Rhys left on the passenger's seat. With everything else that happened tonight, I'd forgotten about our little deal, about the money he'd offered me to "spend the night with him."

Without hesitation, I reach over and grab the stash, momentarily surprised by the thickness of the stack. There are a bunch of twenties, and even a few fifties. I'm almost scared to count them all, but I do.

Five hundred dollars.

And with it, a withdrawal receipt from the gas station ATM with the same amount.

My breath halts when realization dawns.

Rhys may or may not have had any cash in his wallet, but he was willing to pay me up to five hundred bucks just to spend a couple of hours with him.

Before I get a chance to break down exactly what he was thinking, the porch light flicks on and the front door opens. I quickly grab the money and pocket it just as Dominic steps outside. In shorts and a T-shirt, he makes his way to Max's door and opens it, asking, "Did he get to sleep okay?"

"Yeah." I get out of the car and wait for Dom to get Max out of his seat before gathering his backpack and iPad from the floor of the truck. "Did you wait up for us?"

"Of course," Dom answers, his dark, loose curls falling across his forehead, over his eyes. He jerks his head back, ridding them from his view.

After closing the truck door, I follow after them. "You didn't have to do that."

Dom waits until we're in the house before he turns to me, saying, "You call and say you hit some random guy with your truck and that you have to take him to emergency... yeah, Ollie, I'm waiting up for you."

"You could've called."

"And have you worried that I was worried?" That's true, and I really shouldn't be surprised that he stayed up for us. That's how we work— Dom and me—I'm the provider, and he's the protector.

I wait until they're up the stairs and out of view before going to my bedroom. Then I shut the door. Lean against it. I take a moment to breathe. Just... breathe.

Tonight has been wild, to say the least, and I'm not quite sure I'm ready to unwrap it. Not that there's a lot to unwrap, besides, you know, whether or not I can trust Rhys—a guy I barely know—with my entire existence.

10

Rhys

A few hours ago, bodies filled the entire floor level of my house, most of them drunk or high. Some of them both. Music blared from the corner of the living room, the bass shaking the walls and rattling the windows. I scrunch my nose as I walk past the kegs sitting on the kitchen island, the smell more potent now than it was when I first tapped it.

Looking back, it's no wonder I wanted to get the fuck out of this place. But now it's quiet—almost *too* quiet. And, honestly, I don't know which I'd prefer.

The glass sliding doors leading to the yard are still wide open, and I step through, my sights set on the pool house only yards away. I kick away empty beer cans, glass bottles, and Solo cups as I approach it, ignoring the rest of my surroundings. I don't have to take full stock of the remnants of the party to know that the house is trashed. Beyond it. I just can't bring myself to give a shit. At least not yet.

I have one hand on the doorknob of the pool house when a familiar voice speaks up from behind me. "That's gotta be your longest run yet."

I stop in my tracks, my shoulders dropping just enough that he wouldn't notice. I expected my friend, Oscar, to still be here, though I thought he'd be passed out in one of the bedrooms of the main house. It's not that I don't want him here; it's just that, right now, I have other priorities.

"I didn't think you were coming back this time."

My chest rises with my inhale, and I turn around to see him lying in one of the loungers, his eyes wide open as he stares at the few visible stars.

Besides ball, there are two things Oscar and I have in common. We crave silence as much as we fear it, and we never, ever trust the darkness to keep us safe.

I take a moment to replay his words. *He didn't think I was coming back?* "Nah," I say calmly, shaking my head as I approach him. "I just lost track of time, is all." I slump down on the lounger beside him and mimic his position, wondering if he realizes he's half the reason I always come back. Probably not. And it's not as if I'd ever share that with him. That's a hell of a lot of pressure to put on any one person's shoulders.

"Rhys," he murmurs, his head rolling to face me.

"Oscar..."

"What do *you* think is in the ocean?"

I chuckle. "Brandon bring that good weed again, huh?"

"Maybe," he states, shrugging. "But I didn't have any of it..." He sucks in a breath, holds it, and I stay quiet, waiting for him to continue. "It's just... they put all this money into NASA, and space exploration, and the sea... What percentage of the ocean is undiscovered again?"

We'd watched a documentary about sea exploration a few nights ago, and I guess he's still thinking about it. "Over eighty percent," I reply.

"Right." Oscar nods, his eyes getting heavier with each passing second. "So what's down there, Garrett?"

"I don't know."

He's quiet a beat, his eyes back on the night sky while his jaw works as he contemplates. I wait, knowing he's not done. "Imagine if there's a whole other world down there. And our world and their world don't know about the other, and we're just here... existing... as if we're the only entity, the most important of them all. Or... imagine if we are to them what ants are to us. Just these tiny blobs of atoms that have no real purpose, no significance. And the choices we make, the mistakes we carry, the regrets we hold on to... they mean *nothing*. I mean... not *really*." Oscar's two years younger than me, but clearly, his age doesn't match his mental maturity. I guess that happens when you're forced to man up too young.

I don't respond. I simply watch his chest rise and fall until it slows to a steady rhythm. When I'm sure he's asleep, I grab his phone from beside him, unlock it quickly, and make sure he's let his mom know where he's crashing. I send her a text from my phone, too, so she has absolutely no reason to worry. Then I send another text to a different number:

> You would not believe the night I've had.

After hitting send, I head inside, grab my laptop from the bedroom, flop down on the couch, and let ESPN play in the background.

I run through the events of the night like I do game tape post-loss.

Post-failure.

Play by play.

Minute by minute.

Second by second.

Each time I run through it in my mind, the buzzer (aka alarm) sounds at the exact same time—the moment Olivia pulled away from the kiss with tears in her eyes. Tears that let me know exactly how she felt—regret, disappointment, fear.

To her, the kiss was nothing more than a fleeting moment of uncontrolled desire, and I was nothing more than a mistake.

But to me...

I flip open my laptop, my fingers flying over the keyboard as I type in her name.

Hit enter.

And laugh to myself as the search results load.
Olivia just became my new sport.
My new discipline.
My new obsession.
And she has no fucking clue what she's in for.

11

Olivia

It takes thirty minutes under a scalding hot shower for me to finally convince myself that everything will be fine. I just have to keep my shit together, which is entirely doable. Besides, it's not as if I'm unfamiliar with the act of lying. I lie to Dominic every day... about a myriad of things, and he has no clue about any of it.

My biggest lie: *I'm good*.

After a heavy exhale, I leave the bathroom, flicking off the light as I pass, and sit on the edge of the bed.

Then I reach into the drawer of my side table and pull out the cash. There's so much I can do with this amount of money, but I can't, for the life of me, come up with a single reason that would justify keeping it. It's *too* much. So much it feels wrong even to hold it.

My phone goes off with a text, and it takes a moment for me to realize that it sounded from *the* phone. Not *my* phone.

I pull it from the same drawer where the money was and quickly open the text:

NOT FRIDGE GUY

> You would not believe the night I've had.

I stare at it a moment, not knowing whether to laugh or cry.

> It's late... but you got me intrigued. Tell me everything!

> I'm okay, don't panic...

> I got hit by a fucking car.

> Okay, not hit, but like... it bumped me, and I was too stunned to react so I just lay there in the middle of the road until the driver came out to check on me.

I laugh under my breath and get comfortable in my bed, phone in one hand and wad of cash in the other. Both of which led to a new version of Rhys I'd never met before.

I reply:

> I hope the car's okay.

> You're such a smartass. How was your night?

My night? With a smile, I close my eyes and allow myself to get lost in the image, the memory, of Rhys's solid body beneath me, his mouth so close to mine I can almost taste his kiss. I stutter an exhale, my mind working, my heart racing, all while the truth weighs heavy on my chest.

A truth that I could only ever admit to myself.

If I'd known how the night would turn out, I probably would've done it for free.

PART II

12

Rhys

The pain is instant. So is the blood that fills my mouth and coats my tongue with copper. I keep my lips sealed, refusing to let him see the bloodshed he caused. I don't fight back. That would be pointless. But I'll never truly surrender, either. I'm trapped—not just in the corner of the room, but in the darkest recesses of my mind. I'm on my hands and knees, the blows to my stomach putting me there. Blood drips from my nose and other places I can't even comprehend. My head pounds, thud thud, thud thud, and pain sears across my ribs when he kicks me there. Once. Twice. Three times. I struggle for breath, finally allowing the blood to fall from my mouth. I try to inhale, but all I can do is cough. Gurgle. Cough some more.

Darkness falls every time my lids become too heavy, and I suppress my grunt when he yanks my hair, pulls it from its roots. His hot breath coats my face when he sneers, "What now, you pretty-boy faggot?"

I shut my eyes just in time to block the spit in my face.

He releases my hair, letting my head drop between my shoulders. "Get up!"

The cement blocks feel cool against my palm, and somehow, I get to my feet. My chest rises, falls, the remnants of my beating painting the floor crim-

son. I lean against the wall and try to square my shoulders, preparing for the blows that will inevitably come. I'll take every one of them. Wear them like badges of honor.

"The fuck are you smiling for?" He's mad. So mad. And when I try to focus, I can't tell if there's one or five of him. With one eye swollen shut, I can't make out shit.

I spit blood on his shoes. "You, you fucking pussy."

He doesn't like that. Not one bit. The next punch cracks my nose wide open and forces my head to hit the wall behind me with so much force I black out for a second. When I come to, I'm on the floor again, kick after kick, blow after blow. I crack one eyelid open just enough to see her picture hidden between the mattress and the bedframe, a reminder of who she is and why I'm here.

"You're a hundred percent of my fifty, Rhys."

I gasp awake, my eyes snapping open. I'm in a pool of sweat, and the first thing I do is make sure I haven't pissed myself. It's been a while since I've been in this state—both physically and mentally, and the only reason I know it was a dream and not a memory is because I laughed in the face of my attackers. In real life, I cowered in the corner like the pathetic, weak little bitch that I was. Sweat coats every inch of me as I fist the sheets beside me. "Fuck," I spit, throwing the covers off me. I make my way to the bathroom, the harsh lights burning into my irises the instant I flip them on. I go straight for the sink and run the cold water, cup my hands beneath the stream before splashing it on my face, ignoring the scars on the "pretty boy" face he loved beating on. I grip the edge of the counter, my head between my shoulders, and I try to settle my breathing.

For seconds that feel like minutes, I keep my eyes closed, my grip firm, and my breaths weak. Then, slowly, slowly, I allow myself to go back there.

"You're a hundred percent of my fifty, Rhys."

13

Rhys

It's incredibly rare for someone to exist in this day and age and leave very little digital footprint behind. Unfortunately for me, Olivia Delgado is one of those people. No matter how many filters I applied to the searches, I couldn't find her. I tried, though. A lot. To the point some might even consider it stalking. But it was the only way I could satisfy the curiosity that's been building since the night we spent together. That was over two weeks ago, and in that time, I've spent way too many hours thinking about her.

Fantasizing about her.

Jerking off to her.

Oh, and I've watched *Lilo and Stitch*.

Twice.

Consider me a fan.

The only thing I could find was from a few years ago—a single picture of her and Dominic from his middle school website. From what I could gather, Dominic and Liv grew up in Wilmington, but they left so Dominic could begin his high school journey at Philips Academy, a standout basketball-focused, private prep high school that hands out scholarships to only the best of the best—the elite. And as much as I want to deny it—Dominic Delgado falls into that category.

The only mention of Liv is the photograph of Dom with his arm around her.

So, they are siblings... somehow.

And it's not that I didn't believe her. It's just... not the entire story.

And it's not as if I want the complete story from her right now. But... I don't know. Like I said, I'm curious.

There's no mention of the "off-limits" boy in the written piece, or their parents, or anything else that could give me a clue into Liv's life, her past, or *her* specifically.

And I'm fully aware that I could solve all my issues by simply knocking on her door and asking her, but I don't think Dominic would like that too much, and I'm not here to cause problems, especially for Olivia.

So.

I don't have her number, and showing up at her house is out of the question.

Therefore, I'm left with no other option besides what I'm doing now: ordering food non-stop, from multiple places, over and over, in the hopes she might be the one to deliver it.

I don't even know if she's working.

Whenever an order's accepted and a driver who isn't Olivia shows up on my screen, my hopes die a little.

Not enough to make me stop.

Even if she isn't on shift, surely she'd be getting the notifications. I don't think she'd know my specific address even though she'd delivered here before, and to prevent her from purposely avoiding me, I used my mom's maiden name to set up the account. Sneaky, right? Also smart.

Olivia can't hide out forever.

I crack a smile.

We have unfinished business...

* * *

Five non-Olivia deliveries later, and I'm losing steam. I kick my legs up on the coffee table and tap my phone against my chin, thinking.

I know what her truck looks like. Kind of. Actually, not really. I know that it's black, and that's about it.

I know she has an ass made for grabbing, slapping, spreading. "Ayyy!" I say out loud, raising a fist in the air. And then I shake my head, cursing myself for being such an idiot. I look around the house to make sure no one heard me, but I'm positive I saw Delaney, our house manager, take off about an hour ago.

What else? What else?

Nothing.

I got nothing.

I try my chances again and order from a place I don't even like. Then I wait, wait, wait...

Ten minutes later, I'm practically skating across the marble floors, stopping momentarily to slip on a cap and grab a sweatshirt, and then I'm out the front door and jogging down the driveway and out the front gate.

I lean against the brick column of the security gate and wait.

And wait.

Within minutes, a black truck rounds the bend, and I stand taller, square my shoulders.

It's like a dream, the way the sun beams through her windshield and lights up her face. With her head ducked, Olivia's eyes narrow as she looks for the house number. And those eyes—those muddy brown eyes I completely lost myself in? They widen when they see me, and I count the number of insecurities in my head.

1. She could drive away, pretend as if I don't exist. As if that night together never happened.

2. She could stop, give me my order, and pretend she doesn't know me.

3. She could slow to a stop, and I don't give her a chance to decide for me.

I choose option 3 and open the door before she comes to a complete stop. After collecting my food from the passenger's seat, I slide my ass into place.

"What the fu—hell?" are the first words she says to me. I'll be sure to memorize them. Write it down in my amateur stalker notebook.

I'm kidding.

Kind of.

Ignoring her, I turn to the kid in the back seat. "What's up, my guy?" I say, offering my fist.

"Off-limits" looks up from the book he's reading to my fist, and then he shrugs and taps it. He's got headphones on, so I don't know if he heard me, but Olivia sure did.

"What are you doing?" Olivia hisses, eyebrows pinched, fire burning behind her glare. God, help me. That glare is like an antidote straight to my dick.

I shrug. "I didn't know how else to see you again," I answer truthfully. I'm not one to play games, to go around in circles. I wanted to see her, so I made that happen. Simple.

"You can't just—"

"Well, I better do something, Cheeks, because my neighbors are nosy, and you and me—sitting out here when it's light out..."

Panic crosses her features, and a second later, her truck rolls forward. She looks in the rearview and says, "Max, you got your headphones on?"

"Ah, he has a name," I murmur. *Max.* I wonder if it's short for Maximus. Maximillian?

Another glare from the girl of my literal dreams, and if she keeps going like this, I might find myself with a new kink.

When Max doesn't respond, she faces me. "What exactly are you doing?"

I grin. "A ride-along." Curtis told me about them when he first joined the police force. I don't know if this is similar, but I guess I'm here to find out.

"Do not engage with him. At all. I mean it." *Him,* meaning Max. Obviously.

I settle into my seat. "Damn, you're feisty... and I'm into it." She just doesn't know how much.

* * *

The first stop we make is at a little strip mall, and even though there are plenty of parking spots, Liv doesn't take any of them. After going through the same aisle twice, I lose patience and point to an empty spot. "There's a space right there... and there... and there."

"Yeah, but I'm going there," she says, pointing to Down Dawgs. I've never been there, but I hear their hot dogs are bomb. "And I need to park close enough to keep an eye on him."

"I'm right here," I tell her, confused. "I'll stay in the car, and you can go in."

"I'll just take him in with me."

I turn around and look at the kid, still focused on his book. "I'm not going to do anything," I say, trailing my gaze back to her. I roll my eyes to emphasize: "I promise I won't engage."

She huffs out a breath, deflating her chest—her breasts—clearly visible by the tight T-shirt she's wearing. "Fine." Then she pulls into the spot, puts the truck in gear, and turns to me. She reaches out, and I instinctively rear back. After clucking her tongue, annoyed, she tugs the brim of my hat lower on my brow. "Try not to look so..."

I smirk. "Sexy?"

"*Visible.*"

I don't watch her ass as she walks away. Or her legs. Damn those legs.

"Hey, Timothy!" Max calls out.

Who the fuck is—oh, right. I'm Timothy. I turn to him, noticing the headphones around his neck now. I keep my promise and don't engage. Just a slight raise of my eyebrows to let him know I'm listening. "Did you know that according to Greek mythology, the word 'clue' comes from the world clew, spelled c l e w? Some guy went into a labyrinth to kill a Minotaur—"

"Those half-man, half-bull things?" Shit, I wasn't supposed to engage, but the kid's got me intrigued.

Max nods enthusiastically. "Yeah, and anyway, for him to find his way back out of the labyrinth, he unraveled a ball of string as he walked around so he could find his way out again. Guess what a ball of string is called?" His voice is high-pitched, and his words are so rushed that they all join. He never takes a breath. Never pauses. It's almost comical.

My lips form a smile, though I don't know why. "A clew?"

Eyes wide, his grin is ridiculous.

"How did you know that?"

He shrugs, as if it's no big deal. Then he sucks in a whopper of breath before gushing, "I'm going through an etymology phase. I'm normally mad into science and tech. Mainly robotics. A little genetics. DNA—so interesting! Did you know DNA is made of two linked strands that wind around each other to resemble a twisted ladder, also known as a double helix?" His immediate intake of breath has me chuckling, and I reach into the neck hole of my T-shirt and pull out the pendant hanging off the gold chain.

Some people believe wearing a cross around their neck offers protection from evil.

I wear a single helix for the same reason... just a different type of evil.

Max offers a megawatt smile as his gaze shifts from the gold DNA symbol up to my eyes. "You're into human biology?"

Shaking my head, I drop the chain back where it belongs... where the pendant sits close to my heart. "Not me," I tell him. "But my sister is, and she's the one who gave it to me."

"I made a necklace for Ohana once," he says, his grin widening with pride. "I made it out of macaroni, so it's not as fancy as yours, but still."

I peer into the window of Down Dawgs, noting that Olivia's still waiting for the order, and turn back to him. "Yeah, but I bet she appreciated it just as much."

"She did!" He nods, positive. "She wore it for a week before it got gross." He pauses a beat, head tilted slightly, and I can tell he's not finished, so I wait. "Does your sister have the same necklace as yours?"

"She does."

"Makes sense," he states. "Because y'all share fifty percent of your DNA, right? So, she has fifty, you have fifty, and together... *bam*! Double helix!"

I smile, happy to share a few seconds of silence with a kid I barely know.

"Me and Ollie don't share any DNA..." he starts, and I'm all fucking ears because this is what I wanted. What I needed. To get in the mind of the girl who's completely infiltrated mine. "...And sometimes I think we have more of a connection than full-blood siblings."

"How the hell old are you?" I question.

He settles back in his seat. "Ollie says I'm smart for my age. That I know too much. And that I've seen too much. She says it's both a blessing and a curse. Sometimes..." He sighs, the single sound drowning out all other thoughts. All other emotions. "Sometimes, I think I am the curse."

14

Rhys

We only did two more deliveries after Down Dawgs, and Max never engaged with me again, so I didn't either. It was probably a good thing, considering I'd somehow trapped myself in his final words.

The kid thinks he's a curse, which is a horrible fucking thought, but swear... I'd never felt so seen in my entire life.

We were quiet for the rest of the night. Olivia drove me home; I said goodbye, she said goodnight, and I haven't been able to get them out of my head since.

That was a week ago, and every night after, I do the same thing:

Order a bottle of water.

Wait for the driver's name to appear.

Cancel it when it isn't Olivia.

I limit myself, though. I only attempt ten orders a night, and if Olivia isn't one of the drivers, I force myself to stop. But after seven nights of this... seven nights of No-Olivia, I think I'm going insane.

I do my best to curb that insanity during the day. I hit the gym, read, work, hang out with Oscar or Curtis and his girls, and avoid my old school friends like the fucking plague.

It hits the hardest at night—whatever this feeling is—and no matter what I do, I can't seem to shake it.

I'm on my ninth order for the night when an alert comes through on the Get Grubby app: *Olivia is picking up your order.*

My girl doesn't seem surprised to see me waiting by my front gate, nor does she bother to get out of her vehicle. She simply waits for me to settle into the seat and buckle up, and then she's off, handing me my bottle of water as she drives. I turn to Max in his car seat, headphones on. "What's up, my guy?"

He looks up, daps my fist, and returns to his book.

Olivia doesn't say a word until we get to the gas station—the same one we went to on our first date. She parks in front of the attached diner, so she's not here for gas or I would've offered to pay. I mean, it is a date, after all—our third, if you include the first night.

Do I sound crazy? Sure. Am I actually? I guess that's yet to be determined.

For the next hour, Olivia and I don't speak, but every time she goes into a place to pick up an order, Max and I secretly do. Well, he speaks, and I listen. So far, I've learned that the word "robot" comes from the Czech word "roboto," meaning "forced labor" and that the Earth has more trees compared to stars in the Milky Way. He also told me about the books he's always reading, *Miles and his Miracles*. It's a trilogy, he explained, but only the first two books are out. I make a mental note to order them the minute I get home so I can read them and discuss them with him.

Now, we're sitting in the parking lot of a Chipotle farther out of town than we've ventured before. Max is reading his book, so I pull out my phone and go through my emails.

A couple of minutes later, Max pipes up. "Avocado."

I slip my phone into my pocket and turn to him, giving him all my attention. "What about avocado?"

"Aztec for this word," he replies, showing me a highlighted word on a website: *ahuacatl.*

I try to say it aloud, though I'm sure I butcher the pronunciation.

"Guess what it means?" he asks, a cheeky little lilt in his tone.

"I have no idea."

"Guess, Timothy," he giggles.

"I... I don't—"

"Testicles!" He breaks out in a fit of giggles so strong, he can barely take a breath, and I find myself doing the same.

"Avocado!" he almost shouts. "The fruit of testicles!"

We lose it. Completely. Our joint laughter fills every inch of the cab, every piece of my soul. It's the uncontrollable, unbreathable type of laughter that has our eyes watering, our need for air forced to come second to our need for momentary joy.

"Want some balls with your nachos?!" he squeals. I kick out my legs, my hand to my stomach to ease the ache. Max does the same, his arms crossed over his waist, and swear, if our seatbelts didn't restrain us, we'd double over.

"Oh, no! Ollie's coming!" he whispers, and we immediately face forward, sit taller, and school our features.

We manage to keep it that way until Olivia's on the road again. Max breaks first, his not-so-quiet snicker ruining my facade. Liv looks between us as if we've lost our damn minds. Then Max busts out a laugh, and I'm right there with him again. "What's so funny?" Liv asks, and when I chance a peek in her direction, she's attempting to hide her grin.

"It's nothing," I assure. At the same time, Max shouts, "Avocado testicles!" He can't stop laughing, and every time he reaches that peak of no return, I end up riding the wave with him. And sure, it's beyond ridiculous how funny we find this, but boys and balls, man... it never gets old.

"You ask," Max hisses the moment Olivia gets back in the car.

She sets the bag of food on my lap like she's done many times before, and I turn to Max, shaking my head, and whisper back, "No, you ask!"

"No, you!" Max returns.

I press my lips tight, and I shake my head more.

"Ask me what?" Olivia says, both hands on the wheel as she looks between us.

I motion for Max to go ahead, and after a sigh, he rushes out, "Timothy wants to know if he can buy us dinner."

Liv's eyes narrow on mine. "I told you not to engage—"

"He engaged with me!" I cut in. "I won't pretend I don't hear him. Besides, I'm hungry. My stomach feels like it's eating itself."

"Then you should probably go to a doctor," Max chimes in, and Liv smirks as if she already knows what's coming. "It's not normal for a stomach to digest itself because of a mechanism which regulates gastric secretion."

I scrunch my nose. "That sounds... interesting."

"Do you want to see what stomach lining looks—"

"No!" Olivia and I say at the same time.

Max shrugs, leaning forward. "So? Can he?"

"Yeah, can I?" I repeat, focusing on Olivia. "We can pick it up and take it to our spot."

"Our spot?" Liv echoes.

"You're the only person I've ever taken there, so yes. Our spot." Besides, after what happened last time we were there, I can never *not* think of it as our spot. "And if we hang out for a bit, we can catch the sunset."

"How romantic," Max giggles, and Olivia gives him a pointed look before an alert comes through on her phone. She's quick to check it, then tap it a few times. "I'm picking up an order from the diner," she says, then turns to Max. "I'll get you those cinnamon balls you like. You can have them in the car."

"But what about Timothy? He's the hungry one."

Liv puts the car in reverse and backs out of the spot, murmuring, "I'm sure Timothy has food at home."

I do. Lots of it. But that's not the point. Still, I keep my disappointment in check and turn to Max. "Sorry, bud."

"It's okay," he assures, but it's clear in both our expressions that it's not. "You tried, and that's all you can do."

Trying is just another word for failing, and I'm not big on it.

Like I said: I failed once. I won't do it again.

15

Olivia

"You have to call every day," I tell Max, sitting down on the edge of his bed. "Not just call. Facetime."

"Every day," he promises, out of breath. Clearly, getting him those cinnamon balls was a bad idea, because now he's hopped up on sugar and has way too much energy to burn right before bed.

"And journal every day," I remind him.

"Every day," he repeats.

"And make sure you listen to Dom, because he's in charge."

"Every day," he says again, which doesn't really make sense but again: *sugar.*

"And I know you already know this, but there are going to be kids who are older than you, and they might treat you a certain way because they think they're better, and..."

"No one is better than me, and I am not better than anyone," Max says, repeating a mantra we use often. He stops jumping and sits down beside me, sighing. "I know all this, Ollie."

"Ohana," Dom says gently, and I lift my eyes to his. He's quiet when he adds, motioning to our little brother, "You're going to give him anxiety with your anxiety."

I inhale a sharp breath and let it out slowly. "I'm sorry," I tell Max, running a hand over his hair.

"It's okay." His smile is soft, as if he's the one consoling me. "I know you worry."

"I do, but I really shouldn't." Besides, it's not like he's going to be there alone. And by *there*, I mean summer camp. For two whole weeks.

Max heard about the STEM-based camp through one of his favorite YouTubers, and when he brought up the idea to me, I was hesitant. Who wouldn't be? I told him he could apply, but not to get his hopes up. Thousands of kids from across the nation apply and only fifty get accepted—the youngest one in history being eight years old. Max is only six. But Max, being as incredible as he is, got his official invitation via email a couple of weeks later.

The way we celebrated, you'd think Max had won the Nobel Prize.

It wasn't until he went to bed that night that Dom and I could discuss how the hell we were actually going to make it happen for him.

We decided to use the money we'd been saving for a more reliable car and put it toward the camp fees, but that only solved one problem. The program operated during school hours only, so most parents would stay at a local hotel or short-term rental, drop their kids off in the morning, and pick them up in the afternoon. There was no way we could afford that. And besides, I had to work. I had three jobs. I could put off Get Grubby and upcycling furniture, but I also managed a small chain of laundromats, and if I wasn't there for two weeks to clean and empty the cash drawers, then it would all go to hell.

Dom's best friend's dad owned a vending machine company, and about a year ago, I spoke to the owner of the laundromats to see if Dominic could set up a couple in each of them, and they'd agreed. So, I can do Dom's job, but he can't do mine, which meant that if we could make it work financially, Dom would have to be the one to take Max.

I hated the idea of us being apart, but it was the only way.

"Leave it with me," Dom had said that night. Two days later, he told me the plan. Since they ran the program on campgrounds, Dom had asked them if he and Max could pitch a tent, and in return, he would work for free. He'd do whatever repairs or odd jobs, or... anything really, as long as Max could go. They agreed, but offered one of the unused cabins instead, and rather than doing odd jobs, they asked Dominic to lead the daily PE sessions for the kids.

I never asked, but I'm sure Dom used our little sob story to get what we needed, and no judgement, because I would've done the same. It was the dream solution, and I couldn't believe Dom had made it happen. But then again, there's not a lot in this world Dom wouldn't do for Max.

Or for me.

"Towels!" Dom says now, pointing to Max.

Max jumps to his feet and practically runs out of the room. "On it, boss!"

Dom chuckles, going through the packing list the camp had provided.

"Have you packed?" I ask him.

Dom shakes his head, distracted by counting socks. "Not yet. I had to put a few things in the washing machine, but I'll get it done tonight."

"Okay."

"The Camry's making that noise again, so don't go driving around too much at night. Dre's on standby, so call him if you need him." Dre is Dominic's best friend, and he and his parents are the closest thing we have to an extended family.

I nod. "I filled the truck with gas earlier, so you don't have to worry about it."

"Thanks."

I double count the socks he just counted.

Dom looks up, eyes narrowed. "Quit worrying."

"I'm not." I *totally am*. "Anyway, it's not as if you're going to be in the middle of nowhere. There's a Walmart within ten minutes so you can get anything you need."

Dom rolls his eyes. "You just had to look it up, didn't you?"

"Ollie!" Max calls from somewhere in the house, saving me from responding. "Your phone's ringing."

I lift the phone in my hand. "I have my phone!"

A few seconds later, Max returns, a stack of towels in one arm and my bag under the other. "Then your bag's ringing!"

"What?" I reach over, take my bag from him, and sure enough... it's beeping, not ringing, but still... I unzip it and pull out a phone I've never seen before. I look up, glancing between my brothers. "Where did this come from?"

Dom shrugs. "It's in *your* bag."

Max fails at hiding his giggle.

"Did you do this?" I ask. "Where the hell did you get an iPhone from?"

"Is someone pinging that?" Dom asks, and I show him the Find My iPhone alert on the screen.

Max all out laughs. "Timothy must have hidden it in your bag."

Oh, no...

Dread forms a knot in the pit of my stomach.

"Who's Timothy?" Dom asks, teasing.

"That guy Ohana hit with the truck."

"I didn't hit him." Irrelevant, but true.

"He loooooves her," Max sings, and I shake my head, glare at him.

"He does not," I deadpan, and the stupid phone won't stop beeping.

Dom dumps the towels into the bag. "You've been hanging out with him?"

I sigh, not sure what I'm more annoyed with. Rhys and his antics, the stupid phone that won't quit, or my brothers teasing me. "He orders food sometimes, and when we deliver it to him, he comes along for the ride. It's happened twice. It's no big deal."

"I bet he wants to take you on a date since he knows I won't be home," Max says.

"You told him about camp?"

Max nods, his grin from ear to ear, and turns to Dom. Unable to keep his giant mouth shut, he adds, "He wanted to buy us dinner tonight and go to some special spot to watch the sunset together."

"Why didn't you?" Dom asks me.

I wave a hand around the room. "We had to pack." The phone pings again, and I almost throw it clear across the room.

"That's a pretty ballsy move," Dom states, crossing his arms as he looks down at me.

"What do you mean?"

"If he's pinging his phone to find out where you live, he can do that without it making a sound. He's opting to play the notification, so it gets your attention. It's smart."

"Smart or stupid?" I ask, because Rhys already knows where I live. He just doesn't know I know he knows.

Or something.

"I gotta get our soap and stuff," Dom mumbles.

I wait for him to leave the room before glancing over at Max. Then I sigh. "I'm a phone call away if you need anything."

"I know," Max says, unplugging his night-light and throwing it in his bag.

"And if Dom is driving too fast on the—"

"Ollie!" Dom shouts, and I grimace, already knowing what's coming. "Can you come here? I can't find something!"

"Ooooh. You're in trouble," Max whispers.

I drop a kiss on his head and make my way to the boys' bathroom. Dom waits until I'm just inside the door to say, "Wait here." He returns seconds later with my bag and practically shoves it at my chest. "You, here, is making him worried. You got him anxious about things he wasn't even thinking about before."

"I know. I'm sorry."

"I'd rather you just not be here at all."

"What?"

"Go," he says, grasping my shoulders, spinning me around, and physically pushing me out the door.

"Go where?"

His smile is wicked. "Go see your boy."

Rolling my eyes, I dig my heels into the floor. "He's not my—"

"Max and I are fine, Ollie. Nothing is going to happen to us," Dom cuts in, his following sigh so dramatic, you'd think he'd been holding it for years. "And please don't take offense to what I'm about to say, but you need to get a life."

"Excuse me?" I scoff.

"You need a life outside of me and Max. A *social* life."

"I have a social life!"

He throws his hand out between us. "Show me your phone."

I hide my phone behind my back. "No!"

"Yeah, because I bet when I look at the call log, it will only be Max's iPad and me." He drops his hand, shaking his head at the glare I throw his way. "And it's not as if you don't have time."

"You're not home that much during the summer, and Max... Maybe when he goes back to school, I'll have a better routine—"

"You said that last summer."

I sigh. "I appreciate what you're trying to do here, Dom, and I get it. I do. But *I* am completely content."

"Content is a state of peaceful satisfaction," Dom points out. "Peace is for the birds, Ollie. Don't you want excitement or adventure or... I don't know, something to feel passionate about?"

Yes.

I stare at him, unblinking, then shake my head. "Not really. No."

He sighs, defeated. "You forget I know when you're lying, Ohana."

The phone in my hand pings again, and I look down at it, then at Dom.

"Excitement..." he teases, and I feel that exact emotion run through my veins... right before it turns ice cold.

"Maybe one day," I say, switching off Rhys's phone completely. "But not today."

* * *

NOT FRIDGE GUY

You ever had your heart broken?

Can't say that I have. Why?

I was going to ask you how it felt, because I'm pretty sure it's happening to me right now.

Your heart is breaking right now?

Yes

...

... what?

Hearts can't break.

?

Hearts are made of cardiac muscle, so they can ache, they can strain, and they can bend, but they can't break. Not in these bodies. Not in this lifetime.

16

Olivia

For three years I've wondered what it would be like to be alone in a room with Rhys Garrett. I just didn't expect that room to be my garage.

Or maybe I did.

Maybe there was a reason I'd left the garage door open long after it needed to be. Either way, he's here, and I don't know how to feel about it. And not knowing how to feel means not knowing what to say, how to act, and so I continue to do the same thing I was doing before he showed up—stripping paint off an old dresser I'd found on the side of the road a few months ago. It's lived in this garage ever since. And while a lot of my other pieces have come and gone, this dresser has sat, waiting for me to show it some love. But it's personal now—this relationship between the dresser and me. I know it needs attention, but the moment I give it some, it'll sell, and I don't want to let it go. So, I keep it in its miserable state for as long as I can, until eventually, one day, it'll leave me.

Whoa.

If I had a psychologist, they'd tell me I was projecting my insecurities onto an inanimate object.

Thank God I don't have a psychologist.

Besides, this—being in a workshop—is my form of therapy. It's where I spent the most time growing up, watching my grandpa work on old furniture, just like I do now. I was his little helper—his apprentice. Looking back, I hindered more than I helped, but he never once made me feel like a nuisance. I'd sit in my little camp chair for hours, sipping my little juice box, watching him sand and plane and stain, and he would talk to me, his tone gentle at every step. He'd tell me what he was doing as he was doing it, and he'd answer all my questions. Not just about woodwork, but about anything and everything. About life. Love. *Heart*.

I remember watching him once, thinking how it should've been impossible for one man to have a heart as big as my grandpa's and still be alive.

Maybe that's what killed him.

The size of his heart.

After every piece he finished, we'd sign our names on the underside as if we were artists. As if I deserved to have my name next to his craftmanship. Now, whenever I finish a piece, I sign both our names...

...because he's here.

With me.

In my garage.

And knowing that is the only way I know how to heal.

Speaking of healing, it suddenly occurs to me that on the two occasions since our not-so meet cute, I haven't once asked Rhys how *he* is healing. I look up, about to do just that, but stop when I catch him focused on a sanding block in his hand. He flips it over. Once. Twice. Then he runs his thumb over the gritty paper. "Huh," he mumbles, as if it's the most fascinating thing in the world. Finally, he lifts his eyes, catches me watching him, and he...

He *blushes*.

Ugh.

Rhys is hot, there's no denying, but he's not supposed to be cute, or coy, or whatever it is that's happening right now. It's been less than twenty-four hours since I'd seen him last, and watching him now—it feels as though I'm seeing a whole other version of him.

He moves on from the sanding block and makes his way toward the shelf filled with half-empty cans of stains. He picks up one and inspects it, taking his time to read the label.

He doesn't say a word.

Neither do I.

It's been like this for a whole ten minutes—ever since he pulled up in a black Range Rover and walked up my driveway, hands in his pockets, cap pulled low on his brow, and proceeded to enter my physical space as easily as he entered my emotional one.

The silence between us has stretched out for so long that it feels like a game now.

Like a dare.

Without a word, I move past him and make a show of closing the garage door. The last thing I need is one of Dom's friends driving by and seeing Rhys Garrett in my garage. Besides, if Rhys wants to play games, I've got time.

What I don't have, unfortunately, is the ability to be unphased by his presence. I can't hide the heat that curls up my neck, to the tips of my ears, or the blush the colors my cheeks when he looks at me the way he is. I can't hide the way my hands twitch, begging to touch him in ways I only fantasize about at night. When I'm in my bed. Eyes closed. Fingers playing beneath my underwear.

And I realize, too late, that it's one thing to have Rhys sitting shotgun in my car, but it's another to have him here, alone, no Max, no buffer. When we're out doing deliveries, there's a beginning, a middle, and an end to our shenanigans. As soon as it gets close to Max's bedtime, we stop accepting orders; I take Rhys home, and we go our separate ways. Now, though? It's barely five in the evening, there's no allocated end time, and we're at my house. Technically, if I want things to end, he's the one who has to leave, and now I'm panicking.

Overthinking.

Because of course, I am.

And Rhys is standing there in his gray tee and black shorts, watching me, *examining* me, and I get why so many girls fall for boys like Rhys, because boys like Rhys have a certain charisma and self-awareness that make it easy to fall for their bullshit.

His phone rings, breaking our little stare-off.

"I thought you left your phone in my bag," I question.

He smiles to one side, pulling his phone from his pocket. "I gotta take this," he says, all carefree and annoying. He answers the video call before holding the phone in front of his face. "Izzy," he says in greeting.

"Reese's Pieces!" his sister squeals, and I crack a smile. "You owe me an entry!"

"Fuck," Rhys responds. "My bad. I'll do it now."

"Is that your brother?" another female voice says, and my pulse rises while Rhys's gaze drops.

"Yes, Mother," his sister replies.

A second later: "Hi, Pookie bear!"

I cover my mouth to stop from busting out a laugh. *Pookie bear?* I die.

"Mother," Rhys deadpans, his teeth gritted through his fake smile.

"If you want to talk to Rhys, then you call him," his sister whines. "This is my time."

"Sorry," his mother says sarcastically.

Silence passes a beat, and I contain my laughter to a silent, simmering giggle.

Pookie bear.

His sister asks, "How are you?"

"I'm good, Iz. How are you?" There's a gentleness in the way he speaks to her, even through a phone, and I wonder what it would be like to have Rhys and Dom in the same room, away from the outside world, because maybe... just maybe, they're more alike than they wish to admit.

"Also good," Izzy replies. "Hey... I forgot to ask you yesterday! How's that girl who tilts your world off its axis? The one who made you want to stay?"

Made him want to stay? What does that even mean?

Rhys clears his throat, and it seems like forever before he replies, "Ah, I'm actually with her right now, so thanks for that."

Aaand, I'm no longer laughing.

Not even a little.

"No problem," Izzy chirps, utterly clueless to the sudden hysteria she's created inside me. "I'll let you go then, but you owe me an entry. A long one."

"You got it," Rhys replies. "Later." He hangs up, and with zero explanation of what the hell just happened, lifts his gaze to mine, then speaks into his phone. "I know I owe you a long one, and I promise you'll get it, but this one's going to have to be short. It's just... I'm standing in front of the girl of my literal dreams right now, and I'm about to shoot my shot, but the longer I stand here, the more confidence I lose, because she's lookin' a little... terrified, and I should probably figure out why, so... I love you and I'll speak to you later." He stops the recording and pockets his phone, never once taking his eyes off mine. And *what is happening right now?* "Is my being here making you uncomfortable?" There's no play in his words. No bite.

"Not *uncomfortable*," I answer truthfully.

"Nervous?" he asks. "Scared?"

"Nervous, I guess."

He tilts his head just an inch, his eyes narrowing. "Why?"

"I don't know." I shrug. "It's a lot for me—you being here and being who you are... and then there's Dominic to think about, and Max, and you seem to continue to find ways to get to me... and yeah, it's a little unnerving because..." I trail off, unsure how to continue.

"Because why?" he asks, stepping forward.

Dropping my arms, I release a breath, let my shoulders fall with it. "Because I don't know what you want from me, Rhys."

"What do you think I want from you?"

"I don't know," I admit. "But I know that every night for the past week, you've ordered a bottle of water from multiple places. You do this ten times a night, and then it stops. So that means you either have a horrible case of OCD that's forcing you to—"

"I don't have OCD," he cuts in.

I didn't think so. "And I don't want to judge you based on your house or car or whatever, but I assume you have money—maybe not mountains of it—but enough to cure boredom, so that's not it."

"Correct."

"And, I know you have friends—at least based on the carload of people you brought here to egg my house last year—"

He grimaces. "You know about that?"

I roll my eyes. "Of course, I do." I know way more about him than he assumes, but that's not the point. "My point is that you're not going to insane efforts every night to hang out with me and Max because of some psychological disorder, or boredom or... loneliness, and if it's about some... physical need—"

"It's not about that," he interrupts.

I stare directly into his eyes, trying to read his thoughts, but they give nothing away. "So, I guess my question remains... What do you want from me, Rhys?"

17

Rhys

What do I want from her?

If Olivia wants another truth from me, then she's asking the wrong questions, because I want nothing from her.

"I just want to get to know you, that's all."

Across from me, Olivia crosses her arms. "There's nothing to know."

That's where she's wrong. "Well, I know your name's not Olivia Delgado."

"I never said it was," she's quick to say, dropping her arms and turning away from me. Today, she's in a crop top and workout shorts with the waistband rolled over. Her bare stomach's on full display, and swear, I'd never been so turned on by an abdomen before. Maybe it's because it's the first time I'm seeing hers, or maybe because it's her, but holy hell. She moves back to an old dresser she was working on when I walked in and continues to scrape the pale pink paint off it. "It makes sense now..."

She has back dimples.

I might just combust.

Turn to ash on her garage floor.

Her hair's up in a messy knot, the way I've always seen it, leaving her nape bare, and I force myself not to go to her and kiss her right in that spot. I take a step forward. Stop myself there. And I try to remember what she just said. "What makes sense?"

"It bothers you that you didn't know about me, and now that you do, you can't figure me out." She turns to me, her eyes widening at how close I am. She tries to hide her reaction, but I notice the way her throat moves with her swallow. "This is all part of some game for you, isn't it? The chase. The—"

"Why are you acting like this?" I cut in, and it comes harsher than intended, but, honestly, I'm getting sick of feeling like I'm in the wrong. Like whatever's happening between us is one-sided. It's not.

"Acting like what?"

I sigh. "Say it is a game for me. Would you want to play?"

"No," she deadpans.

I meet her glare across the room. "Bullshit."

Her eye roll makes me smile. Makes me kind of hard, too.

"Say what you need to make yourself feel better, Cheeks, but I know you want me."

She scoffs.

"You know how I know?"

"Enlighten me."

"The first time we met was an accident." I pause a beat, narrow my eyes at her. "I think..."

She smiles, lowering her defenses.

I grin wider. "The second time took a little coercing, sure, but the third time? You accepted my order, picked it up, drove all the way to my house, and let me get in your car. And now?"

"What about now?"

"Are you always in here with the door open?"

"You've never worked with wood before, have you?"

I chuckle. Turn *twelve*. "I usually have other people working on my wood for me."

She smiles behind her scoff. "You're an idiot."

"And yet... you haven't asked me to leave, so..."

"So... what?"

"So..." I lean against a workbench, my legs crossed at the ankles, and watch her closely. "What do *you* want, Liv?"

A strangled laugh pours out of her. "It doesn't matter what I want."

Not the answer I was expecting. "Play a game with me?" I ask, and I usually hate going in circles like this, but for her, I don't mind the dizziness.

"What game?"

"Technically, it's your game, but with my twist. Let's call it... trading truths." I wait for a response, and when nothing comes, I continue, "Rules are simple. For every truth I get out of you, I'll owe you two."

She taps her chin, eyes to the ceiling, and it's so fucking cute, I almost break my bravado. "Fine," she says. "I'll go first."

My smile is stupid.

"What did your sister mean before?"

I'd have to be blind not to see that one coming. "About you making me want to stay?"

"Not about me, specifically," she says, shaking her head. "The staying part. Were you planning to leave? Where were you going?"

"That's two questions."

She shrugs. "So, I'll owe you a truth."

I grip the edges of the workbench, wondering how much to divulge. "Yes, I was planning to leave, but... I don't know where I was going." Not a lie.

"I thought this was about truths?"

"That is the truth." I choose my next words carefully. "I was planning to leave, but I didn't have solid plans. It was more a *wake up and see where life takes me* kind of thing."

Even from across the room, she can see through my bullshit. "And your sister was okay with that?"

I avert my gaze, saying, "As long as she knew where I was when I got there, then yes." Also not a lie, but further from the truth than I'm comfortable with, so I add, "It wasn't permanent. When summer's over, my ass will be in Colorado with her and my parents, so what I do between now and then is... irrelevant." My discomfort has me itching to change the subject. "Tell me about how you and Dom are siblings."

"That's not a question."

It's my turn to roll my eyes. "Fine. Why do you and Dom have different last names?"

After a heavy sigh, she sets down the scrapey thing she'd been holding on to and leans against the dresser opposite me, giving me her full attention. "I have my mother's last name. He has my grandparents'—my grandma and step-grandpa."

"So how—"

"That's your one question, Garrett." My shoulders drop while her lips curve into a wicked smile. "How did you know about our different last names?"

This, I can answer. "I have a... thing for numbers. Statistics, to be precise, and I also have a thing for basketball. Those two things combined had me studying certain players. Your brother's stats were— are..." It physically pains me to say the words, and I'm sure she can sense that. With a suffering sigh, I mumble, "Dom's stats throughout his younger years stood out, and so I studied him."

"You *studied* him?"

"Yes." I nod. "And I know it sounds crazy, but it's the truth. I knew of him before he even made his way to Philips."

She contemplates this a moment, before stating, "But studying him, his gameplay and his stats don't lead to knowing about our last names..."

"Once I knew what middle school he went to, finding you wasn't hard."

"So, what else do you know about me, you creep?" There's a hint of playfulness in her tone, and I almost feel bad for diving as deep as I have, because the truth is: I know way more than I should about Olivia *Mitchell*. But the things I've learned about her should come from her. Not a handful of archived news stories that someone worked really fucking hard to delete from existence. "I know you were fifteen when you went into your senior year. Graduate at sixteen? That's kind of baller."

Her gaze drops to the floor as she shakes her head slowly. "You dove real deep, huh?"

"It was in your high school newsletter," I cut in, trying to brush it off. Exposing my extensive knowledge on all things Olivia might get me arrested for stalking. A class H felony if I recall correctly. "It was really all I could find, so..."

Her eyes lift, lock on mine. "Who's turn is it to ask?" she questions, and I can see her interest fading.

Trying to keep her with me, I ask, "Is this one of your three jobs Max mentioned?" I motion to the literal piles of furniture covering the length of an entire wall. "You flip old furniture?"

"How much did Max tell you?"

"Not a lot." I pause a beat. "Actually, yeah, he told me everything. The STEM camp, and how Dominic's working there, so they had a place to stay, and how much he appreciates how hard you work so you could afford to send him."

She doesn't speak, and I get it. It's an awkward topic.

"So?" I ask.

"So what?"

"Is this one of your three jobs?"

After a sigh, she answers, "Why don't you ask your new best friend?"

I grin. Like an idiot. "I would, but he's at summer camp."

Her eye roll is as playful as her tone when she says, "Yes, it's one of them."

I nod, looking around the garage. There's sawdust on every surface, all over the floor, clumps of it heaped in corners. Usually, a space like this would bother me, but having Olivia be the center of it all is almost... calming. "How did you get into it?"

"My grandpa," she answers, and it's the easiest response she's given so far. "But he was much better at it than me. His specialty was restoring antique furniture to its original condition. People would send him pieces from all over; he was that good..."

I wait, wanting more, because I know this means more than she's letting on. Instead, she switches it up and asks, "Truth?"

I nod in response.

"Are you here because you want to kiss me again?" Liv, like any living human, has sides, and I'd happily spend the rest of my existence uncovering every single one of them. This side of Liv—this coy, playful, teasing side—is possibly my favorite.

"I think I've made it pretty clear that I want to do more than just kiss you, Liv." I smirk when her cheeks bloom pink. "But all that aside, you have something that belongs to me."

"Right." She nods once, taking a moment to tear her eyes away from me before moving to a door. She opens it, saying over her shoulder, "Are you coming?"

18

Olivia

The only thing I want to show Rhys seems to be the last thing he notices when he enters my room. Maybe it's because he wasn't expecting to walk directly into a bedroom from the garage, or maybe it's because of the room itself.

I try to see things through his eyes: the many plants that hang from the ceiling, sit on the window ledge, or on the floor. Rather than books placed neatly on shelves, I have years' worth of things Max has made for me: LEGO builds, drawings, pieces he'd crafted at school. My bed is nothing more than a mattress that sits on a raised floor by the full-length window. I'd dreamed about it one night, designed it the next morning, and had Dom help me build it within days. Right now, the bed is unmade, with multiple pillows scattered about. A pile of dirty clothes sits on the floor in the corner, and sure, I'd considered cleaning my room, assuming Rhys would show up, but what would be the point? It's not as if I was trying to impress him. Besides, I don't plan on him staying all that long.

The neatest thing in my room is the stack of Rhys' possessions that sits on the corner of the bed—hoodie, cash, phone. All things I plan on him taking when he leaves.

I know that he's noticed it, but he doesn't give it a second glance. So, I stand in place, watching Rhys walk around, fixated on his surroundings while I fixate on him.

I study his presence like I've studied his texts.

Rhys picks up a completed Rubik's Cube and scrutinizes it before trailing his eyes to mine. "Max solved it when he was three," I explain, even though he didn't ask. Rhys doesn't respond, just flips the cube over in his hands a few times.

There's a certain innocence to Rhys I hadn't expected. An almost childlike wonder in the way he studies things, the way he sees things as if it's his first time.

And as I watch him, I try to imagine him as a kid.

I can't.

In my mind, he appeared out of thin air, age sixteen, and everything before that is... static.

No movement. No change. No clear picture of who he was prior. Then again, he's never told me about his past, and I've never asked because I was warned not to. Not that it ever mattered to me. The version of him I've come to know is all I've ever wanted.

All I've ever needed.

He sets down the Rubik's Cube as if it's fragile and picks up a bouquet made of LEGO sitting in a glass vase. "Max again," I tell him and leave it at that. Divulging that he'd given it to me for Mother's Day would just open a line of questioning I'm not ready to endure. After putting the fake flowers back, Rhys glances around, saying, "You have a lot of plants."

"I like to challenge myself."

"How so?"

I shrug. "See if I can keep things alive."

His eyes snap to mine, filled with an emotion I can't decipher, and I have to wonder exactly how much he's uncovered in his recent stalking. Silence fills the air until he finally says, "This is dope." He makes his way over to the raised part of the room, sits on the edge of the bed with his legs out in front of him, and motions to my dollhouse. "Your grandpa make this?"

I sit next to him and nod, even though he's not looking at me. At nearly four feet high, it took us almost a year to build the dollhouse. "It's a replica of our old house." And my most prized possession.

"The one in Wilmington?" he asks.

I turn to him. "How did you—"

"I studied your brother, remember?" He pauses a beat. "You know Michael Jordan's from Wilmington?"

"You don't say?" I mock.

With a low chuckle, he pushes into my side, then leans forward to pull out the two wooden figures from the play kitchen. One white. One brown. "You and Dom?" he asks, and I nod. He points to the two other figures in the living room of the dollhouse. "Mom and Dad?"

"Grandma and Grandpa for me. Mom and Dad for Dom. But they raised us as siblings."

Rhys's quiet a moment, and so I turn to him, watch his eyebrows lower with each passing second. "So is Dom a brother to one of your parents or...?"

"No."

Rhys turns to me, catches me watching him, but I don't care.

"My grandparents used to foster kids. Usually they were emergencies, but some of them were more long-term. They did it mainly when my mom was growing up." I don't tell him that I'm almost certain it's the reason she hates kids as much as she does.

"Dominic was a foster kid?"

"He was," I answer, nodding. "Until they adopted him. He was four when he came to us. I was five. My mom had given over legal rights of me to my grandparents within weeks of having me, so I'd lived there all my life. I'd seen foster kids come and go, but Dominic... he was... special." A knot forms in my throat, and I lower my gaze, try to breathe through the sudden ache in my chest.

"Did he give you the name *Ohana*?" Rhys asks, his tone gentle.

"Yeah." I nod, just once. "That's kind of how my grandparents knew they had to make it official," I say through bated breaths. "We were so close—Dom and me. We still are... which is why being with you like this feels like such a betrayal to him."

"I get that," Rhys says, so quietly I barely hear him. "And if you want me to leave, I understand."

I do. But also: "I don't." Besides, it was Dom who wanted me to strive for more than peaceful satisfaction, right? To seek some excitement or adventure, or something to feel passionate about... Rhys ticks all those boxes... at least for one night.

"And where does Max fit into all of this? Did they adopt him, too?"

"Max and Dom are half-brothers. Same mom." I release all the air in my lungs, let my shoulders deflate with heaviness of the truth. "Dominic was given up for adoption because his parents were super young when they had him. By the time his mom had Max, she was in a far better place in her life, but... there was an incident that claimed both his parents. That's how the authorities found out about Dominic and why they reached out to my grandparents. Max had only been with us for a couple of months before..." Before it all happened again. "They didn't get a chance to legally adopt him. So, for now, he still has his biological parents' last name. We have a Mitchell, a Delgado, and a Harris." I take out my phone and find the last picture we took of all of us together, then show it to him. "We're probably the most diverse family you'll ever meet."

He smiles as he looks at the picture of me and my brothers with my grandparents standing in front of our old house. My grandma is white, and my (step) grandpa is Filipino—the source of Delgado. Then there's Dom, half black, half Iranian, and Max, whose parents were both black, and me, the only kid with an accessible parent, but whose parent won't say who or where half my DNA is from. Dominic says I should take one of those DNA test kits, but I'm almost afraid of what I'll find out. That, and the rabbit hole it might lead me down.

Rhys is still staring at my phone, his eyebrows drawn, mind racing a million miles a minute, trying to piece it all together. "Does that mean that Dom is technically your uncle?" he asks, and of all the things he could've said, I'm glad he went with something light.

"Yes." I roll my eyes, locking my phone and setting it beside me.

"And believe me, he reminds me of it whenever I try to tell him what to do."

"Do you do that a lot?"

"No," I say truthfully. "He has too much to lose if he steps out of line, so..."

"Huh," he says, and that's all he says before reaching back into the dollhouse. I try to see what he's aiming for, and when realization kicks in, I almost choke on air. On *dread*. I'd forgotten the book was in there, and now he's pulling it out, inspecting it. "What's this?"

I shrug, try to play it cool, but my stomach twists. "A book."

"I can see that, Einstein, but why's it in there?"

"I don't know," I lie, my pulse racing beneath my flesh. Nerves swarm through my veins, twist in my stomach. I swallow the sudden fear in my throat, then add, "It was in one of those top ten must-read-before-you-die lists, and I had every intention to, but it's *so* long." I laugh and hope he doesn't pick up on the awkwardness of it.

"It's 464,000 words."

I glance at him, and even though I already know the answer, I ask, "I take it you've read it?"

"It's my favorite book." I already knew that, too.

I try to settle my breathing, try to calm my thoughts, and as nonchalantly as physically possible, ask, "What's it about?"

He contemplates for a moment, his jaw working. "It's about this guy who was falsely imprisoned for fourteen years. Most of the story is him seeking revenge for the ones who framed him, but there's this girl—"

"There's always a girl," I try to joke, but I don't think he hears me.

"—*Mercedes*. He was engaged to her when everything went down, so when he gets out, he goes to see her..."

I know what happens next. Still, I ask, "And they live happily ever after?"

He turns to me, a smile tugging on his lips. "The happily ever after isn't the point, Cheeks."

"What *is* the point?"

"That the love he felt for Mercedes, and the idea of being with her once it was all over... that's what kept him going all that time." He pauses a breath. "Sometimes I wonder if that's all life is. The constant search for that one person who gives you hope. Who inspires you. Someone you're willing to wait years for, even when the outcome may not always be forever."

I stare at his profile. At the way his lashes fall against his cheeks when he blinks. "Do you have someone like that?" I ask, because I know I do, and he's sitting right next to me.

"Maybe." He turns to me, his eyes meeting mine. "I just don't know how she feels."

I hold his stare for one second, two, and then I look away, slowly filling my lungs with some much-needed air.

Am *I* she?

Or is *she* the version of me trapped in his phone?

Or has he somehow worked out that we're one and the same?

Neither answer is okay, and with that thought in mind, I stand up, stop a few feet away, and turn to him. "Do you ever think about what would've happened that night we met? I mean, how far we would've gone if Max wasn't in the car or if my alarm didn't go off..."

Chin raised to look up at me, his eyebrows knit, just slightly, but he doesn't respond.

"Because I think about it," I rush out, for no other reason than to fill the silence. "I think—for me, anyway—the reason I'm so drawn to you is *curiosity*."

"Curiosity?" he repeats.

I nod. "Yep. The *what if* of it all." His stare is blank, as if he has no clue where this is going. "I think we should do it. Just once. Get it out of our system and move on."

After inhaling a huge breath, he raises a finger between us, saying, "Just to be clear, when you say *it*, you mean sex, right?"

I roll my eyes. "Yes."

"As in *penetration*?"

"Oh, my God," I murmur. "Yes."

He cracks a smile, right before he hooks a single finger into my waistband and pulls me toward him. I'm so surprised by the sudden move that I don't have time to react until I'm standing between his legs.

I stutter on a breath and grip his shoulders for balance. His hands find my hips, fingertips digging into me. Eyes half-hooded, he pulls me closer, looks up at me. Voice deep, smooth, he says, "As in my hard cock in your wet pussy?"

Jesus.

Fire licks at my flesh, simmers beneath the surface. I nod once, my throat suddenly dry. "Yes."

His grin turns mischievous and he pushes forward, his eyes never leaving mine. Breath hot against my bare stomach, he runs his lips along my skin, so light I barely feel it. My eyes drift shut when he kisses my belly button, then snap open when he parts his lips, his hot tongue snaking across my abdomen to my hips. First one. Then the other. He takes his time, gliding his hands up my sides until his thumbs near the underside of my breasts. He strokes me there, and I let out a moan. Or a groan. I can't tell if I'm frustrated or turned on. I just know that I want more. *Need* more. "Rhys," I whisper and dig my nails into his shoulders when I feel him smile against my stomach. He's so wicked in his ways—his lips, his hands, his words—all just enough to tease, but not enough to torture. He keeps his eyes on mine when he lowers the band of my shorts, just an inch. Then he kisses where I'm newly exposed, again and again, his breath faltering with every press of his lips.

My muscles clench, my breath trapped within my rib cage, and I'm done with his games.

I pull away from his mouth and grasp his head in my hands, forcing him to look up at me. Then I lower my mouth to his. But before I can make contact, he rolls out from beneath me, and I fall onto the mattress, face-first, and *what the fuck?*

I flip onto my back just in time to watch him shove his hand down his shorts to adjust himself. "Where do you consider home?" he asks.

I repeat, "What the fuck?" Only this time, I say it out loud.

"Where do you consider home?" he asks again, all lazy and cool, and I throw a pillow at his head. Of course, he blocks it, then uses it to cover his junk. And then he does something that makes me wish I had something far more solid to throw at him. He *laughs*. "You never said we had to have sex now... or tonight, even."

I sit up in the middle of the bed. "What is wrong with you?"

"You said one time, and it's over." He shrugs. "What if I'm not ready for it to be over yet?"

"Rhys…" His name is a sigh. "That's not…" I don't even know what to say to that.

"What? We can't hang out until then?"

I shake my head. He may not know the full truth of who we are to each other, but he knows enough. "We shouldn't be hanging out at all."

"So, ask me to leave then," he deadpans, and it's the second time he's brought it up. If I weren't so in tune with the ways of Rhys Garrett, I'd almost assume he *wants* me to ask him, but that's not what this is. This is him, constantly throwing the ball in my court and waiting for me to decide what the hell to do with it. That way, should anything actually happen between us, he won't be responsible. It's smart—just like every decision, every play, every move Rhys makes.

I wonder how many times he's gotten away with it.

Probably not as many times as I'll look back on this moment and regret what I could've/should've/would've done.

I'm supposed to have said something by now, told him to leave, or asked him to stay, but my feelings aren't binary. I can't simply pick one or the other.

"I told you before," Rhys says, breaking through my thoughts. "This isn't just about sex for me, Liv. I want to get to know you. Anything else is a bonus."

"What if sex is the only thing I can offer right now?" Or *ever*… at least with him.

With a heavy sigh, he gets on the bed, kneeling opposite me, and mumbles, "Then I guess I'll have to take it."

"Jeez." It's annoying how easily he can make me giggle like an idiot. "Don't get too excited."

He chuckles, gently pushing on my shoulder until I'm flat on my back. "This is what happens when you don't give me options." He grabs my thighs, forcing them apart, then effortlessly drags me toward him until he's in between my legs. He settles a warm hand on my stomach, fingers splayed, and inches it higher, higher, slowly, slowly. I watch his eyes lose focus when he gets to the space between my breasts. Arching my back, I writhe against him. "Fuck," he spits, removing his hand and falling back on his haunches. "If we're going to do this, you have to at least let me buy you dinner first."

I drop my head to the mattress, stare up at the ceiling. "Why are you cock-blocking yourself like this?"

Reaching into his pocket, he mumbles, "Because I'm a sucker for pain." After pulling out his phone, he taps it a few times, then hands it to me. "Find something on that menu you like." Then he lowers himself on top of me and nuzzles my neck. He kisses the spot just below my ear, his weight held up on his forearms, and then he parts his lips, his tongue like flames flickering against me, burning through my flesh, into my veins and it's so much all at once...

...until it's nothing at all.

Rhys pulls back, extending his arm, and then he smirks.

I push on his shoulder—a feather touch versus a brick wall. "Stop teasing me."

"Pick something from the menu," he reminds me, and I'd forgotten about the phone in my hand.

"Fine," I say, tugging on his nape and guiding him back to where I want him. His breath warms my neck when he chuckles, and I wrap my legs around his torso and pull him down to position. I smile when he groans, bites down on my shoulder. Then sucks. *Hard*. "You're going to mark me."

"That's the point." He scrapes his teeth along my neck until his mouth finds my ear. "Food, Cheeks."

"Stop distracting me then." I raise his phone behind his head and start scrolling through the menu. Then pause. "You realize you've given me full access to your phone, right?"

"Don't care," he says, making his way down to my breasts.

"Instagram. Snapchat... your photos... probably some nudes..."

He tugs my top down with his teeth, repeating, "Don't care."

"I could go through your messages..." Now *that's* tempting.

He traces the top of my bra with his tongue. "Have at it."

I take it as an invitation and open his messages in search of something scandalous. Something to tease him about. The most recent contacts are his sister, his mom, and Curtis—his cop friend who I'd met. After Curtis is Oscar, and I assume it's Oscar Mendoza—a kid on his team with a good arm, at least according to his egg-throwing capabilities.

After Oscar is a name I'm all too familiar with. A name that has my pulse racing and breath catching. It's a name that appears over 260 times in a 464-thousand-word book.

I click on *Mercedes*, my heart as thirsty as my eyes.

MERCEDES

Hearts are made of cardiac muscle, so they can ache, they can strain, and they can bend, but they can't break. Not in these bodies. Not in this lifetime.

Rhys hadn't responded to the message I'd sent last night, even though he'd read it right away, and I'd spent the next few hours wishing I could take back my words. Just because I'm cynical about all matters pertaining to the heart, that doesn't mean that everyone else should be. In fact, most days, I wish I was the opposite. I wish vulnerability lived inside me the way I see it in others. The way I see it in Rhys. But every piece of tenderness—of *warmth*—I've ever held on to has only burned me in the past.

Now, I live in an ice chest, guarded by walls so thick and so high that even sunlight can't break through.

I exit the messages and lock the phone, drop it as if it's fire in my hands.

"Have you decided?" Rhys asks, kissing just above my belly button.

"You order for me," I say, then shove down the knot in my throat, bury it deep inside me. "I suck at deciding."

He sits up, still between my legs, and I hand him his phone. I watch his face, his brow furrowing as he seems to type out a text, then throw the phone on the mattress beside me. Finally, his eyes meet mine, widening slightly. "You okay?"

I nod. "Yeah," I lie. "Why?"

He runs a thumb over my cheek, his touch cold against my blush. "You're all flushed," he says, pressing his lips to my cheeks. First one. Then the other. I gently grasp his nape, holding me to him, and catch his mouth before he can pull away.

And then I kiss him.

I kiss him just like I did the first time—as if I've been starved of his taste, deprived of his touch.

And it feels the same now as it did that night.

Kissing Rhys Garrett is like breathing in sunshine, warming me from the inside, thawing my heart, my soul, until cracks appear in my ice-cold armor.

19

Rhys

Swear to God, I try so hard not to laugh, but the emotion takes over my body, and I can't stop the sound that forms deep in my gut. I nuzzle Liv's neck to stifle it, but it's useless.

"Stop it," she whines, tightening her hold around my neck. We're both sitting up on her bed, only she's straddling my lap, and at some point, not quite sure when, she'd ripped off my T-shirt. Not *ripped*, as in literally, but she may as well have.

Our mouths had been so busy locked on each other's that it's the first time we've spoken since she kissed me. And, honestly, I can't fucking remember the last time I made out with a girl just for the sake of making out.

No complaints.

I still have one hand in her hair, the other on her ass, where it's spent the past few minutes, my fingers digging deep into her flesh, guiding her while she shifted her hips, grinding in slow circles as she pressed down on my cock. I was so fucking hard, and she was so warm, and minutes later, her breathing hitched, her hips jerked, and her moans—goddamn her moans—and it took me a second to realize what was happening. At first, it was an assumption, but then she started cursing with every exhale, "*fuck fuck fuck*", and I knew for sure she was coming. Or close to it. I let her ride it out, and by that, I mean *ride me*, meeting her thrust for thrust, until she bit down on my shoulder to muffle her *scream*. She shook in my arms, and I held her close, not knowing what to be more shocked about—the fact that I'm pretty certain she broke skin with her teeth or the sound she made when she did it. Or maybe it's that she was able to get there by *dry humping*.

Or, even more surprising, that I was about two fucking seconds away from doing the same.

Hence, why I can't stop laughing.

"I'm not laughing *at* you," I tell her between chuckles. I kiss her neck, her jaw, her mouth. "Swear it."

"Then what's funny?" she asks, pressing down on me again. Girls have it good when it comes to sex, as long as they're with a giving partner. They can go multiple times. I have one shot, and in Liv's scenario, that one shot is my *only* shot.

"I'm just insanely turned on, that's all." I pull back, smiling when I see the state of her. Beads of sweat form along her hairline and join the freckles on her nose. Her cheeks are flushed, rosy red, and I remove my hand off her ass to swipe my thumb along the warmth there. "God, you're beautiful," I tell her, and I mean it in every sense of the word.

She kisses me once. Twice. And then over and over again. She ends on a sigh, the sound of contentment, and adjusts on my lap, sitting slightly higher. Forehead resting against mine, she asks, "Where do you keep your condoms?"

Eyes narrowed, I pull back slightly. "This isn't my house."

She rears back even more, keeps her forearms on my shoulders. "Don't you keep some in your wallet?"

"Who the fuck carries a wallet?"

"You did!" she retorts. "Remember? The night we met..."

"Oh yeah. I lied." I glance around her room, ending on her nightstand, and motion to it. "Don't you keep some in there?"

"Who am I having sex with?"

I grin, liking that answer. Then stop. Because what now?

"Don't you have some in your car?" she asks.

I shake my head. "What about Dom—"

She squeals, interrupting me. "I don't want to know." She pulls back an inch, squeezing my nape as she glares down at me. "How are you this unprepared?"

"It's not as if I came here intending to fuck you."

She pouts, pushing out her bottom lip. "You didn't?"

I roll my eyes. "I'm not having this conversation again."

She nods, looking down at the problem between us. I'm still rock hard, and she likely wants to get off again.

"Want me to blow you?" she asks, all even toned and casual.

I almost come at the thought. Right there and then. Instead, I throw her off of me in one swift move. She lands on her back, and I flip onto my stomach beside her. I grip my cock, delaying the inevitable.

"I've never done it before," she says, her tone pensive, and if she's still talking about sucking dick, then I'll lose my mind, and my load, all at once. "You'll have to show me what you like so I can get it right."

"Fuck me." I rise, half over her, and cover her mouth with my hand. "Stop."

Eyebrows bunched, she asks, her words muffled by my palm, "Stop what?"

"Stop talking, you're fucking..." I growl into the pillow, and now I'*m* dry humping her fucking mattress. *Great.* "I'm going to lower my hand, and you have to help me, okay?"

"Help how?"

"Talk to me. Take me off the edge."

She nods, and I slowly lower my hand. "But why can't I just put your dick in my mouth?"

I slam my face into her pillow, again and again, until she laughs into my arm. "It's not funny, Cheeks!" But I'm laughing, too.

This whole thing is ridiculous.

She strokes what little hair is on my head, and I almost regret keeping it short. I close my eyes, ready to bask in the feeling of her fingertips stroking my skull, but as soon as darkness fills my surroundings, I'm reminded of why I keep my hair short.

I suppress my grunt when he yanks my hair, pulls it from its roots. His hot breath coats my face when he sneers, "What now, you pretty-boy faggot?"

A shiver wracks up my spine, and I force my eyes open, suddenly too aware of my surroundings, of the shakiness of my breaths. Of Olivia lying next to me, *watching* me.

There's an obvious switch in the air, a heaviness blanketed by my stupid emotions. My pathetic fears. I hate this part of my life. I hate the darkness I can't seem to shake no matter how bright the light is that envelops me.

"Wilmington," Liv says, and I turn to her, but not completely. Biting down on her bottom lip, she looks directly into my eyes, and she must sense the unanswered questions swarming inside me, because she adds, "You asked me before where I considered home, and my answer is Wilmington."

It takes a moment for her words to kick in, and when they do, the tension in my chest dissipates, unfurls through my bloodline. Not only is Liv doing what I asked, talking me off the physical edge of release, but she's giving me what I came here for.

She's giving me *her.*

"What about you?" she asks.

I wait a few seconds before flipping over and extending my arm. Liv takes the cue, moving in close until she's in the crook of my arm. I twist a strand of her hair between my fingers and sweep my gaze around her room, trying to pinpoint exactly what it is about it that's creating a familiar feeling in my chest. I felt it the moment I stepped inside, but I can't for the life of me figure out why. "What about me?"

"Is the house you live in now where you consider home?"

"Nah," I'm quick to answer. "We used to live... a couple blocks away, actually."

"You lie."

"True story." I tug gently on the strand I'd been playing with and add, "I was pretty young when my parents made their money, so we weren't there long, but I remember it." I don't tell her that it's still ours. That I still go there often because my friend, Oscar, lives there now, and his mom forces me to have dinner with them at least once a week. "The house is small, only two bedrooms, so my sister and I shared, and..."

"And?"

"Nothing." I shake my head, refusing to continue. I have a feeling that the things she misses from her childhood were ripped away from her, making the things I miss from mine completely inconsequential.

"That must be a big contrast to where you live now?"

I nod. "This house reminds me of my old one," I tell her, adding as an afterthought, "not because it's small or whatever; it just feels... I don't know... lived in?"

"Your house doesn't feel like that?"

"No." I laugh at the thought. "My house feels like a hospital." Sometimes, it feels like a psych ward, and I'm the only patient. Obviously, I don't tell Liv that. "I moved into the pool house thinking it would help with feeling so..."

"Isolated?" she offers.

My lips thin with my forced smile. "I guess, yeah."

"I'm sorry," she says, scrunching her nose, shifting the freckles there.

One day soon, I'm going to kiss every single one of those freckles. Starting now. I press my lips to her nose, then her cheeks, her shoulder.

She squirms in my arms until she's out of my embrace. "You ever build a pillow fort?" she asks, and I feel every bit of tension inside me slowly unravel.

Smiling at the absolute randomness of her, I answer. "Not that I can recall."

Her grin is instant, innocent and pure, and it only draws me further into her web. "Wait right there," she says, palm up between us as she gets off the bed. "Don't move, okay?"

"Okay," I chuckle, and then she's gone, disappearing out the door that leads to the rest of the house.

I take the opportunity to glance around her room again. String lights hang above her bed, but they're not on right now, and I imagine what they'd look like in the middle of the night while I'm lying here beside her, talking about nothing and everything and all the tiny parts in between.

There's a nagging in my gut that *almost* feels like guilt, like a silent reminder that I've had these thoughts before. Only I had them with a different girl. A girl I've never even met before.

Things had been a little off between me and Mercedes the past few months, and I have no idea why. Or even if it's real or in my head. When I've asked if she's okay, she says that nothing's changed on her end. Still, the text she'd sent last night proves otherwise.

I peer over at the empty doorway before finding my phone to check my messages. My heart falters a beat when there's nothing new—not that I really expected there to be.

I didn't know how to respond to her last message, so I left her on read.

Just because she hadn't experienced heartbreak in her lifetime, that didn't mean it didn't exist. I've opened the texts a few times today, ready to respond, but I didn't want to say something I'd regret. Something like: *If heartbreak isn't real, then what caused the endless tears my mom and sister shed?*

What causes mine?

"One second!" Liv calls out, throwing a bunch of pillows through the open door. A moment later, she enters with an armful of couch cushions.

I start to get up, but she stops me with a hand up between us. "Lie down! I'm going to build you the best damn pillow fort you've ever seen."

"Yes, ma'am," I chuckle, lying on my back. It's only now I notice the posters of space, forests, and coastlines stuck to her ceiling. With a few childish grunts, Liv throws all the pillows and cushions on the bed and, true to her word, starts building a pillow fort around me.

Occasionally, she'll pause, contemplating what to put where or swap things around, and when she's done, she announces it to the world. "Ta-da!" she sings, arms swinging around us. A vision of her as a little kid pops into my mind, only it's not me she's making it for. It's Dominic. And honestly, *fuck that guy.*

"What do you think?" she asks, lying down beside me.

I extend my arm and wait for her to lift her head, rest her cheek on my bicep again. I look around—at nothing but pillows surrounding us and posters above us. "I think you were right. This is the best damn pillow fort I've ever seen."

She snorts/giggles, holding my arm to her chest. I switch positions and hug her to me, noting how small she feels in my arms. *One wrong move, and I could break her.* "The next time you feel isolated, just build a pillow fort," she tells me.

"Won't that make me feel more isolated?"

She nods. "That way, when you're in there, you can just think... *it could always be worse...*"

I understand her sentiment, in theory, I guess. It just doesn't really make sense. I tell her as much.

She's quiet a beat, and just when I think I've offended her, she laughs, clearing my airways of the nerves that had built there. "Yeah, I guess you're right. But you have to admit, it's a pretty gnarly pillow fort."

"Are you kidding? It's the best pillow fort that ever existed. They should write books about it—deem it the eighth wonder of the world."

She lifts her chin, looks up at me. "Maybe in the future, but for right now, I'll accept a simple thank you."

I press my lips to hers, linger for just a moment, before pulling away. "Thank you." In sync, we settle back into position—me on my back with her tucked in beside me, and I'm pretty sure I could spend the entirety of my life just like this, and I wouldn't miss a thing. "Your turn," I tell her. "Why Wilmington?"

She's quiet a beat, before answering just above a whisper, "It's where I grew up. Where I learned who I was..." she trails off, her slow exhale warming my chest. "I don't know how much you know about me and my brothers, or what happened to us," she says, "but my mom— she's our legal guardian now, and she works out of state a lot, so it's just me and my brothers most of the time."

Guardianships are court proceedings, which makes them open to the public unless circumstances deem otherwise. So, thanks to my undeniable stalking, I already knew about her mom. Though, it made me wonder... if her mom is their guardian now, where has she been the rest of Liv's life?

I take Liv's hand in mine, link our fingers, and kiss the inside of her wrist, just once, just to show her that I'm listening and that I'm grateful she's saying anything at all. "That must be hard," I tell her, even though I have no real clue.

"It could've been a lot worse," she replies, shrugging, and I don't know what she means by that, but I don't ask. "Sometimes..." she sighs, shifting closer. And it's almost as if she doesn't *want* to say what she says next. She just *needs* to say it out loud, and not even to me, but into the universe. Into the void. "Sometimes living here feels like a job. Like I wake up and I go to work, and not even for one of my actual jobs, but for my family. For my brothers. And that's a choice I made. I know that. But I feel like I never really rest. Physically, sure, but there's no off switch for my mind. For my worries, and—" She stops there, her eyes wide when she peers up at me. I have a feeling it's the first time she's admitted all this to herself, let alone to anyone else.

I kiss her forehead, keep her close, and stay quiet, giving her the space she might need to process her feelings, her *truths*. I wait until she's ready to speak—all the while replaying her words in my mind, over and over, trying to imagine a life I know nothing about.

After seconds that feel like hours, she finally breaks the silence. "Your turn," she says.

"My turn to what?"

"Talk me off the edge—emotional, not physical."

I've never understood a single statement more.

I motion to the ceiling. "Did you know that Earth has more trees compared to stars in the Milky Way?"

She laughs, a breathy little sound I want to bottle up and keep forever. "Did Max tell you that?"

"Maybe..." I freeze. "Did *you* tell him that?"

"Maybe," she repeats, rolling onto her back. "But three trillion trees on Earth is nothing compared to 7.5 *sextillion* grains of sand."

"That's not a real number."

"It is so. It's seventy-five, followed by seventeen zeros."

"Why do you know this?"

She shrugs. "You're not the only one who likes stats."

"Fair," I say, "but I don't go to sleep with them every night."

Her shoulders shake with her silent laugh, and she turns into me again, eyes focused on my single helix pendant she's toying with.

She doesn't ask about the necklace, just says, "I keep them there as a reminder that the world is vast, filled with so many singular objects, and we, as individual humans, are just one of those *things*. We're so small. All of us. So insignificant."

Maybe so, but... "Why do you *want* to be reminded of that?"

Her mouth snaps shut, and she looks away, eyebrows drawn as if thrown off by the question. "Can I ask for your truth now?"

"You can just ask me for the sake of asking, Cheeks."

Forearm on my chest, she lifts herself half on top of me, all so she can look directly in my eyes when she asks, "How much do you know about what happened to my grandparents?"

Even though I was expecting this question at some point, I hadn't decided exactly how to answer it. I hesitate, but keep my eyes on hers. She deserves that much. "I know there was a car accident that involved two cars—your grandparents' and one with three teens inside. Both your grandparents died along with a passenger from the other car. The driver was a sixteen-year-old boy who had been drinking."

The kid's blood alcohol *barely* registered during testing, so he was far from drunk. In fact, had he been over twenty-one, it would have been a non-issue. There were other factors involved, too. It was pouring rain, and the road they were on was winding, with no barriers on either side. Speed may have been a factor, too, but it was never proven. From what I could tell, it was the absolute definition of a literal accident.

I keep all these thoughts to myself, because the last thing I want is to come across as if I'm defending the boy, now man, who played a hand in her grandparents' death.

Biting back a sigh, I say, "I know the driver is the son of a wealthy politician, and that politician paid a hell of a lot of money to make the whole thing disappear, at least from the courts and the media." And this is where I struggle with the circumstances around her grandparents' death. My dad would, and has, done the same for me (and himself, his family, and his empire). To be fair, though, I've never actually killed anyone.

The one time I wanted to, I failed.

Nodding slowly, she asks, "I assume you were around here when it happened... Is that how you know?"

I shake my head. "I wasn't." And I don't know how to maneuver this part. Telling Olivia the truth wouldn't make her the first person in my life to know about it, but it would make her the first person I'd have to explain myself to. And, honestly, I'm not ready to walk that path.

I could give her the same lie I give to everyone else, but that puts her in the same category as the rest of the word, and that doesn't feel right either.

So, I say, hoping my deception doesn't show, "It happened the beginning of my sophomore year, and I was abroad for the first semester, so..."

"Abroad..." she says, quirking an eyebrow. She can ask me to elaborate, and that'd be fine. By now, I've got the lie seared so deep in my memory that it rolls off my tongue without a second thought. But she doesn't ask that of me. Instead, she says, "What else do you know?"

I inhale a sharp breath, let it out slowly. "I know that there was a payout for an undisclosed amount, and... I know they sentenced the driver to a year at a boarding school for troubled boys." In other words, his dad's power and money saved his ass.

I refused both when it came to my sentencing.

Liv's eyes widen as she stares at me, as if surprised I held that knowledge. "So... you know a lot..."

"Maybe..." I answer, shrugging. "But that's not all of it, is it?"

20

Olivia

I shouldn't be surprised that Rhys has uncovered as much as he has. If money can make what happened to my grandparents disappear, then money sure as hell can make it resurface. And I'm not saying that Rhys is crazy enough to spend money just to uncover it, but I have a feeling he might already have the resources in place to do so.

"But that's not all of it, is it?" His question weighs heavily on my chest as I sit in his car for the first time. Or, *one* of his cars, if he still has the bright yellow Lambo he paraded around last year.

What was I saying?

Oh, right. The stories I've told him, and the feelings involved, are far from *all of it*, but I don't know where I should make the truth end and the lies start.

Luckily for me, his phone rang before I needed to answer him. I couldn't hear who was on the other end, but their exchange was brief. Rhys hung up after a few seconds, and with his eyes still lingering on the posters on my ceiling, asked, "Are you coming?"

I didn't even think. Didn't hesitate. I simply changed out of my work clothes and into an old dress before I let him lead me out of my house and toward his car. He's been driving for a good five minutes now, and neither of us has spoken. I don't know where his head's at, but I'm confused. As I should be. "Where are we going?"

Without taking his eyes off the road, he answers, "Pino's."

Oh.

Oh, *no.*

I probably should have paid more attention when I was looking over the menu on Rhys's phone because Pino's is, by far, the fanciest and most expensive restaurant in town, and I was wearing the most *un*fanciest, most inexpensive clothes I own. Not only that, but—

"Don't worry," he says, cutting through my thoughts. "I'm just picking it up." He glances over at me, a smile tugging at his lips. "As much as I'd love to piss off your brother by publicly claiming you as mine, I'm assuming you're not up for such chaos."

"Your assumption is correct," I tell him and leave it at that. There's no way I'm adding fuel to that fire. "I thought Pino's only did dine in."

His eyes snap to mine. "Is that bad?"

"I don't know. I've never been there," I rush out. "Why are you, so..." I trail off, unsure how to finish.

"My parents own Pino's," he says, and I don't respond because I already knew that.

I'd just... *forgotten* that I knew that.

He adds, "I've kind of been running it the past year—"

"Weren't you a high school senior the past year?"

"Yes."

"And co-captain of the basketball team?"

"Stalk much?"

I roll my eyes "Pot meet kettle, and guess what?"

"What?"

"We're both black."

His shoulders bounce with his chuckle. "See?" he says, placing his hand on my thigh and squeezing once. "We're perfect for each other."

The rest of the drive to Pino's is spent with Rhys telling me the history of the restaurant, which also included the history of his parents.

When I first found out about Rhys and his family, I did as much online research as I could. From what I could gather, Rhys's parents were born and raised a couple towns over and were high school sweethearts. They both skipped college, and instead, worked full-time so they could move in together, get married, have kids, and live happily ever after.

That's how Rhys's dad—Troy Garrett—found himself bussing tables at Pino's when, one day, the owner called a meeting to let staff know they were financially struggling to stay open. From the stories they've told to those rich people magazines, Mr. Garrett begged the owner to give him six months to turn things around, and if he could make that happen, then he asked for shares in the business. Back then, Mr. Garrett knew nothing about marketing, let alone running a restaurant. But he did his research, worked his ass off while his kids were still in diapers, and hustled hard to made the dream work. Within six months, Pino's was booming again, and within a year, the owner offered to sell the whole thing to Rhys's Dad. Within two years, his parents had paid off the loan they took out to buy the restaurant and used their extra earnings to start another business.

I had learned all the above through many online interviews and articles I'd sifted through, but hearing it from Rhys's perspective is so much better.

"So, Pino's is how they gained their success?" I ask.

Rhys pulls up to the restaurant, bypassing the valet and opting to park at the rear. "I like that," he says, putting the car in park.

"Like what?"

"That you used *success* instead of wealth."

"Wealth is subjective." So is success, if I'm being honest, but, unlike my mother, I've never really looked at financial wealth as something to strive for, or in her case, something to marry into.

"Hey," Rhys says, and as soon as I've turned to him, he's kissing me. Taking my bottom lip between his, his hand finds my neck, willing me closer while his tongue coaxes my mouth open.

The first stroke of his tongue against mine has me gasping. Heat and desire flow through my bloodline, simmer below the surface, until it pools at my core, and I...

I push him away. "You should get that food," I whisper.

He nods, eyes unfocused as he reaches between us and to the back seat. He pulls out a cap and dumps it on my head, tugging the brim low on my brow like I've done with him. "Just so we're clear," he starts, kissing me once. "I hate hiding you."

Moments later, I have a giant pile of take-out containers on my lap, and it smells so good I'm tempted to open each one and have my own little grazing session. "Where do you want to go?"

Honestly, I hadn't thought this far ahead.

He continues, "We can go back to your house, or we can go to the rooftop, or..."

"Or?" I ask, shoving my entire face in the paper bag just to sniff the food some more.

Rhys chuckles at my antics, but he has no clue what a treat this is for me. At home, I do the laundry, and Dom does the dishes and the trash. We both tidy and take turns with cooking dinners. I do four days; he does three, and it's only less for him because of his insane training schedule. Eating out for us is the diner once a month and pizza whenever Dom is too drained to cook.

He waits for me to sit upright before saying, "Or we could go back to my house, eat by the pool, and go for a swim after."

"I didn't bring anything to swim in."

Rhys trails his eyes down my entire length, from the top of my head to the tips of my toes. "You have underwear and a bra. It's practically the same thing..."

"Yes, but then I won't have anything to wear after that."

His smirk is the smirkiest I've ever seen. "What a shame..."

I *should* say no. I should draw a line. *Yeah, right.* The only line I could draw right now would be in the sand, and the moment Rhys so much as breathes in my direction, it would blow away. But the sand would still be there, and I'd draw another line, somewhere else, somewhere new, and the same thing would happen again and again, because I can't control myself or my feelings when it comes to Rhys.

What harm could it do to just *see* his house? It's not as if I haven't wondered about it in the past. There's only one problem. "I bet your house has a ton of cameras, huh?"

"Yeah," he says, putting the car in drive. "But I'm the only one who has access to them."

"What about your parents?" I ask.

Rhys scoffs. "If you knew the shit that went on at that house..." he trails off, which is fine, because I don't need the details. I have to bite back a smile when he squirms in his seat, his discomfort showing. Has he forgotten that I know about the giant three-foot dildo he super-glued to his school's door? Because if that shit's happening in public, I can only imagine what goes on in private. "I blocked my parents from the cameras." He taps the steering wheel twice, before facing me. "You better decide, Cheeks, because the food's getting cold."

21

Olivia

Rhys's house is beautiful. And ridiculous. Especially for one person. Not that I'm judging (maybe a little).

It's the type of house you see on the cover of architecture magazines or the ones you see in movies, surrounded by snow, somewhere in the Swiss Alps.

Only we're not in the Swiss Alps, or anywhere near snow, and those houses usually hold entire families and their staff. Rhys is just one singular guy. A grain of sand, if you will.

I notice all of this from the front seat of his car as we make our way up the driveway. Rhys slows while we near the top of the arch but doesn't stop. As we pass the front doors, I take in the mansion for all its beauty. A mixture of dark wood and light brick makes up most of the exterior, including the two large pillars that bracket the massive double doors to the house.

Four brick steps lead up to the concrete patio by the doors, and aside from all of that, the only major thing of note is the windows. So many windows. All of them with curtains open. I wonder if they stay open all day and night or if someone goes through the entire house every morning to let sunlight in.

I wonder if Rhys does it.

Unlikely.

And I'd ask, but I don't know if that's being too nosy, and besides, Rhys is too busy entering some code into his phone while reversing into the million-car garage. He parks between a yellow Lamborghini, answering my earlier question, and an older Honda Civic that looks out of place in a mansion surrounded by luxury cars.

I step out of the car when Rhys does, struggling with the bag of food on my lap. Rhys takes the bag off me as soon as I'm upright. "I was coming to open your door," he says, his mind seemingly elsewhere.

He takes my hand and leads the way, my two steps for every one of his. He walks quickly, almost dragging me behind him, and I don't even have time to register the gym that sits behind floor-to-ceiling glass as we pass it, or the size of it, or the quality of the equipment in there, or what appears to be an indoor pool made to look like a beach that's on the other side of the gym.

We've literally *just* entered his home, and this is what greets me.

This isn't a house.

This is a hotel.

We continue to walk down a long, wide hallway, and it feels endless. Like too much space and not enough of it at the same time.

I can't explain it.

The interior is white on white on white—walls, ceiling, marble floors. The only thing that breaks up the starkness is the stunningly bold exposed beams. Those, I *love*. But there are no personal touches, no family photos hanging on walls or on the pieces of furniture I spot here and there. The furniture is all decorative, with no real purpose. Modern, shiny black or blindingly white, accented with marble or glass, and I understand that "old" isn't to everyone's taste, but they don't suit the house as much as antique furniture would.

Again, I'm judging. Or maybe I'm just observing.

Regardless, I feel as if you could fill the entire house with wall-to-wall furniture, and it would still feel... empty.

I guess I kind of understand it now—Rhys's need to be alone, but *want* to be with people, because besides our rushed footsteps hitting the floors, the house is silent.

Dead.

Desolate.

I wonder what it must feel like in his head.

Rhys is still grasping my hand as we finally make it to the massive kitchen (white again) and to the large sliding doors that lead to the backyard. Remaining quiet, he opens the door, and it's only once we are outside does he slow his steps.

It's almost as if he couldn't escape the house fast enough.

His backyard seems to stretch as far as the eye can see, lined by lush, tall trees. His pool is exactly how I'd imagined it, and as we walk across light pavers, passing several seating areas made of rattan, he asks, "Should we eat in or out?"

I'm so busy taking in my surroundings that I don't even realize we've stopped in front of the pool house and he's opening the door. The pool house is designed the same as the main, with large columns bracketing the entrance. The entire front wall is made of glass, facing the pool. Rhys opens the door, holds it open for me, and waits.

I step inside, and that's as far as I get before an overwhelming sense of recognition washes over me. I've never been here before. I know that to be a fact. But I've imagined his surroundings when he texts me throughout the day and sometimes late into the night. I've pictured him standing in this exact kitchen, his phone in one hand while holding a fork in the other, waiting for the microwave to finish. And I've imagined him sitting on the huge sectional couch with his feet up on the coffee table, watching a game while he texts me the highlights, even though I'm watching the same game only miles away.

"What's up?" he asks, pulling me from my thoughts.

I drag my eyes to his, but he hasn't moved far. Only steps away, he rests against the arm of the couch, watching me.

"Nothing," I say, but it comes out in a whisper. Heat burns in my cheeks, and I know he can see it, because somehow, his smirk gets smirkier. I shift my gaze to the side, embarrassed. I've pictured him in this space. A lot. And not all the things I imagined him doing were... family friendly.

He pushes off the couch. "You want a tour?"

"Sure." Anything to get me out of the images circling my mind.

He takes my hand in his, and the first thing he shows me is his bedroom.

Because *of course* it is.

I go straight for the stack of books on his bedside table to give my hands something to do. I pick up one, and then another, inspecting them as if they're precious ancient artifacts that will disintegrate in my hands.

Rhys chuckles, catching onto my bullshit. "You good, Cheeks?"

"Yep," I say, turning to him. He's sitting on the edge of the bed, as relaxed as always.

I run my hand over the bedsheets. "This is nice," I say, because I don't know why. "What is it? A million-count goose-egg feather down?"

He laughs at this, his head throwing back, and then he takes my hand, tugs until I'm standing between his legs. He guides me to sit sideways on his thigh, my legs still between us. "What are you thinking right now?" he asks, his hand on my leg, not moving, not squeezing, just *teasing*.

I put my arm around his neck and get comfortable. "Honestly?"

He blinks.

"I'm thinking about how many times you've jerked off in this bed and if you've ever done it while thinking about me."

"Four times," he answers, not skipping a beat. He shifts his hand, his fingers splaying on my inner thigh as he glides it higher, higher. "And only since I met you, so all four times have been about you."

I squirm, my legs parting as if on their own. "What am I doing to you when you think about it?"

His eyes narrow, just a tad. "You're naked, legs spread..." He squeezes my thigh, hard, and I let out a moan. "While I lick your pussy..."

My vision blurs, heat crawling up my spine, and I shift forward an inch, so the tips of his fingers touch my center. "Rhys," I almost beg, and he answers by running the back of his fingers against me. I'm sure he can feel how warm I am. How *wet*.

He brings his mouth to my shoulder, kissing, licking, sucking, then makes his way up my neck, all the way to my ear. I force myself to breathe when he flicks my earlobe, takes it between his teeth. "I want to take my time with you, baby."

I puff out an exhale, my hips circling, trying to create more friction. I try to remember what he said, but when his mouth meets mine, his tongue gliding along the seam of my lips, I open up to him and forget everything else.

He kisses me as if he's been waiting for this moment, fantasizing about it, and within seconds, I'm removing his shirt and he's lifting my dress off of me, and then I'm on my back in the middle of his bed with him between my legs. His erection presses against my core, moving in ways that bring me close to the edge, over and over.

He holds both my wrists above my head with one hand, while the other brings my thigh up and around him, giving him better access. Our kisses are wet, all tongue, filthy, and so perfect, I can't handle it. He pulls back from the kiss, and I moan in protest as he moves down my neck to my chest. My blood simmers, heating every inch of me. He releases my hands so he can move lower down my body, kissing my stomach, then making his way back up again until he gets to my bra. He tugs down the fabric, his tongue burning hot when he flicks my bare nipple for the first time. I thrust my hips up, searching for more, and he sucks my nipple into his mouth, then bites gently, before moving to the other. I whisper his name, stare up at the ceiling. But the world is a blur, and all I see are stars. So many of them. For minutes, he just stays there moving from one to the other, while whispering words of appreciation in between. He tells me that I'm perfect, that I'm beautiful, that he's never wanted anything more than he's wanted *me*. And then, slowly, he makes his way down, down, down. He doesn't remove my underwear like I thought he would. Instead, he settles his head between my thighs, and he kisses me—over the fabric. He licks me, tasting the liquid pleasure he's created. I close my eyes, try to focus on the pure bliss he's giving. He tugs on the sides of my underwear, pulling the fabric taut against me. The white cotton sticks to my soaked flesh, revealing my slit. "Such a perfect fucking pussy," he moans, and I look down at him, almost lose it at the sight of him. He glances up, his eyes half-hooded. "You ever touch yourself, baby?"

I nod, breathless, flames of wanton need blazing inside me.

"Show me," he says, almost *demands*.

"Rhys," I whisper. *Plead*. I don't want to play these games. I just want him to touch me. Skin-on-skin. I want him on me. Around me. Inside me.

"Show me," he repeats, and I lower my hand, reach beneath my underwear, until the tips of my fingers touch my clit. I'm gentle with my movements, careful not to send myself over the edge. I want him to be the one to take me there. I circle my nub, slowly, and he watches intently, focused.

"Fuck, baby," he groans, and then his mouth comes down. He kisses, open mouth, over my fingers and just beneath them, sucking on the cotton as if thirsty for every drop of my pleasure.

"Rhys!" I cry.

"Soon, baby," he murmurs, and then he pulls my panties to the side, licks my fingers clean, before removing my hand completely. His tongue replaces my finger, and I lose it. My eyes shut tight, and I almost cry at the intensity of the pleasure he creates with just his tongue alone. I peel one eye open so I can watch him, and it's almost as if he was waiting for me to look at him. Because he's been watching me. Anticipating. And then he slides a finger inside me. Again and again. And I'm done. Pleasure crashes through me, momentarily flashing white in and all around me, and I *scream* out my release, my thighs shaking, and he grabs them, his fingers digging deep to keep me *right there*. Wave after wave after wave, and he never lets up, never takes his mouth off me until my release consumes every part of me.

Unable to grasp a full breath, I force his head away with my hands. "Enough," I huff. "I can't take anymore."

He kneels up, freeing his erection from his boxer shorts, and I lick my lips. God, I can't wait to wrap my mouth—

"Later," he says, reading my mind. He reaches into his side table and pulls out a condom. Then he kisses my cheeks. One, then the other. "You okay with this?"

"Please," I beg.

"I need you to say it, Cheeks," he murmurs against my neck while slipping the condom over him.

I don't say it. Instead, I wait until the condom's all the way on, and then I reach for his cock, ignoring the way my body tingles at the feel of him in my hand, and bring him to my wet center...

He enters me slowly, carefully, his face in my neck the entire time. It hurts at first—his size, my lack of experience, the tension coiling inside me, telling me that nothing good can come of this, that it's wrong for me to lead him this way... even when it feels so, *so* right.

22

Olivia

Dressed in a pair of Rhys's boxer shorts and one of his shirts, I watch him from the other side of the counter while he heats the food we let get cold.

"I can probably find you a hair dryer if you want one," he says, the remnants of his exertion still visible in his cheeks. We'd showered together afterward, and now we're here... standing in his kitchen, playing house, as if this is all completely normal.

"I'm good," I tell him, wrapping my hair in a towel. I glance around, taking everything in.

He has piles of books scattered around, and it's clear they aren't just there for decoration. There are books on the shelf behind his couch, on the side tables, and on the kitchen counter. And it's not just the books that hint that this is where he spends his time. He doesn't have dirty clothes scattered everywhere or posters of pro athletes on his walls like Dom does, but the space is very... Rhys.

Clean. Confident. Masculine.

It also kind of maybe smells like him, not that I noticed.

It's obvious that the main house is a house, but this pool house is

Rhys's *home*. Even if he hadn't told me earlier, I'd felt it the moment I stepped inside. The place is *clean*—not a hint of dirt or dust and no pictures on the wall, just like the main house. Along with the couch are two armchairs in front of a window, facing the pool, and between the chairs is a vintage barrel coffee table. I smile. I can't help it. Because the table reminds me of my grandfather.

"You want to snoop, don't you?" he asks.

I should be ashamed, but I'm not. "So bad," I admit.

He chuckles, grabbing plates from an overhead cabinet. "Have at it, Cheeks."

I go straight for the barrel coffee table, get on my knees beside it, and run a finger along the woodgrain. "It's beautiful," I say, but it's barely a whisper. I note the books stacked in the center: *The Catcher in the Rye*, *Don Quixote*, *The Secret Garden*, and *1984*.

Back on my feet, I spot the bookshelf by the bedroom door and make my way over. It's only once I'm close enough to read the spines that I realize what the books are.

Or *book*, in this case.

Multiple different editions, different bindings, different covers and even different languages, but all the same title.

The same story.

I hover a hand in front of the only one facing forward, while the rest only show their spines. "May I?" I ask, glancing over at Rhys standing in the kitchen with his arms crossed, watching me.

He nods once, eyebrows set.

I pick up the small, worn paperback of *The Count of Monte Cristo* and flip it to the page that's bookmarked. Then I zone in on the highlighted words, even though I already know what they'll be.

I knew it even before I cracked open the book.

The one and only voice message Rhys had ever sent me was a recital of his favorite line in the book. The same line that's highlighted in the copy I keep in my dollhouse.

I make my way over to him, the book still open in my hands, and read out loud, "All human wisdom is contained in these two words - Wait and Hope."

He doesn't respond, and when I look up at him, he's watching me, his eyes holding more emotion than I'm comfortable with. I square my shoulders, level my breathing. Then ask, "What are you waiting for?"

He takes the book from me, closing it carefully before placing it on the kitchen counter behind me. He doesn't speak, doesn't answer my question. He simply holds my hips, gently pushing me back until my back hits the counter. And then he grasps my face in both his hands, as if he's afraid I'll fly away. I lose my breath when he tilts my head back, brings his mouth so close to mine the only air I can breathe has lived inside him. My chest rises, falls, and he shifts his hand to the small of my back, then forcefully tugs me forward until there's nothing between us. No air. No space. "Ask me the next part," he whispers against my lips.

Heat burns behind my nose, my eyes, and I blink the tears away. Fear and anticipation pump through my veins, come out in the shakiness of my voice. "What are you *hoping* for, Rhys?"

His answer is simple.

Fast.

To the point.

"*You.*"

PART III

23

Olivia

Three years earlier

My grandparents used to tell me that hate was a bad word—equivalent to shit, fuck, and... wait for it... hell.

At barely sixteen, I still can't say the words out loud, but that doesn't mean I don't think them.

I fucking hate the hell out of this shitty life that's been handed to me.

I hate the coldness of the water soaking through my sneakers, making my toes numb.

I hate the weight of the rain as it pounds down on me.

I hate each and every one of the cars that drives by, splashing dirty water on us, completely oblivious to the fact that I'm already drowning.

"Ohana," Max whimpers.

I hate the pain in my hips from having to carry a three-year-old.

"Why running?"

I hate the tears that hide so comfortably amongst the raindrops.

"Because I'm late, Max." By a whole twenty minutes. It'll be a miracle if the woman conducting the job interview is still there. She said it was fine when I'd called earlier—that she was in no rush. Still, this isn't the first impression I'd hoped for, and I *need* this job. Any job.

"I'm sorry," he whispers, and my soaked feet falter on the pavement beneath me. I shut my eyes and take a breath. And then another. *I can't hate Max*, I remind myself. None of this is his fault.

But, I can hate the world... hate that it continues to spin when there are two fewer souls on this earth who once made up my universe.

24

Olivia

"I hate it," Dom deadpans, his gaze landing on the crest embroidered on my shirt's pocket. I'd literally just stepped out of my bathroom and into my bedroom, and that's the first thing he has to say? *Asshole.* He quickly looks away, feigning disgust, and I try not to roll my eyes at him. Instead, I focus on my reflection in my full-length mirror and grasp the blazer's lapels, tugging gently to get used to my new school uniform.

Fortunately, my scholarship to St. Luke's included a clothing budget because there's no way I'd be willing to spend—I check the tag that's still on the sleeve and almost dry heave at the price. Dom moves closer, shifting the tag so he can see, then scoffs. "Thank fuck Philips isn't run by a bunch of rich pricks with sticks up their asses."

"Swear jar!" Max shouts, glancing up from his iPad just long enough to glare at Dominic. Max has set himself up in the middle of my bed—headphones on, iPad, books, and snacks all around him.

"How the hell can you hear me with your headphones on?" Dom asks him.

Max taps the piece covering his ears. "Superhuman hearing."

Dom rolls his eyes, his lips curled as he spots some loose change on my dresser. He collects a handful and throws it over to Max. "What I meant to say was..." he starts, glaring at Max playfully, "I'm glad our school doesn't make us dress like this." He motions to me via the mirror, and I follow his gaze. "You look like your own worst nightmare, Ollie."

I don't retort because he's right. I do. And it has nothing to do with socioeconomics and everything to do with jealousy. At one point, not too long ago, I wanted so badly to be part of the elite, and now...

Now, it just feels pointless.

I agree with him about Philips Academy, though. I'm grateful they don't have a uniform like this, or we'd be broke—especially since Dom's grown the equivalent of two heads in the same number of years. He's about to enter his senior year at Phillips, and since it's a K-12 school, Max started there last year. Their uniform is simple—gray slacks, white button-up shirt, and a black tie. No logos. No brands.

Unlike St. Luke's Academy—a prestigious religious institution with a history that goes back generations—Philips is a private prep school funded by alums who like to feel good about giving chances to "at-risk" kids. Or, in Dom's case, a middle-class kid bound to make a name for himself in the NBA. They also have a killer STEM program, so it suits Max perfectly.

"You're mean," Max says, speaking to Dom, who flops down on my bed. Max makes a show of glaring at Dom before offering me a cheesy grin. "I think you look good, Ollie." Sweet, sweet Maxy—always my protector. "What do you think?"

I suck in a breath, hold it, and take stock of the girl in the mirror. The shirt I'm wearing is plain, blindingly white, crisp to the touch, and tucked into a black, plaid, pleated skirt. Throw in the school-issued knee-high socks and blazer with bright orange trim, and... what do I think?

I think I could grace the thumbnail of the top three searches on Pornhub.

Obviously, I don't state that opinion out loud. Instead, I shrug. From tomorrow onwards, I'll be stuck in the uniform five days a week, so how I feel about it is irrelevant. "It is what it is."

Dom sits up from his half-lying position. "As long as you don't come home one day with black and orange pom-poms, screaming *Wildcats! Wildcats! Wildcats!* then we're good," he mumbles, and I sigh as I continue to stare at my reflection. He adds, eyes narrowing, "It could always be worse, I suppose."

I meet his gaze in the mirror. "What could be worse?"

He stands to move in front of me now, a relaxed smile gracing his lips as a lock of curls falls over his eyebrow. "You could end up *dating* a Wildcat." He shivers at the thought, and I don't think it's voluntary. Neither is my reaction to his words. Heat rushes to my neck as thoughts and images of a boy with slate-gray eyes, a killer smirk, and expert hands come to mind. "Would it really be so bad?" I murmur, pretending to focus on removing the blazer.

Dom stills, his spine straightening as he looks down his nose at me. "You're kidding, right?"

With a shrug, I lie, saying, "I guess I don't understand the whole school rivalry thing, that's all."

"Ohana," he scoffs, crowding me while I attempt to fold the blazer. "You may wear that uniform, but your blood is Phantom."

"Phaaantoms!" Max cheers, and Dom chuckles. Max has as much interest in sports as Dom has in genetic engineering, but they'll support each other to the end of the earth because *brotherhood*.

I remove the tie from around my neck while Dom sits on the edge of my bed. "Tell me again why you have to go to St. Luke's?"

"Because that's where the scholarship is."

"And they can't, like, give you the cash, and you go to Philips instead?"

"That's not how it works," I sigh out and leave it at that.

Sometimes, it gets hard to keep track of all the things I keep hidden from him.

25

Olivia

The student parking lot at St. Luke's Academy is only dotted with cars when I enter it for the first time. I left the house super early this morning, wanting to be prepared, because—as Dom teased—I'm a giant fucking nerd.

I put the Camry in park, undo my belt, then take a moment to breathe while staring up at the school. The best way to describe the building I'm about to enter is... *a beautiful monstrosity*. It's two stories high with a red brick facade crawling with ivy. There are a ton of windows, all spaced out symmetrically, and the yard is so immaculate it wouldn't surprise me if the maintenance team trims the grass and brush with tiny scissors. And, like any real reputable private school with a history as rich as St. Luke's, there's a bell tower.

A single laugh filters out of me, built from nothing but nerves, because I've never felt so out of place in my life. Sure, my high school back in Wilmington was exclusive, but it was nothing like this.

I grab my phone from my bag and quickly find the voice recording app. A smile tugs at my lips as I remember how Rhys and his sister communicate this way—and I wonder if it started before or after "Mercedes" told him about it.

I'd lied when I'd mentioned it, said that I pretended to speak to my non-existent dad hoping, one day, I might meet him and I'd have all these recordings of my life to show him.

In reality, I was talking to my dead grandparents.

"Well, I'm still here," I say into my phone. "We made it through another summer, and I can't believe it's the first day of school again. Max and Dom are still at Philips, and Max is in first grade. He's thriving, as we all knew he would. Dominic's a senior now. He's six-five right now, and I don't think he plans on stopping anytime soon. I'm not sure if I mentioned it earlier, but he ended junior year fifth in his class. He'll most definitely be captain of his basketball team this season, so we'll see how well he can maintain it. I'm sure he'll do great, and if not, we all know he'll be the hardest on himself about it. His coach is still amazing, and he assures us that his spot at Indiana State is a sure thing just as long as he stays out of trouble...

"As for me, I'm sitting in my car in the parking lot of St. Luke's Academy, going into my senior year three years later than we'd planned, and since I'll be nineteen in a few weeks, I'm most likely the oldest student here—which, I know means nothing in the grand scheme of things, but... I don't know... I can't stop thinking about it, I guess.

"Also, I have to wear this uniform that I hate, and I'm sure I look as ridiculous as I feel, and how I feel is... *afraid*. Not that I'll ever let it show. Truth is, I don't really know what I'm so fearful of. It's not as if I won't be able to stand on my own here. I know I'll be fine. At least academically. But everything else... the people, the socializing... I can guarantee I have zero in common with a single soul at this school, and... and sometimes, I have to wonder if any of this is worth it. Like, what difference will it make if I graduate from high school or not? A part of me feels like my entire life is already planned out... but then I remember what happened to you guys and what happened to us, and it reminds me that, in the end, plans don't mean shit.

"Anyway... I love you both, and I miss you. So much. And I hope I'm doing okay, and that I'm making you proud... because swear, most days, I feel like I'm failing..."

I choke on an exhale and close my eyes, try to keep the tears at bay. Then I count to ten in my head, like my grandma taught me to, and when I open my eyes again, the world remains as unclear as it was ten seconds ago.

I stop the recording and attach it to an email, then send it to an address that no one's checked since my grandparents died. And, with one final breath, I ignore the shakiness of my hands as I open my door, slip on my mask, and take my first step toward another false persona.

26

Olivia

Surprisingly, I'm not the first student to be herded into an empty meeting room next to the front office. The middle-aged woman with striking dark hair and pronounced eyebrows ushered me through the threshold with a stern "Sit and wait," and then disappeared.

There are three other students who've already had the same treatment, and they sit, waiting, scattered as far apart as humanly possible. I take the seat in the back corner and do my best to hide in plain sight. No one dares to speak, and I watch, fascinated by how different fears can create such a vast range of reactions.

Some fear has you screaming so loud, the action burns your throat, forces heated tears that come on so quick and so thick that it momentarily blinds you. And then there's the type of fear that steals your breath, rattles your rib cage, and knocks you into a state of silence.

That's the type of fear that fills this room right now. The type that creates a thickness in the air made up solely of our mixed exhales.

Two new students enter within the same number of minutes, and they quickly find their own pocket of anxiety to sit in and wait.

Time passes, and the only sound that can be heard is *terror*.

Thankfully, Principal Brown—whom I met a few days ago when I was doing my final interview—enters the room followed by a handful of students.

What happens next is pure and instant chaos. Everyone who was once seated quickly gets to their feet, standing so straight that I'm surprised there's no salute and shout of, "Sir!" Yes, sir!"

Still seated, I glance around at my fellow newbies, eyes wide, and then I giggle. Because it's what I do in painfully awkward situations. I *laugh*. But no one else seems to find it funny. Just me. Well, me and the tall, dark-haired boy standing next to Principal Brown. His honey-colored eyes meet mine, lit up with his smile—not a smirk, but a genuine smile—and it's as warm as it is welcoming. He lowers his head a moment later, but his shoulders bounce with his withheld laugh, and it takes a moment for the recognition to hit me. I know the boy... though I wish I didn't.

"Stand down," Brown says, dismissing the overly ambitious students with a wave of his hand. He doesn't even wait for everyone to regain their seat before saying, "You're each going to be paired with someone from student council who's going to show you around the school, go through your schedule with you, and talk you through some of the more important rules of St. Luke's Academy. Welcome. Have fun. But not too much. This is a place of education, after all." He turns swiftly, exiting the room, and I don't hold back my eye roll.

The dark-haired boy catches that, too, and his smile only widens.

"Jared!" the blonde pixie-cut girl next to him announces, reading off a sheet of paper. I notice the way her hands tremble, causing the paper to shake, and maybe people don't limit fear to first days around here.

Maybe this place is built on it.

A boy at the front of the room stands, walks over to her, and one by one, people find their pairs and leave the room until there are only two people left. "Olivia?" the familiar boy asks, his smile still in place.

I nod.

He returns the gesture, flicking his inky dark hair away from his eyes, saying, "I'm Oscar."

I know his name. Just like I know he was the one riding shotgun when Rhys pulled up to my house at three in the morning during regional finals to throw eggs at it.

I stand, about to grab my messenger bag off the floor, but he beats me to it. "Oh no! I got it," I say, but he's quick to swing it over his shoulder, gently slapping my hand away.

"Don't be annoying," he mumbles, and *what?* He doesn't even know me. He turns, heading for the door, and I follow behind.

If I wasn't afraid of breaking the laptop in my bag, I'd be tearing it from his grasp. "I can carry my own things."

"Olivia," he says again, more to himself than to me, and we've walked out of the room now, and we're passing the front office. "Do you go by Liv?"

I falter a step. "I prefer Ollie," I tell him, and it's a blatant lie, but what am I supposed to say? That there's only one person in the entire world who calls me Liv, and I'd like to keep it that way?

Oscar stops in his tracks, his smile goofy as hell as he faces me. "Oscar and Ollie!" His eyes dance with amusement, almost childishly so, and it reminds me of the first time Rhys was in my room. "We're already so fucking cute I can't even stand it!"

I laugh with him, and I hate that I do. *He egged my house*, I remind myself. And even if I take that away, he's clearly close with Rhys, or at least he was. I don't know what their relationship is like now, and I'm really trying to force myself not to care.

It's been about a month since I'd seen Rhys last and just over a week since I'd had contact with Not Fridge Guy. Last time I heard from him, he was looking for apartments in Colorado. As far as I know, that's where he is right now.

Oscar stops in front of a door, his fingers resting loosely on the handle as he turns to me, his tone suddenly serious. "If you forget everything else I show you today, just remember this door right here," he says, knocking twice.

"Come in!" a woman answers.

"Trust me," Oscar murmurs. "This room and the person behind it have saved my sanity more than once. And to be honest, you're going to need her if you want to make it through this hellhole alive." He ignores my wide-eyed reaction and pushes open the door. I peer into what I'm sure was once a janitor's closet. It's unexpected and completely anti-climactic, and I wonder if Oscar's always this dramatic.

There's a brunette woman behind the desk who can't be more than a few years older than me, and, like Oscar, she smiles with her eyes. "Good morning and happy Wednesday, Oscar!" It almost sounds like she's *teasing* him. Like how an older sister teases their little brother.

"Miss T," Oscar says in greeting. "This is Olivia Mitchell. She's starting today, so I thought I'd introduce you first."

"Olivia!" she sings, standing and pushing her hand out for me. "I'm Miss Turner, the school therapist. I think you're on my list this year!"

I take her hand just as Oscar says, "She prefers Ollie over Liv, just so you know."

"Noted," Miss Turner responds, nodding and releasing my hand.

I open my mouth to reply, but Oscar's too quick. "I have to show her the rest of the school!" He's already pushing me out the door, both hands on my shoulders, walking me backward. "Later, Miss T!"

He waits until we're both back in the hallway before closing the door behind him. After adjusting my bag on his shoulder, he asks, "Ready for the tour?"

27

Olivia

I was diagnosed with general anxiety disorder at the ripe old age of ten. I hated the label, but too many incidents at school forced my grandparents to get some answers. Personally, I think I just like to be prepared for anything. Prepared probably isn't the right term. It's more like I need to be in control of everything. Which, even I can admit, is a dumb take on life. Especially since I know firsthand how little control we have over anything.

I didn't go on any form of medication until after my grandparents died, and even then, I hated the way they made me feel dependent on them to function like a regular human. Needless to say, I wasn't on them for very long.

Growing up, my grandma found ways to help me cope emotionally, and my grandpa was in charge of giving me physical tasks, mainly in his workshop. We'd discovered early on that keeping my hands busy meant my mind was, too, and that helped not to derail every single one of my completely rational thoughts.

Since they're no longer around, I've had to double down on the use of my coping mechanisms and force myself to see the signs before I spiral.

What some people might see as simple, everyday tasks can set off a chain of thoughts so chaotic that I don't even realize I'm mid panic attack until it's too late. Something as basic as parking in an unknown area has set me off before. Dominic, who used to believe that my anxiety was nothing more than a fear of failure (or, more specifically, a fear of not making my absent mother proud), was in the passenger's seat at the time of said parking lot meltdown and witnessed, for the first time, what it was like to be around me when I couldn't do something as fundamental as *breathe*.

From that moment on, he's made it his mission to make sure I never find myself in that position again. If we're going somewhere new, he'll usually drive for the first time. And if, for whatever reason, he can't be there, then we'll sit on Google Maps and plan it *precisely*. Satellite view. Aerial view. Street view. Whatever it takes to make sure I'm comfortable.

I say all this as an insight into how prepared I was to enter St. Luke's Academy today. I'd downloaded multiple maps of the school and studied them as much as I'd studied for my SAT prep exam years ago. I'd been waiting almost three years for today, and I was determined not to let my stupid anxiety break me.

At least on the first day.

I tell all of this to Oscar (minus the parts about Dominic and taking years off) as he skims over my schedule, and clearly, it's an over-share, because he glances up from the paper when I'm done talking, his eyebrows drawn. He doesn't speak. Not right away.

I rock on my heels in the middle of the hallway just outside the cafeteria and bite my lip, look anywhere but at him.

From my peripheral, I see him fold my schedule in half once, twice, then hold it out between us. I take it from him, shove it into my hidden skirt pocket. "Ollie," he says, and I hesitate to meet his eyes. When I finally do, he smiles—that soft, warm, welcoming smile. "I hope saying this doesn't minimize what you've been through, but I get scared some-times, too."

"Of parking lots?" I joke, and his grin widens.

"Not of parking lots, but of—" He breaks off when his phone rings, and he's quick to reveal it from his pocket, then curse under his breath when he sees who's calling. "Sorry," he tells me, then answers the call. "Coach?"

I don't hear the words that are spoken on the other end. I just hear the loudness of them. Oscar's entire body turns rigid, his jaw set in a way that switches him from comforting to *cold*. "Yes, Coach," he says into the phone. "I'll be right there."

He hangs up and spins on his heels, saying over his shoulder, "We need to make a slight detour..."

Even if I hadn't memorized the school's layout, I could have easily assumed where we were going based solely on who Oscar had just spoken to.

The athletic department at St. Luke's takes up about a quarter of the school grounds. And that was *before* they had the new basketball stadium built over summer break. Now, St. Luke's is home to a total of three basketball courts appropriately named Old Gym, New Gym, and the brand-spanking-new Mega Gym.

Dumb name.

According to the information I found online, the Mega Gym is for games, the New Gym is for practice, and the Old Gym is now for... wait for it... the *girls*.

You gotta love blatant sexism.

These are the thoughts that sit stagnant in my mind as Oscar and I walk side by side. Oscar doesn't speak. Not once. He walks, determined, even though his head is lowered, and he remains that way until we get to a set of large, wooden double doors. He doesn't stop, doesn't hesitate, doesn't even warn that I'm about to get an eyeful of shirtless boys lifting weights.

I quickly avert my gaze.

Oscar waits until I've stepped all the way into the room before handing me my messenger bag. "Wait here," he says, "I'll be right back."

I take the bag from him and practically glue my back to the wall, my eyes on him and only him as he retreats to an office in the corner of the weight room. There's a window into the office, and behind it is a man wearing what I assume is the St. Luke's coaching staff uniform—white polo shirt with orange trim and a black Wildcat's logo with the word *staff* printed beneath it. The coach's biceps are so big, so bulging, I'm surprised he hasn't torn the sleeves apart. He stands tall, his hands on his hips, glaring at Oscar as he waits for him. Oscar's barely stepped foot in the room before the same shouting on the phone happens face to face, and just like the phone call, I can't hear the actual words, just the loudness of them.

I grimace, tearing my eyes away from the train wreck, while unease crawls up my spine, all the way to the tips of my ears. I look around, wondering if everyone else in the room is having the same reaction. Maybe this level of *asshole* isn't a common occurrence here because everyone seems to have stopped what they're doing. They might be trying to listen to what's being said in that room, but their eyes... they're all focused on me.

I swallow, thick, and push down the nervous giggle that wants to jump out of me. Instead, I lock eyes with my audience, one after the other, after the—

I choke on a breath, blinking hard, once, twice, three times. But no matter how many times I blink, the view from my pupils remains the same.

Just like the man yelling at Oscar, the one I'm locked in a stare-off with has the same white polo, with same orange trim, but it's his eyes I'm drawn to.

Slate-gray and searching mine—creating the type of fear that steals your breath and renders you speechless.

"Let's go," Oscar says, and I quickly avert my gaze. He's already taking my bag strap from my shoulder and throwing it over his. He guides me, his hand gentle on my elbow, until I'm turned around and facing the door. One hand on my back, he leads me out the same doors we came in through. It's only once the doors slam shut behind us that I'm able to take my first full breath.

Rhys is here.

In this school.

And he's what? Part of the coaching staff?

That doesn't—

"Are you okay?" Oscar asks, derailing my thoughts.

We're walking side by side, and I have no idea which way we're going. I replay the past couple of minutes in my mind, only to remember why we went there to begin with. "I'm good," I tell him. "Are *you* okay?"

"I'm fine," he answers. "But I'm not the one who looks like they've just seen a ghost."

28

Rhys

What.

The.

And I cannot stress this enough...

Fuck?

Olivia's here.

And she's here as a student.

It doesn't make sense. If Olivia needed to return to school for whatever reason, then why isn't she at Philips with her brothers?

Why is she here?

How is she here?

And why didn't she tell me?

So many questions.

But most importantly: Did she think I was here for her? Because contrary to what one might believe, I didn't stay here for Liv.

I would've, if she asked me to, but she never did.

She'd been honest from the beginning—that whatever was to happen between us was to a) stay between us and b) end as soon as her brothers got back. And by "end," she meant full no-contact.

It was my choice whether I agreed with her terms: I could have her for a limited time, or I couldn't have her at all.

To me, the decision was easy.

What wasn't easy was the aftermath. The non-goodbye, followed by every single waking minute after.

But I respected Olivia, which meant that I had to respect her wishes, too. I did what she asked, and I kept my distance, hoping that one day, it would be enough to erase the visceral need to be with her. Then... eventually, that same distance mixed with time would make her nothing more than a memory. And that memory wouldn't include the heartache I felt when she found the strength to walk away—even while I was still weakened by her presence.

29

Olivia

I try to scream, but the hand covering my mouth mutes all sound, and any attempt to fend off the arm around my waist is futile. He's too damn strong, or I'm too damn weak, or maybe...

Maybe I'm not all that determined to fight him...

I knew the second my back slammed into his chest that there was nothing to fear about the boy who'd literally lifted me off my feet and carried me into the dark room, closing the door after us.

Mouth to my ear, his chuckle warms my neck, flooding my mind with memories of other times he'd done exactly that... while we were in his bed...

Naked.

Sweating.

Satisfied.

It takes a moment to clear those thoughts. To remember where I am, how I got here, and, most importantly, who I'm with.

Oscar must be really good at reading people, because swear, "seeing a ghost" is exactly how I felt when I saw Rhys this morning. And don't get me wrong; it's not as if I thought I'd never see him again. I figured one day I might run into him—when he came home to visit or check on the restaurant, but *here*? In this capacity? Me as a student and him as a *coach*? The thought never even crossed my mind. How could it? He was supposed to be in Colorado. He told me so himself. *"When summer's over, my ass will be in Colorado with her and my parents."* They were his exact words, verbatim. I memorized them—all so I could reason the choices I made that night...

...and the twelve nights after.

The problem with being with Rhys is that one time isn't enough. I became addicted, like I'd been a fiend for years and he was the only drug that could cure me. It all happened so fast—the hunger and cravings—that I didn't realize what was happening until it was too late. And it wasn't even just the physical pleasure that occurred when we were together. I became addicted to his presence, to the way he made me feel.

He made me believe I was *more* than I was.

That I was bigger. Braver. *Better* than I was.

Who wouldn't want to feel that way always?

But we were on borrowed time, and we both knew and accepted that. We didn't make plans or promises. We simply existed together in the time Max and Dominic were away, and the night before they were to return, I kissed him in his sleep, whispered goodnight, snuck out of his bed, and drove away. I didn't get far before my tears made it impossible to see straight. I pulled over on the same street where I'd hit him —where all of this started, and I gave myself one minute, and one minute only. I let out all my emotions. Then I took a deep breath, wiped the liquid heartache from my cheeks, and carried on with my life as if twelve days with Rhys Garrett meant nothing. As if being with him didn't dig up all my selfish wants and desires and bring them to the surface...

All so I could bury them deep again.

Now, I blindly turn in his arms, unsure of what to say, because my mind's suddenly foggy with the mere *scent* of him. I'm a mess. Truly. My lips part, ready to speak, but even in the darkness, his mouth finds mine and they become perfectly succinct, as if drawn to each other—

like magnets attracting, *colliding*. He tilts his head, begging for access, and I give in to his wants. To *my* needs. And then he *kisses* me. Warm. Wet. *Perfect*. As if his mouth was made for nothing more than this single act. Not for speech. Not for taste. Just for kissing me. He swipes his tongue along mine in long, slow strokes, exactly the way he's licked my—

I moan against his lips, my knees weakening at the memories. He catches me, holding my head in place so he can deepen the kiss even more. One hand on the side of my face, the other cradles my neck, squeezing gently. And I lose myself to him.

Again.

My mind plays back all these same moments with him.

Kissing him in my bed.

In his.

His sofa.

His pool.

His gym.

And my favorite kiss of all—the one in his car while we were still in his garage. It was just after midnight, and I'd just spent the past hour lying in his arms while I told him how much I missed home. Not the home fifteen minutes away, but the one in Wilmington—the home I grew up in. I told him about all my favorite places to eat. About the diner we'd go to on my birthday every year. About the playground my grandpa would take us to every Saturday morning. I even told him about the basketball courts where I taught Dominic to play. He paid attention to every word and made sure I was done talking before he smacked my ass, kissed me once, and practically pushed me out of his bed. He got up, got dressed, then grabbed his phone and keys. Over his shoulder, he said, "Are you coming?"

For the second time in my life, I got into Rhys Garrett's car, having no solid proof of where we were going. Only this time, I had an idea. Still, I asked, "Where are you taking me?"

His voice was deep, rough, and in the most nonchalant, yet most earth-shattering way, he replied, "I'm taking my girl home."

I kissed him then, the way he kisses me now. As if us, together, was nothing more than a dream, and we were so afraid to wake up. Afraid of The End. But The End was only *nearing* then. It's *passed* us now. Or, at least, I thought it had. And with that in mind, I force myself back to reality and push Rhys away, something I should've done from the very beginning.

He doesn't argue, doesn't resist. He simply stays silent, waiting for my next move.

Breathless, I pull out my phone from my skirt pocket and quickly turn on the flash so I can finally see where he's dragged me into.

I roll my eyes when I figure it out because it's perfect, really. It's my first day of school, and I'm already *that* girl—making out with guys in *storage closets*. I haven't even made it through lunch.

And now I'm annoyed. Unjustifiably so.

I search for the light switch so I can see clearly.

"Kids always break the globe in here, so the switch won't matter," Rhys says, all calm, as if he hasn't just taken the exact steps that define *kidnapping*.

"Why would they—" I cut off when I realize I don't care and then glare at the boy in front of me.

He smiles back.

"What are you doing here, Garrett?"

"Well, I can't go making out with you in the halls. I'd get my ass fired." I cross my arms, and it only makes him smile wider. His eye roll is playful, as if this is all a game. To him, it might be. "Don't look at me like that, Cheeks."

"Like what?"

"As if I'm the only one who has some explaining to do."

I hold my phone between us, shining the flash right in his eyes, just so I can scan his face for any signs that he's joking. If him being here is all some kind of prank.

He cowers away from the light, taking my phone from me and putting it on a low shelf beside him. A dim glow filters through the air, creating shadows across his features. He hasn't changed much in the month since I'd seen him. His facial hair isn't longer, but it's thicker, and I hide my hands behind my back to stop from reaching out and running my fingers through it.

"You never mentioned you were going to be a Wildcat."

"Please," I scoff, throw in an eye roll for good measure, and repeat Dom's words from earlier. "I may wear this uniform, but my blood bleeds Phantom, and you know that."

His smile falters. Just enough that I notice. "Fair, but my point remains." He crosses his arms, too, matching my position. Then he steps forward and stands to full height. I have to crane my neck to keep my eyes on his. "Didn't you start senior year when you were—" He breaks off when my gaze drops, and I know all I have to do is wait.

Rhys is smart, incredibly so, and it won't take long for him to figure it out. I count the seconds in my head as I focus on the floor between us.

One.

Two.

"Oh," he says.

Oh, *indeed.* I was only two weeks into my senior year of high school when my grandparents died. I'd been living with my best friend's family, but I'd been on my way here when it happened.

I never went back to Wilmington after that.

And I never went back to school, either.

Until now.

"I didn't mention it because I didn't think it was important," I tell him, saving us from the awkward silence. "Aren't you supposed to be in Colorado? What the hell are you doing *here*?"

"Nice to know where I'm *not* wanted," he says through a chuckle, hand over his heart to feign hurt.

I push on his shoulder. "You know that's not what I meant."

"Do I?" he asks, grabbing my hand before I can claim it back. He grasps it in both of his, gentle yet firm, and I hold my breath when he closes the distance between us.

"I thought about you a lot," he says, the sincerity in his words, his eyes, making me lose my breath. "Kind of hard not to when you kiss me while I'm sleeping, say goodnight, and then disappear, never to be seen again."

"You were awake?"

He shrugs.

"Why didn't you stop me?"

"Was I supposed to?"

He *shouldn't* have.

But that doesn't mean there wasn't a part of me that wanted him to. "I'm surprised you didn't just show up one day."

"You told me not to."

"I know."

"Did you *want* me to?" My non-answer is answer enough, because he chuckles, this deep rumble of a sound that sets off the butterflies. "Good thing I'll be seeing you a lot more now."

He starts in on me again, and I hold my hand up between us, stopping him.

He looks down at my hand, then up at me. "You're right," he says. "At least one of us should have some self-control. At least here."

It's not about self-control, I want to tell him. *It's about fear.* "Rhys, we can't do—" The bell rings, signaling the end of lunch. "I need to get to class," I rush out, reaching for the door handle.

"Aww, so cute," he teases, flattening his hand on the door just beside my head.

I grab his wrist, trying to remove it, but I may as well be hanging off a statue. "I really have to go," I whine.

"Yeah, I'd probably wait if I were you."

Confused, I let go of his wrist and ask, "Why?"

"Because the hallway's packed right now, and this is kind of a known spot."

"Known for what?"

He doesn't answer. He just... pinches my cheek.

I click my tongue, swat his hand away. "Known for what?" I repeat.

Rhys drops both his hands to his sides. "Blowjobs."

I lick my lips and instinctively look down at his... a mistake on my part. Obviously. So much for self-control.

"Unless..." he trails off.

I lift my eyes to his, shaking my head at the cocky smirk on his lips. "I bet you've been blown in all corners of this school, huh?"

He laughs at that but doesn't deny it. "Did I mention I miss you?"

"Miss *me* or the head you taught me to give you?"

His throat moves with his swallow, his eyes softening on mine. "You, Liv." And then he kisses me again, but it's different this time. This kiss is slow. Delicate. Tender, almost. And just as I'm about to give in to him completely, he pulls away. "I missed *you*," he reiterates, then reaches around me to open the door. "Here." He hands me my phone and a slip of paper and sends me on my way.

It takes a second for my eyes to adjust to the harsh hallway lights when I step out. Rhys remains in the closet, the door closed between us. I make it halfway to my locker before I get the nerve to look at the paper he'd handed me.

It's a late pass with my name, for my next class, addressed to my specific teacher.

I pause in my tracks, look back at the empty hallway, wondering exactly how much power Rhys has at this school.

And how much that power can ruin me.

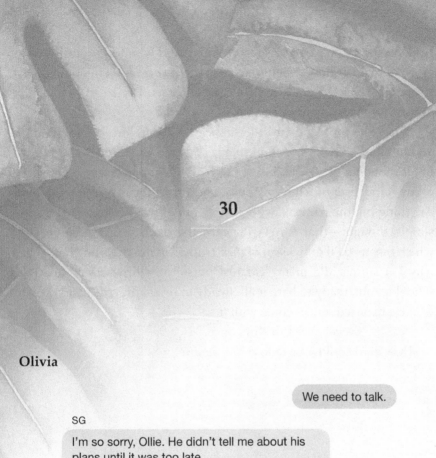

30

Olivia

> We need to talk.

SG

> I'm so sorry, Ollie. He didn't tell me about his plans until it was too late.

> You should have told me.

> I know.

> What am I supposed to do now?

> Just wait, please. I'll be in touch tomorrow.

I read over the text exchange from only minutes after I left Rhys in the storage closet. I'd snuck out my phone while Mr. Finn went over the syllabus for this semester's English class, urgently searching for answers.

That was on Wednesday, and I'd waited all of Thursday for a

response that never came. Now it's Friday, and without clear directions on what to do or how to behave, I've spent the past few days doing what I thought I should do: avoid Rhys at all costs. But I can't avoid him forever, and I can't continue to live in this limbo.

That's the problem with the silence I'm being forced into. It's built and built, and now it's so loud that it's taken over all other sounds. All other thoughts. Now it's nothing but fear—taking up every spare space of my mind, every inch of my body, and I can't focus on anything else. Anything but the panic clawing its way out of me. Panic caused by one simple thought—that Rhys will learn the truth from someone else, which means he'll only learn of *their* truth. Not mine. And I guess that's why I'm sitting idle in my car just outside his driveway hours after school let out, ready to bare it all. Ready to reveal the truth and take on whatever consequences come with it.

Besides, I've already lost Rhys once.

How hard could it be to lose him again?

31

Rhys

Liv's copy of The Count of Monte Cristo lives on the nightstand on her side of my bed, and yes, I realize how insane it is that she has a side of the bed, especially considering how short-lived we were, but whatever.

I refuse to move it. Moving it means letting go, and as hard as it is to admit, I'm not there yet.

Even if she is.

I grab my phone off the nightstand next to her book and then pick up the open cardboard box by the foot of the bed. I snap a picture of the contents from multiple angles, then flip through them, trying to find the perfect one to send. The package had arrived a few days ago, but I wanted to take advantage of it first. Worth it. And, if I'm being honest, I don't think I'd ever been so excited to receive something that wasn't even mine. I select the picture I want to send, delete the rest, then open my messages, pausing momentarily when I notice the single unopened text from Mercedes that was sent over an hour ago.

MERCEDES

How's Colorado?

My stomach turns. Dips a little. But doesn't drop completely. A year ago, Mercedes and I talked daily, sometimes non-stop. We were as close as two people in our situation could be. Yeah, we had our secrets, but she would've been the one I talked to about whether I should stay. At least, back then. Now, I don't know what we are, and worse? I don't know how to feel. I just know that I wasn't the one who started pulling away from this... *whatever*ship we'd formed over the past three years. She'd been such a constant in my life during those years, such a *force*, such a saving grace more times than I can count, and maybe...

Maybe I made her out to be something she wasn't. Or maybe my feelings for Olivia tainted my fantasy of a girl I'd never met before. Never even spoken to in person.

Still, there was a part of me that wanted to *wait* for Mercedes.

Wanted to *hope* for her.

No matter how pathetic that was.

I type out a reply:

> About that...

Then I stare at the blinking curser and inhale a deep breath, unsure what to type next. A notification from the security cameras distracts me, and I click into the livestream just in time to watch Liv's car coming up my driveway. Heart hammering against my rib cage, I drop the phone and race through the main house, to the front door, and swing that fucker open.

Liv stands on the other side, eyes wide, finger an inch away from the doorbell.

Without thinking, I grab her hand and pull her inside.

We're halfway across the foyer before she says, "Rhys, stop!" She tugs on my arm and waits for me to face her. "I came here to talk to you. Not to... you know..."

"Have sex?" I ask, shrugging. "That's cool, but can I show you something before the talking part?"

"Are you about to show me your dick and balls, because I've—"

I bust out a laugh, and she does the same, and it all feels so...

natural. So normal. But it had always been like that with Liv and me. Easy. *Effortless.* "How the fuck do you struggle to say *sex*, but dick and balls... no problem..."

She holds on to my wrist hanging loosely over her shoulder and shrugs. "I don't know."

"How was school?" I ask, only slightly teasing. Seeing Liv at that school, in that uniform, is wild to me. I don't think that I'll ever get used to it. I don't know if I ever want to.

It's obvious she's avoided me since our little closet encounter, but that doesn't mean I don't see her. *Watch* her. From afar. Like the serial-stalker than I am.

From what I can I tell, the only friend she's made so far is Oscar, and I wonder if that's by choice.

"It's..." She sighs. "It's been an adjustment. How was... *work*? That's what you're doing, right? You're coaching your old team?"

"Kind of," I reply. "Coach Sykes retired at the end of last season, and this new coach they've hired is... different." I pause a beat, contemplating how much to tell her. "Let's just say you're not the only one adjusting to new normals."

We're outside now, walking from the main house to mine, and she asks, "Is that why you stayed?"

I'm not dumb. I can read between the lines. "I didn't stay for you, if that's what you're wondering." I stayed because Oscar asked me to, and I'd do pretty much anything he asks of me.

Two minutes later, we're sitting on an outdoor lounge, poolside, while Olivia stares down at the open box, silent, her eyes wide and coated with tears.

Finally, she looks up, my name nothing but a whisper as it falls from her lips. "This is... so... so..." Her grin splits her face in two now, and I wish I had the security cameras pointing right at her so I could replay the look on her face over and over. "Max is... he will..." she stutters, her gaze shifting to mine, eyes bright like blazing embers against the setting sun.

Swear there's something to be said about making a girl speechless that doesn't involve sex or designer gifts. To surprise a girl and make her happy like this, to have her single smile consume every part of you... I get it now—why people choose one over everyone else.

Everything else.

I shrug, trying to play it off. "Max said you guys were entering contests to win a copy and you haven't yet, so..."

Liv picks up all three books in the *Miles and His Miracles* Trilogy, in hardback, gold foil, signed and personalized to Max. "How did you get this?"

"I reached out to the author."

She scoffs, but a snort comes with it. *Hot.* "I did that, too, and never got a response."

"Must've been my lucky day."

"That easy, huh?" It's clear by how she's looking at me that we both know I'm full of shit.

I nod anyway. It wasn't *that* easy, but Olivia doesn't need to know that. I did reach out to the author, who sent me a generic email back telling me to contact his publisher. After an hour of research, I discovered that Jeffrey Grayson, the author of the *Miles and his Miracles* Trilogy, was a board member of a charity my mom heavily supports. And when I say heavily, I mean that in the obvious way: through monetary donations. So, I called her, asked if she could pull some strings, and, as always, she came through for me. A somewhat large donation from my bank account later, and here we are.

Olivia's been silently watching me for a few seconds now, and I force myself to look away. Lying comes second nature to me, but it feels wrong doing it with Liv.

"I'd organized it before the whole never-seeing-each-other-again thing... and you can say it's from you," I tell her, my voice weak from being under her scrutiny. "Say that you won it or something. Get the credit." I force a smile.

Olivia keeps staring, and I can't seem to look away. "Max is going to love it. Thank you so much," she says finally. She reaches up, arm going around my neck to pull me close, right before her lips meet my cheek.

Her hair's down today, like it is when she's at school, and the smell of it overwhelms my senses. So does the way her body feels pressed against mine. The way her touch fills all the shallow, hollow parts of me, and, *fuck*, I've missed her.

And as selfish as it is, I've missed the way she makes me feel. Like I'm invincible.

Unbreakable.

It suddenly dawns on me that I don't just want her. I *need* her. Not just in the physical sense, like my brain's wired to think, but in every way possible. Don't get me wrong; I like what we have going on. This back and forth, and push and pull. But, right now, I want to jump into an ocean of her. Surround myself with nothing but infinite moments of her.

All day.

All night.

Time stands still as I watch her eyes light up, watch her lips form a smile as she watches me back.

I could live in this ocean.

Drown in it.

I stand quickly, suddenly unable to sit still. I pace. Three steps one way. Three steps back.

Liv stands, too, but she stays in one spot, watching me. "What just happened?"

I rub the back of my neck, frustrated. "I thought I was okay," I murmur. "I mean, I'm not over you yet, but I assumed one day I might be, but I don't know if I will be. If I even *can* be. Because I fucking *want* you, Liv—so bad—but I'm also pissed."

"Pissed?"

I face her. "Yes!"

"At me?"

"Yes!"

She rears back, eyes narrowed. "Why?"

"Because you never said goodbye to me, and you never gave me the chance to do the same."

Eyes right on mine now, she shakes her head, as if she can't believe the words coming out of me. "You knew the terms," she almost shouts. "And I said goodnight to you!"

"You said *goodnight*, Liv! Not *goodbye!*"

Her entire demeanor shifts at my words. At my tone. Shoulders dropped, she closes in on herself, and I hate that I caused it. "Liv..."

"I've *never* said goodbye to you, Rhys," she murmurs, arms around her waist as she talks to the ground beneath us.

I step toward her, expecting her to pull back. She doesn't.

"It's always *goodnight* with you," she says. "Never goodbye."

I stop breathing. Start thinking. I go back to all the times we've parted ways, scrutinize every word she's ever said. She's right. Always *goodnight* or *see you later*. Never goodbye. "Why is that?"

She looks up, teary eyes locked on mine. "Because goodbye is forever. And I'll never be ready to say goodbye—"

I kiss her.

I hold her face in my hands, because I'm so afraid she'll somehow disappear, and I kiss her as if she's the only form of oxygen and I've been underwater for years. Her breaths become mine, inhaled into my lungs, pumped into my veins, all so the smallest part of her can live inside me forever. Maybe that's all I need. Just a fragment of her. A single particle. Maybe it'll be enough to get me through my dark days. To get me up and out of bed and living my life in the light. And maybe
—

I freeze when I taste her tears on my tongue, then pull back. My stomach twists at the sight of her cries. At the sound of her destruction. And even though there's a part of me that doesn't want to know, I have to ask, "What's wrong?"

She wipes her tears, refuses to meet my eyes. "I came here to talk to you, remember? Not for... *this.*"

"Okay." I try not to smile. "But can we do *this* first, talk after?"

32

Rhys

"We have no self-control," Liv says, laughing as she drops her full weight on top of me. For minutes, we lie in silence, naked, satisfied, and trying to catch our breaths.

She nuzzles into my neck as I run a fingertip down her spine, back up again. "That's on you," I say, my voice scratchy. "I'm not trying for control."

She lifts her head, just enough to meet my eyes. "Oh yeah, because sleeping with me isn't grounds for instant dismissal, *Coach*."

"Fuck," I grimace. "I forgot about that."

"How did that even come about?"

"It's a long story, and not mine to tell." I guide her off of me carefully, so we don't make a mess of the sheets, then slap her ass. "Don't move," I tell her, getting out of bed. I turn just as I get to the bathroom door and add, "I mean it, Cheeks. Don't fucking leave me."

Within minutes, I'm back in the bedroom, and she's nowhere to be seen. "You're fucking kidding me," I murmur, but really, why I am surprised? I find my shorts, slip them on, then grab my phone and sit my ass on the edge of the bed, thinking. I could call her, but what would be the point? It's clear—

"What's wrong?"

My eyes snap to Liv standing in my doorway with the box of books in her arms. "Motherfucker," I spit.

"What?" she giggles, and she knows exactly *what*.

"You scared the shit out of me. I thought you left. *Again*."

Pouting, she sets the box on the chair by the door, then makes her way over. "We left the books outside," she explains. "I didn't want to get them ruined." She bypasses me and lies down on her side of the bed, then pats the spot beside her.

Of course, I comply and lie down beside her, settle my hand on her waist. She's in the T-shirt I'd been wearing and—I glide my hand down her hip, then back up under her shirt, and *yep*—nothing else. A sound emits from deep in my throat—one I have no control over.

Liv reaches up, kisses me once, then scratches the hair on my jaw. "I like this," she says.

I squeeze her thigh, just below her ass. "I like *all* of this."

She laughs at that, then moves in closer, so our faces are only inches apart. "So, these books..." she starts. "I probably should've checked before I bought the first two for him, but they're age appropriate, right?"

I scoff. "I think that kid could read Dostoevsky and understand it better than most adults."

Olivia's smile widens, her pride evident. "What's it about?" she asks, shifting on her pillow to get comfortable. I smile, giddy for no other reason than the fact that she's here. With me. And it doesn't look like she plans on leaving for a while. "I always assumed it was about a kid named Miles with superpowers."

"Like Miles Morales?"

She scrunches her nose. "Who's that?"

"The animated Spider-Man," I say slowly, because who the hell doesn't know Miles Morales? "You know... *Into the Spider-Verse*?"

At lightning speed, she lifts both her fists between us, fingers out, web shooters ready, and then, in the cutest fucking voice possible: *"Pew! Pew!"*

"Holy shit!" I laugh out, covering her hands. "Web shooters do *not* go *Pew! Pew!"*

She laughs, too, the uncontrollable kind that forces her eyes shut, her teeth showing with her smile. She tries to take back her hands, but I refuse to let them go. If the girl's going to walk around *pew pew*ing web shooters, she needs to be stopped. Immediately. "How would you describe it, then?"

"It's a well-known fact that it goes *Thwip! Thwip!"*

"Thwip?" she repeats, her voice so loud it echoes off the floorboards. "You lie!"

"I spit nothing but facts, Cheeks."

She shakes her head but accepts defeat. "Okay, so Miles and His Miracles… not about a superhero?"

"Correct," I answer. "It's about Miles, this boy around Max's age, and he lives in this giant mansion surrounded by all these servants and… adults, basically. He's home-schooled by a tutor, so he rarely leaves the house. And he doesn't really have any friends, so he's alone most of the time." Alone and *lonely*. "But he has the Internet, so he sees the world through that. Anyway, he has this obsession with miracles." I stop. Inhale a huge breath.

"Go on," Olivia says, and I chuckle, wondering if I sound like Max and if this is her way of showing she's listening.

"So, Miles goes online and starts looking up miracles, but he doesn't quite understand what they mean, and so he finds people online who swear they've experienced one, and he talks to them and eventually convinces them to meet him at his home to tell him all about it."

"Are the books about stranger danger—"

"No," I cut in, shaking my head. "The first book is basically about his life, and the second is about the people he meets and the miracles they've experienced. It never really explains why Miles is so captivated by the idea of miracles, but then in the third book…" I trail off and chew my lip, recalling how I'd spent the past couple of weeks immersed in these books and how deep they got to me. A lonely boy living in a giant mansion, searching the world for something else? Something *more*? Yeah, it hit a little too close to home... until the third book. "You know what? You should read them. I think you'd like them."

Her eyes search mine, but she says nothing in response, and the longer she stares, the deeper I fall. Silence stretches between us until, finally, she asks, "Does Miles ever find what he's looking for?"

In a way, yes. But in the end, what he was searching for wasn't there to be found. Not in the way the author made us believe. "You should just read them."

"I will," she states, "and it's really sweet that you would read them so you could talk about it with him. I didn't know..." she trails off, and I wish she'd end the sentence.

She didn't know what? That Max had told me about them? Or that I felt such an intense connection with him that I wanted to do this one simple thing just to make him happy? Or maybe she didn't know that walking away from me meant taking him away, too, and that was a different type of heartache all on its own.

"It's no big deal." I shrug, hiding my true emotions. "You know I enjoy reading."

She watches me a beat, her eyes shifting between mine, and I wish I knew what she was thinking. "Have you always liked it?"

I hesitate to answer, unsure of what to say. Some people enjoy reading because it takes them to another world without them ever leaving their couch. I feel the same way... only my couch was a bed made of concrete and a mattress so thin it may as well have been cardboard. The walls of the room were cinderblocks, and the only door in and out was made of steel and glass so thick it was unbreakable.

Sometimes people would enter.

But I would always remain.

Just me and my books.

So... *have I always enjoyed reading?*

"Not really," I answer.

But reading saved my life.

In more ways than one.

33

Rhys

I've hit play on the short, thirty-second video so many times I've lost count. Still, I could watch it a thousand times over and I'd never get sick of it. The clip starts just as Olivia pushes open the door to what I assume is Max's bedroom. He's in his pajamas, sitting at his desk beneath a loft bed, inspecting what looks to be a circuit board. "I have something for you," Olivia says, holding out the books between them. She'd wrapped them at some point between leaving my house last night and giving them to him this morning, so he takes the gift-wrap covered box from her and puts it on his lap, then looks up at her. "You know it's not my birthday, right?"

"I know," Liv says, and I can imagine her rolling her eyes. "And anyway, it's not from me."

He hasn't even started to unwrap the gift, too busy trying to uncover the mystery first, and I get it. I'd do the same. "Then who's it from?"

"Remember Timothy?"

"My guy?" he asks, his eyes lighting up, and this is the part of the video that steals my breath, holds it hostage. "I miss him! What happened to him? Did you guys have a fight?"

"No," Liv says, and that's all she gives him. "Are you going to open it or not?"

Max looks from the box to her and back again. Then, without another moment of hesitation, he rips off the wrapping paper and tears into the box.

What happens next—his reaction to the gift—the pure joy mixed with awe and excitement... it's the reason I've watched it as many times as I have.

I tap out of Liv's messages and ignore the unopened text from Mercedes before setting my phone on the cement block beside me.

I'm on the rooftop again, sitting on the half wall facing the alley with my legs hanging over the edge. It's the same way I've spent most nights lately. Four floors high. Approximately sixty-two feet in the air. I might not die if I fell, but it would probably kill the people around me.

I haven't been able to sleep much.

It's likely why I'm having these thoughts again.

Ever since I told my parents that I wanted to stay, the nightmares have returned. And I don't know if I'm losing sleep because I'm struggling to find the connection between the two or if I'm suddenly afraid of the dark again. And not the dark that's real and alive and ever changing, but the darkness I see behind my closed eyelids.

I never had nightmares when Liv was beside me—a realization that hit me just now. Though, to be fair, I'd never truly spent a night with anyone else before. I mean, yes, I've been with girls and spent nights with them, but those nights didn't involve a lot of sleep.

Not until Olivia.

I pick up my phone again—my thumbs deft with bringing up her contact—and I type out a new text. Three simple words that tell her everything she needs to know.

> I need you.

34

Rhys

Alley. Text me when you're here.

Liv's house is next to an alley—a path between two houses that's used as a walk-through to the community playground behind her house. There's a gate in her fence from the alley that leads to a little garden patio just outside her bedroom door. Through that gate is the only way I've entered her house since the first time I showed up. According to Liv, her brother had sent her screenshots of me walking up her driveway from a security camera they had installed above the garage door. I didn't see the camera, but then again, I wasn't really looking. Luckily, the footage was grainy as hell and my cap covered my face, so Delgado had no idea it was me. It didn't stop him from teasing her about it in that annoying brotherly way—the same way I tease my sister about her boyfriend. But there's a difference between Delgado and me.

He's a fucking dickhead.

I'm not.

Anyway...

It's safe to say my opinion on the guy hasn't changed just because I've developed feelings for his sister.

Liv opens the side gate just as I get to it, dressed in baggy sleep pants and a tight tank, and I immediately wrap her in my arms and lift her off her feet until her legs wrap around me. She laughs into my neck, hugging me close, and *this*.

This is what I needed.

Nothing more than Olivia's touch.

Olivia's presence.

"You have to be quiet," she whispers. "Dom's home."

Truly, fuck that guy.

I graze my teeth along her bare shoulder, then bite gently. "I'm not the one who needs to be quiet," I say, walking her into her room. I set her on her feet the second we're inside and close the glass sliding door behind us.

When I turn back around, Liv's on the floor with tin cans and a clew (thanks, Max) of thick twine in front of her. "Let me just pack up real quick," she says, unplugging a glue gun.

"You don't have to pack up," I rush out. There's cardboard laid out beneath all the supplies—to protect the floors, I assume—and I make sure not to disturb anything as I sit down opposite her. "What are you making?"

She laughs once. "It's nothing."

"Obviously, it's not nothing," I say, motioning to the stuff between us. "What is it?"

"I'm making some new planters." She lifts one that's already made. "I just glue the twine around it, and then I'll probably dip the bottom in white paint to make it look a little nicer. Then I'll go to a few thrift stores to find little plates for underneath them, and then Max and I— we like to walk around the neighborhood and steal cuttings from people's front yards."

"So, *you're* the one doing the burglary," I tease, throwing back her assumption of me from the first night we met. "How hypocritical."

"Hardly the same," she says, rolling her eyes, before pointing to the window. "I think I'm going to line them up on the ledge there."

I follow her gaze, try to picture it in my mind. "That'll look pretty," I tell her.

She giggles.

"What?"

"The word *pretty*, from your mouth, it's like a dichotomy."

"That's a big word," I muse, picking up the twine and rolling it between my fingers. "And I've said 'pretty' before."

"Not around me, you haven't."

"Maybe." I shrug. "But I've definitely said it *about* you." I pick up an unused can. "Are you just making these for you, or do you plan to sell them?" For a long moment, she doesn't respond, and so I look up, catch those muddy brown eyes staring back at me. "What's up?"

"You just called me pretty."

"And?"

She shrugs.

I look back down, focus on the project in front of me. "You're insanely pretty, Liv, and if you don't know this, then I'm sorry you're surrounding yourself with people who haven't already convinced you of it." I lift the can up between us. "Can I make one?"

"Rhys..."

I glance up. "Yeah?"

Liv tilts her head, just a tad, and spends the next few seconds silently scrutinizing me. "You didn't come here to craft with me."

"I came to *be* with you. This included."

"So, you didn't come here for..."

I raise my eyebrows, wait for her to say the word. S E X. It's really not that hard. But the longer I watch her, the redder her cheeks get. "Did I come here for you to play with my dick and balls—"

She busts out a laugh, and now I'm the one reminding her to be quiet. Not that I'd care if Delgado found me in here, but I'm not here to complicate things for her. Also, she mentioned that he'd asked her if the rumors were true—that I was now an assistant coach at his rival school. Liv said she played dumb; told him she didn't know. But if Delgado discovers me in here, with his sister, a *student* at the very school where I'm coaching, then there's no way I'd be able to keep the job, which means I'd leave Oscar on his own, and *fuck*... maybe my being here is a bad idea.

"I have a spare glue gun," she whispers.

My smile is stupid.

I don't know how long we spend in comfortable silence, hot-glueing twine to tin cans, but I don't think I've ever felt so... weightless. So at ease. "This is kind of therapeutic, no?"

"It is," she agrees. "Keep my hands busy, keep the anxiety at bay."

I lift my gaze. "You get anxious?"

"Who doesn't these days?" she murmurs, focused on removing the sticky residue from a can. "Crafting is cheaper than therapy, so there's that."

"You know the school has a therapist—Miss Turner. She's great."

She nods. "She must be amazing, considering she was the first thing Oscar showed me on his tour of the school."

"Speaking of school," I edge, and I don't know if now's the right time to bring this up, but I don't know if there ever will be. "I have questions."

"I figured you might."

I take a moment to find the right words. The last thing I want to do is dig up horrible memories. "After your grandparents died, did you just drop out of school altogether?"

"Yep," she says, as if it's no big deal. "I was enrolled in a fast-track program that isn't offered at a lot of schools, so the best option for me was to stay in Wilmington for my senior year while they all moved up here for Dominic's scholarship."

"He couldn't wait a year until you graduated?"

She doesn't respond, just gives me a pointed look as if I should know the answer and, unfortunately, I do. Scholarship placements to schools like Philips are one in a million, even for players as good as her brother. "It's not a big deal," Liv says. "We'd planned that I live with my best friend's family for that year, which at the time, felt like the greatest thing in the world. I'd be living with my best friend who had a brother, and her brother had a friend who also happened to be my boyfriend—"

"I hate him," I cut in. Then shake my head at myself. It may not be a lie, but it's an incredibly inappropriate time to be exposing my jealousy like this.

Liv watches me a moment, brow dipped in confusion, and I stare back... glue gun in one hand, tin can in the other, not knowing how to react to my childish outburst. "Anyway..." she says, and I release the breath I'd been holding. "After they died, Dominic wasn't sure what his immediate future looked like, and Philips was eager to keep him, so they offered me a scholarship, too. But with Max and everything else going on, it just wasn't the right time. They let us defer and use it for Max, and thank God, because Max is thriving there."

"So how did you end up at St. Luke's?"

"Anonymous scholarship," she says. "I guess whoever it is found out about what happened and wanted to help. They had ties with St. Luke's, and I sure as hell wasn't going to look a gift horse in the mouth —" She stops to think a moment. "Is that the phrase?"

"Yeah."

"Cool." She unwinds some twine, before adding, "St. Luke's name alone reads great on my transcripts—if I ever want to go the college route—which is important considering there's a three-year gap filled with literally *nothing*."

I nod, trying to wrap my mind around it all, and I'm sure I had more questions, but I can't seem to come up with one. Besides, Liv's watching me now, her eyes almost as wide as her smile. "How cute was Max's reaction?"

"Oh my God." I drop everything in my hands. "I've watched it a thousand times, and I still can't get enough. Thank you for recording it and sending it to me. You made my fucking life!"

"You're adorable," she says through a giggle, getting up on her knees to kiss me. Just once. "And you're welcome."

I return the kiss threefold, then wait until she's seated again before bringing up something I've wanted to for a while. "I feel like I need to tell you something, but I don't know if I should because I don't know if I'm betraying his trust, or if—"

"Max?" she cuts in.

"Yeah."

"What happened?"

I lean back on my outstretched arms and ready myself. "This one time, you were picking up a delivery and Max and I were in the car alone, and he mentioned that..." I sigh, discomfort crawling up my spine. "He said he thought he was a curse."

Liv lowers her gaze, her shoulders dropping, chest caving in. "He said that?"

"I'm sorry," I say, and I don't really know what I'm sorry for. That I'm telling her he mentioned it or that he feels like that in the first place?

She lifts her eyes again, red and raw from her withheld emotions. "You care about him a lot, don't you?

I shrug, tell her the truth. "I feel a connection with him, and I can't really explain why."

"You don't need to," she says through a half-hearted smile. "He has that effect on people."

I nod, agreeing, but don't say anything more. I just watch her—watch the myriad of emotions that flash through her eyes. "The night of the accident... I was coming up to visit for the weekend. I didn't drive, so my boyfriend offered to take me. I was navigating us, and so I had his phone in my hand. We were about twenty minutes out when a text came through from this girl. It was a picture of them together from the night before. I was so... I don't even know how I felt. I just knew that I couldn't sit in the car with him for the next twenty minutes, so... I asked him to let me out. He refused at first, but I was..." She clears her throat, clears the tears from her eyes with the heels of her palms. "I was in this blackout rage, and I don't even remember what I said or did. I just know that at one point, he finally conceded and pulled over. It was pouring rain, but I didn't care. I got out and watched him peel away, never looking back. I was soaking wet, on a winding road, with nothing but trees around me, and so I called my grandparents to pick me up. They were already on the way to a meet and greet that Dom was at with the team and their families, but... they turned around... for *me*..."

My eyes drift shut, while my heart plummets to my stomach. "You can't blame yourself," I tell her, at the same time she sniffs, says, "I'm always trying to convince myself that it wasn't my fault, but they wouldn't even have been on that road if I hadn't asked them to. And the worst part is that I could've just sucked it up for twenty more minutes, just dealt with it. But I forced myself into a situation where I felt unsafe, stranded on the side of the road, in the pouring rain, with no real clue of where I was. My grandpa was tracking my location on my phone, but every second that went by, the more scared and anxious I got, and my grandma was on the phone trying to calm me down when—" She breaks off on a sob that wretches through her entire body, and I go to her, sit behind her, lift her onto my lap. I hold her while she cries. While she relays the memory with no filters. "The *sound* of it, Rhys... it was so loud, and then it was silent, and then..." Her eyes widen, and she chokes on a breath.

I hold her tighter, almost too afraid to ask. "Then what?"

"Max..." Her eyes meet mine again. "I could hear him crying, screaming, *wailing*."

I can't breathe.

"He'd only been on this earth for three years, and it was the second time he was in a car accident that took the lives of both his parents."

"Jesus Christ," I murmur, unable to see straight.

Arms around my neck, she folds into me, as if I'm the one who can save her. I can't even save myself. "He wouldn't stop crying, and I think it's the only reason the kids from the other car got out. They could hear him. And I could hear them, and I was yelling, screaming through the phone..." she trails off, her breaths ragged, her tears so big, so constant, they soak through my T-shirt and into my flesh. "Do you believe in miracles, Rhys?" I start to answer, but she doesn't give me time to speak. "Because I don't. Never have. But this couple driving past somehow saw me standing on the side of road, hysterical, and they pulled over to see if I was okay. I could barely see a foot in front of me, that's how heavy the rain was... but they saw me. Somehow. Someway... There were no sirens. I remember that much. Why hadn't they called anybody?" She's rambling, lost in the memories, in the anguish, and she's moving, rocking back and forth, taking me with her. "But then I remembered I could track their location, so I found them, and the woman who had pulled over, she called 911 for me, and then they offered to drive me to the scene and I wish... I wish I'd said no, because..." She tries to settle her breathing—an impossible task. "And then there was the aftermath. The guilt and the shame and the lawyers, and my mom, abandoning me again—"

Wait. "What?"

"She's not working out of state, Rhys." She sniffs back the pain. The heartache. "I took my share of the hush money from the boy who killed my grandparents and paid my own mother to sign off as our guardian so they wouldn't split us up. Dominic and Max, they're blood, and they'd just found each other, and Dom... God, he was so hurt, so confused, so worried about all of us, about our futures, and it was the only thing I could think to do to save us. My mom agreed, took my money, hung around for long enough to remember how much she hated being a mom. How much she hated me. And one morning, I woke up, and she was gone... She took my money, took my trust, and just left. And you know what's so fucked up? I wasn't even surprised. Wasn't even *mad.* I didn't have time to be." She stops there, eyes wide as if surprised by everything she's just revealed. "But no one can know about it, Rhys," she rushes out. "If anyone finds out..." She picks up the twine and twists it between her fingers. *Keep my hands busy, keep the anxiety at bay.* "There's so much more, so much I want to say, but I don't know how to tell you or if I'll ever be ready to—"

"So don't," I interrupt, finally finding my voice.

I push back my emotions and rear back, just enough so I can focus on her sad, sad eyes. "You don't have to give me everything all at once."

I realize now that it's how my feelings for Liv started: *everything,* all at once.

But it doesn't need to be like that *always.*

I can take my time with her. Go slow. Uncover her heart first, then later, discover all the fragments that make her who she is.

"I have to tell you something, Liv..." Swirls of emotions pump through my bloodline. Pride. Pity. Perpetual hope. I reach up, wipe away her liquid heartache, and give her a tiny sliver of my soul. "That night when you obliterated me with your monster truck and put me in a coma—" She laughs through her tears, the single sound expanding the beating organ inside my chest. "I mentioned I was escaping my party, but what I didn't tell you, or anyone else who was there, was that it was a farewell party. For me. I'd planned to leave that night." And where I'd planned to go isn't important anymore. "I'd been in this... *slump*." Or, as my therapist would say, a deep state of depression. "I was already dreading the rest of summer. It felt like every day was a repeat of the last. Like I was forcing myself to wake up just so I could prepare to wake up the day after. It was the same mundane minutes that built into hours, into days, and I felt like I was standing still, and the world was moving around me..." I reach up, coat my thumb with the remnants of her sorrow. "And then you and Max showed up, and you flipped my entire world off its axis." I lick the dryness off my lips, my heart heavy. "It's funny... Miles-*not*-*Morales* spent his lonely days searching for a miracle, and here I am—the luckiest guy on earth because *my* miracle crashed right into me... and I didn't even know I was looking for it."

35

Olivia

"Ohana! Get up!"

I gasp awake, and my first and only thought is Rhys. I'd fallen asleep in his arms, and now Max is at my open bedroom door, smiling from ear to ear, and I quickly check the spot next to me.

Empty.

All but for a torn piece of paper lying on his pillow. I inhale a sharp breath, release it slowly. Carefully. "Morning, Maxy," I croak, my voice scratchy from sleep. As inconspicuous as possible, I grab the note and hide it beneath my pillow. Leaning up on my elbows, I ask, "What time is it?"

"Time to get your ass up!" Dom says, coming in behind Max with a coffee and...

I sit up taller to get a better look. "Is that an apple cinnamon muffin from the diner?"

"Yep!" Max grins, skips his way from the door to my bedside. "Dom and I went out and got it for you."

Again, I ask, taking the coffee and muffin from my brother, "What time is it?"

"Almost midday," Dom answers.

"*What?*"

He pokes the spot between my eyebrows. "Sleepy head."

I push his hand away, murmur, "I haven't slept in like that since... ever."

"I wouldn't have woken you, but I'm meeting the guys at the sports park soon," Dom says.

"And you and I are going for a walk to steal some cuttings!" Max adds.

"Right." I take a sip of my coffee. "Maybe let's not use the word *steal...*"

Max ponders for a moment. "Acquire without prior permission?"

"Nerd!" Dom yells, picking him up and throwing him over his shoulder. "Let's give Ollie some time to wake and enjoy her breakfast." He turns just before my door. "I have to leave in thirty."

"I'll be up," I assure.

He exits, turning Max to face me. "Best wishes, m'lady," he says.

I lift my coffee. "And warm regards to you, good sir."

I wait until I'm sure they're not lurking just outside my room to search for the torn paper beneath my pillow. I'm quick to find it, to read the handwritten words from a boy who'd so easily stolen my heart— acquired it without prior permission...

It's four simple words.

A million different emotions.

My miracle is you.

36

Olivia

"You good, Ollie?" Dom asks, closing the dishwasher and switching it on.

I tear my eyes away from my phone to focus on him. "Yeah. Why?"

"You've been glued to your phone all day. Even throughout dinner," he says, teasing. "You waiting on someone?"

I rest my hip against the kitchen counter and shrug, my mind elsewhere.

After reading Rhys's note this morning, I'd sent him a text. A heart emoji. Lame, sure, but I didn't know how else to convey what I felt. A heart was as close to *love* as it gets without saying the actual word. Besides, the interaction wasn't supposed to end there. He was supposed to respond, and we'd do our regular back and forth, but that's the problem.

He read the message, but he hasn't responded.

It's been *hours*. Six, almost. And it wouldn't usually worry me, but he's never done this before. Never just blatantly ignored me. As *Not Fridge Guy*, sure, but never as Rhys.

I almost jump out of my skin when my phone vibrates in my hand.

Pulse pounding against my flesh, I check the notification. My stomach drops when it isn't from Rhys. It is, however, related to him.

SG

> I got home earlier today and told him everything.

I read the words a thousand times in the space of a second. Stare at them until they become nothing but a blur of letters that mean way too much but give too little.

"Ohana?" Dom says, but he sounds so far away. So distant. As if he's in another world...

And I'm lost, walking through an inferno with no end in sight.

"It's work," I mumble, avoiding his stare so he can't witness the pain burning behind my eyes.

"The laundromats?"

"Yeah..." I head for my room, dazed and distracted, saying over my shoulder, "I gotta deal with this..." The second I'm behind closed doors, I make the call, ignoring the way my hand trembles as I bring the phone to my ear.

She answers on the first ring, and I don't wait for her greeting. "Define *everything*," I demand, my jaw clenched. Tears coat my lashes, but I refuse to let them fall.

Not now.

Not yet.

"*Everything*, Olivia."

I empty my lungs, struggle to fill them again. A sob clogs my airways, making it almost impossible to ask, "Does he know who I am?"

"Yes, but—"

I hang up, not needing to know the rest, and immediately call Rhys. I can barely make out the sound of the phone ringing through my pulse pounding in my ears, through the blood pumping in my veins, through my harsh breaths clawing at my throat with every inhale, every exhale. The call goes to voicemail, so I hang up, throw my phone on the bed. The drawer of my side table falls out completely with my urgency to open it. I grab the phone that was given to me almost three years ago and open the only contact in there—Not Fridge Guy—and for the first time ever, I hit *call*. It's the same number I'd just dialed, and I get the same outcome: voicemail.

Thick, heated tears well in my eyes, overflow to my cheeks and soak into my flesh.

I can barely see.

Barely breathe.

Barely steady my hands long enough to type out a text.

> Please talk to me, Rhys. At least give me a chance to explain.

I drop that phone on my pillow and grab my other one.

My real one.

My *Rhys* one.

And I type out another text. Same meaning. Different words. Words he used on me less than twenty-four hours ago.

> I need you.

37

Olivia

Three years earlier

"I need you to be good for me, okay?" I tell Max, helping him out of his rain-soaked jacket just inside the doors of Cup of Cake. I ignore the way my body aches from carrying him for the past thirty minutes and drop to his level. Eye to eye, I explain, "I'm just going to talk to a lady about getting a job here, and as soon as we're done, we can go back home, get you nice and warm again."

He nods but doesn't speak. Not that I can blame him. I'm practically a stranger to the kid.

My grandparents had gotten the call about him two weeks into summer break. A week from moving their entire lives so Dom could play basketball at a school that guaranteed him a scholarship to a Division I college. They changed whatever plans they needed to fit Max into their new lives, and I stayed in Wilmington, preparing for the rest of mine.

I don't *know* Max. Not really. While he and Dom had the entire summer to create a bond, I was thrown into the deep end without a single clue on how to float. I wasn't even given a life jacket. And now, I'm supposed to be responsible for him?

I've just turned sixteen. Dom's fourteen. Max is three.

We're babies raising babies, and it doesn't matter how much that thought terrifies me, there isn't a choice. At least, I was never given one.

There's a puddle on the tiled floor beneath us now, created by us alone, and I grimace, look around the small cake shop. Besides the one girl behind the counter, restocking the tubs of smashed-up cakes, there's a lone woman in a corner booth, sipping a coffee. Neither of them is watching us, and I'm grateful for that.

I stand, patting down my wet hair, attempting to look somewhat put together. A delusional desire considering I've literally just waded through a storm without an umbrella.

With a muted sigh, I take Max's hand and step up to the counter. I wait for the girl in the light pink apron to look up at me, smile. I smile back. Or at least I try to. "I have a job interview..." I tell her, my voice as weak as the organ beating beneath my chest. "I'm a little late, so..."

The girl, who can't be over twenty, points behind me to the woman sitting in the booth, waving me over. I guess I was so flustered when I first noticed her that I didn't really take her in. Middle-aged, sandy-blond hair cut just above her shoulders and styled in a way that screams *composed*. In other words: the complete opposite of me. I almost slip on my wet shoes as I lead Max over to her, holding his dripping wet coat to my chest. I help him into the booth first, then slide in after him. And then I just stare at the table, picking at a worn spot, while my stomach turns, my heart so heavy I can't even tell if it's still beating—if the weight of my grief and the pressure to do the right thing hasn't already crushed it to death.

"It's Olivia, right?" the woman says, and I give her the courtesy of meeting her eyes.

"Yes, ma'am."

"And you're here for which position?"

I swallow, nervous. "The one that's evenings and weekends. I can't work during school hours because..." I glance at Max, but don't say anything more.

The woman smiles, but it's so forced it makes me uncomfortable. "How old is your son?"

"He's not—" I stop there, because who Max is to me isn't important. The less people know, the better. "I don't have a lot of experience," I say, deflecting, "But I'm a very fast learner, and I'm not at school, so I'm somewhat flexible with hours, as long as I can find..." I realize I'm not breathing. That the fear of releasing my withheld tears has blocked oxygen in my airways. "Um... I—"

"Olivia, I'm going to be honest with you, the position you're applying for has already been filled."

My heart drops. "Oh."

"But—"

"I understand," I interrupt, looking up at her. "If I had gotten here on time, would it have made a difference?"

Her gaze shifts, moving between my eyes, as if trying to decide how much the truth will hurt.

"I'm really sorry for wasting your time," I tell her. "And thank you for your patience. With waiting for me and talking to me even though I'm... a lot right now."

"You know what always helps me when I'm feeling a little over-whelmed?" Her smile is forced, made of nothing but pity, and she reaches across the table to cover my hand. I hate her pity almost as much as I need her touch. Her warmth coats my cold flesh, warms my icy heart. "A cup of cake!" Her grin widens as she looks over at Max. "I have just the right thing for both of you," she says, sliding out of the booth. "It's in the kitchen. I'll be right back."

The moment she's out of my vision, I slip out of the booth and help Max do the same. I rush to put Max's coat back on him and then exit the building. As much as I appreciate the sentiment, a Cup of Cake isn't going to save us. And neither is her pity. And I know that the longer we stay, the more questions she'll have, and that's the last thing we need.

The rain hasn't eased up outside, and I squeeze Max's hand, look down at him. "Can you please walk until you can't anymore, and then I'll carry you, okay?"

Max squeezes my hand back, and I smile. Genuine. And then I look up and ahead of us, through the sheath of rainfall so thick it's impossible to see too far in front of us. I'm about to step out from under the sheltered eave when the shop door opens behind us. I cringe, turn to the woman. "I'm really sorry for wasting your time."

She doesn't disagree with me, just looks out at the rain. "I have a car. At least let me drive you home."

"I can't," I say and step out into the storm. "I'm really sorry," I repeat, because I truly am.

Max and I walk hand in hand, our heads lowered, his tiny steps forcing me to go slow. "I like the rain," he says out of nowhere, and I turn toward him. He looks up, his dark eyes squinting as droplets crash against his face. "It means there's something above us. And all around us. Maybe it comes from heaven. Like tears. From my mom and dad. From Dominic's. And yours, too."

I slow my steps even more. "So why do you like it, then?" I ask. "If it's made of tears..."

"You can have happy tears, right?" he says, gripping my hand tighter as he jumps in a puddle. "Maybe they're happy for us!"

I don't understand how they could be, but I'm not here to argue with a three-year-old.

Max jumps in one puddle, and then another, and I watch him, transfixed, wondering how nice it must be to be too young to comprehend the realities of *life*.

He turns, raindrops clinging to the tip of his nose when he looks up at me. "Maybe they're happy because we're still here... even if they can't be."

By the age of sixteen, I'd experienced three defining moments in my life.

The first was my mother's reaction to me calling her "mom" to her face. I was only four years old, but I remember it clearly. She was so mad at me, so disgusted, so angry that this little girl had the audacity to remind her of her mistakes. Some days, I still see myself through her eyes, and I hate that I do.

The second was when Dominic called me Ohana for the first time. I'd just turned six, and he was four, and he'd been with us for a few months already. We were sitting next to each other on the couch when it happened. The final credits of *Lilo and Stitch* played on the television, and my grandparents were cleaning up the empty bowls of popcorn and juice boxes. Dominic took my hand in his, patted the back of it a few times, kissed my cheek, and said, "You're my Ohana." My grandparents stopped what they were doing and looked between us. I looked at them, conveying with my eyes what my heart knew it wanted. Within months, he was a Delgado. And I would forever be his Ohana.

The third defining moment was watching my grandparents being taken away in body bags. That's... self-explanatory.

And I wondered—as I spent a few minutes puddle jumping in the rain with my three-year-old brother on the sidewalk—if this was another one of those moments. While he laughed along, squealing in delight to be rained on by the "happy tears" of our dead parents, I stomped in the pools of water, one after the other, and let the rain hide the tears of my anger, my frustration.

"Go, Ohana!" Max jumps up and down in glee, cheering me on. And so I *go*. And I can't stop *going*. I keep stomping on the rain-covered ground until my feet sting with the force of my actions. I push through the tears, through the silent sobs that wreak havoc on my insides. And I don't stop... can't. Even when a black SUV pulls up beside us and rolls down the rear window. The woman from the cake store pokes her head out, yells over the thunder cracking above us, "Get in!"

I kick a pool of water at her car. "We can't!" I yell back and continue my path to self-destruction. Stomp after stomp, kick after kick.

"I'm tired now," Max says, tugging on my arm. I hear him; I know I do. But at the same time... I feel like I'm not *here*. Like I'm not *present*. I know I exist, and I know that I'm real—that I'm flesh and bones and working organs—but I don't *feel* like it. I don't feel like I'm living or breathing. I don't *feel* alive.

The car door opens, and I slow my steps but don't stop completely. "Get in the car, Olivia," she repeats, her tone laced with pity.

I stop then. Face her head on. "I told you already. We *can't*," I repeat, jaw locked, teeth clenched. The rain falls on my eyelids until they become so heavy, I'm forced to blink them away.

"Why not?" she asks, getting out of the car. "I promise, I won't hurt you."

"Because *he*—" I say, pointing at Max, "has been in horrible car accidents that have killed people. People really fucking important to us. So now he has PTSD, and he won't get in a moving car unless his brother's sitting in the back with him. And that can't happen right now because his brother's at school, and so that's why I was late! And that's why I'm standing here in the pouring rain with a boy I barely know, trying to find a way to make money so we can survive, because you know what? Everyone else who's supposed to be doing this shit is dead or chose to abandon me. Again!" I break down. In front of my new brother and a complete stranger, and I *shatter*. Right there, in front of their eyes. "I'm barely sixteen, and suddenly, I have to be the one to pick up the pieces because no one else will! No one else—"

I stop there, my words caught in my throat as she pulls me into her arms, holds me until her warmth replaces the frigidness of our surroundings, of my life. She strokes my back, soothing my pain, and before I'm ready, she releases me and goes to Max. She drops to her knees, right in the middle of a puddle, her bare knees exposed by her pencil skirt—and looks Max right in the eyes. "What if we just sit in the car?" she asks him. "We won't drive. We'll just sit. All three of us in the back."

Max looks at me, then at her. And then he nods.

We settle into the back of the SUV, the hazard lights on, with the warmth of the heater blowing directly on us. Max sits across my lap, his head on my shoulder, and he wasn't lying before when he said he was tired. He's struggling to keep his eyes open now, and I should've listened to him. "I'm sorry," I tell him, holding him close. I stroke his hair, keep my sob contained when he stutters a breath. "I'm sorry."

Then I face the woman beside me, and for the third time in the space of minutes, I say, "I'm sorry."

She's in a skirt and a sleeveless blouse, and she sits in that way posh people do—crossed at the ankles and knees to the side. I don't think I've ever been in the presence of someone so... together. "Sorry for what?"

"For leaving the way I did. I figured I wasn't getting the job after the way I... *am*." I don't say *the way I behaved,* because that implies I can somewhat control myself. Right now, I can't. I don't. I just... *am*. "And I'm sorry for my outburst before. For yelling at you like you were the one who killed my grandparents."

She smiles, made of nothing but pity, and motions to Max, now asleep on my lap. "He's out like a light."

"Yeah," I say through a sigh. "He'll be out for a while."

"Can we drive you home if he's sleeping?"

"Yeah." I return her smile, grateful. "I'd really appreciate it."

I give the driver my address, and within minutes, we're pulling up to my house. "Thank you for the ride," I say and start to get out, but she stops me with a hand on my arm.

"Olivia."

I turn to her. "Yes?"

"I want to help you."

"With a job?" I ask, eyebrows drawn.

"With a job, with your family, your house, your education, anything you need."

My shoulders drop, and I bite back a scoff. "And what do you get in return? My *soul*?"

"No." She shakes her head. "Hopefully, I get my son back."

I turn my entire body to hers, my back against the door with Max still on my lap. There are as many questions floating through my mind as there are red flags, but the only thing that comes out of my mouth is: "You never told me your name."

"It's Skylar," she tells me. "Skylar Garrett."

PART IV

38

Olivia

Three Years Earlier

Picture book held to my chest, I roll my head to the side and ignore the dampness of my tears staining the pillow. Max lies beside me, his eyes closed, breaths even, in a state of peacefulness I haven't felt since my grandparents died.

It's only been a few months, but God... the days seem like forever when you feel like you're drowning.

Max stirs and shifts onto his back, releasing a sigh. He fell asleep twenty minutes ago, but I haven't been able to move—too paralyzed by my thoughts, by my fears.

I'm not ready to leave the comfort and safety of his bed. Leaving would mean facing reality, and reality means the unknown.

I hate the unknown.

My phone vibrates on the nightstand, and I wipe at my tears before reaching for it.

THEO

I'll be there around 7 tomorrow, but I have to
leave early the next morning. Good?

Most sixteen-year-old girls would feel giddy at the thought of their
boyfriends driving two hours to spend the night with them, but I just
feel... empty.

And I've felt that way for so long now that I'm starting to wonder if
there's something wrong with me. And worse, I wonder if I'm always
going to feel this way.

I reply *"good"* to Theo's message and wait a few minutes to see if he
responds. The hopeful part of me wants him to ask what I'd like to do,
if I want to go somewhere, or if I want him to bring anything, or just... I
don't even know. And it doesn't even matter because he doesn't write
back. Why would he? There's nothing more to say. He'll show up
tomorrow for two reasons. Sex and pity. Luckily, not the two combined,
because if that were the case, I'd rather dig a hole between my grandparents and peace out of this life.

And with that thought in mind, I force myself out of Max's bed and
onto my feet. With one hand on the doorknob, I make sure there's no
evidence of the tears I've shed, plaster on a smile, and open the door.
Then stop in my tracks.

Dom's sitting in the hallway, his back against the wall, knees up,
head lowered.

"Dom?" I quietly close the door behind me. "Are you okay?"

He lifts his head, just an inch, and I break down at the utter devasta-
tion swimming in his eyes.

"Dom," I whisper, my heart dropping. I get to my knees in front of
him, settle a hand on his shoulder, and it's as if that single act—that
touch—breaks the walls of the dam that he'd built inside him. His
entire body trembles, overflowing with emotions.

I hold him to me, push back my own sobs as he falls apart in my
arms. "I don't know what to do," he cries.

There's just over a year between us, a good foot difference in height,
and even at fourteen, he has the physical strength to carry my weight.

And Max's, too. Maybe he has been. Maybe I haven't been doing enough, because right now, he feels so small. So fragile. It's been years since I've held him like this. Years since he's *needed* me like this.

"We'll get through this," I assure, though I don't know how. Mom left two weeks ago, without a word, and she hasn't made contact since.

He pulls back, lifting his sad, defeated eyes to mine. "I'm scared, Ollie."

"Of what?"

"Everything."

I sit beside him, take his hand in mine like he did when we were little. Right before he declared me *his* Ohana.

I'm scared too, I want to say. And I almost do. The words are right there, on the tip of my tongue, but no good can come from revealing my truths.

I worry about Max. About raising him on our own.

I worry about Dominic and how he's going to get through these critical years without the male guidance most boys need to get there.

I worry we won't be able to survive on our own. Financially, especially, but in all the other ways that matter.

But most of all, I worry that someone's going to find out about my mom leaving. That they're going to see we have no one. That it's just the three of us. And that they're going to separate us. Tear us apart.

"What are we going to do for money?" Dom asks. He has his share of the will and the payout from the accident, but he can't touch it until he's twenty-one.

"I'll get a job," I reply.

"What about school?" he says, his cries subsiding. He squeezes my hand tighter with one hand, the other wiping his eyes.

"I'll go back one day. It's not a big deal."

"I'll quit, too. We'll both work."

"No," I'm quick to say. "You focus on school and basketball. I'll take care of the rest."

He's quiet a beat, and so I turn to him. He's already watching me, his eyes holding so much pain and anguish that I have to look away. "You think I'll really get into the NBA?"

"Of course. I have full faith that you'll get there, Dom. But only if that's what you really want."

"I do," he says, nodding. "And once I get there, I'll take care of all of us. Forever. I promise."

The tears I'd held on to slip from my eyes, cling to my lashes. "I know you will," I state. "Get into the NBA, I mean. Anything else is a bonus."

He smiles, or at least attempts to. And then sniffs once, his green eyes holding mine. "Promise you won't leave us—"

"Dom..."

"I'm serious, Ohana. That's what I fear the most. That you'll resent us one day, and—"

"I'm not my mother," I cut in, a flicker of anger heating my words.

"I know," he says, and his hand tightens around mine again. "But Max isn't your brother. He's mine."

"He's *ours*."

Dom watches me, his eyes shifting between mine. And then he laughs. Just once. But it's sad. So, so sad. "Remember what Dad used to say?"

I nod, knowing what he's thinking, because the same words have lived inside me for as long as I can remember. But they've never been as clear as they have been since my mother walked out. "The family we create means more than the family who created us."

* * *

Sleep evades me, as it has most nights lately, and no amount of tossing and turning puts my mind at ease. With a frustrated sigh, I throw the covers off me and open the drawer of my nightstand, pull out the phone Mrs. Garrett had given me a few days ago. I unlock it and go straight to the text messages from the only contact stored in the phone, then read through our exchange from a couple of days ago.

> Hey. I'm at the front of the address you gave me to pick up the fridge, but no one's answering the door.

UNKNOWN

Wrong number

> I just checked, and this is the number you gave me through Messenger.

I don't know what to tell you, but I don't have a fridge for sale.

> Did you block me on Messenger?

I didn't, but whoever scammed you obviously did.

> Are you serious? I drove all this way...

I fail to see how that's my problem, but sorry (for you), I guess.

> Fuck you.

Life already has.

The next day, I tried again.

> Hey

UNKNOWN

Still wrong number.

> I know.

> I just wanted to say sorry about yesterday. Obviously, I wasn't in the best mood, and I took it out on you, a random stranger, who might possibly be having a worse day than I was. So. Sorry.

He didn't respond, and I didn't know what to say, so I left it at that.

The contract I have hidden in the bottom drawer of my dresser states that any contact I have with Mrs. Garrett's son should be via text only. No identifying myself. No phone calls. No meet ups. In fact, it's stipulated that we are never, *ever*, to meet in person.

I figured she had her reasons, so I didn't ask why.

All she told me is that her son had been through something recently and that they would be separated from each other for the foreseeable future. So, she needed a way to "keep tabs on him" ... *emotionally*.

I'm not exactly sure what that means to her, or him, or me even, but then she told me what I'd get in return.

Mrs. Garrett offered me an *actual* job managing a group of laundromats, and with it came a salary that far exceeded anything I could ever hope for. On top of that, she'll cover day care for Max if I decide I need it, and she'll also pay for me to go back to school. And not just any school, but St. Luke's Academy, one of the most prestigious schools in all of North Carolina. The only problem is that her son currently attends there, so I'll have to wait until he graduates. In three years. Three years seems like a hell of a long time, but it's not as if I'm ready to go back now, and who knows what will happen between now and then? It's a bridge I'll cross when the time comes.

I signed off on her terms, along with a non-disclosure agreement, because I couldn't *not*. Her offer was too good to refuse.

But here's the problem: the job, the contract, will only come into play if or when my contact with her son is reciprocated, and so far, we're not at that stage. And I'm struggling to figure out a way to get there.

I change his name in the phone to *Not Fridge Guy,* then watch the cursor flash before my eyes as I try come up with something to say. I can't cling to the whole wrong number story, and since I know nothing about him and can't reveal too much about me, I don't know how to slide into a conversation that I know he'll engage in. I can't—

The sound of a door opening stops my thoughts. I drop the phone on my bed and make my way to the door leading to the garage, press my ear to it. Dominic's steady footfalls land on the concrete, drag across the floor, and I turn the door handle and pull. Dom's standing in the middle of the garage, his hands at his sides.

My grandpa's incomplete projects fill the garage, along with his tools and random pieces of timber he'd collected throughout the years. Once Dominic got the scholarship to Philips, my grandparents sold our old house and bought this one. When they moved, they took everything with them, along with every single piece of my grandpa's old workshop. I'd helped with the initial move but didn't have time to come back once they'd settled into the house.

I'd been too afraid of the memories behind the garage door... so much so that I hadn't yet found the courage to open it.

Until now.

Emotion clogs my throat, blocks my airways. Still standing in the doorway, I ask, "You okay?"

"Can't sleep." Dominic picks up a plane sitting sideways on a bookshelf and moves it to the bench. It doesn't belong there. It lives under the bench in a wooden box my grandpa and I made from an old pallet. But Dom wouldn't know that, because he didn't spend as much time in the workshop as I did. "Help me with this?" he asks, motioning to a toy chest.

I step foot in the garage for the first time and ignore the intense ache in my chest. "Where do you want it?"

He looks around the garage, ending on me. "I don't know."

We don't move the toy chest.

We don't do much of anything, really.

For the next hour, we sit on the cold, hard concrete floor of the garage, our silence broken only by our cries. We don't talk. We don't make plans. We don't make promises. We just... sit. Together, but alone. And then Dominic stands, says, "Goodnight, Ohana."

"Goodnight, Dom."

I watch him enter the house, then spend a few minutes stewing in the silence before getting up myself. Before I go back to my room, I put the plane back where it belongs.

. . .

The phone's still on my bed, right where I left it, and I grab it before lying down. Back under the covers for the third time tonight, I stare up at my bare ceiling, wondering if Dominic's doing the same.

I check the time on the phone. It's just after three. Thankfully, there's no school tomorrow. Not that I'd force him to go. Not that I could.

After a heavy exhale, I unlock the phone and go back to the messages, back to the blinking cursor. And, without a single thought and even fewer fucks left to give, I let my thumbs relay my feelings.

> I know you don't know me, and I sure as hell don't know you, but... to be honest, I don't know a lot of people. I just moved to a new town where the only person I have is my brother, and I guess I just needed someone to talk to who isn't him. You don't need to respond to what I'm saying. In fact, I almost prefer that you don't.

> Do you ever feel like you're not breathing? Like, physically, you are, because otherwise you'd be dead, but sometimes I feel like no matter how many breaths I take, no matter how full of oxygen my lungs are, I just... I don't even know.

> And don't get me wrong, I don't feel like this always. Just lately. And it comes in waves. But the waves are so big, and so strong, and so powerful, and they drag me under... and I know I should gasp for air, but... lately, the feeling of drowning is the only thing that makes me feel alive.

> And I know that's a pretty fucked up thing to feel, let alone tell someone, but there it is.

> I need to feel like I'm dying in order to feel alive.

> That sounds a hell of a lot worse than it actually is.

Sorry if all this wakes you. And I'm sorry if you're someone who carries the weight of other people's emotions. Please don't carry mine. I'm not worth it. But also, if you are one of those people. Welcome, and hi.

I lock the screen and practically throw the phone back in my nightstand, but just as I'm about to shut the drawer, a text comes through. And it's strange—how badly I wanted a response from him, how quickly I'd jumped at every other message he'd sent, but this time... I hesitate, almost fearful of what he has to say. With bated breath, I grab the phone, read his words.

NOT FRIDGE GUY

I get it.

And I'm sorry that you have to get it too.

I fall asleep with tears in my eyes, dreaming of oceans and waves dragging me under.

I wake up to the sunlight streaming through my window, and the first thing I do is check the phone. My breath catches, heart racing at the sight of the unread text message waiting for me.

NOT FRIDGE GUY

I was thinking about what you said—about the waves knocking you down, taking you under... and I think I figured it out—why you don't gasp for air. You said it yourself; your lungs are already filled with oxygen. You can't drown. You float. So just keep doing that. Breathe. One more time. Every time. And I promise to do the same. – Rhys

39

Rhys

In the third and final book of the *Miles and His Miracles Trilogy*, the readers find out that Miles is dying.

Pretty fucked up, right?

It turns out that the giant house he claimed to live in was, in reality, a hospital, and all his tutors and nannies? They were his nurses. And the reason he was so fascinated with miracles is that he once overheard his doctors telling his mother that, in order for him to live, they would need a *miracle*.

Miles had no clue what a miracle was, and even throughout his search for it, he still failed to comprehend it completely. Regardless, the search continued, as far as his mom and Internet strangers would allow, for this mysterious, ever-elusive miracle.

And this is where things get messy because at some point throughout the captivating storytelling that lasts three full-length novels, we, the readers, forget one crucial fact.

Miles is *six*.

He wasn't the one searching the Internet for people who had experienced miracles.

He wasn't the one inviting them into his hospital room to tell him all about it.

And he sure as hell wasn't the one forcing false hope down his throat, as if swallowing the lies would be enough to save him.

Miles was dying, and he'd been dying since the day he was born. The life he'd been living was all he'd ever experienced. All he'd ever known. Sure, he'd seen things in movies or on YouTube videos, but that's all they were. Digital moving pictures that were created for his entertainment. He knew of nothing else but the sickness that lived inside him, clawing at his insides until there was nothing left to take. Even so, he was happy. He was surrounded by people who cared about him. People who wanted to see good happen to him. He was content in his life until his life itself wasn't enough.

Toward the end of his time, his parents and all his doctors and nurses threw an elaborate celebration that included—you guessed it— a *miracle*. A fake one, of course. Just like the fake stories they'd drilled into his head about the mansion he lived in and the maids and the tutors and everything in between. And as Miles lay in his bed, dying, he forced a smile at the people who had curated his life for him. A life filled with nothing but lies. And he was torn.

Torn between *their* truth and *the* truth.

And as Miles struggled to breathe as he walked the path from this life to the next, it suddenly occurred to him that everyone had spent his entire life trying to keep him alive, but in the end, Miles never actually got to *live*.

Miles' mom stood at the side of his deathbed, his hand in hers, and on his final breath, she said four simple words that put an end to the misery.

To the trilogy.

"My miracle is you."

It was then, as Miles's eyes closed for the last time, that he finally realized the truth of his life.

It was never him who needed the miracle.

40

Olivia

The chairs just outside Miss Turner's office have to be the most uncomfortable ones in the history of ever. Either that, or my physical inability to sit still makes it feel that way. Probably the latter. My knees bounce so vigorously, the floor beneath me shakes and I'm surprised no one's told me to stop, leave, and take my crazy with me.

And then there are my hands...

God, I hate my hands.

I hate the way they sweat, the way they tremble, the way they expose the truths I fight to hide.

I'm on edge, obviously. I didn't sleep a wink last night. All the thoughts racing through my mind made it impossible for my eyes to close long enough for the darkness to take over. I did a lot of other things, though. Like sand back an entire sideboard, by hand, while also checking my phone every few seconds.

Rhys never responded to my texts.

Never returned any of my calls.

I'm living off four cups of coffee, an abundance of heartache, and the tiniest amount of hope. But it's that hope that got my ass dressed and out the door this morning, so it's all I have left to cling to.

The door to Miss Turner's office opens, and I immediately hide my hands. Look up. Honey-brown eyes stare back at me. "You look like shit."

"Oscar!" Miss Turner admonishes, backhanding his chest. Oscar shrugs, and Miss Turner adds, "That's not something you say to—"

"It's fine," I tell them both, getting to my feet. "I was actually hoping to run into you."

Casually leaning against the doorframe, legs crossed at the ankles, Oscar tilts his head, eyes narrowed when he asks, "What's up?"

"Do you know where Rhys is?"

"Garrett?" The slightest smirk graces his lips, and I wonder how much he knows.

With a nod, I say, "His car's here, in the parking lot, but I can't find him, and I need to talk to him about—"

"Olivia," Miss Turner interrupts, and I cut my eyes to her.

"Ollie," Oscar corrects her.

Miss Turner ignores him. "If you and Rhys have a past, that's somewhat... personal, then—"

"Get in line?" Oscar chimes in.

My stomach turns at the thought, though it really shouldn't.

Miss Turner continues, "Coach Garrett is faculty now, so whatever your past might be, it can't continue. There are..." I don't hear what she says next over the pounding in my ears. I stare down at the floor, ignoring the heaviness of my eyelids and the weakness of my muscles caused by fatigue.

"Ollie?" Oscar steps forward, places a hand on my shoulder. I force myself to look up and into his eyes. I can only imagine what I look like. No sleep. No shower. Not even a brush through my hair. The second the tears return, filling my eyes with liquid pain, I know I've lost the fight to fake it. My shoulders drop, and a knot forms in my throat, but I force myself to breathe.

One more time.

Every time.

I focus on Oscar and plead with my eyes and my eyes alone, and just like the first day I met him, Oscar reads me perfectly.

Smirk gone completely, his expression reveals his thoughts: *poor, pathetic little girl.*

He sighs, jerking his head to somewhere behind me. "He has the entire Old Gym to himself," he says, and my pulse picks up as I walk away. "His office is the old AV and stats room. Take the stairs to the left when you get through the doors."

"Thank you!" I turn around, run.

"What about our session?" Miss Turner calls out.

"Next time! Sorry!"

"Ollie!" Oscar shouts.

I stop, spin on my heels, and give him the respect he deserves. "Yeah?"

"Whatever he did, he didn't mean it."

My chest tightens at the thought. "It wasn't him," I say, breathless. "It was *never* him."

I take the stairs to Rhys's office two at a time, never once looking back or down—always ahead. The stairs lead to a narrow hallway with two doors, two windows, and through the cracks of the blinds, I can see Rhys sitting behind a desk.

I force myself to stop just outside his door and take a few long breaths to calm the hell down. Shaking out my hands to release my pent-up anxiety, I close my eyes, count to ten. Then knock.

"Yeah?" Rhys calls.

I suck in a breath, hold it, then open the door.

Darkness surrounds Rhys's eyes when they look up from his desk, and just as quickly, he drops his gaze again, never actually looking at me. He sighs, a palpable sound that fills the entire room. "What's up?"

I had so many things I had planned to tell him, but now that he's in front of me, I can't think of one. "We should talk," I say, just above a whisper, and start to close the door behind me.

"Leave it open."

I freeze.

"The last thing I need is people making assumptions because a female student is in my office with the door closed."

Female student? That's what he's minimized me to in his head. *A female fucking student.*

I leave the door open and step farther into his office. There's not a lot here. A desk with a chair on either side and a couch pushed up against a wall. I take the seat opposite him and wait for him to look at me. Seconds pass. Nothing changes.

Tears well in my eyes, and I plead, "Rhys, come on...."

"Come on, *what?*" he all but yells, lifting his eyes to mine. But when I see the anger there, and the hatred that goes with it, I wish he'd never looked at me at all.

I lock my hands together, squeeze as hard as my minimal strength will allow. "I need to explain—"

"You don't need to explain shit, Olivia." He leans forward, elbows resting on his desk, and spits each word like venom—made to hurt me, destroy me from the inside. "My mom showed me the contract. I was nothing but a fucking job to you. Understood. Loud and clear."

"Rhys..."

"What?" he yells, and I rear back at the loudness of it. He stands, walks around the desk, to the other side of the room, as far away from me as possible. "What the fuck do you want from me?"

I stand, too, and go to him, but he holds his hand up between us, stopping me. "No," he fumes, shaking his head, and I choke on the giant knot in my throat, let it block my airways completely. A single tear falls from my lashes, but he doesn't notice. Or if he does, he doesn't care. "You know what the most fucked up thing is?" he says, his jaw so tense it doesn't even move when he speaks. "Two nights ago, I lay in your bed with you in my arms, and I was so fucking close to telling you I was falling—" He stops there—at the point of no return. And I drown on the inside, wave after wave dragging me under. "There's nothing you can say that will make any of this okay."

I try to look him in the eyes, even though I can't see him through my tears. He has to understand. Surely. "Taking that job was the only way I could save us, Rhys."

"I genuinely don't give a fuck."

I've always believed in pain.

Believed in agony and grief and suffering.

But I never believed in heartbreak.

Until now.

And whatever that sudden realization looks like on me has Rhys's entire demeanor shifting. His shoulders drop. His eyes do too. And he takes a step forward. Just one. But he doesn't come to me. Why would he?

"I didn't mean that I don't care about you, or your brothers being in the situation you were in, because you know I do. And I don't care that you agreed to do it. I'm not even mad that you signed a fucking contract where *I* was the clause." His anger returns, replaces his sympathy. "I'm pissed that you didn't tell me."

"I tried," I cry.

"When?"

"Friday!" I rush out. "I went to your house, but—"

His disbelieving scoff cuts me off. "Right. When you realized I wasn't going anywhere. But prior to that, you were more than happy to let me believe we were something more than we were!" The corner of his lip lifts into a snarl, and his eyes search mine, looking for... something. "Was any of it real?"

"Of course it was!"

"I can't even tell your bullshit from your truths." And then he laughs, cynical. "I don't even know you."

"Yes, you do," I urge. "You know me better than anyone!"

He drops his head again, shakes it.

I take one more step closer to him. "Sometimes, I think she knew..."

He lifts his gaze but keeps his head down. "What are you talking about?"

"Your mom," I explain, my chest rising and falling with each of my cries. "Maybe she could tell, you know? She could see that we needed each other. Maybe she knew that... that we were meant to be..."

"Maybe." He laughs. Right in my face. Cold. *Ruthless.* "But we're sure as fuck not made to last."

41

Olivia

Something is different.

And it's more than what's happening between Rhys and me.

Something is off.

I left Rhys's office with enough time to slip my mask back on, hide my emotions, and make it to first period. But, as soon as I stepped foot in the classroom, I *felt* it.

Something is *wrong*.

I should've left then, and I don't know why I didn't, because by second period, all eyes were on me.

By third, the whispers had begun.

And by lunch, those whispers had turned into openly snide remarks.

"Mole."

"Spy."

"Traitor."

It didn't take a rocket scientist to figure it out. Someone has worked out who I am. Or, more importantly, who my brother is. I just hope that someone isn't Rhys because it's one thing to hate me for what I've done. It's another to take that hatred out on my family.

He couldn't.

He *wouldn't*.

He's not that cruel.

And I'm not naïve. It's not as if I didn't anticipate this exact thing to happen at some point, but not this early into the school year, and *fuck*.

Fuck.

Fuck.

Fuck.

As if life hadn't screwed me enough today, it needed to kick me while I was down. I shouldn't be surprised... but I guess that's the thing about surprises—they come out of nowhere, when you least expect it. One minute you're in the arms of the boy you've dreamed about for years and the next...

Unease settles in the pit of my stomach, spreads through my blood-line until I can no longer think. No longer breathe. I push my untouched tray of food away from me and stand, ignoring the amused looks and snickers from everyone in the cafeteria.

This is all one giant joke to them.

I am one giant joke to them.

I wait until I'm outside the cafeteria doors to pull out my phone and send Dom a text.

It's out.

Adrenaline replaces my fatigue, and I keep my eyes glued to my phone, waiting for a response as I rush toward my locker. I need to grab my things, get to my car, and I'll figure out the rest once I'm there.

I'm leaving now.

I take the last corner to my locker and falter a step before slowing, then stopping completely. A group surrounds my locker, all facing it, laughing, and I should turn around. Leave. Never come back. But I can't.

My feet feel like lead as I take step after step toward my demise. The people around me step back, parting to let me through. They all watch, anticipating the moment I see what's waiting for me.

Potted plants—so many of them—all cut off at the stems. Some pots are tipped over on their sides, leaving a mess of dirt and remnants of plants and leaves on the marble floors. My mind races, trying to make sense of it all. Why would...

And then I remember.

And I wish I could forget.

"You have a lot of plants," he said.

"I like to challenge myself."

"How so?"

"See if I can keep things alive."

But there's nothing alive about these plants. They're all dead. Just like me on the inside.

"What's up, *Mini Delgado?*" some motherfucker says from behind, too much of a pussy to say it to my face.

You'd think at some point, tears have to dry up, right? I guess I'm proof that they don't.

I turn swiftly, my heart in my throat, and push past the crowd and right into a solid chest. I try to move past him, but he won't get out of the way. "Move," I grind out, but there's no sound to my heartache.

"Don't," he says, his single word just for me.

I attempt to shove him, but he grasps my elbows, bends at his knees to look at my face. Honey brown and filled with pity, Oscar puts his mouth to my ear. "Don't let them win." And then he turns to stand beside me, his hand still on my elbow as he guides me away. "Keep your head up, Ollie. Eyes clear."

A strangled sound forms in my throat.

"Don't let them win," he repeats, and before I even know what's happening, he's opening the door to Miss Turner's office.

She looks up from behind her desk, but she's not alone. Rhys glances in our direction, his eyebrows drawn, "What—"

"Fuck you!" I yell, just as Oscar slams the door shut behind us.

"Ollie," he says, but I'm too broken to hear him.

Everyone has their breaking point. I reached mine three years ago.

"What's going on?" Miss Turner asks, eyes wide as she gets to her feet.

I ignore her, march right up to Rhys. "Fuck you!" I cry, finger pointed right at him. "You knew what this would do to me! To us! How could you be so fucking—"

"Olivia!" Miss Turner chides.

But I don't hear her. Not really. I'm lost, drowning in a sea of hurt, and because I have nowhere else to direct my emotions, I slam my closed fists against Rhys's chest. Again and again. And I can feel the arms around my waist, trying to pull me away, but I can't stop moving. Can't stop crying. "How long do you think it's going to take for someone to find out?" My eyes overflow with tears... tears that coat my cheeks with liquid agony. "They're going to take Max away from us, and it's all your fault!" I scream now, spit flying from my lips. And Rhys just stands there. Like a solid fucking statue. Not speaking. Not fighting back.

I break down. Fall apart in the arms of a practical stranger. I choke on my words. "Do you think my life is some kind of joke?" I push Oscar's arms off of me and throw mine in the air. "Her grandparents died, and her mother left, and it's just her and her brothers! Fucking *ha! ha!* Let's see how much we can ruin her—"

Rhys steps forward so fast, I don't have time to stop him from grabbing me. One hand on the back of my head, the other covering my mouth. I breathe through my nose, my eyes wide and right on his. "Enough," he deadpans, his jaw unmoving, nostrils flaring with anger.

I kick him in the shin.

Hard.

He winces but doesn't let go of me. He only repeats, "Enough, Olivia." But the way he says it—soft and *deadly serious*—it solidifies every inch of my insides, hardens me, freezes the blood pumping through my veins. Slowly, purposefully, his eyes shift to Miss Turner standing beside us...

And I realize too late how I've acted.

What I've done.

What I've *said.*

And slowly, painfully, I return to myself... return to a reality I have no control over.

I choke on a sob, my entire body turning languid in his arms. Rhys drops his gaze and, cautiously, lowers his hands. He takes a step back, and I hold still, not allowing myself a full breath. The room is silent. My mind is, too.

I turn to Miss Turner, who watches me with more pity in her single stare than I'll ever deserve. "You have to report it now, don't you?"

42

Rhys

I keep my eyes on Belinda as she stands behind her desk, waiting for Oscar to help Olivia back to her class. I don't know if Olivia actually plans to go back to class, but that's what Belinda asked Oscar to do, so of course, that's what he'll do.

As soon as Oscar closes the door behind him, she flicks her eyes to mine and motions to the chair on the other side of the desk. "Take a seat."

I scoff, cross my arms. "In case you haven't noticed, I'm not a student anymore. Therefore, I'm not your patient."

She returns my scoff with one of her own. "So that suddenly means we're not friends?"

My shoulders drop, along with my facade.

"Because if that's the case," she continues, "then let me know, so I can tell my daughter that her godfather won't be around anymore."

I die a little at the thought, and Belinda must sense that because she offers a smile and motions to the chair again.

This time, I sit.

So does she. "What did I miss?"

I get comfortable. Or as comfortable as one can get, considering I'm sitting on a plastic chair. I've spent many, many hours in this room. Or closet, really. It used to be storage for cleaning supplies, and no matter how many incense and oils Belinda burns, most days, you can still smell the bleach in the air.

"Rhys?" she says, gaining my attention.

After a heavy sigh, I ask what I came here to ask—you know, before Oscar and Olivia barged in. "Did you know?"

"Obviously not, considering I have no clue what you're talking about."

"So, my mom didn't tell you about her?"

"Olivia?"

I nod, focused on my hands while I try to rub the tension out of them.

"Rhys..." she says, and after a few seconds, I force my eyes up, but keep my head low. "I've never met Olivia before, and I'm almost certain I didn't know of her existence until a few days ago."

"But you did," I tell her, and I hesitate to go on. To speak the truth out loud. Because saying it means it's real, and I don't know how to process that. "Olivia is *Mercedes.*"

Belinda attempts and fails at silencing her gasp. "Oh." And then her eyes narrow, go distant as her mind works. Finally, she forms the pieces of the puzzle, but it's obvious she doesn't quite know how they fit.

Belinda is the only person in my life who knows about Mercedes and what she means to me. What she *meant* to me. I spent so many sessions just relaying the conversations I've had with Mercedes. She knows about the first time we'd exchanged meaningful text messages. About how that initial conversation sparked something inside of me that had sat dormant for months. She knows the meaning of the name *Mercedes.* She knows exactly why my favorite line in a book with over 464,000 words is *"All human wisdom is contained in these two words - Wait and Hope."* And she knows exactly what those words mean to me. What I was willing to do for someone I'd never met: *wait and hope.*

Belinda looks at me, watches me fight through the myriad of

emotions I can't seem to escape. "What does your mom have to do with Mercedes—or *Olivia*?"

I suck in a breath, hold it, then stand, because sitting seems to agitate the anger inside me. "She paid Olivia to keep tabs on me."

"Holy fuck."

"No shit."

"Wait." She lifts both hands, palms up, as if she needs time to slow down. I get it. I've felt like that since my mom dropped the fucking bomb on my lap, then walked away as if it wouldn't explode. News flash: that's the whole fucking purpose of a bomb. "I'm so confused."

I was, too. But then I spent the past twenty-four hours going over everything in my mind and really, it all makes sense. I think what really pushed me over the edge is the timing of it all. The text from my mom is what woke me yesterday morning while I was in Olivia's bed. She said she was home and that she needed to see me, and so I snuck out of Liv's room after leaving her a dumb fucking note on the pillow and went home.

There's no way I would've even guessed the seriousness of what she was about to say going by the way she acted. All calm and aloof, as if her actions had no consequences. "You've been speaking to a girl via text for the past three years," she said. "I don't know how you refer to her, but her name is Olivia. Olivia Mitchell."

It felt like the walls caved in and covered the hole the ground had created—the same ground that swallowed me the moment Liv's name left my mother's mouth. "I wish I didn't have to tell you this, but since you'll be seeing her every day at this new—" she air-quoted "—'job' of yours, then you'll likely find out the truth. And the truth is this... I hired her to talk to you. To get close to you. And to pass on anything she might think is important so I had at least some knowledge of what was going on with you since you were so adamant on pushing us all away after—" She stopped there. She doesn't talk about what happened that caused the "after." No one in my family does. "You have to understand the position I was in, Rhys. You had shut down completely, and you refused to move to Colorado, even though you knew we needed to be there for your sister."

We were sitting at the kitchen counter with the blinds wide open, and the morning sun felt like it was burning me alive. Still, I remained frozen.

Silent.

She slid a bunch of documents across the counter and under my nose: a signed contract and non-disclosure agreement with both her and Olivia's signatures. "And Olivia... that poor, sweet girl was going through—"

I cleared my throat, cutting her off. "Is that it?"

My mom stuttered an exhale, her head tilted as she watched me. I made sure to stare back, keep my expression neutral, so I gave nothing away. "I had no other choice, sweetheart."

In my mind, I yelled, cursed at the top of my lungs and called her out on her bullshit. In reality, I stood up, documents in hand, walked out of the kitchen and out of the house.

I haven't been back since.

I tell Belinda all of this while I wear out the carpet with my constant pacing. Back and forth. Back and forth.

"Has she tried calling you?" Belinda asks, and I give her a pointed look. She nods. "Right," she says. "Of course she has."

I'm fully aware that the moment this conversation ends, Belinda will be on the phone to my mom, telling her that I am, at the very least, *alive*. And you know how I know this? Because Belinda, the therapist of the high school I just graduated from, is also on my mother's payroll. The difference is that I *know* about their little arrangement because I'm the one who came up with it. It was part of the deal when, as my mother puts it, I "pushed them all away."

"So..." Belinda says, her elbows on her desk while her fingers tap, tap, tap away. "I'm just trying to grasp the situation here..."

I hold back an eye roll. There's nothing to grasp. Betrayal is a bitch, and I've suffered it twofold.

"As of right this moment," Belinda starts, "who is Olivia to you?"

"She's..." I don't even know how to explain it, because I think, of everything, this is the part that fucks me the most. "She's the only girl I've ever met who's come even close to replacing Mercedes."

"But she *is* Mercedes."

"But she's not," I'm quick to argue.

"But she *is*," Belinda contends. "The only difference I can see is that Olivia is *real*. She's not some dream girl you've made up who only—"

"You don't get it," I interrupt, and why would she? *How* could she? My frustration rattles through my rib cage, reveals itself in the way I ball my fists and the way I recklessly release oxygen through my airways.

"You're mad?" Belinda says, and this is what she's so fucking good at. Forcing me to face my flaws and then making me explain them away.

"Of course I am," I spit out. "You have no idea what it feels like to know that every single person who's important to me is here, with me, because I fucking pay them to be. You, Curtis, even Oscar!"

"You saved Oscar," she points out.

I stop pacing, press the heels of my palms to my temple and groan, irritated.

Belinda stands, makes her way toward me, and it takes everything in me to stay grounded. Not to pull back from her closeness.

"Breathe," she says, settling a hand on my shoulder.

I do as she says.

"One more time."

I blink back the heat burning behind my eyes and nod, then finish the mantra she urges me to live by. "Every time."

She waits; with the patience of a thousand saints, she holds on to my emotions, to my *sanity*, until I'm ready to reclaim them.

"I'm sorry, but I have to ask..." she edges. "Does the timeline of Olivia's grandparents dying and her mother leaving match up with the proposition your mother offered her?"

I sigh, and that's all she needs to witness.

"I really don't want to take sides, Rhys, but maybe step away from your emotions for just a tiny second and try to consider what position Olivia was in to make her feel like she had no other options." She pauses a beat, gauging my reaction before adding, "It must've been difficult for her... to know that her sole purpose in your life was to keep you above water. Right?"

I don't respond.

"And to dedicate three years of her life to do that? There's no way that she didn't form feelings for you, too, Rhys. That's impossible."

"You're missing the point," I murmur. Every single person who isn't me seems to miss the fucking point. "She's had every opportunity to come clean and tell me the truth. And she never did."

And I'll never forgive her for it.

Done with the conversation, I head for the door, but stop with my hand on the knob and face her. "What are you going to do?"

"About what?"

"About her situation... at home..."

"You know that I'm a mandatory reporter... if there are concerns about the safety, welfare or well-being of a child—"

"I didn't ask for a summary of the handbook."

Belinda's shoulders drop. "What exactly are you asking me then?"

"Are you going to report it?"

Her gaze drops, and I know the answer before she voices it. "I don't *want* to, but I have to."

43

Olivia

When I was younger, maybe around ten, I couldn't sleep one night because my mind was too busy thinking, thinking, and so I got out of bed just for something else to do. My grandparents must have heard me creeping around because they called out for me from their bedroom.

"Can't sleep?" my grandma asked once I'd opened the door. She patted the space between her and my grandpa, and I climbed onto their bed and under the covers in the middle of them. Even now, when I look back on my life and try to remember the time I felt the safest, I think about that moment.

They were watching TV, something they did together most nights, and a show was on about mind control. It fascinated me to no end. Not because I didn't believe it was possible, but because it blew my mind that there were people out there who could control other's minds while I couldn't even control my own.

And as I sit here, on the front steps of a house my grandparents had handpicked to start their new life, waiting for the inevitable to occur, my mind wants to play games with me. Games I never agreed to partici- pate in. See, my mind wants me to compare the absolute worst moment of my life to this current one. What is more terrifying? Losing my grandparents or losing my brothers?

The screen door behind me opens, and I quickly swipe at the tears coating my cheeks. "What are you doing out here?" Dom asks.

He'd called while I was driving home from school after my mental breakdown and forced me to pull over and tell him what happened. And because I'm weak and ashamed of my actions, I gave him the footnotes: that the kids at school know about him, and when he asked how I knew that, I held back on what truly happened and simply told him that one of them called me *Mini Delgado*. "I'm sorry," he'd said, and not in an *"I'm sorry that happened to you"* way, but in an *"I'm sorry I exist and that I'm good at what I do"* way. He felt *guilty*... for something he had absolutely no control over.

"I just needed some air," I answer.

"Here?" he asks, skeptical, and he has every reason to be. We have an entire backyard and my little garden patio where I usually go when I need time.

Space.

Air.

When moments pass and I don't respond, he steps out onto the porch, letting the screen door close behind him. "Ollie?" He places a hand on my shoulder, and still... I refuse to turn to him. To face him. "Ohana?"

It's that single word that breaks me, and I drop my head in my hands and release the flood of tears I can no longer hold on to. He's quick to sit beside me, to take me in his arms and hold me through my sobs. "I'm sorry," he says, and it only makes me cry harder, because he has no clue. No idea of what's about to happen.

An hour earlier, I'd gotten a text from an unknown number. All it said was:

UNKNOWN

They're coming at 7.

Last time I checked the time, it was 6:58.

"Talk it out with me, Ollie," he pleads, rubbing my back in slow circles the way he'd watched my grandma do for me in the past.

"I can't," I cry. I wouldn't even know what to say. But I don't need to. Because as soon as those words leave my mouth, a police cruiser slows to a stop in front of us.

"Ollie..." Dom says, and the fear in his voice only makes me cry harder.

"I'm so sorry, Dom," I sob, holding on to him tighter. "I did my best."

Dominic releases me and stands up, and I keep my head down, refusing to face reality. I stay that way even when Dominic steps off the porch. When I hear the car doors open. Close. And I give in to my mind's games. To the decision I have to make. The worst moment in my life is this.

Right now.

Because I'm the one who caused it.

"Can I help you, officer?" Dom asks.

"Olivia..." Miss Turner's voice forces my hand, and I shudder a breath, rub the liquid pain from my eyes so I can see clearer. I get up, take the few steps to stand beside my brother. Holding his hand in mine, I tighten my grip. I don't want to let go, but at some point, I know I'll have to.

Miss Turner's eyes drop to where Dom and I connect. Then up to Max, opening our front door. "Ohana? What's happening?"

I swallow another round of cries as Miss Turner steps forward. "I'm Belinda Turner," she says to Dominic. "I'm the therapist at St. Luke's."

Dom shifts, turning to me, but I won't look at him. "Ollie..."

My emotions wreak havoc on my stomach. On my heart.

Miss Turner motions to the police officer standing beside her. "And this is my fiancé, Curtis."

Curtis. I know that name. Know the man wearing the uniform. But...

"We've met," Curtis says, and realization dawns when he adds, "Hi, Olivia."

The first time I met Curtis, I was sitting in my car with Rhys beside me and Max fast asleep in the back seat. We'd just spent the night at the hospital and then on the rooftop. It feels like forever ago, but I remember it as if it were yesterday.

Miss Turner is engaged to Curtis? And Rhys... Rhys is the godfather to their daughter?

I swallow the knot in my throat, push through the agony pumping through my veins.

"We just need to have a look through your house," Curtis says.

"Dom?" Max makes his way down the porch steps, stopping on the other side of our brother. Even though I can't see it, I know Max has taken Dom's other hand. "What's happening?"

Finally, I find the courage to look up at Dom. He stands tall, his chin raised as he holds on to the only family he has. I've always been the provider. But Dom... Dom's always been the protector. His throat moves with his swallow, as he nods once. "Come in."

* * *

It's the oddest feeling, watching strangers go through your entire house, opening drawers, closets, *everything*. Miss Turner and Curtis go through the food in our fridge, the supplies in our pantry. They look through the drawers of Dominic's dresser, and Max—sweet, *innocent* Maxy—is so excited to show them his room. All his toys, his LEGO builds, his printed designs for a flying submarine. They go through the garage, picking up tools only to put them back down, and the entire time, Dominic and I watch. Silent. Waiting for our entire life to come crashing down.

The minutes pass, feeling like an eternity, and suddenly, in the middle of my bedroom, they turn to each other and communicate in that silent way that couples do. Then Curtis faces us, all standing in the open doorway, and nods once. "Thanks for your time," he says, and that's all he says before they leave the house through the same way they entered.

We stand on the porch, watching their backs as they return to the police cruiser. Max says, "I like them!"

Dom doesn't respond.

And I...

"Wait!" I call out, getting to them just as Curtis opens Miss Turner's door for her. Chest rising and falling, I force air into my lungs. Again and again. And through tear-filled eyes and a heavy heart, I tell them, "My brothers are blood. Dom will be eighteen in a few months, and I don't know if that matters, but I just feel you should know that. We can't afford a lawyer right now, but one of us will adopt Max as soon as we can. That's the plan. That's *always* been the plan. And Dominic—he has to do a year of college ball before he can go up for the NBA draft, but when he does, we can..." I don't even know what I'm saying; I just know that I need to say it. Say *something*. I have to fight for us. Protect us. "I'm eighteen. I'll be nineteen soon... I just... I'll be okay. Somehow. But please, don't separate them. Max—he needs Dominic. But they don't need me. Just *please*—"

Miss Turner hugs me, her arms tight around my neck. She *holds* me. And for the second time today, I cry in the arms of a practical stranger. "Please," I beg. Cry some more. My shoulders shake with the force of each sob. And Miss Turner doesn't let go. Doesn't loosen her hold. She just continues to embrace me, her hand stroking the back of my head.

"Just breathe," she says. "One more time... *every time.*"

I pull back, eyes wide and right on hers, and I whisper his name —*Rhys*—just loud enough for only us to hear.

Miss Turner smiles, shifting my hair stuck to my cheeks. "You've made a beautiful home, Olivia," she says. "And an even more beautiful family."

44

Olivia

I throw up.

As soon as I got back in the house, I ran to my bathroom and dropped to my knees. All the adrenaline that had been pumping through my veins since I left Miss Turner's office earlier expels from my body in waves.

Dominic kneels on the bathroom floor beside me, holding my hair as my entire body shakes, shudders with every purge.

It's not the first time he's done this for me, but it's been years since he's had to.

When I find a pocket of calm, I ask, "Max?"

"He's in my room. I told him we could have a sleepover. He's fine. Take the time you need. But when you're done..."

I nod, try to inhale through my nose to settle my breaths.

I know Dom wants answers, and I'll give him what I can. When I can. But right now... I need to focus on finding enough calm to settle my racing heart.

I fall back on my haunches, and Dom hands me a towel to wipe my mouth. Then I rest against the bathtub, and he sits against the sink, waiting.

For minutes, we sit opposite each other, my sniffs the only sound in the room. Finally, he cracks. "When we decided to take care of Max, we said we'd do it together. *Always.*"

Vision blurred from my endless tears, I say, "I know."

"So, are you going to tell me what happened, or should I just keep guessing?"

I pull my knees up to my chest, drop my forehead between them. "You're going to hate me."

"Try me."

I sniff back my heartache. "I don't even know where to start, Dom."

His brow dips in confusion. "Did it start earlier than today?"

"You're going to hate me," I repeat.

"Ollie..."

I wish, more than anything, that I could give him the details without including Rhys. But... Rhys is the puppet master, controlling all the strings.

"Remember over the summer when I hit that guy with the truck?"

Dom sits taller, giving me all his attention. "Yeah?"

"I told you that his name was Timothy, but I lied."

"Why?"

"Because it was Rhys." I watch his face for a reaction, and when nothing comes, I add, "Rhys Garrett..."

45

Rhys

"So, she didn't respond to your text?"

Oscar collects the dirty paper plates and empty cans of soda from the table and dumps them in a trash bag before saying, "For the third time, *no*."

I follow him as he heads back to the food truck. "What exactly did you send her?"

Tying a knot in the bag, he answers, "Exactly what you told me to. *They're coming at 7.* That's *all* I wrote."

"And she didn't respond?"

"Jesus Christ!" He throws his hands up, waving the bag in the air. "What is *wrong* with you?"

"She wasn't at school today!"

He puts the trash bag next to the truck, then reaches in there for the cleaning spray and cloth. When he faces me again, he says, "Would you go after what happened yesterday?"

I press my lips shut, because he's right. There's no fucking way I'd show up to my living nightmare. We're halfway back to the table when

Oscar's mom calls out from the food truck window. "Have you eaten, Rhys?"

I turn to her. "Yes, Miss Mendoza," I lie. There's no way I'd be able to keep anything down with the amount of nerves creating havoc inside me since the moment I left Belinda's office yesterday.

"You make sure to eat, okay?" She goes back to work, mumbling something like, "Growing boy in that big house all by yourself..."

"Have a good night," Oscar says, smiling at a young family getting up from one of the tables.

When Oscar moved here, his mom needed a job, and the sports park needed a food truck. And since his mom loved feeding the entire neighborhood *just because*, it only made sense that I use the money I didn't earn and invest it into a business for them. The initial investment was a loan, one they paid back within months of opening. His mom continues to love feeding people, and Oscar gets to hang out at a sports park in his free time. It's a win-win.

"Wipe down that table," Oscar says, slamming the spray and cloth to my chest. I take them from him and start wiping down one table while he clears the other. "If you're so curious about what happened, why don't you just ask Belinda?"

Like me, Oscar refers to Miss Turner as Belinda because we know her better outside of her job than we do within it. Sure, she sees us as her patients, but above all, we're friends. Actually, we're more like *family*. "I don't know," I answer truthfully. "I don't want to overstep the boundaries."

Oscar doesn't respond, and so I stop wiping and look over at him. He's already watching me, his head tilted slightly, eyes narrowed.

"What?"

"I've been patient with you," he tells me. "I figured at some point you're bound to tell me what the hell happened between you and Ollie..." I like that he calls her Ollie, as if they're actually friends, and if they are, I'm glad it's Oscar she has by her side. "But I've waited, all yesterday and all today, and it's—" He checks his watch. "It's almost nine now, so the day's already gone, and still, no explanation from you."

I sigh. "She didn't tell you?"

"I've spoken to the girl twice. Once on the first day and then again yesterday. I don't know shit about shit."

"No swearing!" his mom yells.

"Sorry, mamá," he yells back, glaring at me as if I forced curse words down his throat.

I roll my eyes and continue to wipe down the already clean table. "We hung out over the summer." Such simple words for such a complex situation, but I'm not sure how much I want to reveal just yet.

"*Hung out?*" he repeats, skeptical.

I stand to full height and heave out a sigh. "We did more than hang out."

He nods, then jerks his head to somewhere behind me. "Is that why Delgado's walking toward us lookin' like he wants to slit your throat and use your decapitated head as a football?"

Fuck.

I turn around, and sure enough... there he is. In the flesh. But he's not alone. His best friend, Dre, is with him, and Oscar's right... Delgado looks *pissed*.

I face Oscar again, but he's too busy on his phone. "Don't start shit here, okay?" he says, as if I regularly go around *starting shit*.

"The fuck?" I mumble.

After pocketing his phone, he shrugs. "Just not around my mom, that's all." Then stands beside me and squares his shoulders, ready for whatever.

"Mendoza," Dominic says as he stops a few feet in front of us. Dre stands next to him, expressionless.

Oscar jerks his chin. "What's up?"

"My sister says that you guys are friends," he says, his arms loose at his sides, making it obvious that he didn't come here to fight. But then again, he probably didn't expect me to be here. "She mentioned that you've looked out for her since she started." Dominic shrugs. "I just wanted to say thanks, man."

"It's nothin'," Oscar says, and I'm sure he means it. Oscar's one of the best guys I know, but anyone would say that about their best friend. I'm sure Dre says it about Dominic, and that should tell you something.

Dominic turns to me, his entire demeanor shifting. I stand my ground, my shoulders squared. He has a couple of inches on me, but I have a couple of pounds. I also have enough rage to kill a small horse. Rage I've kept contained for far too long. I've *been* ready to release it. All he has to say is *when*. He glares at me, his jaw working. "Did you do it to fuck with me?" he asks. "Like you did with Dani?"

Right. Because of course he'd be thinking about his pathetic ex-girlfriend who left him after two years for one night with me. Oh, and the offer of a Birkin bag. Like I said, *pathetic*.

If I were someone who actually wants to start shit, I'd tell him all that. Instead, I just say, "No." And besides, what Liv and I had is none of his fucking business.

"Bullshit!"

I scoff. "You won't believe what I have to say anyway, so fuck you."

"Fuck me?" He steps forward until we're almost touching.

"Yo, guys..." Oscar says, ready to jump between us.

"Go ahead, tell me your truth then," Dominic spits, looking me up and down. "Tell me you didn't know who she was to me."

"I didn't."

He ignores me, says, "Or that you actually care about her?"

"I *do* care about her." Or at least, I did. I don't know how I feel anymore.

Dominic laughs, bitter and conceited. He pulls back an inch, but his eyes stay on mine. I hold his glare. "If you really cared about her, then you'd know what getting everyone to call her Mini Delgado is doing to her." He pauses a beat. "You and everyone else at your fucked up school might associate that name with me, but she doesn't. You know what she thinks of?"

I drop my gaze, just the tiniest bit.

Dom keeps talking. "Our dead parents. And now, thanks to you, she'll be reminded of them fifty times a day."

I don't respond, because what the hell can I say?

"Let's go," Dre says, one hand on Dominic's chest as he pushes him back. "You said what you had to say."

Dominic shoves his friend's hand off him and focuses on Oscar again. "You have ice baths at your school, right?"

My brow bunches in confusion, and Oscar must feel the same. He looks between us before answering, "Yeah."

Dominic nods. "If what happened to Ollie yesterday ever happens again, then I need you to get a bucket of ice for her. Fill it with water. She dunks her head in there. It helps her re-circuit her brain or something. I don't know. I just know that it helps her." He inhales a sharp breath, his shoulders deflating with his exhale. "And then I need you to call me. And I need you to stay with her until I can get her." His voice cracks with emotion, and it suddenly hits me, all at once: Dominic might be a fuckwit, but he's Olivia's brother, and it's clear he cares about her in the same way I care about my sister.

We love them beyond words.

Protect them beyond reason.

I'm sure facing me just to get to Oscar was the last thing he wanted, but here he is...

And I never thought I'd one day *respect* Dominic Delgado, but here I am...

"Whatever you do," Dominic continues, "please don't leave her side, because she'll want to leave. She'll want to get in her car and drive away, and when she's like that, she's in absolutely no condition—"

"Ice bucket. Call you. Stay with her. I got it, man," Oscar interrupts, saving Dominic from revealing his hand—that Olivia is his weakness.

And *I get it*, I almost tell him.

She's mine, too.

46

Olivia

For the second night in a row, I find myself sitting on the porch steps, waiting for the inevitable.

It's almost like a repeat of yesterday.

A text message from an unknown number that leads to a full-blown panic attack.

> UNKNOWN
>
> Your two boys are about to throw down.

I should've expected it, really, and I don't know why I hadn't prepared myself for such a visceral reaction from my brother. Dominic's hotheaded. He always has been. But that energy that ignites the stands when he's on the court is the same one he has to work to control in real life.

Last night, we stayed in my bathroom for however long it took me to tell him as much as I could, even the parts that made me uncomfortable.

I told him about the first night Rhys and I met. How I'd hit Rhys with the truck, taken him to the emergency room, then spent the next few hours with him.

I told him about the weeks after that, when Rhys sought me out through the Get Grubby app and how he'd invited himself to ride with us a couple of times.

Dominic already knew about that, only in his mind it was some random guy named Timothy he'd linked all those events to.

He didn't know about the days after, while he was with Max at summer camp. It was hard to tell him those details. So *incredibly* hard. How do you tell your brother that you've been in bed with someone he despises? And worse? That I allowed that someone into our home. I apologized for lying to him and for revealing things to Rhys that we swore we'd never tell a soul. "I thought I could trust him," I told Dom.

"Well, you thought wrong, Ollie."

And he was right, obviously, because Rhys took all my secrets, along with my pain, and he released them to the world as if it meant nothing.

As if *I* meant nothing.

Years ago, when I told Dominic I'd gotten a scholarship to St. Luke's, he told me it was a bad idea. That they would crucify me for who he was. I didn't believe him. Not really. But I trusted his instincts, and when he told me that in order for me to even make it through one year at St. Luke's, we should (as much as possible) hide who we were to each other. I'd agreed with him. School was important to me, and I wanted to see it through. Sure, I could've gone to a different school, a public one, but I *wanted* St. Luke's. I wanted something close to what I'd had before. So, for years, I've gone to Dom's games and sat in the back while Max sat with his best friend, Dre's, family. I watched from afar, unable to truly celebrate all the greatness that Dom had achieved, and later, all the things that Max would achieve at that same school.

All three of us, including Max, kept up the lie that my mom always worked out of town. We kept our lives private and our home our sanctuary.

Until I ruined it all with one stupid, selfish decision.

I let Rhys into my life.

And into my heart.

* * *

As soon as the truck pulls into the driveway, I get to my feet and rush over to it. The second Dom's out of the car, I'm running my hands across his face, over his body, touching every bit of exposed skin, searching.

He grasps my wrists, carefully lowering my hands. "What the hell are you doing?"

"Checking for injuries."

"What?"

"I got a text," I tell him.

He closes the car door and starts for the house. "What did it say?" he asks over his shoulder.

I follow him. "That you and Rhys were about to throw down."

"Pshh. As if I couldn't take that fucking asshole." Dominic turns to me. "That motherfucker's lucky he's still walking."

I stop in my tracks, my gaze lowering. I don't know why it pains me to hear Rhys referred to in such a way. Dom only sees him as the Rhys he knows, and I wish that I could, too, but sometimes, like now, I see him as the boy who was there for me during my darkest times. A boy who told me to keep breathing. To keep going. A boy I made a pact with all those years ago...

Breathe. One more time. Every time. And I promise to do the same.

Clearly, I suck at hiding my emotions, because Dom dips his head to look right at me. "You're fucking kidding me, Ollie."

"What?"

"He actually means something to you, doesn't he?"

I shake my head. "It doesn't matter."

"I don't get it," he laughs, disbelieving. "How can you *still* feel something there? Even after what he did... after he hurt you like that?"

I release my breath and close my eyes. Count to ten. And reveal the truth only I know. "Because I hurt him first..."

47

Rhys

I thought the idea was brilliant when I initially came up with it, and I was angry with myself for not thinking of it earlier.

For years, Belinda had been working out of a dingy old janitor's closet, and for what? Because I was too damn selfish to come up with something else. Something better. It was me who had asked her and Curtis to pack up their entire lives and move close to me—all because I was a pussy who didn't think I'd survive without them.

Sure, we'd set them up with a house and jobs, but I really should've taken better care of them than I have.

From now on, I will. Starting with moving Belinda's office to the one next to mine. We even have an adjoining door. I couldn't just give her an empty office, so I've filled it with new furniture. A desk, a nice cushy chair for her and more comfortable ones for the students. A new couch is being delivered tomorrow. The decorating or whatever—I'll leave to her. When I first showed her, she told me to "get the fuck out" in that excited way she does. Then she hugged me, wouldn't let go for a whole-ass minute.

Worth it.

But, like I said, I *thought* it was a brilliant idea.

I guess I didn't take into consideration that she needed a space for students who were waiting to see her. She set up some chairs in the hallway—in direct view of *my* office—and, of course, the first person waiting to see her in her new office is Olivia.

According to what I read in her contract with my mother, her enrollment at St. Luke's came with two specific caveats.

1. She couldn't attend while I was enrolled.

and

2. She had to see the school's therapist.

Oscar's "scholarship" has the same last caveat.

The difference between those two is that Oscar would look horrid in the school-issued skirt. Olivia... not so much.

After what happened to her locker, and my little run-in with her brother last night, I wondered if she'd ever show again. Clearly, she's braver than I thought she was.

And I...

I'm in way deeper than I want to be.

Because just *seeing* her sets off something visceral inside of me, and I wish I could say that it was purely physical, because that would be easy to ignore, or even replace. But no...

I think the fucked up part of all of this is that at one point, I felt *guilty* about the feelings I'd developed for Liv because it felt like I was emotionally cheating on Mercedes. Not that me and Mercedes were ever—

Scratch that.

Mercedes never existed.

And the sooner I can wrap my brain around that, the better off we'll all be.

I glance up from the playbook spread open on my desk to see Olivia still sitting there, her eyes downcast, holding on to a potted plant. Tin can and twine wrapped around it. I wonder if it's the one I made, and if so, I wonder if she's doing it to fuck with me.

The top two buttons on her shirt are undone, exposing her neck and part of her breastbone, and it's the perfect fit for her. It hides what it needs to and tight where it counts. When standing, her skirt stops just below the knees, but it's bunched up a little now, exposing an inch of her thighs, and my blood heats at the memories of those same thighs pressed against my ears, with her hand on the back of my head to keep me in place as she ground her pussy on my tongue. "Right there," she'd say, over and over. "Don't stop." I'd complied every time, because I got off on it as much as she did.

I'm hard.

And I really shouldn't be.

But then I remember the marks I left on those thighs from my fingers digging into her flesh when she'd been on the edge of the pool, legs spread, and—

Olivia pulls down her skirt now, hiding that sliver of exposed skin, and my eyes lift to hers. She stares right back. Unblinking. She must've been watching me for long enough to pick up on my thoughts, and maybe I should be ashamed, but I'm not. Besides, if I walked over to her right now and ran the backs of my fingers along her cheeks, she'd practically set me on fire.

Olivia's cheeks, my favorite part of her, give off a blush like no other.

Belinda's door opens, and Olivia jumps to her feet so fast she almost forgets the plant she'd been holding on to.

I chuckle under my breath and look down at the playbook again. "Come in, Olivia," Belinda says, and I glance up again. Belinda's just outside my door, her arm out, guiding Olivia into her office. After a few seconds, she turns to me, does that lame two fingers to her eye "I'm watching you" motion, and it only makes me laugh harder.

As soon as I hear the door closed, I get up, close the blinds to my office and shut the door. Then I put my ear to the door leading directly into Belinda's office.

If Olivia, as Mercedes, can get into my head without my permission, the least I can do is get into hers.

Olivia

"For me?" Miss Turner asks, taking the plant I'm offering.

"A thank-you," I say, nodding. "It's not much, but I think it resembles who you are."

She sets the plant right next to her computer screen. "How so?"

"I feel like you have a way of finding people when they're at their smallest, like this," I say, pointing to the tiny piece of green stem sprouting from the dirt, "and you nurture them, help them grow until they're ready to stand on their own."

Miss Turner looks from the plant to me, a sad smile tugging on her lips. "That's how you see me?"

I nod again, push down my emotions.

She motions to the chair on the opposite side of her desk, and we both sit at the same time. "Is that how you felt about yourself the other night, when I went to your house... that you were at your smallest?"

With a shrug, I answer in truth. "Yes."

"Have there been other times when you've felt like that?"

"Yes, but that night was the worst."

"Tell me about the other times."

I laugh only because I'm nervous. "We're just going to jump straight in, huh?"

"I've opened your dresser drawers and seen your underwear, Olivia. I'm pretty sure we're past pleasantries."

"Right." I clear my throat, my vision immediately blurred by my tears. "Three years ago—today—my grandparents died."

"I'm so sorry."

"I sat in an ambulance, holding the hand of my then three-year-old brother while the paramedics took their bodies away. There was a cop there with us, and he kept asking if there was anyone I'd like him to call, and my mind went blank. There was nobody else. Nobody but Dominic. He was at this event with his new team, and somehow, I had to get to him. I had to be the one to tell him that.... that it was the worst day of our lives. And it was only just beginning..."

* * *

By the time I finish unloading all my trauma on Miss Turner, it's already halfway through second period. She asked if I wanted to stop before classes started, but I was already in her office, bare and vulnerable like I'd planned to be, and honestly, I don't think I could've mustered up the courage to go another round, at another time.

Late pass in hand, I leave her office feeling emotionally drained, yet, somehow, accomplished.

I don't make it far.

Rhys is in his doorway, leaning against the frame, his head bowed, and it's obvious he's been waiting for me.

"Hey," he says, no affect in his tone.

I stop a foot away. "Hey."

He attempts a smile, but it doesn't quite reach his eyes.

Internally, I die a little. Externally, I say, "I heard you saw Dominic last night."

Pushing off the door, he crosses his arms and stands to full height. "You heard that, huh?"

I don't really know how to respond, so I don't. But I've come to terms with the fact that I'll be seeing Rhys, in some capacity, until I graduate, so regardless of who we once were to each other or what he's done since, I have to at least acknowledge him.

Last night, after Dominic came home from the sports park, we sat on the front steps of the house, and I handed him all the missing pieces of the puzzle. I told him about the job interview with Rhys's mom and everything that happened after. He told me I should've stopped the moment I realized Rhys played for St. Luke's. That would've been a ridiculous reason to deny our main paycheck, and I told him as much. He'd agreed, somewhat, until I told him the truth—that Rhys had become a friend to me. Sometimes, it felt like more. Rhys had been there during some of my darkest times—times that I'd kept hidden from Dominic because I didn't want my stress to fall on his shoulders. There were moments when I felt guilty, sure, but at the end of the day, Rhys and his mother—they saved me. Saved us. In more ways than I can count. Even Dominic's work—the vending machines—exists because Mrs. Garrett allows it. And sure, I had pulled back a lot once the whole Rhys-stealing-his-girl thing happened, but I was still obligated to complete what I had started.

It was in the contract.

And that contract was supposed to end as soon as he left town and moved to Colorado with his family. The job with the laundromats was still mine until I no longer wanted it. But things have changed, obviously, and as of right now, I don't know where I stand.

Regardless of all of that, I had to (finally) be real with Dom. I couldn't be mad at Rhys for the things he'd done, because like I said—I hurt him first.

I *betrayed* him.

In so many ways.

And on so many levels.

"Can we talk?" Rhys asks now, pulling me from my thoughts.

It's so sudden—the fear that makes its way up my spine, to my neck, tightening its hold. I don't know if I'm ready to hear what he has to say. But I know that I have to. "Sure."

He motions into his office but leaves the door open. I stand in the middle, unsure of whether to sit, or stand, or...

"The couch is comfortable," he says, deciding for me.

I sit on the couch, and he leans on his desk, opposite, his ankles crossed. And then he just looks at me. Right into my eyes. And I wish I knew what he was thinking, because maybe it wouldn't be so bad that I'm thinking the same.

I miss him.

Both versions of him.

"Do you know a kid named Silas Carney?"

My eyes narrow—in confusion at first and then in thought. "No," I answer. "Should I?"

Rhys grabs a printout from his desk and hands it to me. It's a picture of a school-issued ID card of this Silas kid. "He's a freshman—just started here," Rhys tells me, then waits a beat. "Still nothing?"

I shake my head, handing it back to him.

"What about Aaron Holmes?"

The name rings a bell, and I try to remember how, but still... *nothing*. Rhys hands me another printout—Dominic's team picture from middle school. "I—"

"Look at the names," Rhys suggests, and so I search for Aaron Holmes and find him in the second row. He's not a player, though. He's a volunteer coach from the local high school back in Wilmington.

"Okay...?" I shrug. "Why is this information important to me?"

"They're half-brothers—Silas and Aaron," he replies. "Turns out Silas is a big fan of basketball. And even bigger fan of his older brother. He used to go to all his games, even the ones Aaron coached..."

Realization falls over me like a cold blanket on an even colder night...

"I assume you attended a lot of Dom's games?"

My heart drops to my stomach, and I choke on my words. "Every single one."

Rhys nods, taking the printout from my hands as I stare ahead, too ashamed to face him. Heat burns behind my eyes. My nose. And I hold my breath, wait for Rhys to deliver the gut-punch.

"I wasn't the one to reveal who you are."

"But the plants..." I say, and it's such a dumb thing to be caught up on, but: "You were the only one who knew about my plants..."

"The *plants*? They did that because that's what they're calling you. Like a spy. An informant. A *plant*."

"Oh..." I inhale slowly, quietly, and face Rhys head on, let him witness the shame as it washes over me. It's the least he deserves.

"I think that's what breaks me the most about all of this..." he says, his eyes holding mine. "Even after everything *you* did to me, I still wanted to believe that you felt something for me."

"I—"

"But that you thought I would do that to you... to your family... that I would go so fucking low as to risk Max's life, and for what? For *my* personal gain?"

"Rhys..."

"I have nothing to gain from anything to do with you, Olivia. Not now. Not anymore."

A single tear escapes, and it's only then that he looks away. "Why didn't you say something?" I ask. "Why let me believe—"

"Because it's so much easier to hate you when the feeling is reciprocated."

48

Rhys

"Mom still refuses to go back to Colorado, so to answer your question, yes, I'm still refusing to enter the main house, and I know how you feel... that she was just trying to help or whatever, and maybe you're right. But come on, Izzy, even you can admit how fucked up all of this is. She's been here almost a week now, and I think I've said two words to her. Don't worry. I know these feelings I have toward her won't last forever, but right now, it's all I have.

"As for how Olivia handled the news when I told her it wasn't me who told the entire school... honestly, I don't know. It's Friday now, and I told her on Wednesday, and she hasn't been to school since. So... there's that. It's the only thing I feel guilty about with this whole thing —the amount of school the girl's missing. She had worked hard all her life for her education, but it was cut short due to reasons beyond her control. She deserves to graduate. To go to college or whatever else she wants to do. So... I guess it's clear that no matter what—I still want the best for her, and that's never going to change..."

I look up at the sound of the pool house doors sliding open. Mom stands in the doorway, her hands clasped together.

From the couch, I stare at her as I say into the phone, "I have to go, Izzy. I love you." I drop my gaze just long enough to hit send, then focus on Mom again.

"You're still doing that voice message thing with your sister?" she asks, and she's smiling, and it irks me that she is. "I love how close you've gotten."

Gotten? We were *always* close. I almost died for my sister. And I'd do it again, a thousand times over.

Apparently, my mom thinks my silence is an invitation to enter my personal space. She sits on the other end of the sectional couch, picking at a spot on the arm. "I came to ask if you knew anyone who needs a job."

I don't even bother hiding my eye roll, because of course she's here about *work*.

Mom doesn't react to my attitude, just continues to speak as if I'll actually talk back. "Olivia came over earlier today..."

If she wanted to get my attention, she succeeded. Though I don't let it show.

"She quit her job, handed me the keys to all the laundromats, and said she could no longer continue to work for me. In any capacity..."

She waits a moment for a response that never comes.

"So, anyway," she says, standing. "If you think the position suits anyone you know, just have them contact me."

I wait until she's well and truly gone before unlocking my phone and opening the app for the security cameras. I'd had the notifications muted since Mom's been home because I got sick of watching her come and go. Now, I skim the footage from the front door until Olivia appears. She'd come around midday, when she knew I wasn't home, and it's Delaney, our house manager, who greets her. Delaney had seen Olivia in passing but had never formally met her before. She recognizes Olivia, though, because she says, "Rhys isn't home right now."

Olivia nods, and I try not to look too long at her face. "I'm here to see Mrs. Garrett."

Only seconds later, my mom appears. "Did you want to come in?" Mom asks her, and she's quick to shake her head, get straight to the point. She hands Mom a set of keys and tells her exactly what Mom had told me, that she's sorry, but she can no longer work for my mom in any capacity. And then she turns, and I think that's all there is, but just as she's about to step down, Mom calls her name.

Slowly, Olivia turns to my mom, and even through the security cameras, I can see her chest rise with her inhale, see the frown marring her lips. Mom asks, stepping toward her, "Why didn't you ever tell him?"

Olivia's quiet a beat, then answers, "For the same reason you didn't." She shrugs. "I was afraid to lose him."

She turns around again, and again, Mom stops her with her words. "Do you remember what I told you? When you asked me what I would get out of our agreement."

Olivia doesn't hesitate. "You said you'd hoped to get your son back."

Mom sniffs, loud enough that I can hear it, but her back is to the camera so I can't see her face. "And I got that, Olivia. For the time you were in his life, I got glimpses of the boy he was before..." Even though I can't see it, I know she's crying, and it tugs at something inside of me, because she's right. And I didn't even realize it until right at this moment. "And I have you to thank for that, I'm sure. And I'm so, *so* sorry that it ended this way. I'm sorry that I told him the way I did, and I'm sorry that it's affected you the way it has. But most of all, I'm sorry that you feel like you've lost him... I know now what it's like to have Rhys shut you out of his life, and I wouldn't wish that upon anyone."

49

Olivia

I wonder what it is about my house—or my open garage in particular—that makes boys think they can just walk right in.

Unlike Rhys, Oscar actually says something when he crosses the threshold. "You know I live two blocks away?"

I continue filling dents on an old side table. "Oh, yeah?"

"Yep," he says, standing beside me to look at my work. He's in running shorts and a loose tank, and he's clearly just gone for a run because the boy is *sweating.*

"So, did you walk home after egging my house that night, or did you get back in Rhys's car?"

"I—" He takes a step back. "You know about that?"

I'm about to answer when Dominic opens the door leading into the house. He looks at Oscar, then me, then Oscar, and back again. "You good?" he asks me.

"Yeah," I say with a sigh. I'm pretty sure I know what Oscar's doing here, and I'm really not in the mood.

As soon as Dom closes the door, Oscar asks, "Come for a walk with me?"

"Didn't you just finish a run?"

"Yes. And now I need to cool down, and I don't want to do it alone."
He tugs on my arm. "Please?"

I roll my eyes, shrug out of his hold. "You know I already have one
annoying little brother, right?"

"Please tell me you're referring to Delgado because that would
make my life."

Shaking my head, I put my supplies down before turning him
around by his shoulders and guiding him out of the garage, rolling the
door shut behind us. Once we're on the sidewalk, I send Dom a text
letting him know what's happening, and as soon as I've pocketed my
phone, Oscar states, "You haven't been to school the past couple of
days."

The sun's just beginning to set on a Friday night, and Oscar could
be anywhere else, doing literally anything else, and I'm sure it'd be
more fun than asking me about my sudden disappearance from
school.

"I need some time away," I tell him.

Oscar nods, looking from left to right, as if deciding which way to
go. He chooses left, and off we walk. Slowly. "But you're coming back,
right?"

"I don't know," I tell him truthfully. I've spent the past couple of
days trying to decide if it's worth it. I can always go to West High, the
district public school. I'd looked it up, and it's a decent school. It's not
St. Luke's, but it might have to do.

"Is it because of Rhys or because of the whole rivalry thing or
what?"

I pull a branch off a tree that lines the street just for something to
do with my hands and answer, "All the above."

A beat of silence passes before he says, "The rivalry thing is so
dumb."

"No shit."

"And it wouldn't even be so bad if your brother hadn't pulled that
shit last year."

I stop in my tracks, turn to him. "What shit?"

Oscar looks down at me, his eyes narrowed, as if I'm stupid. "The whole breaking into St. Luke's and glueing that motherfucker of a dildo to the front door thing." He starts walking again, clueless to my reaction, and I try to focus on the details of that event. It happened right before the regional final between Philips and St. Luke's. Rhys and another kid from the team got a one game suspension. Philips won, pushing them into the state finals and putting an end to St. Luke's season. If St. Luke's had a full team...

"I mean, to be fair, it was pretty smart," Oscar continues. "I don't even know how he got one of Rhys's game day jerseys to wear that night or where the hell he and his boys got a yellow Lamborghini from. It would've taken a lot of planning and effort, but damn, they got us good..."

After the suspension, a clip of Rhys talking about it circulated like wildfire. *When someone had asked him if regretted his actions, Rhys took a moment to respond, looking pensive, before asking the interviewer if he thought a hundred unarmed men could take on an adult-size gorilla.*

He made a joke of the situation, but... there was nothing funny about it.

"Does Dom still have that jersey, though, because he should—"

"Oscar." I stop walking and tug on his arm, forcing him to do the same.

He turns to me, almost surprised by whatever emotion I'm displaying. "What?"

"I don't know about any of this."

"Oh." He grimaces, then asks, "Like, *none* of this?"

"I knew about what happened, but I had no idea Dominic was involved. *Obviously.* There's no way I would've—"

"Well, it's out now..." Oscar sighs, starts walking again as if he didn't just unclip a grenade and hand it to me. "That's why Rhys started messing with your brother's girl—to fuck with his head a little before the play-offs. It didn't work, clearly, because Philips still won state, and all Rhys got out of it was a security company he's been trying to offload since the moment he bought it."

"Hold up." I tug on his arm again. "What the fuck are you talking about?"

"Rhys didn't do anything with Dominic's girl, if that's what you're thinking. He flirted with her until she broke it off with Dominic, and once it was done, Rhys ghosted her. But she told everyone they slept together, and Rhys didn't care enough to deny it, so he just let it go."

Good to know, but far from the fucking point. "Not that part, the security company bit! What—"

"Rhys bought the company that manages the security cameras for St. Luke's." Oscar says all this as if it's something I should have already known.

I stare at him, wide-eyed.

He sighs, and that sigh may as well be a yawn with how bored he seems to have to tell me all this. "So the morning after it all went down, Rhys's mom got a call from Principal Brown explaining what they knew —that there was a big black rubber dick on the door and according to what the footage the off-sight security company could see, a guy wearing Rhys's jersey was the one to do it—which, if it *were* Rhys who did it, he wouldn't be that dumb, but anyway, Rhys's mom called him and told him, and Rhys contacted the owner of the security company and bribed him, as in *paid* him, to send him the footage before he sent it to the school. Rhys saw what he saw, knew it was Dominic, and then asked them not to forward the video to Brown until he decided what to do with it. Personally, I would've ratted him out, but Rhys isn't like that. Anyway, the owner of the security place declined, wanted more money... like, enough money to buy the whole-ass company from him, and so Rhys's crazy ass did it. He still owns it, but it's not really his thing, so..."

I turn, walk away.

"Where are you going?" Oscar calls out.

"To beat the shit out of my brother!"

* * *

Within minutes, I'm doing exactly what I said I'd do: I'm beating the shit out of my brother.

"Yo, what the fuck?" Dominic huffs, pushing me off him.

Seconds earlier, I'd marched in through the front door and entered the living room. Max was on his iPad, and Dom was on the PlayStation I bought him with the money Rhys had given me to "spend a few hours with him."

I told Max to go to his room, waited until I knew he was far enough away, and then attacked Dominic with as much strength and anger as my body could muster. Which isn't much compared to my brother but fuck him. Honestly. "Fuck you, Dom!"

"Jesus Christ, Ollie," he fumes, as if he has any right to be the angry one in this station. He throws the PlayStation controller on the couch and gets to his feet. "What the fuck is wrong with you?"

"You!" I slam a finger into his chest. "You're what's fucking wrong with me!"

"What the fuck did Mendoza say to you to get you—"

"Shut up!" I yell, and I cry, and I hate that I cry because it shows weakness when I'm feeling anything but. "For years, I've been *so* careful, walking on eggshells, so fucking worried that I was going to make one wrong move that could split us up or have Max taken away..." I cry because I'm angry. Because I'm so fucking livid, I can't see straight. "And here you are, perfect fucking Dominic Delgado, breaking into schools for some bullshit high school prank!"

Dom's shoulders drop. So does his anger. "Ollie."

"No!" I grasp my hair, adrenaline pumping through my veins so fast it makes me dizzy. "Three years, I've dedicated to making sure we can survive, and you! You have no problem risking it all, and for what? For nothing! And you sit there like you're a fucking victim of it all. Poor me, Rhys stole my girl... boo fucking hoo!"

"Ollie!"

"And then you have the fucking audacity to sit there and make *me* feel guilty for the things *I'd* done. When all I've ever done is put you first. You and your friends. You and school. You and basketball. You you you! It's always about you! Well, fuck you, Dom. Honestly, fuck you!" I gasp for air, but it never comes. And I cry harder, this time... for different reasons. "I have lost so much of myself that there's nothing left of me, Dominic. *Nothing.*"

50

Olivia

Dominic spent most of the day out of the house, which is fine with me. After what happened last night, I wouldn't want to be around me either.

It was the first time anything like that had ever happened between us. Sure, we have stupid, immature spats, but we don't *fight*. I don't yell. And I definitely don't hit. And don't get me wrong; I'm not ashamed of the things I said, but I do regret the actions that came with it.

Now, we're cleaning up after dinner, and we've barely said two words to each other all day. Max doesn't seem to notice the friction between us, and if he has, he hasn't mentioned it.

"Ohana!" Max says, rushing down the stairs. "It's finished!" He holds up a LEGO build he'd been working on for days. It's green and yellow and shaped like an oval, with wheels. He'd shown it to me a few times, but he didn't want to tell me exactly what it was until it was done. Now it is.

"That's awesome, bud," I tell him, wiping down the table. "Are you going to tell me what it is now?"

His teeth show with his smile. "I have to show Timothy first. Can we go see him now?"

I pause mid-wipe and glance over at him. "Why do you need to show Timothy?"

"Because I made it for him," Max answers. "To say thank you for getting me the last Miles book."

"Oh." With a heavy sigh, I drop the cloth on the table and sit on the chair, then give Max my full attention. "I have to tell you something," I start, tugging on his shirt to bring him closer. "His name's not Timothy, and I shouldn't have lied to you about it, but there was a reason." And that reason is standing beside us, listening in on our conversation with a dip in his brow. He doesn't speak up—a smart move on his part.

Max's eyebrows lower, confused, and why wouldn't he be? "What's his name then?"

"His name is Rhys."

"Okay." Max shrugs. "Well... can we go see *Rhys* now?" He holds the LEGO between us. "I want to give him his present."

For the first time since last night, I make eye contact with Dominic. I don't really know why, because truthfully, it doesn't matter how he feels. And it doesn't even matter how *I* feel. This is about Max. Nothing else. "I'll text him," I say, grabbing my phone from the kitchen counter. "But it's a Saturday night, bud, and he might be busy."

I write out a message without overthinking it.

> Max has something he wants to give you. Any chance we can meet up?

Rhys responds within seconds.

TIMOTHY
> I'm at the rooftop if you want to come now.

I change his phone contact from Timothy to Rhys, because I'm done with keeping secrets, and reply:

> We'll be there in 15.

Then I look over at Max, his eyebrows raised in anticipation. I force a smile. "Get your shoes on."

"If Max is going, then I'm going with you." Dom scoffs. "And I'm driving."

I turn away to hide my disdain. "Whatever."

* * *

Dominic doesn't speak on the drive. He doesn't ask where we're going or how I have a code for the boom gates of an empty building. He just sits behind the driver's seat, listening to my instructions and stewing on his bitterness while occasionally puffing out his annoyance.

Rhys is shooting hoops when we arrive at the rooftop but stops the minute we pull up next to his black SUV. Ball held at his side, his face remains passive when he watches all three of us get out of the truck. He stays that way until Max runs toward him, holding the LEGO in the air as if it's a trophy. Rhys smiles—the same smile I see in my dreams. "My guy," he says, squatting down, fist out for a bump. But Max bypasses that and hugs him instead.

Dom and I stay a few yards away, leaning on opposite ends of the hood, and watch their interaction. As soon as Max hands Rhys the LEGO, Rhys laughs. The kind of genuine, carefree laugh I'd heard many times before. I push back my emotions, my longing to hear that sound again and again. "I can't believe you made me an avocado!" Rhys says, shaking his head.

Max takes it from him and sets in on the ground, then pushes it forward. "Rolling testicles!" he cackles, and Rhys laughs with him as they watch it roll away.

"Is this what you guys did?" Dom asks, and I can hear the contempt in his tone. "Go to abandoned buildings and talked about nutsacks?"

"It's not abandoned; it's empty, and shut up."

"How often were you bringing Max around this guy?"

"*This guy* saved your ass, in case you've forgotten." I face him completely. "And maybe I should've brought Max around him more. At least then he'd have a decent male role model!"

"Oh, real nice," Dom chides, pushing off the hood and stepping closer. "Now I really know where your loyalty lies."

"Don't fucking talk to me about loyalty," I spit out. "I haven't taken a single breath that was *for me* in years!"

"You're going to keep pulling that card?" Dom yells, throwing his hands up. "In case you forgot, Ollie, no one made you stay—"

"Go to hell!"

Somewhere in the distance, Rhys says, "Guys?" But we both ignore him.

"Seriously!?" Dom booms. "How long are you going to make *me* feel guilty over *your* choices?"

"However long it takes to get through your thick fucking skull that what you did—"

"Guys!" Rhys shouts now, and Dom and I pull back and turn to him... and *Max*. And *fuck*. I'd been so heated in my anger toward Dominic that I'd forgotten where we were and who else was here. My chest tightens at the sight of Max, his head lowered, hand on his stomach, looking down at his feet. Rhys squeezes Max's shoulder, saying, "Max says his stomach's hurting."

Shame washes over me while Dom rushes to his side. "Are you okay, buddy?"

Max shakes his head, and I turn away when Dom embraces him. "We'll get you home, and make you a nice tea, get you cozy in bed, okay?

"Okay," Max responds, the dejection in his voice palpable.

I can't look at them as they pass, and I don't move to get in the car because I already know what's coming before Dom says the words. "You can find your own way home."

* * *

As soon as the truck's no longer in view, I grab my phone from my back pocket. "What's the address here?" I ask, pulling up the Uber app.

Rhys covers my phone with his hand and pushes it away. "I'll give you a ride."

Honestly, I don't know what's worse. Being forced in the car with Dominic or trapped in the car with Rhys—a guy who's openly admitted to hating me.

"Let me guess..." Rhys says, walking toward his car. He drops the basketball into the open rear window, then leans against the passenger's side door, adding, "Whatever's happening between you and your brother has everything to do with what Oscar told you last night."

I stand beside him, match his position, but don't respond.

"He wasn't supposed to tell you shit," Rhys says. "He was just supposed to convince you to go back to school."

"How do you know?" I ask, then shake my head at myself. *Rhys is the puppet master,* I remind myself, *always pulling the strings.* "So, it's true... about the dumbass prank?"

Rhys remains silent, and I turn to face him, resting my hip on the car.

"Why not rat him out? Why take the fall for him? And worse, why let your team suffer—"

"My team was the *only* reason I had to think twice about what I did," he cuts in, a tinge of anger in his tone. "Your brother didn't just mess with me. He ended my team's season, and some of those guys—"

"So why do it?"

He shakes his head, then pushes off the car so he can stand in front of me. "Do you know what they would've done to literally anyone else who isn't me for pulling that kind of shit? At a school like St. Luke's? The disrespect alone... Not to mention that your brother is *the* star player at Philips!" He scoffs. "Jesus, Liv. They would've dragged his ass through the coals, pinned every single charge they could on him, and laughed in his face during sentencing."

"You honestly think he would've done *time?*" Surely not.

"That new Mega Gym is *my* punishment, and I'm a fucking God at that school," he rants, clearly heated. "So, yes, Cheeks, they would've sent him to juvie and thrown away the key. And trust me, I've *been* to juvie. I wouldn't wish that upon anyone... even Dominic."

51

Rhys

Liv's mouth opens, shuts, again and again, and I watch, confused, until I realize what I've just revealed.

"You've been to juvie?"

I genuinely have no fucking clue what I was thinking, and maybe that's the problem. I wasn't thinking at all. But my time at the detention center has been on my mind lately, and so maybe that's why it slipped out the way it did. "Yes," I answer, then heave out a sigh. "Obviously, it's not a well-known fact, so I'd appreciate if it stayed between us."

"Right." Liv shakes her head, as if clearing her thoughts. "Of course, yeah." And then comes the silence I'd expect from anyone in her situation. Not that I have a lot of experience with it. The people who already know about that part of my past are either family or were there to experience it alongside me.

I've never had to tell the story.

Never had to explain the how, why, when.

But the way Liv's looking at me now—discomfort mixed with unease—I feel compelled to give her *something*. With a heavy sigh, I stand next to her again, rocking the SUV when I rest my weight on it. "Do you remember Curtis?"

"Ah, so I'm not the only one versed in subject changes," she muses, and I don't respond to that. I just wait. "If you mean your cop friend, Curtis... The one who showed up at my house, entered my home and proceeded to invade every inch of my privacy... *that* Curtis? Then yes, he's kind of hard to forget."

If I didn't have a good read on Olivia, I'd think she was talking shit. But she's just being a smartass. Petty as hell, but still... a smartass.

"I met him in juvie."

"Oh." After a beat of silence, she asks, "He was in juvie with your or..."

"He was a guard," I tell her, then slide down the car until my ass hits the concrete. I'm exhausted. The memories that usually consume my dreams are working overtime while I'm awake, so it's safe to say that sleep hasn't been my friend lately. Nor is it my enemy. Knees bent, I rest my forearms on them and wait for Liv to mimic my position. Instead, she sits opposite, so we're facing each other, and it's a move I wasn't expecting, so I sure as shit wasn't prepared to be eye to eye like this.

I avert my gaze and look down at my hands, unable to face her. "I know you want to ask *why* I was there, but truthfully, I can't say. Just know that I don't regret it..." My throat closes in as the memories flood my mind. My knees bounce, uncontrollable, until—

Until Liv grasps the tips of my fingers—the touch so light I have to physically see the connection to know that it's real. "You don't have to..." she says, just above a whisper.

But I'm already past that point, and so is she. According to the contract between Liv and my mom—Liv was never to ask about my past. Truth is, if she had, I probably would have told her. Not *her*, but Mercedes. And yes, I realize they're the same person, but try telling my brain that.

Liv's still grasping my fingers when I feel the need to tell her, "I was only in there for six months, but... it was brutal. The absolute worst time of my life."

"Rhys..."

I force my eyes up and onto hers and immediately look back down again because I know what she's thinking. "No," I rush out. "I wasn't assaulted—*sexually*—if that's what you're wondering, but... a guy like me, with a face like this, in a place like that..." I push forward, grasp her fingers that had been holding mine, and guide them to my lips. I press her fingers to the deepest scar there and ignore the tightening in my chest when I hear her shaky exhale. "That ones from this motherfucker of a guard, Williams, who ran his own little gang in there." Then I lower my head between my shoulders and place her fingers on the back of my head, right over those scars. "Sixteen stitches," I murmur. "From the leader of that gang." I hold out my hand between us, palm down, and run her touch over the scar tissue on my middle finger. "Five boys almost beat the life out of me, then held me up while one put my hand on the doorframe and continuously kicked the door closed on my fingers... all while that piece-of-shit guard watched." I know Liv's crying only by the way her hands tremble, the way her breaths fall shakily between us. But I don't look at her. I *can't*. "I can still hear his laugh," I continue. It used to only be in my dreams, but ever since I found out the truth about what Liv and my mom did, I've been hearing it *every-where*. "It's like a fucking soundtrack to my nightmares. That day... it was the one and only time I cried out in pain. And that cry is how Curtis found me. I was fifteen and scared out of my mind, and I thought I was strong... invincible." I almost laugh at the thought. "But Curtis— he taught me what true strength was. Through discipline, hard work, and mental mind shifts. And *books*. God, those books got me through endless days of darkness."

"*The Count of Monte Cristo...*" Liv whispers, and my eyes snap to hers.

I nod, releasing her hand so I can wipe the endless tears staining her cheeks. I'm not heartless. I realize that both versions of the girl I've come to know feel *something* for me, whatever it is, and I know what I'm saying is hurting her. "All human wisdom is contained in these two words..."

"Wait and hope," she finishes for me.

I attempt a smile but fall short when I remember how Mercedes and I spent an entire night talking about the book after she'd read it and how Olivia keeps a copy in her dollhouse—her self-proclaimed most prized possession. I release her face and sit back against the car, angry at myself for allowing our closeness to let me forget she lied to me.

A lot.

After clearing my throat, I disassociate from all other emotions and push forward. "My mom and sister used to visit me every other day, but when the beatings became a regular thing, I forced them to stop." Some days, I was still bleeding from the night before, and I didn't want them to see me like that. But they still showed up, like clockwork, and I refused to go out and see them—no matter how hard Curtis tried to convince me otherwise. Eventually, it was only my mom who would sit in that room. Waiting. Hoping. And that hope never ebbed. Even once I was out. "I guess that was the beginning of me pushing them away... and after a while, it just became too hard to let them back in. That's why..."

"That's why she asked *me* to try," Liv says, and I glance up at her, nodding.

"She's my mom... and she felt like she had no other choice," I say, and I don't know why I feel the need to explain. "I can't continue to be mad at her."

Liv nods, her eyes overflowing with tears again. "But you can continue to be mad at me?"

"I don't know where else to direct my feelings..."

"I understand," she says, and I don't know if she *truly* does, but it doesn't matter. I can't get caught up in her heartbreak more than my own. "You said your mom and sister visited you a lot... what about your dad?"

"My dad hasn't been able to look me in the eye since," I admit, the words flowing out of me easier than I'd thought. "I put shame on our family, so I get it." It didn't help that I refused his assistance once I was arrested. Sure, his money could've saved me. Could've made the whole thing disappear, just like with that kid who killed her grandparents. But I'd be the absolute worst kind of hypocrite if I allowed that to happen.

The reason I was arrested in the first place was because I was trying to prove a point—that there has to be a punishment to fit the crime. I wanted my victim's punishment to be death; therefore, mine was juvie. I stand, wait for Liv to do the same. "It sucks, though," I tell her, opening the passenger door. "This building contains the first office he ever rented, and I thought by buying the place it would somehow bring us closer."

"Has it?" she asks.

"He's never even seen it since."

52

Olivia

Rhys keeps Max's gift on his lap the entire drive to my house, one hand on it at all times. He doesn't speak, and I have nothing left to say. Well, that's a lie. There's a lot I wish I could say, but doing so would achieve nothing. Besides, I wouldn't even know where to start.

Rhys pulls up in front of my house, but doesn't kill the engine, doesn't even put the car in gear. Message heard, loud and clear.

I hop out without another word and don't turn around, even when he takes off. I don't go into the house though. Instead, I take the alley beside it, bypass the gate that leads to the side yard, until I get to the playground.

The sun's only just beginning to set, but it's late enough that no one else is here. It's a small playground—just a set of swings and a rocket structure with a couple of slides. We used to take Max here a lot, but according to him, "There's only so many times you can do the same thing before it gets boring."

I sit on a swing, my legs crossed at the ankles, and push off the ground. I don't really *swing*; I just... sway. And I cry. Because apparently crying here is something you can do many times, for many reasons, and it never gets boring.

I barely move as I watch the sky turn from orange to red, then red to purple, and I get lost in my thoughts, in my anguish, to the point I can no longer pinpoint the reason for my tears. They're just there—existing in a world under a multicolored sky. I'm so lost in my heartache that I don't notice the black SUV pull up to the curb until Rhys steps out, makes his way over to me.

He waits until he's only feet in front of me to say, "You don't want to go home, huh?"

I stare at his Nike-covered feet and shake my head. The last thing I want is him, *here*. But at the same time... it only makes sense that he is.

"You want me to take you somewhere else?"

I laugh through my cries. "I don't *have* anywhere else." Then I push off the ground, wishing it would swallow me whole. "What are you doing, Rhys?"

"I was on my way home from Oscar's. Saw you here..."

"And thought you needed to get out, and what?"

"I don't know," he says with a sigh. The entire swing set groans under his weight when he sits beside me. "Are you afraid to go home? Is Dom—"

"I'm not *afraid* to go home," I cut in. "I'm *ashamed* to."

"Why?"

I shake my head, keep my eyes downcast so he can't witness the new onset of tears. "After the accident... Max developed a fear of being in the car, which is completely understandable. And we didn't realize it at first—that that's what the problem was—but every time we'd leave to go somewhere, he'd complain of a stomachache..."

It doesn't take long for Rhys to understand. "Like he did tonight."

I nod. "It's the way his body reacts to fear..." I exhale a shaky breath. "Once we'd figured it out, we slowly built his courage back up. He's half the reason we do food deliveries together. He keeps all the tips... that's what I'm supposed to do, you know? I'm supposed to be the one who protects him... who fights his fears for him. I'm not supposed to cause them."

"I'm sorry," he's quick to say, and I don't know what he's sorry for. I don't think he does either. "And I can't believe I'm saying this, but... as a little brother who's made a hell of a lot of mistakes, Dominic's not such a bad guy. Until last night, you and Max thought the world of him." He's quiet a beat, then adds, "This is completely unsolicited advice to do with what you will, but I don't know, Cheeks... I don't think it's fair to judge him based on one bad decision."

I wipe the remnants of my tears with the back of my hand and sniff back my emotions. Then I repeat his words, throw them right back at him. "This is completely unsolicited advice to do with what you will, but your dad's not dead, Rhys." I stand and turn to him but keep my head down. "You still have time to make it right. If you *want* to." I make it one step toward my house before I force myself to stop, face him for the first time since he got here. Then I tell him something I've been holding on to since his mom revealed the truth about our past. "I get why you're mad at me, and I get why you want to hate me. I don't even know how I would react if I were in your shoes. I betrayed you in ways I can't even comprehend... but, Rhys..." I choke on a sob, but don't let it escape. "You lost someone you just met. I've lost my *best friend*. You've known me for weeks... I've *loved* you for years."

53

Olivia

When I get home, Dominic's sitting at the bottom of the stairs just by the front door, and it's clear by the look on his face that he's been stewing on his feelings as much as I have.

He waits until I've closed the door behind me and slipped off my shoes before speaking. "You've never, not once, ever made me feel like a burden... until lately."

I suck in air through my nose, release it slowly, slowly. And then I sit on the step beside him and lean into him. Physically. Metaphorically. In every way possible. I take out my phone, open the voice recording app, and release the words that lighten the load on my too-heavy heart.

"Hey, Grandma. Grandpa. Dom and I—we're not doing the best, and if you could see us right now, you'd be so disappointed. You used to always say that the family we create means more than the family who created us, and I think, sometimes, we forget that..."

54

Rhys

The world is crimson, made of nothing but blood and the flames that blaze inside me. I press my cheek to the floor, my eyes drifting shut when the cool concrete coats my flesh. Broken bones held to my stomach, I choke on the blood filling my airways, spreading through my lungs.

Suffocating me.

In the distance, their laughter fades along with their footsteps, and I wish it did something to ease my fears.

I groan when the pain soars, ricochets through me with every beat of my heart, thump thump, thump thump, and I wish I could die.

Not would, but could.

I wish I could take my own life and not care how much it would hurt my family. My sister, especially. I wish I could end it all and fall into the darkness and never come up for light.

I wish I could die.

I wish I had the strength not to flinch the next time Williams put his gun to my throat for his own sick, twisted pleasure.

I wish my eyes didn't convey my fear when the metal pressed against my neck.

*I wish I could look into his deranged eyes and beg him to pull the trigger.
I wish—*

*Footfalls sound, coming nearer, and my eyes snap open as I gasp for air. I
try to move, try to hide, but my body is as broken as my spirit. Black leather
boots beneath a gray guard uniform fill the doorway, fill my vision. He drops
to his knees, in the middle of the utility room, and places a hand on my shoulder, rolling me to my back. His name tag reads Murphy, but he tells us to call
him Curtis. "Jesus, Garrett, what the fuck happened to you?"*

I gasp awake, sitting upright, and blink blink blink the darkness
away. "Alexa, lights," I murmur, inhaling only when the room fills with
brightness.

I throw the covers off me and rush to the bathroom, my hands
immediately finding the light switch, then the tap. I run the cold water
until it's almost freezing, then splash it on my face, again and again,
until my head, neck, and shoulders are soaked.

I breathe.

One more time.

Every time.

Until my pulse finds a rhythm that doesn't make my entire body
tremble. Throat dry, I glance up at the vent in the bathroom, knowing
exactly what's there and how I could use it.

I wish I could die...

But I don't.

Not in this life.

When I've reached a level of calm trustworthy enough to move, I
grab my phone from my side table and exit the pool house from the
bedroom doors. It's dark out, but the pool lights give off enough light
that I can see my surroundings.

I sit on a lounge chair and peer over at the window of my parents'
bedroom. The lights are off. My mom is home, but my dad...

*"Your dad's not dead, Rhys. You still have time to make it right. If you
want to."*

Olivia's words have replayed in my mind so many times I've lost count.

After our conversation tonight, I'm not at all surprised that the nightmares came to pay a visit. Though, to be fair, it wasn't just Liv who triggered all the fucked-up memories to return. Mainly, it was when and *how* my mom's need to *fix me* came to light.

With a sigh, I check the time on my phone—it's just after 2 a.m. here, so just after midnight in Colorado. My dad will most likely be asleep, but I have to stop making excuses to keep putting this off.

Without another thought, I pull up his contact—something I've done many times in the past. But the difference between now and all those other times is that now, I finally hit *call*.

Dad answers on the third ring, his voice scratchy from sleep. "Rhys?" he asks. "What's wrong?"

It's been over three years since I'd heard Dad's voice aside from in the background of a call between me and my mom, or me and my sister. He seems older somehow. Tired. And not just from lack of sleep. But tired from *life*.

"I'm sorry to call so late," I tell him, staring down at my lap. "I just wanted to talk to you..."

"You don't need a reason to call, son."

My chest tightens at his unexpected words. At the tone in which he says them. As if he, too, has been putting off this conversation for years. "Do you need a reason to call me?"

Silence fills the space between us, and I swallow, nervous of his reaction. "It's something I should've done a long time ago, and I'm sorry that I haven't."

I sit up taller, fill my lungs through my nose, and let the quiet fall between us while my mind races, until it slows, then stops completely. "You know Belinda?"

"Of course I do," he says. I can hear movement at his end, and I imagine him getting up and out of bed. "How's your goddaughter? It's Layla, right?"

"Layla's awesome. Growing up way too fast."

Even through the phone, I can hear his smile. "I bet she loves her uncle Reese's Pieces."

I chuckle. "How do you know she calls me her uncle?"

"Your mom told me about it," he says, then after a beat: "So, what about Belinda?"

I drop my gaze, let my shoulders relax a little. "She does this thing —when we talk about regrets... she has us start the sentence with '*I wish I would have*' or '*I wish they would have...*'"

"Okay..."

I feel small, like the little boy he used to carry on his shoulders. "And so I was thinking maybe I could do it with you? And we switch, and you can say something..."

"Okay..." he repeats, even more unsure than the first time.

I clear my throat, clear the fear and insecurities from my mind. Then I throw it all out there between us. "I wish you would've visited me at least once while I was in there."

The silence that falls is so heavy, it lands with a crash so loud it's almost deafening. "My turn?" he asks, and I nod, even though he can't see me.

"Yeah..."

"I wish you would've told me of your plans before you went off and did it..." he says, and the break in his voice gives me reason to pause, "... so that I could've gone with you, and you wouldn't have had to do it alone."

55

Rhys

By the time I get back into bed, a couple of hours have passed, and Dad and I spent those hours talking, in depth, about everything that happened and how those things affected us.

For years, I'd held on to the shame of disappointing my family, never once realizing that my father carried his own shame, and that shame is the reason he couldn't face me, even after all this time.

He was embarrassed that he didn't have the guts to do what I did and humiliated that it fell on the shoulders of his fifteen-year-old son to right the wrongs that had been done to his family.

His reasons never even occurred to me, and the more we spoke, the more he opened up. He regretted, almost more than anything, that he didn't have the strength I did to pick up the phone and make the call we both needed in order to move on.

Swear, I've never felt as light as I did after hanging up the phone with him. As soon as that call disconnected, I sent my sister a voice message telling her what had just happened and that I'd go into detail about it more the next time we spoke. And then I told her something I knew would make her smile. I told her I was *happy*.

And for the first time since I can remember, I actually meant it.

I crawl back into bed, my mind clearer than it has been for a while, but just as I settle in and close my eyes, my phone rings.

Oscar's face lights up on my screen, and I'm quick to answer it. "What's up?"

"I need you to pick me up," he whispers.

I'm already on my feet with my keys in my hand when I answer, "Where?"

* * *

There's a water tower a couple of towns away, in the middle of a field, surrounded by a chain-link fence. Years back, someone cut a hole in the fence, and most weekends, kids around here find themselves at the field when nothing else is going on. I've done it dozens, if not hundreds, of times. For a while, cops, as well as surrounding residents, turned a blind eye to it... until some dickhead ruined it by wanting to give a Harry Houdini performance inside the tank.

Spoiler alert: he was no Houdini.

There's usually a kid from West High who keeps a police scanner in his truck, so he'll alert everyone before the cops get there. I guess he wasn't there tonight, or if he was, the cops were too quick, because according to Oscar, he was too late to flee the scene but was able to hide out in a bush while the cops cruised around for a few minutes after.

When I get to the empty industrial parking lot that lines the fence into the field, I keep an eye out for Oscar. He'd gone there with a couple of guys from the team, but they fled without him. I would bring it up at the next practice, but the fact is: if it was anyone but Oscar, I wouldn't give a shit.

A figure appears a few feet ahead, and I slow my SUV to a stop and unwind the passenger side window. Oscar ducks, poking his head through the open window, and says, "I need your help."

I shrug. "I'm here, aren't I?"

Oscar grimaces, looks at the bush behind him, then back at me. "I'm kind of maybe not alone."

* * *

Delgado is fast asleep, on dirt ground, in a fetal position, and it takes everything in me not to be an immature asshole and snap a picture to post on Instagram for the world to see. It's the least he deserves.

"I think his boys bailed on him," Oscar explains. "But he was already out of it by the time I came across him."

"Jesus."

"I had to drag his ass from the field to here, and you know I lift, bruh, but that dude is one beefy motherfucker."

I look from Dom to my car and back again. "I say we leave him."

"Fuck you, Garrett," Dom groans.

Oscar chuckles. "He has a point."

* * *

Dominic is trashed—to the point he can't even sit up straight. Even with the two of us helping him into the car—dead weight that's alive enough to fight you off is an absolute bitch to maneuver. We manage to slide him into the back seat, in the same fetal position we found him in, and off we go.

It doesn't take long to get to Oscar's neighborhood—the same one Dominic lives in—and when we're only blocks away from his house, Oscar makes a call, puts it on speaker.

"Hello?" Liv answers in that sleepy, croaky voice, and I push aside memories of all the times I've heard that voice... when she was lying next to me, completely spent from the hours of pleasure we'd just endured.

Oscar breathes heavily into the phone before growling, "What are you wearing?"

"Dangit, Oscar, it's the middle of the night," Liv hisses, and it only makes Oscar chuckle.

"I have a package for you, but you'll need to accept it at the front door."

"Please don't egg my house again," she pleads. "It smelled for months after. I had to hire a pressure washer for the driveway."

"No eggs," he assures. "Just a six-foot-five Prince of Persia currently filled with enough alcohol to kill a small horse."

Liv sighs before hanging up, and we pull up to the front of her house just as the porch light flicks on.

In unison, Oscar and I look between the seats at Dominic. "Yo, Dominator?" Oscar says, shaking him.

"Fuck you, too," Dominic murmurs.

I lock eyes with Oscar. "Told you we should've left his ass there."

"Yeah, but then Ollie would be all worried about him, and I like Ollie."

"Ollie, Ollie, Ollie," Dom mumbles.

I glance over at Olivia standing out on her front porch now, arms crossed. Tank top. Sleep shorts. Hair a complete mess. Even when she's not trying, she looks good enough to eat. I say, "She's waiting for you to get in the house, bro."

"I couldn't pronounce my V's," Dom stammers, half drunk, half sleeping. "I would say Olibya or Libby. Then I just started calling her Ollie... Ollie, Ollie, Ollie. We're fighting, you know? She hates me because I'm a fuckup... and I could've ruined everything."

Oscar's sigh fills the entire cab of the car. "We need to at least get him in the house."

I push open my door. "I know."

* * *

Dominic barely makes it up the porch steps with Oscar and me on either side of him, so when Liv looks at the staircase, then me, I shake my head. "No chance."

Oscar's phone rings, and he shuffles his hold on Dominic to answer it. There's only one person who would call him at this hour, and my assumption's proven correct when I hear his mom's shrill scream through the phone. "Mamá!" Oscar yells, followed by groveling in Spanish. Once he hangs up, he practically pushes Dom into my arms. "I gotta go!" He leaves on foot, and swear, I didn't think it was possible for someone under the influence to flee as fast as he does.

And then it's just me and Olivia, standing in her entryway. Well, me, Olivia, and her drunk brother. "You think he can make it to my bed?"

I shrug. "We can try."

Olivia replaces Oscar, and we guide him to her room and up the step to her bed. "Lie down and sleep it off," Liv tells him, clearly done with his shit. Dom turns to her, then proceeds to empty his stomach all down her front and the floorboards by her feet.

"Fuck, Dom!"

Dom flops onto the bed, face-first, feet off the edge, mumbling, "Ollie, Ollie, Ollie."

I step back, holding my breath, and Olivia looks down at her puke-stained clothes. "What the fuck did you eat?"

Dom snores.

Olivia faces me. "Can you stay while I shower? Just make sure he doesn't choke on his own vomit?"

Last thing I want to do, but... "Sure."

After getting Dom onto his side and wiping the puke from his chin, cleaning as much as she can off herself and the floorboards, then opening the windows, Olivia finds a bucket and hands it to me. "Just in case." Then she goes into her bathroom, closes the door, and a moment later, the water pipes clank when the shower turns on.

I pull up her desk chair and sit beside the bed, bucket in hand, just in case. If you'd told me a year ago, I'd be sitting at Dominic's bedside at five in the morning, somewhat taking care of him, I'd have told you to kick rocks.

Dom groans, shifting onto his back, his eyes opening just the slightest. And then he... he *laughs*.

"These fucking posters," he mumbles, and I glance up at the ceiling —space, forests, coastlines—and I'm reminded of what she said all those weeks ago.

"I keep them there as a reminder that the world is vast, filled with so many singular objects, and we, as individual humans, are just one of those things. We're so small. All of us. So insignificant."

"She put them up after she found out her mom left us. Or maybe it was when she found out her ex-boyfriend was seeing her best friend. The motherfucker didn't even break up with her."

"The fuck?"

"Right?" Dom rolls his eyes. "He used to come here on weekends just to screw her. I guess... eventually, he figured he could get the same thing without traveling over two hours for it. He just stopped coming 'round, stopped answering her calls." Dom peers over at me. "Makes you want to punch something, right?"

I don't respond, just keep my lips pressed tight while I imagine a younger Olivia having to deal with that on top of everything else.

"She tried to play it off," he says, his eyelids heavy. He'll be out soon, but until then, he keeps talking. "She says she wasn't in a good place back then... that she had nothing else to offer him."

My initial thoughts on the guy remain the same. *I hate him.* But... the story sounds familiar because she felt the same way with me. The difference is that I wasn't enough of an asshole to take advantage of her because of it.

"Anyway..." Dom says, shifting to his side as his eyes lose the fight to stay open. "That's why she put the posters up... She wanted a daily reminder that she was nothing more than a single object amongst millions of other things. Things so small and insignificant.... She felt like if she gave herself more importance than that, then she'd be forced to believe that these things happen for a reason. To her. And then she'll take things personally." He sighs, ending his ramble with, "How fucked up is that?"

Again, I don't respond—too busy replaying his words in my mind.

"You got a sister, Garrett?"

I speak for the first time since Liv left us alone. "Yes."

"Do you love her?"

She's a hundred percent of my fifty. "Yes."

"Do you hurt her, too?"

Also "Yes."

56

Olivia

This entire shitshow of a day/night/early the next morning is laughable. It's the only way I can describe it. And as Rhys watches me from the doorway of the laundry room while I dump vomit-covered clothes into the washing machine, it's exactly what I do. *Laugh.* In a disbelieving, almost psychotic way.

"Are you good?" he asks, hands in the pockets of his gray sweatpants. I bet the fucker wore them on purpose, just to fuck with me.

"I'm *great*," I say, tampering down my insane cackle to a simmering giggle. I slam my fingers on the buttons of the washer to start the cycle, then turn to him. "You know what's funny?" I don't wait for a response. "Weeks ago, you were the one stalking me, and now you want distance, but you can't get rid of me."

He doesn't deny my assumption, because why would he?

"Thanks for taking care of shit tonight," I murmur, lowering my gaze. "I'll walk you out." I flick off the light, then try to pass him in the doorway, but his hand on my stomach stops me.

Heat emits from his touch, spreads throughout my entire body. I stop breathing when he moves his hand from my stomach to my hip, and he pulls gently, forcing me to turn to him. "Liv," he says, his voice a low hum. We're close. Closer than we've been in weeks. And he shortens that space even more when he dips his head, places his mouth right to my ear, and says, "You're not small... and you're definitely not *insignificant.*"

I find bravery in his words, courage in his touch, and I look up and into his eyes—those slate-gray eyes that have seen more than they should. "Why are you saying this?" I choke out.

"Because you have the right to know."

I glide my hands up between us, flattening my palms on his chest. "Rhys..."

His fingers find my jaw, thumb stroking my cheek. I shudder a breath when his forehead meets mine, and he inhales that air right into his lungs before his lips skim across mine. My eyes drift shut, my exhales pouring from me in tiny spurts, one after the other. My chest rises, falls, and I fist his T-shirt when his lips press to mine.

For weeks, I've dreamed of this moment. *Prayed* for it.

He tilts his head, mouth parting just enough to glide his tongue along the seam of my lips. I fall. Into his arms and into the light. He presses me up against the doorframe, holding me steady as he deepens the kiss. His hand's in my hair now, tugging gently, and I tilt my head so he has access to my neck. "Fuck," he murmurs into my skin, and then his hands are everywhere, all at once, and my feet are no longer on the ground. They're moving around him while he lifts me in the air. He steps into the laundry room and closes the door, shrouding the room with darkness. My ass lands on the washer, and his mouth lands on my breast, over my tank top, and I'm so dizzy with desire I can't see straight. But I don't need to see. I just need to feel him. His head. His shoulders. His back. His chest. His abs. His hardened cock beneath the fabric of his sweats. He moans against me, his hand on my thigh, squeezing hard, just once, before slipping in through the leg hole of my loose shorts. His hand works fast, expertly, as he shifts my panties to the side and slides a finger inside me. I moan, so loud and so wanton, that he feels the need to cover my mouth with his. His tongue glides along mine while his fingers slide inside me, again and again, and then his thumb.... He flicks his thumb over my nub, and I tremor in his arms. I push down the band of his sweatpants, then his boxers, and wrap my fingers around his heated length. Fuck, I missed this. Miss him. Miss *us*. He tugs me forward until I'm at the edge of the washer and pulls my shorts and underwear completely aside. Pulse pounding in my ears, I guide him to my warm center, but...

But he doesn't push inside me right away, and when I try to deepen the kiss...

... he doesn't kiss back.

"Liv," he says, his entire body stiff beneath my touch. He drops his head to my shoulder but doesn't release me completely. "I'm so sorry."

I push him away as gently as possible and wipe away the sudden onset of tears, grateful he can't see them in the dark. "It's okay..." I was dreaming to think he'd actually want this. Want *me*. I swallow the pain. The *shame*. And throw back the words he'd said the first night we let our physical desires consume us. *"It's just biology, right?"*

"Olivia, that's not..." He doesn't finish the thought. He doesn't need to.

I replace my clothes back where they belong and jump off the washing machine, ignoring the way he's still close to me. Too close. I push past him, forcing my breaths to stay stagnant in my lungs so my cries don't expel with my exhales. I open the door, wincing at the bright lights of the kitchen, and start for the front door. His footsteps follow behind, and I don't stop. Don't look back at him when he calls my name. I make it all the way to the entryway before he catches me. Hand on my wrist, he tugs, forcing me to face him.

"I'm sorry," he repeats.

"It's okay," I tell him. Again. And I don't know if it is, but whatever I'm feeling—it's not something I want to dissect with him standing right in front of me.

"Just give me a minute to explain." His clothes are all skewed, sweatpants hanging off his hips, exposing the band of his boxer shorts. "I don't know how to separate you."

What the fuck does that mean? "What?" I huff, meeting his eyes.

"In my mind," he explains. "You're still two different people, and I don't know how to separate you. And not even *you*—as in the two different versions of you—but I don't know how to separate what was real and what wasn't."

"All of it was real, Rhys."

"But I don't know that!" He takes a step forward and lowers his voice. "I keep going through every interaction we've ever had, trying to determine what was genuine or if any of it was, and now, somehow, I'm supposed to move forward with this and just stop questioning every move you make, every word you say...." He pauses a breath, his eyes shifting between mine as if searching for answers. "If you can tell me how to do that, how to stop feeling like I'm some kind of game to you, then *please* tell me, because I'd love to know."

Even if I had all the answers in all the world, he wouldn't listen to me. "I've tried, Rhys. I've tried to make you accept who I am and what you mean to me, but if you can't see that, or feel that, then I don't know want to tell you..."

His gaze drops, along with his shoulders, "Then I guess there's nothing left to say."

57

Olivia

"Ollie?" *Knock, knock.* "You decent?" Dom asks.

"It's better if you're not!" a voice yells from the other side of my door, and I can't help but smile.

"Dude, that's my sister."

I open the door just in time to see Oscar shrug, say, "She ain't my sister."

I tug on his arm and pull him inside, telling Dominic, "I'll start dinner in half an hour."

Dom starts to leave, then hesitates, turns back to us. Going by how chipper he is, one would never know that less than twelve hours ago he was passed out drunk in my bed. "Do we need to have an open-door policy in this house, because I can't handle taking care of another kid..."

Idiot. And gross.

"Nope," Oscar says, at the same time I say, "It's just Oscar."

Oscar, always the dramatic, grasps his chest, just above his heart. "Direct hit," he groans, then slides down the doorframe until he's nothing but a mess of limbs on my floor.

Dominic looks from him to me. "Is he always like this?"

Oscar moans.

"Always," I tell him.

Dom nods. "Good to know," he says, turning his back on us.

Oscar waits until he's no longer in view to suddenly come back to life. He enters my room, closing the door behind him. Then he just stands there, looking around. "Your room's dope," he murmurs, then focuses on me. "What are you doing?"

I point to the open laptop on my bed. "Updating my resume."

"So... you're not coming back to school?"

I shut the laptop and place it on my desk. "Did Rhys send you again?" Because after last night, I'm pretty sure I'm off Rhys's radar for good.

When he doesn't reply, I turn to him. Lips clamped shut, he pretends to be focused on a vine hanging from the ceiling.

I laugh, because what else can I do?

"I haven't decided," I admit. "About coming back or not."

Oscar nods. "It's just that school started, like, three weeks ago, and you've been there for maybe four days. You're going to get kicked out if you don't come back soon. Belinda—I mean, *Miss Turner*—she's been vouching for you, but she can't do it forever."

"I never asked her to."

"You do realize who Rhys is, right? You don't have to ask for shit. He'll take care of it for you." He takes the step up to my bed and throws himself on it, landing on his back. He looks at the posters on my ceiling, then says, his voice low, just above a whisper. "Speaking of Rhys... he mentioned he told you about juvie."

I'm not surprised that he knows about Rhys's past, but I am surprised he wants to openly discuss it. "Yeah, he did."

"I bet he didn't tell you that's how we met..."

A breath catches in my throat, and I freeze in the middle of my room. "You were in juvie?"

"Yep," he says, patting the spot beside him.

I don't think twice. I just lie down beside him and let him take my hand, and sure, it should feel weird to have a boy in my bed, a boy who isn't Rhys, but there's nothing between Oscar and me. At least nothing physical.

"My stepdad used to beat on my mom, and I got tired of it," he says, and I squeeze his hand, let him know I'm listening. He keeps his eyes on the posters, adding, "One day, I went to his work and beat the fuck out of him with a massive wrench. Almost killed him. I had to do time because they said it was unprovoked." He rolls his head to the side so he can face me. "It could've been self-defense if I'd done it mid-him-attacking-her, which I knew, but I didn't want my mom to see me act as horrible as he does."

I flip to my side, give him all my attention. "I'm so sorry, Oscar."

He shrugs. "I thought that was the worst of it, you know? But it was just as bad in there..." He clears his throat, eyes downcast. "The same guard who used to beat on Rhys did the same to me. Until one day Rhys intervened. I guess the guard took it personally, and the day after... Let's just say I'm the reason Rhys can't bend all his fingers fully..."

"Oscar..."

"Don't cry," he tells me, and I wipe my eyes against my pillow to rid the tears. "It's not all bad. Rhys took me under his wing, and Curtis and Belinda took both of us under theirs. You ever hear Belinda tell me the days when she greets me?" He heightens the pitch of his voice to mimic her. "*Good morning and happy Wednesday, Oscar!*"

I nod.

"She started doing it when I told her that one of the worst parts of being in there was that all the days merged into one, and it felt like life was never moving forward. Now, she reminds me it's a new day, every day." He laughs, and I don't know how he does it while talking about something so devastating. "Thanks to Rhys and his parents, we created a family. Our little family. And it's awesome."

"I'm glad you have them," I say.

He nods. "Me, too." Then he inhales a sharp breath, focuses on the ceiling again. "But sometimes, I still have that fear, you know? Of men like my stepdad. Of that guard. The new coach..."

I recall the way the coach yelled at him the first time I met him, and I wish I could've done something about it then, but I didn't know...

JAY MCLEAN

"That's why Rhys is working at the school," he continues. "I told him I was scared, and he found a way to be there for me. He saved my ass. Like he did in juvie and like he's done every day since." His eyes meet mine again. "Ollie... when Rhys loves, he loves with everything inside of him."

I lower my gaze. "So, what you're saying is that I'm not worthy of that love?"

"No. What I'm saying is that now, it's his turn to be loved. And that love better come with everything inside of you. Because he deserves nothing less."

58

Rhys

"This is a decent view," Dad says, looking through the window of my office and out onto the basketball court beneath. He turns to me, his smile from ear to ear. "You ever just go down there to play?"

"All the time," I answer, half sitting on my desk.

The day after what I'm now officially referring to as the longest day in history—the rooftop with Liv, then the playground, followed by my phone call with Dad, and we can't forget Drunk Delgado and Liv's laundry room—Dad called me again, and we spoke for another two hours. He mentioned he had some business to take care of, but he was clearing a few days off his schedule so he could come down and spend time with me.

He flew in last night, a few days post-longest day in history and, as sappy as it sounds, his presence means the world to me. And my mom —she couldn't be happier.

Dad and I spent last night poolside, while I caught him up with everything that had been going on with me. *Everything*. And he listened to every word, giving advice only when I asked for it. He didn't have a lot to offer—mainly to do what makes me happy, which...

I don't really know what that looks like right now, but I'll figure it out.

Eventually.

"Alright," Dad says, "I better go check in on the restaurant."

I push off the desk. "No days off, huh?"

He chuckles. "I'm trying." My dad has always worked hard, no matter the job. It's his work ethic and dedication that allowed my mom to live out her childhood dream of owning a one-of-a-kind cake shop. Smashed cake, served in a cup, with your choice of icing and toppings. It was the Subway of cakes, and they appropriately called it A Cup of Cake. Simple and to the point, sure, but A Cup of Cake has over 170 locations within the U.S. and even more worldwide, so while my dad got the ball rolling, my mom is the one who took that ball and turned it into what it is today. They now spend their days buying and selling businesses. My job, should I have taken it, would have been to expand their portfolio into the sports and tech space. I chose, instead, to be an assistant coach of a high school basketball team. But I have my reasons, and now that Dad is fully aware of those reasons, he backs me a hundred percent.

"Call me when you're leaving here so I can meet you at that building of yours," Dad says, stopping at the doorway. "Good job on snapping that one up. The things you can do there are endless."

"Thanks," I tell him, trying to hide my reaction to the pride in his voice.

He takes a step out, and that's as far as he gets before "*oomph*."

I rush to the door, only to see Olivia standing just outside, holding a potted plant to her chest. "I'm so sorry," Dad tells her, grasping her elbow to keep her upright.

I watch, wide-eyed, as Olivia finds her footing, then smiles up at him. "It's okay," she says, and she's... smiling. And I don't know what's more surprising—the tone in her voice or that she's *here*. It's a Thursday morning, which means that Oscar's in with Belinda, so...

"You must be Olivia," Dad says, and *what the fuck?* I'd told him about Olivia, filled him in on the parts Mom wouldn't have known, and... maybe I spent a little too long describing her in detail, but that was supposed to be between him and me. He turns to me, his grin as goofy as the thumbs-up he offers. "You're right, son, she really is something else."

"Dad..."

Olivia giggles, her cheeks flaming pink. "You must be Mr. Garrett?" Liv says, tucking the plant under one arm to shake his hand. "I've heard horrible things about you."

"Liv..."

Dad... *laughs*. This *boom* of a sound that came from deep in his gut. "I've heard some pretty horrible things about you, too," he says, but he's smiling, and so is she, and what the fuck universe am I in right now?

Liv grins from ear to ear, and again, *what the fuck?* "And, yet, here we both are," she muses.

"That we are," Dad agrees, nodding. He turns to me. "Call me later."

I nod in return, and that's all I can do because their interaction has left me speechless.

Liv watches Dad walk away until his footsteps thud down the staircase, and then she faces me. "Good morning."

"Morning," I reply, giving her the side-eye. "You're back."

She enters my office as if I invited her. I didn't. "Sure am," she says, placing the potted plant on the corner of my desk, right next to the LEGO avocado Max had given me. She turns the avocado an inch in the wrong direction, just to mess with me. Then she sits on the couch, not a care in the world, and I move the avocado back to the right position before resting on the edge of my desk again. I cross my arms, give her my full attention. "What's up?"

"Nothing." She shrugs. "I just woke up with this realization, and it compelled me to get my shit together."

"Well..." I lower my arms to my sides. "I'm happy for you?" It comes out as a question, because I really don't know what to say. And I definitely don't know how to react to her being here. Besides, you know... wanting to throw her down face-first onto my desk so I can lift her skirt and fuck my insecurities away. But... I've tried that and it didn't end well, so...

"I never realized how lucky I was."

I scoff, unable to comprehend how the hell she got to that conclu-
sion. "You're the least lucky person I know, Liv."

"Nah," she says, waving a hand in the air. "I've had a few days to
think about it, and I realized that until my grandparents died, I had a
pretty great life. I had an amazing childhood that only they could offer.
I had a best friend in my brother, who I got to—and still get to—do life
with. And I had you."

A breath catches in my throat, but I don't let it show. "Me?"

Liv nods, then smiles—and that smile fills my lungs with oxygen
again. "Most people spend their entire lives searching for their soul
mate, all so they can fall in love." She stands, steps closer, but doesn't
quite touch me. "And you know why I'm lucky, *Coach Garrett*?"

I lift my chin but keep my eyes on her, all the while gripping the
edge of the desk to control my hands, stop them from reaching out and
grabbing her. "Why?"

"Because I've gotten to experience that twice in my lifetime." She
turns away before I can come up with a response and is already at my
door when I call out her name. She stops in her tracks, turns to me.

And then I ask her something I've been stewing over for days. "The
other day, at the playground, you said something..."

For the first time since she showed up, she drops the bravado, lets
her vulnerability show. "That I've loved you for years?"

I nod. "Did you mean it?"

Her gaze drops, and I wait. Wait. Wait some more. Finally, she looks
up, a reverence in her stare that steals my breath. "I love you, Rhys
Garrett," she says, and it's more than just words. It's a declaration. "And
I'll make you believe me again. But more, I'll make you believe *in* me.
Even if it takes another three years. Hell, even if it takes the rest of my
life."

59

Olivia

I don't know what I expected to happen after I made my stupid declaration to "win Rhys back"—whatever that means—but it seems to have had the opposite effect. He didn't return to school for the rest of the week, nor did he reply to the two text messages I sent him over the weekend. He also didn't answer the one time I tried to call.

There's only so much a girl can do before her desperation turns to humiliation, and I think I passed that point when Miss Turner caught me trying to break into his office early Monday morning. To be fair, I was there to water the plant I'd given him. Or, at least, that was my excuse. It's Thursday now—an entire week since I'd seen him—and I'm losing my mind. And a little self-esteem, if I'm being honest. I guess it wouldn't be so bad if he'd just communicate with me, even if it's to tell me he wants nothing to do with me. I'd accept that over whatever is happening because it doesn't make sense.

It's not like Rhys to shy away from facing things head on.

Something is off.

I can feel it deep in my gut.

And I'm going to get to the bottom of it.

There are two people in this world who would know where he is, and they're both sitting in the same room right now. I wait until the door to Miss Turner's office opens and Oscar appears before pressing my hands to his chest and forcing him back inside. I shut the door behind me, determined, and turn to them.

Their eyes shift from me to each other, silently communicating something I have no perception of.

"Where is he?" I ask, and I sound deranged. No sleep and no answers can do that to someone.

Miss Turner sighs, while Oscar shrugs, says, "What are you talking about?"

Yeah, something is definitely wrong.

"Olivia," Miss Turner says. "You can't come barging in here like that. It's not—"

"What?" I huff. "Not appropriate? You know what else isn't appropriate? Leaving me in the dark like this. I know you know where he is, and I just wish someone would tell me, because—"

"He's out of town," Oscar cuts in.

"Oscar," Miss Turner scolds.

Oscar shrugs again. "It's a family thing."

"Bullshit," I snap. "If that's all it was, he'd tell me." I look between them, but their pitiful stares have me pulling back an inch. My anger ebbs, turns to confusion. "Right?" I ask. "He'd tell me..."

They don't respond, just look at each other before facing me again. There's an ache in my chest, a tightness I can't ignore. I lower my gaze, the veil of denial suddenly lifting from my eyes. "Well..." Heat burns behind my eyes, but I blink it away. I ask, only so I know when to prepare for the inevitable. "Do you know when he'll be back?"

"No, Olivia. We don't," Miss Turner says, her eyes downcast.

"Oscar?" I ask, looking right at him, but he refuses to meet my eyes.

I take a step back, my heart heavy. "You guys are horrible liars, you know that, right?" I don't wait for a response because I know it won't come. I just turn for the door, put my hand on the knob.

"Olivia," says Miss Turner. I pause, but I don't turn around. "There are a lot of things in this life that you have every right to take personally. Please don't let this be one of them."

60

Olivia

My grandpa always kept his tools in pristine condition, and everything had its place. I... do not. I remember him telling me once that your workspace is an extension of your mind, and I didn't quite grasp what that meant... until now, apparently. Because my mind is a mess and so is my workspace. And my room. And the entire house, if I'm being honest. And since I can't do much about my mental state, I may as well do something about my physical one. Who knows? Maybe it will help. It better. Or else I don't know why I'm out here at midnight, on a Saturday night, sorting out sandpaper by grit.

Dom sets down my water bottle on the bench beside a stack of sandpaper, and I should really put a bell around his neck, because I had no idea he was even in here. I remove my headphones to glare at him.

"You're not drinking enough water," he tells me. "You'll get sick."

I roll my eyes. "Thanks, *Dad*." I expect him to leave, but he just stands there, his hip on the workbench, watching me. "Was there something else?"

"Are you okay?"

I focus on the sandpaper, start sorting again. "I'm fine."

"Ollie..." He covers my hand with his, stopping me from my task. "You know you can talk to me, right? Even if it's about Garrett."

"It's nothing."

"You moping around the way you have been doesn't seem like nothing."

I sigh, try to push down my emotions, and Dom grasps my shoulders, forcing me to face him. "Talk to me." My exhale comes out shaky, and he dips his head to meet my gaze. "Please?"

I sniff back my heartache. "I told him I loved him, and he... bailed."

"*Bailed?*"

I shrug. "I don't know where he's gone, but he's not at school, and he's not answering my calls or replying to my texts. He's not even reading them. And everyone—" I roll my eyes. "Not *everyone,* but the two people who would know where he might be are covering for him, and—"

"Did you ask Oscar?"

"He's one of the two people."

Dom's shoulders drop, the pity in his eyes only making things worse.

"I don't know what I did," I cry, and then I fall into my brother's embrace because there's no one else to catch me. My tears soak into his T-shirt while he holds me, soothes me with his hand on my back. "I thought I could make him love me back, but I guess he can't. Not after what I did to him."

"Ollie." He pulls away, knees bent to look me in the eyes. In my mind, he's always been my little brother, but right now... I feel so frighteningly small. "He'd be the luckiest guy on earth to be at the receiving end of your love. It's *his* loss."

I want to believe him. I do. But... "I can't imagine my life without—" My phone rings on the bench, and I'm quick to check it. Rhys's name flashes on the screen, and Dom and I look from the phone to each other. "It's him," I whisper.

"Answer it," Dom urges. "Maybe you'll get the closure you need."

I wipe the tears from my eyes and take a breath. Then another. And then I square my shoulders before hitting *answer.* "Hello?"

There's nothing at his end... nothing but heavy, uneven exhales, as if he can't catch his breath.

"Rhys?" My heart picks up, and I step away from my brother as if that will somehow help me hear better. "Are you there?"

The same breathing, only now, a strangled sound comes with it. Almost like a cry. And then comes a sob that wretches through every inch of me.

Gaze scattered, I ignore the sharp ache in my chest and try again. This time, his name is a plea. "Rhys!"

The heavy breathing stops, just for a moment, just long enough for him to shudder three simple words that stop my heart from beating. *"I need you."*

* * *

The drive to Rhys's house feels endless, and by the time I get there, I'm so filled with adrenaline I can't see straight. My tires screech as I come to a stop just outside his iron gates. His closed gates. I stumble out of the car and press the buzzer on the panel, again and again.

Again and again.

No one answers.

Nothing moves.

I step back to look at the height of the fence, wishing I could climb it, but it's so damn high, and I'm so damn weak, but that adrenaline... It fools me into thinking otherwise. Rhys's house backs up into the woods on one side, and I find a tree close enough to the fence line and climb it. The skin on my palms and shin tear from the sharp bark, but I ignore the pain, and run up the driveway—the ache in my bones nothing compared to the fear in my heart. I race up the front steps, ignoring my body screaming in pain. Physical. Emotional. I slam my fist on the door. Press the doorbell. Scream. Kick. Over and over. Again and again.

After what feels like forever, a light turns on overhead, and the door opens just a tad. "What in—" Rhys's dad doesn't have time to finish before I'm pushing the door open on him and *running*. Through the foyer and into the kitchen, stopping at the rear sliding doors. His dad runs after me, calling for his wife, and I slide the door open and crash into outdoor furniture to get to the pool house. It's dark. Everywhere. Out in the yard. Into the pool house. Inside me. Nothing but darkness. I try to slide the glass door open, but it won't budge. My open palms meet the glass, slam against it until a shooting pain ricochets up my arm and directly into my heart. "Rhys!"

"Olivia," Skylar yells. "What are you doing?"

"Get the *fucking* keys!" I try to open the door again, but of course, nothing's changed. I peer into the glass, into the darkness and I see him... "Oh God..." He's nothing but a silhouette on the floor of the kitchen, his back against the island, one hand in his hair, the other beside him... holding a gun. "Rhys!" I scream.

I turn around, face three sets of eyes all on me. His mom, dad, sister. I almost choke on my words. "He's got a gun."

"No no no no no," his mom whispers, and she's off, running back into the house while his dad tries to forcefully open the door.

I grab the nearest metal chair and yell, "Move!"

"Dad?" Rhys's sister cries, and Mr. Garrett moves out of the way just in time to miss the chair I throw at the door. Glass shatters so fast, yet so slow... and I jump through the opening and rush toward Rhys, dropping to my knees and pushing the gun away. "Rhys." I hold his head in my hands, force him to look at me.

His shoulders shake, his chest rising and falling, but his gaze is so far in the distance, there's no way he can see me. "I can't— I can't—"

"Breathe," I cry, and he shakes his head.

Tiny breaths, spurts of it, like hiccups... "Liv..."

"Where the hell did he get a gun?" his dad asks, and I don't know who he's talking to.

"Rhys..." A light flicks on, followed by Mrs. Garrett's gasp. "I need you to look at me, baby."

He can't see me. Can't feel me here with him. I look around, not sure for what, and then I get to my feet while his mother drops to her knees beside him.

I round the island and find a mixing bowl, then open the fridge to detach the ice container from the dispenser. I dump all the ice into the bowl, then fill it with water, never once stopping to wipe the flood of tears pouring out of me. "Grab a chair," I tell Mr. Garrett. "Put it in front of him." He rushes to do as I say, and I place the bowl on the chair. Then I kneel beside Rhys again, help him up just enough so I can guide his face into the water.

Bubbles of oxygen float to the surface of the bowl while I count to three, then pull him back by his shoulders. "Again," I whisper, unable to take a full breath through the strength of my cries. "One more time."

61

Rhys

I get curious about death.

Not the finality of death or even the act of dying. More like... what would happen if?

I can't see her.

But I can *feel* her with me.

I can hear her voice.

Feel her touch.

Feel her eyes on me as she wipes away the ice-cold water from my face, only to lead me to it again. Every time she does it, I feel my entire body turn to ice, feel my heart slow, feel my lungs expand... even while I feel like I'm drowning.

But I can't drown, I remind myself.

Every breath I take is for her.

And the more breaths I take, the more I get to float.

I can barely keep my head up, but she's here, stopping me from falling into the liquid darkness.

She's *here.*

And so am I. "I made you a promise," I try to tell her, but my throat's closed in on itself, and nothing comes out.

"What?" She holds my face again—cold, wet hands keeping me steady. Keeping me safe. "What did you say?"

"I made you a promise," I croak, my words finally audible. "You breathe, *I* breathe."

62

Olivia

There was a stillness in the air during the aftermath of my grandparents' death. It felt like it was instant, though I'm sure it wasn't. One second there were flashing lights and people everywhere, and once they'd taken the bodies away, there was just me.

And Max.

And the stillness that surrounded us.

At least that's how it felt.

I know, in reality, that was far from what happened, but most days, when the memories of that night flood my mind, that's all I can remember.

The stillness.

I don't know how many times Rhys's face lowers to that bowl, but eventually, he no longer needs me to guide him. He does it himself, holding air in his lungs for longer than I'm comfortable... and when he brings his face back up again, I run a towel over his eyes first, then his entire face.

"I love you," I whisper, in between dunks.

And we repeat the process. Again and again. And I don't know how much time passes while he does this, and I don't care.

I'll wait for an eternity for my hope to arrive.

With every ice bath to his face, his shoulders loosen, his breaths even, and his vision clears.

And then comes the stillness.

The silence.

"Liv," he breathes, his hands reaching for mine. He pulls me toward him, and I willingly fall into his arms. For minutes, he holds me, drenching me in his embrace. "Please, Liv..."

"What do you need?" I choke out.

"You," he says. "I need *you*... take me with you."

I glance over my shoulder at the three bodies all huddled together, holding on to each other as they watch us. "My car's outside the gates. The keys are still in the ignition." I focus on Mr. Garrett. "Please bring it up to the top of the driveway."

"Rhys, no!" his mom cries. "Stay, so we can—"

"Let him go," his sister cuts in, an edge of finality in her tone. She moves away from her parents and kneels next to Rhys, cups his face in her tiny, shaky hands. "You're a hundred percent of my fifty, Rhys."

* * *

Dominic's sitting on the bottom of the stairs when I open the door, and he stands when Rhys and I enter. "Is everything okay?" he asks, rushing toward me. "Jesus, Ollie, you're bleeding."

"What?" Rhys speaks for the first time since we left his house. He turns to me just as Dom reaches for my forehead.

I shy away from his touch, and he lowers his hand. "I'm fine," I tell them, pressing my fingers to the spot on my head that's been throbbing. I know I hit it on something when I jumped down from the fence, but I didn't realize...

"I'm sorry," Rhys whispers, his gaze lowered.

"Stop." I take his one hand in both of mine and face Dom head on. "I'm fine," I repeat. "I promise. And I promise I'll explain everything, but right now..." I trail off, shifting my eyes to Rhys standing beside me. "We just need to get to bed."

Dom looks from Rhys to me, and whatever he sees has him nodding slowly. "Okay."

"Thank you," I mouth, before turning us away.

As soon as we're in my room, I tell Rhys to get into bed while I clean up. I wait until he's sitting on the edge of my bed to go to the bathroom, close the door between us. The harshness of the bathroom lights has me squinting, and I stand in front of the mirror, unable to recognize my reflection. Eyes half-hooded, blood trickling from my hairline... I run the tap and soak a washcloth under the stream, then dab at the crimson coating my flesh.

The door opens, and Rhys appears, stepping right up to me. I lower my gaze when he takes the washcloth from me to finish what I started. "I'm sorry," he says again, and I shake my head.

"Please, don't be sorry."

"You were the only one..." he murmurs, sniffing once. He turns me to him, lifting me up so I can sit on the counter. Then he holds my head in his hands, wiping a line across my forehead. The warmth of his harsh breaths coats my face, and I stare into his eyes—his sad, all-consuming slate-colored eyes. "You were the only one I thought to call. The only one who could stop me. But I didn't think..."

I grasp his wrists, pull them down and wrap my legs around him to bring him closer. So close I can feel his heartbeat change the air between us. "Didn't think what?"

"I saw your face, Liv. It was all I could see. And I saw the fear in your eyes and I..." He drops his gaze between us. "Your grandparents..."

I'd held it together from the stillness and all the way on the drive here, but now... Now I break down in his arms, the events of the night catching up to me. I cry, the sobs so strong they're uncontrollable. He holds me, just like I hold him.

"I'm sorry, baby."

"I don't want you to be sorry," I cry. "I just want you to *be*."

63

Rhys

Liv and I don't sleep. We lie in the semi-darkness of her room, our hands held between us, and our eyes never leaving each other. We don't talk about what happened. We don't talk about what will happen. We don't talk at all. We just exist, in the same room, in the same life, in the same heartbeat.

The darkness turns to light, night turns to day, and nothing has changed.

We hear Max and Dominic moving and talking, getting ready for school, and right before they leave, Liv gets a text. It's the only time the entire night she checks her phone. "I'll be back," she says, pressing her lips to mine.

My pulse immediately picks up when she's gone, my throat closing in, and *I can't breathe without her*.

The realization dawns, slow but solid, and it puts my feelings into perspective. Into words.

I can't breathe without her.

It's the only thought that's made sense ever since—

I reach over to her nightstand for my phone, see the missed calls and texts from my family. I ignore every one of the notifications but the lone message from my sister.

IZZY

> I would've killed for you, too, Rhys... but please don't die for me.

I sit up, suddenly aware of the position I put her in. My parents. Liv... I heave out a breath, the realization making my head spin.

"You okay?" Liv asks when she's back in the room.

"Yeah," I lie, then hate myself for it.

Liv nods, sitting on the edge of the bed. "Dom told Max you were here, and he made you this." She hands me a sheet of paper—a drawing of an avocado. My heart smiles, even though my body can't. She points to the words written beneath it—*The Fruit of Testicles*. "He made Dom write testicles because he couldn't spell it."

I stare at the drawing for a long moment before placing it on the bed beside me. "Do you think it would be okay if my sister comes over?"

"Of course," she answers, then pauses a beat. "Your mom has called me so many times, and I don't like—"

"I know," I cut in. "I'll handle it. But first, I need to speak to my sister."

* * *

By midday, Liv's house is filled with more bodies than she's had people walk through her front door. Ever. My sister got here a couple of hours ago, and we had the talk that's been a long time coming. As soon as I had her approval, I called my parents. Then Belinda and Curtis. And then Oscar. They all dropped everything to be here.

It's obvious Liv has no clue what's happening, so she doesn't know what to do, how to act, how to *feel*. She sits on the couch, her gaze distant while the world moves on around her.

My sister sits in an armchair in the corner of the room, her legs tucked in beneath her. My mom, Belinda, and Curtis are on chairs brought in from the kitchen. Dad stands behind Mom, and Oscar sits on the floor.

I sit on the couch next to Liv, my focus shifting to everyone in the room. One by one, I lock eyes with them, finding pockets of encouragement and determination between the anguish. I finish on my sister, the *hundred percent of my fifty*. Until I met Liv, my sister was the strongest person I knew. Now they're on par with each other. "Are you sure, Iz?"

She nods, and I expect her to drop her gaze or at least look away, but she doesn't. She stares right into my eyes, and I take a fragment of her strength and face Olivia.

"There's so much—" I start to say, but I'm interrupted by her front door opening. Dominic freezes in the doorway between the living room and entryway, his eyes going wide at the number of people in the room. "I had some free periods," he murmurs, then throws a thumb over his shoulder. "But I'll come back."

"You should stay," I say, surprising myself. "This involves Liv, so it involves you, too."

Dom glances around the room before crossing the threshold and silently sits next to Oscar on the floor.

They don't greet each other.

No one says a word.

They just wait, watching me, because I'm the only one who has something to say.

I turn to Liv. "Do you remember the night I came over, and we did that thing with the twine?"

Liv nods, her brow dipped slightly. "Yes?"

"Do you have something like that I can do?" I flex my fingers. "I need something to do with my hands if I'm—"

She turns her entire body to mine, one leg up on the couch, and offers me her hands. "Right here," she says, wiggling her fingers.

I match her position, hold on to her hands, and brush my thumbs along the backs of her fingers. And I don't know how she does it. How this simple touch can set off something so ingrained, so visceral, inside me. Lifting her hands, I kiss the tips of her fingers, then lower them again.

I look from our touch to my sister—one last time. One last out. She simply nods, urging me to go on. And so I do...

"It was the summer after my freshman year..."

64

Rhys

It was the summer after my freshman year and my sister's junior. A couple of months earlier, she secretly applied for a job as a lifeguard at a summer camp, and they offered her the position. She kept it from everyone because she knew how my parents would feel about it. My sister, Izzy, is incredibly smart. Gifted, really. But the level of intelligence that Izzy has, unfortunately, comes with a slew of other problems.

Socially, she struggles with awareness and the emotional cues of others. The first time I noticed it was in elementary school—when a bunch of kids teased her about the food she ate and *how* she ate it. The next day, she returned with enough food for them all. She gathered them in a circle to teach them how to divide carrot sticks into equal segments for consumption—just like she does. Even during this, they continued to tease her, and she... she continued to smile, carry on as if nothing was happening. The day after that, I punched the ringleader of those asshole kids right in his nose. Broke it. I was in third grade.

It was those types of situations that had my parents weary of her decision while also wanting to encourage her to be independent. She was seventeen, but her developmental mind was that of someone much younger.

In the end, they caved and allowed her to go on the condition that she call every day.

She was supposed to be gone for eight weeks.

She returned after two.

And the Izzy who came back was not the same one who left.

She was guarded; didn't like to be in a room alone, didn't like the quiet, didn't want to be hugged... even by me—someone she used to have to force to give her affection. I knew something was wrong, but when I asked her, she just shrugged. And when I asked my parents, they greeted me with silence. But there were whispers throughout the house and heated conversations behind closed doors.

I'd catch my dad in fits of anger... my mom constantly in tears...

And my sister...

...it's like she wasn't even there.

One day, I answered a knock on the door, and there was a woman on the other side. She introduced herself as a detective and asked to see my parents. I sat in Izzy's room, watching her stare out the window... and she was just... blank. Empty. I asked her if she wanted a hug, just to test the waters...

She shook her head and looked at me... and the tears in her eyes... I'd never felt heartbreak until that moment. It was the first time she said it...

"You're a hundred percent of my fifty, Rhys."

My mom came into her room not long after and gently coaxed her away, locked her in her office with the detective. I tried to listen in through the door, but all I could hear was muffled conversation.

And my sister's cries.

That night, I lay on the floor of her room, and she lay in her bed. She had a night-light on. She didn't turn it off like she normally did, and when I offered to do it for her, she said to leave it. I remember lying there, looking at the glow of stars on her ceiling created by a light she had when she was a fucking toddler, and I don't know why...

I don't know why it was that moment that fueled a sudden rage inside of me. She'd reverted to being a child... a hopeless child who was afraid of the fucking dark. And I knew it wasn't her fault. I just knew it...

I waited until I knew my parents had gone to bed and found the key to my mom's office. I went in there and sifted through her desk drawers looking for... I don't even know what I expected to find; I just know that it wasn't there. So, I turned on her computer, went through her emails, and then her files... and I found it... the police report.

I sat in there with the door locked and the computer screen my only source of light, and I read

Every

Single

Word

In the voice of my sister.

Nick Harper was a camp counselor in his mid-thirties who had spent days grooming my sister—taking advantage of her young mind and then... taking advantage of *her*.

After my sister's allegation, the camp suspended him from his position and put him on *paid* leave. I couldn't see through my tears. Through my anger. But when I saw a note attached to the file stating "Not enough evidence", I couldn't see through my rage.

* * *

Nick was easy to find. His name and address were listed and his socials were open for anyone to see. He had a wife. Three kids. All girls. I don't know why that last piece of information sent me spiraling, but it did.

The car picked me up just outside my house at close to one in the morning and drove me the two hours to Nick's house. I walked around the neighborhood, waiting for darkness to turn into light, and then hid behind an oak tree on the opposite side of the street, waiting for my opportunity.

I didn't know what I planned to do once I came face to face with him. I just knew that I wanted to hurt him.

It was close to seven in the morning when the front door to Nick's house opened. I watched as his wife and daughters got into the car and left, and then I crossed the street and onto their property. The house was small, single story, and I walked around it, looking for an open window or something.

Anything.

The backyard had a kiddie pool, and there were these dolls lying in the dirt... the same dolls my sister used to play with, and seeing them... seeing them just doubled my rage. The screen door on the rear of the house was closed but not locked, and the main door was wide open. I stepped inside as quietly as possible and right into a laundry room. The house was dead silent. No TV, no movement. Nothing. I found myself in the small living room filled with toys, and I ignored everything else around me when I saw the fire poker next to the fireplace.

He was asleep—face down, his arm tucked beneath the pillow, and—

There wasn't a single thought in my mind.

Just this... outburst of fury.

Rage.

Violence.

The first blow was to the back of his head, and I remember being surprised by how much blood sprayed across the room. He awoke, flipped over, and shielded his face with his arms. But I just kept going, holding the fire poker in both my hands and swinging downward. Over and over. I didn't aim for a specific spot. Didn't look at the damage. I just... kept going. And then—

Then there was this squeal, and I think it was the only thing that could've made me pause. I looked to the doorway, to the little girl standing there, and I remember... I remember cursing at myself because I didn't count the number of girls that got in the car.

There were only two.

Her eyes were big, blue, and so full of fear when she looked at her blood-covered dad and then me... and as soon as she looked in my eyes... she pissed herself... I saw it trickle down her pajama bottoms...

She ran out of the house.

And I should've run, too. Not to follow her, but to flee. But there was this man on the bed, groaning in pain, and he was still breathing while my sister was at home, afraid to be alone, afraid to be touched, afraid of the dark... She was dead inside, and in my mind, it only made sense that he should be dead too.

He was coughing blood, his arms at his sides, and there was blood *everywhere*. It didn't stop me from dropping the fire poker and climbing on top of him. I wrapped my hands around his throat and squeezed.

His eyes were brown, bloodshot, and I squeezed harder, harder, harder.

I couldn't stop.

Even when I heard the sirens...

Even when the cops were pulling me off him... I couldn't...

I couldn't finish the job.

I was arrested, pleaded guilty, because there needed to be a punishment that fit the crime.

It was the sole reason I was there in the first place.

I don't go into the details about juvie because Liv, the only person who I'm really telling all this to, already knows about it. But, after Curtis found me the way he did, he wrote up a report, and we sued that guard—Williams—and the entire detention center, and we won. Williams was immediately dismissed and stripped of any future benefits.

Days after I got out, I bought a gun and hid it in a vent in the bathroom. I thought Williams would come for me, and this time, I wanted to be prepared. He was in my head all the time. I'd have horrible nightmares—*flashbacks*—of him, the other boys, the beatings...

At the beginning, they were so bad that the only way I thought to stop them was to end it all. One night, I was about to do just that. I was sitting at the edge of the pool, loading the gun, when I got a text...

I look up for the first time since I started talking and right into Liv's tear-filled eyes. I release her hands, just long enough to wipe at her cheeks. "You asked me if I ever felt like I wasn't breathing. Do you remember that?"

Liv nods, releasing a sob that tears through her.

"Swear, Liv, your words... I'd never felt so seen. So protected by someone who didn't even know me. And then that night when you hit me with your truck? I told you I left my farewell party, and I meant it... that night, I was going to..." I trail off, not needed to say anymore. "You saved me, more times than you even know... Every time I felt that darkness creeping in, I picked up my phone and you were there. Always. But... I think I'd somehow blocked out the events of the day that got me thrown in juvie—the day I entered Nick's house and did what I did. I blocked it all out, and I never thought about it, until last week..." I swallow the knot in my throat. "Last week, we found out that another girl had accused that motherfucker of the same thing. But this time, she had proof—video footage from one of those nanny cams. When the investigators looked into him, they saw *multiple* accusations, all with the same ending—*not enough evidence*. The prosecutors reached out to all the girls, including Izzy, and they wanted her to testify in court. She agreed to do it, and I wanted to be there for her, but I didn't think about how seeing him would affect me... mentally. I hadn't slept in days. I still haven't. Every time I close my eyes, I see his face covered in crimson, see his bloodshot eyes staring back at me, fucking *pleading* for his life. I keep feeling his neck between my hands... and I keep thinking about how... how if I'd just finished him then... maybe I could've saved the other girls. And that's what I was thinking about last night when I grabbed the gun, but... I told you I needed you, and you came for me. You protected me. You stopped me from drowning. You forced me to *breathe*. One more time. Every time." I press my lips to hers. "I've loved you for years, Olivia. From the first time you saved me and all the times in between. I loved you then, now, and always."

For the first time since I started bleeding my soul to a filled room, I look around. My mom and sister are crying. So is Belinda. My dad's looking out the window, his fists balled, and Oscar and Dominic have their heads bowed. Curtis has left the room, and I know why. He's heard this story before, and it's ruined him in ways I can't even fathom.

Curtis and Belinda have two girls, and even though he's seen the worst of the worst, it's different when it's someone he knows. I focus on Dad again. "Dad?" I say and wait for him to turn to me. "I know you guys will want me to move back into the house, but I can't... I can't go back there. There's just too much—"

"I can buy you another house by the end of the day, son," he says, already pulling out his phone.

Mom wipes at her tears. "And I can have it furnished by tomorrow."

Dad adds, "And for now, we're staying here. All of us. And your mother and I can take turns staying with each of you, until your sister graduates, and then—"

"And then we can see what happens then. But we'll make it work. Whatever you need. As long as it's not pushing us away."

"I'm not pushing away," I say, exhausted. "That's not what I want."

"Then what do you want?"

I tighten my grasp on Liv's hand. "I don't..."

"I'll buy another house," Dad says.

"No." All attention shifts to Dominic, who's sat silent this entire time. He lifts his head, his eyes red, raw, and right on mine. "You're staying here with us."

65

Rhys

It's been almost a week of me staying with Liv, and I can't sleep. Again. And not for the same reasons as before. I don't have those same dreams or thoughts when I have Liv in my arms, but my mind is restless, and so my body is, too.

I haven't gone back to St. Luke's yet, and I don't know if I ever will, which means I'm going to have to have that conversation with Oscar, and I don't know if I'm ready for it.

I'm up and out of the house before everyone else, and I don't come back until after dinner. I keep Liv posted on where I am and who I'm with... what I'm doing. Usually, I spend the days hanging out with my sister while she's still in town, and a few nights, I've babysat for Belinda and Curtis so they could go on dates—something they don't do often enough, according to Belinda. I also annoy Oscar at his work. Basically, I do whatever I can to avoid being at the house, because I don't want to disrupt their routine. In other words, I don't want to be a burden. I don't want them to feel like they have to feed me or care for me or... I guess I don't want them to pity me. I feel emasculated enough. And, yes, I know that I shouldn't be feeling that way, but it is what it is.

It's just after 3 a.m. now and the house is quiet, but the thoughts inside my head are screaming so loud that I can't lie still.

Liv's fast asleep beside me, her head on my chest, arms and legs over me as if she's afraid I'm going to up and leave and never come back. Just so we're clear, I would *never* do that to her. She's my entire world, and I don't see that changing. Ever.

Slowly, carefully, I remove her arms from around me and get out of bed. I slip on my running clothes, my shoes, and grab the set of keys she had cut for me. I leave through the glass sliding door onto her patio and then out through the side gate. The first thing I do is text her to let her know where I am, and then I run, hoping to rid my body of the nervous energy that's been simmering inside me for days.

I can't stay here forever, and I can't take Liv away from her brothers... I also need to figure out what the fuck to do with my life, because this wandering around aimlessly isn't fulfilling. Neither is running around aimlessly, apparently, because I do it for an entire hour before I'm back at the house and nothing has changed. No decisions have been made. No solutions have been found. I stand in front of her house a moment, trying to catch my breath. The only lights come from the staircase and Max's room. Max... the kid fills me with so much unexpected joy; I genuinely don't know how he does it.

Since I'm clearly not ready to get back into bed, I take the side alley to the playground behind the house and sit at the spot where I found Olivia that one time. It's weird—how long ago that interaction seems. It's only been two weeks, but it may as well be a different lifetime.

I was guarded then—still protecting my space. My heart. I was fooling myself, clearly.

The swing set groans under my weight, and I hold on to the chains as I slowly push off the ground. For minutes, I listen to the world sleep. Until I hear footsteps approaching from behind me. I turn swiftly, ready for an attack. But it's only Dominic... wrapped in a blanket... "You know I can see you from my bedroom," he says. "You good, man?"

I don't ask what he's doing out here. Or why he opted for a blanket instead of clothes, because I'm almost certain the only thing he has on underneath is boxer shorts. Instead, I stare ahead and tell him the truth. "Couldn't sleep, and I didn't want to wake Liv, so I went for a run." I shrug. "Now I'm here."

I expect him to leave, but instead, he sits on a bench beside the swings. Then he lets out a yawn, pulling the blanket tighter around him, and *this*. This is what I didn't want. To feel like a burden.

"You can stay for as long as you need," he says, and here comes the pity. "Don't feel like you have to leave."

I focus on the ground. "Thanks," I tell him, my voice low. It's not that I don't appreciate what he's saying; I do. I just... I don't know how I feel. "How did you know?" I ask.

"Know what?"

"That it had nothing to do with going back home and everything to do with—"

"Olivia?"

I nod, staring ahead.

He clears his throat, and it forces me to give him all my attention. "You know, I won't say I know what you've been through, because *fuck that*. But... I *understand* what it's like to need Ollie. After our parents died, she was the one who kept it all together. Kept *us* together. She was barely sixteen and acting like a grown-ass adult, working three jobs to make ends meet, and doing it all for us..." He pauses a breath. "This one time, Max asked me if he could call her mom, and I didn't know what to say."

I stay quiet, listening to every word.

"It's pretty messed up. Max will never get to call anyone *mom*. Liv's mom is an asshole, but she still exists, and she had my mom—her grandma. But Max... all he'll ever have is a big brother and sister."

"Yeah, but he's got some pretty great ones," I say. "That's a whole lot more than many kids have."

Dom doesn't respond right away, and so I look over at him. He's smiling from ear to ear. "You just called me *great*."

"No," I deny the truth. "What I meant was as a brother, you're great... I guess."

"You called me *great*."

"Liv thinks the world of you, so that has to mean something, right?"

Dom laughs. "Not really. She thinks highly of you, and you're a dick."

I chuckle, shaking my head as I push off the ground.

"Yo, did you see Luka Dončić play today?"

"Dude, that guy is next fucking level."

"Right? I never really enjoyed watching the Mavs until him."

"I've got a signed rookie card of his."

"Shut the fuck up."

I nod. "My dad does business with Mark Cuban, so he got it for me."

"Honestly, genuinely, and I mean this from the bottom of my heart, Garrett, *shut the fuck up*."

I bust out a laugh, and holy shit... I'd not only forgotten what my laughter sounds like, but I'd forgotten how it *feels*.

Weightless.

Free.

Floating.

The house across the road lights up, and Dom groans. "Oh, look, you've gone and woken the neighborhood."

I bite back a smile.

"I hate those fuckers," he adds, and then he flashes a middle finger to the woman peering at us through a window. The lights switch off immediately, and Dominic chuckles. "Did Ollie ever tell you about them?"

I shake my head, facing him. "No."

He gets more comfortable on the bench, then says, "So this one time I come home from a run, and there's a package on my door, right?"

"Yeah..."

"But they delivered it to the wrong house." He points to the house that was just lit up. "So, I'm like, okay, I'll do the right thing and take it over to them. I'd just been for a run, and it was raining out, so I had my sweats, hoodie up. I don't even knock on the door. I just leave the package by the door and leave. Next thing you know, the old hag who lives there posts my picture on that Next Door app, telling everyone to look out for me because I stole a fucking package from her."

Eyes wide in disbelief, I murmur, "No, she fucking didn't."

"She fucking did, Garrett!" Dominic all but shouts, sitting forward. "I didn't see it, but Ollie did, and *goddamn...*"

"Did she think you did it?"

"No!" He scoffs. "Yo, up until your boy Oscar ratted my ass out, Ollie thought I walked on water."

I shake my head, chuckling.

"So anyway... Ollie comes storming into my room, dragging my ass out of the house and all the way there—and remember, I have no idea what's going on at this point—I'm literally being dragged, barefoot, through the streets, by my hoodie..."

I can't stop laughing at the mental image because Dominic's twice the size of Liv, and he could've stopped her, I'm sure, but he just let her do it, and it's funny because I'd let my sister do the same. No doubt.

"So, she's slamming her hand on the fucking door, yelling, 'Open up, you ugly bitch!'"

I'm holding my stomach, trying to ease the ache from laughing so hard.

"The ugly bitch opens the door, and Ollie practically pushes me into her. And she goes: 'This is my little brother Dominic Delgado! He's the starting power forward for Philips Academy and top of his class! He has better things to do than steal your shit! Now take down that fucking post, or I'm going to come back here, fuck your husband, and give him a kid he's actually proud of!'"

I'm *dying*. "She did not say that!"

"The fuck she did!" he yells. "And then... as we're leaving, still dragging me by my hood, she turns back to the woman and says, 'And if you so much as think about posting this anywhere on the Internet, I'm going to come back in the middle of the night and burn down your fucking house, with you and all your ugly-ass kids inside it!'"

I bust out a guffaw. "The fuck am I getting myself into?"

"Someone who's got your back, one hundred," he says, turning serious.

I let the remnants of my laughter filter out of me until it's quiet again.

Then he says, "Hey, I know! Maybe we should egg it."

I roll my eyes at his dig. "We could always superglue a giant dick to the front door."

He laughs at that, and I'm right there with him. "Yo," he says, jerking his head to the street. "Is that your boy?"

I squint, trying to get a better look, and sure enough, "Oscar!" I call out.

Oscar stops in his tracks, looks over at us before making his way over. "Garrett," he greets, then nods at Dominic. "Delgado." He looks between us, shoving his hands in his pockets. "Well well well, how the turntables..."

With a chuckle, I ask, "What are you doing up so early?"

"Up? Early?" He parks his ass on the swing beside me. "Brother, I haven't been to bed yet."

I sigh. "Does your mom know?"

"She thinks I'm staying at your house," he says, kicking off the ground. He actually *swings,* shifting the entire metal frame. "So, what's good, motherfuckers?" he asks, just as more lights flick on at the house across the road.

Oscar groans. "Not this fucking Karen."

"She's the worst, right?" Dom murmurs.

"Speaking of Karen," Oscar says, his tone picking up. "She's coming home this weekend, right?"

Karen's one of our good friends, and even though many rumors have spread about the two of us, I consider her one of the boys. "Yeah, I think so," I answer.

Dom pipes up. "Karen Thatcher?"

I turn to him, try to hide my grin. "Yeah, why?"

Dom looks away, attempts to play it cool. "Nothin'."

"Delgado and Karen, sittin' in tree..." Oscar sings, and I chuckle under my breath.

"We're hanging out this weekend—" I start to tell Dominic, but he interrupts me.

"Does my sister know?"

"Yes, she'll be there too." I roll my eyes. "So, I take it you don't want to come with?"

"I never said that," Dom's quick to respond, while Oscar continues his song, "f u c k i n g, first comes..." he trails off when a police cruiser pulls up to the curb.

"Oh shit," Dominic murmurs.

Oscar looks past me and at him. "Are you naked under that blanket?"

The cruiser's door opens, and even in the darkness, I can make out Curtis's silhouette. He walks toward us while Dom asks, "Should we bail?"

"Nah," I tell him.

When Curtis gets close enough to be lit up by the lamp post nearby, he asks, "What's good, boys?" He takes a seat on the bench next to Dominic, stretching out his arms on the back of it.

"Just chillin'," I tell him, while Dominic looks at him sideways, and Oscar...

Oscar laughs so loud I'm sure he's waking the neighborhood. "Aren't we a bunch of mismatched motherfuckin' misfits!"

66

Rhys

It's close to five when I get back into bed, and Liv hisses the moment I touch her, turning in my arms. "What the fuck?" she croaks, half asleep. "Why are you so cold?" She sniffs my bare chest. "And why do you smell like outside?"

"Outside has a smell?" I muse, wrapping her in my arms... and legs. "Warm me up."

She pulls back, just her head, because I've got a pretty tight hold on every other part of her. "Where have you been?"

"At the playground."

"Doing...?"

"Just hanging out with your brother."

"Okay." She twists out of my hold and reaches over me to flick on her lamp. "You were just *hanging out* with my brother?"

I take advantage of her position and grab her ass, set her right down where I want her. "We need to get you some smart lights," I tell her.

After adjusting her position so she's comfortable on me, she sits up taller, flattens her hands on my chest. Her hair's an absolute mess, and her clothes are all skewed, and she only has one eye open, but God, she's never been more beautiful. "What are smart lights?"

"The ones you can control by voice."

Her head tilts while a smile tugs on her lips. "Oh, yeah. I want those."

"I'll order some tomorrow." I run my hand up her bare thigh, stroke my thumb just beneath her sleep shorts.

"So, you were out with Dominic?"

I nod. "I'll explain later."

"Why not now?"

I sit up, just enough so I can kiss her neck. "Because we're busy right now."

"Wait." She pushes on my shoulders until I'm flat on my back again. "What's going on?"

I can understand why she's questioning me, because even though we've stayed in the same bed for almost a week now, we haven't had sex. We've found intimacy in other ways, sure. We've held each other, kissed (a lot) and we've been close... but I don't know. I didn't want her to think I was *only* here for that, and besides, my mind hasn't been all that clear.

Until now.

"I just forgot for a moment," I tell her.

"Forgot what?"

"What I have and how good I have it." I pause a breath, trying to catch my thoughts. "I guess I didn't want you to think that I was pouring my emotions into you, physically..."

"Okay..." She smiles to one side, then lowers herself onto me. Breasts pressed to my chest, she kisses my collarbone, makes her way up my neck, and I raise my hips. "But can you pour *other things* into me, physically..."

"Fuck, baby." I slide my hand under her tank top, all the way to her neck, and tug her hair just enough so she pulls away. "You'll have to be quiet."

Liv sits up, grinding her hips on my too-hard cock, and I help her remove her top. My mouth instantly finds her nipple, rock hard against my tongue. She arches her back, a moan falling from her lips. I cover her mouth, and the single move has her eyes rolling back in pleasure. I flip us until she's on her back and I'm on top. I continue with her nipples, smiling when she writhes beneath me. One after the other, I lick, suck, bite. All the while covering her mouth with my hand. When I hear her high-pitched moan, begging for more, I make my way down her stomach, my wet tongue leaving a trail behind. I tug down her shorts, and her shorts alone. Leave her in her white underwear. She sits up on her elbows, watching my every move. And I don't waste any time. I run my tongue along her slit, over her underwear. "Rhys..." she whispers, and I do it again. "Stop teasing me."

I glide the pad of my fingers over her underwear, moaning when the wet fabric outlines her slit. "I'll fucking tease you as much as I want," I say, tugging on the fabric until I get a perfect view of her pussy. "For as long as I want."

She puffs out a breath, her tits rising when her back arches again. "Lie back, baby," I tell her. "I'm going to be here a while."

67

Olivia

"How the heck are we blood?" Dom murmurs, just loud enough for me and Rhys to hear, but not Max. "This kid does not have an athletic bone in his body."

Max swings a foam bat at a foam ball atop a T-ball stand and misses completely.

"Oh my God," Dom groans.

I giggle, my head bouncing from the way Rhys's chest shakes with his own laughter.

It's a Saturday—almost an entire month since Rhys started staying with us, and we're on the back porch, watching Max attempt to show us how good he is at T-ball.

Dom's on the porch, manning the grill, and I'm sitting on the steps. One step above me, Rhys sits, his legs out on either side of me, his arm around my middle.

"You just gotta keep your eye on the ball," Dre, Dominic's best friend, calls out. He's sitting at the outdoor table on the porch, laptop in front of him. He and Dom are supposed to be working on a project together, but not much is getting done.

"Watch!" Max yells, and we all mumble the same response, but in different words.

"Yeah!"

"We are!"

"Go for it, bud!"

"You better hit it this time!"

That last one is Dom, of course.

Max swings again.

Misses again.

Only this time, he swings so hard, he spins with the bat, turns a full circle, and falls flat on his butt.

"Nice try," Rhys calls. "You'll get it next time!"

"The fuck he will," Dominic murmurs, and Rhys chuckles at that. Obviously, they've been getting along, and it's as much of a surprise to them as it is to everyone. Everyone but me. I always knew they would get along if they just put their bullshit aside, because regardless of all the petty pranks and drama—their hearts are the same. Pure. Loyal. *Good.*

I jump a little when a giant duffle bag lands just inside the fence, then relax when I see Oscar's head pop up from the other side, followed by the rest of him. He lands on the grass with a thud and loses balance, ends up on his side. Max goes up to him with his bat, starts beating him with it. "Yo!" Oscar laughs, but Max laughs louder.

"We have a door, you know?" I call out.

Oscar raises his arms, blocking the blows. "But it's not as fun!" he answers, then points to the side. "Look, a UFO!"

"UFO!" Max spins, his nose and gaze at the sky, and Oscar takes the opportunity to stand, picking up the duffel before joining us on the porch. He dumps it beside Rhys, bowing and saying, "Your clothes, as requested, your Highness."

Rhys says, "Thanks," right before he shoves him off the steps. From what Rhys has told me, he's been back to the house a few times to see his parents, who go back and forth between here and Colorado. They're still looking for a new house, but the market hasn't been all that great around here, and since we've told Rhys he can stay for as long as he wants, they're taking the time to find the right property.

"What kind of clothes?" Dominic asks.

"Ask Oscar. He packed them."

Oscar zips open the bag, starts pulling out clothes, and suddenly, it's a free for all to see who wants what.

Three boys, fighting over clothes to steal.

I tilt me head all the way back to see Rhys's reaction, but he's too busy watching Max still looking for a UFO that doesn't exist.

I nudge him. "You see what's happening, right?"

He grasps my neck, tilting my head back even more, and kisses me longer than what's probably appropriate in front of an audience. He pulls away. Kisses me one last time. The shrugs. "It's just clothes, Cheeks."

"Is this Gucci?" Dom all but yells.

"Mrs. Garrett has a contact there. She gets a bunch of stuff for free. Give her your measurements and she'll take care of it," Oscar responds.

I turn to Rhys. "You didn't tell me that. I want clothes."

Another shrug from my boyfriend. "You talk to my mom more than I do. Give her your size. Max!"

I look over just in time to see Max turn to us.

"There's no UFO, buddy. Oscar was tricking you!"

"Speaking of tricking, you'll never fucking guess what Coach did," Oscar says.

"Swear jar!" Max yells.

"Dangit," Oscar spits, taking out his wallet. He pulls out a dollar, sets it on the floor beside him.

"What did your coach do?" Dom asks, obviously done with the clothes theft. Rhys's duffle is now empty, and Dom, Oscar and Dre have a pile of clothes each.

"He's making me go through tryouts."

Rhys shifts, facing Oscar. "That ain't right," he says, and I can hear the anger in his tone. He grasps a strand of my hair—twisting it between his fingers. *Keeps your hands busy, keeps the anxiety at bay.* Rhys quit coaching for a number of reasons. One: his heart was no longer in it, and two: he can't work there while dating a student. But, quitting his position also meant he couldn't be there for Oscar, so I know it was a tough decision to make. "You made varsity as a sophomore."

"No shit."

"Swear jar!" Max yells.

"Dangit!" Another dollar added to the pile later, Oscar continues. "I'm the only one he's making tryout, so I know it's personal.

Dom pipes up. "I made varsity as a freshman."

"I made varsity as a freshman," Oscar repeats, clearly mocking him.

Dom points a spatula at him. "I'ma throw your fucking hot dog in the trash."

"Swear jar!"

Dom groans.

"He's really making you try out?" Dre asks. "You're the best center St. Luke's has seen in decades."

"Thanks, and tell him that!"

"We'd kill for a decent center," Dre murmurs. "We've been subbing ours for the past two years, and they ain't shit."

"Swear jar!"

"Jesus," Dre sighs, lowers his voice. "You got to get this kid a fucking Venmo."

"Swear jar!"

"How the fuck can he hear us?" he snaps.

"Swear jar!"

Then, out of nowhere, Dominic says, thinking out loud, "You should move to Philips. You'd walk on the team."

"Ya think?" Oscar asks, as if he's actually contemplating it.

"We could definitely use you," Dre says. "Plus, our coach isn't an asshole."

"Swear jar!"

Dre gets to his feet, screams at the top of his lungs. "God fucking dammit!"

Everyone cracks up. Everyone but Max. "Double swear for using the Lord's name in vain!"

Dre sits back down. "I swear..." he mumbles under his breath.

"You should seriously think about it, though," Dom tells Oscar.

Oscar shakes his head. "I can't. Mrs. Garrett's already dropped a house deposit on my tuition at St. Luke's."

Rhys releases my hair. "If that's the only thing that's stopping you, then don't let it. She won't care. You know she just wants you to be happy."

I turn to look at Oscar. "You can't leave St. Luke's." I almost cry at the thought. "You're the only reason I make it through each day."

Dom grunts, "Say that shit again, Ollie, and I'm going to blow up that fucking school."

"Swear jar!"

"I mean, it's not *that* bad," I try to backpedal. The dumb pranks have stopped, and for the most part, so has the blatant name calling. Either that, or I'm just too busy keeping my head down to pay attention to it. During school hours, I don't speak unless necessary, and if I do, there are only two people my words are directed to— Oscar and Miss Turner. It's tough, sure, but I like Oscar said: *don't let them win.*

"You can go to Philips, too," Rhys says, turning me to him. "You never mentioned it before."

I shrug. "I didn't think it was an option for me."

"How fucking—" Dom starts.

"Swear jar!"

Dom continues, "—good would it be if we graduated together?"

A spark of hope ignites in my chest, but I push it down quickly. Mrs. Garrett covering Oscar so he can play ball is one thing, but there's no reason I can't stay at St. Luke's. Besides, "I like my sessions with Miss Turner."

Oscar scoffs. "Your boyfriend's her daughter's godfather. You can see her outside of school, you *dingbat.*"

"These dogs are ready," Dominic announces, and Max runs toward us while Dre and Oscar get to their feet.

"How much do I owe this six-year-old millionaire?" Dre asks.

Oscar laughs. "Doesn't matter," he says, rubbing Rhys's shoulders. "Garrett's got us, right?"

"Heck no," Rhys answers, his hand on my neck, tilting my head up again. "I got Liv, and only Liv." He presses his lips to mine.

"I didn't even swear!"

Rhys chuckles. "Exactly." Then he turns to Oscar. "You'd really want to play with Double D's?"

"Double D's?" Dre and Dom ask at the same time.

Rhys presses his lips tight while Oscar laughs. "Ask Rhys. He made it up."

My phone alerts me to a Venmo payment from Rhys with the description "Swear jar!" Then he gets up, looking between Dominic and Dre. "Because you're a pair of *tits*."

68

Rhys

If you'd ask me a year ago if I could ever picture myself sitting in the stands of the gym at Philips Academy, I would've laughed in your face and told you to go fuck yourself.

On the court, sure. I've done it plenty of times. But here? *Supporting* the Phantoms? Never.

Ever.

The volume in the gym doubles suddenly, and next to me, Max stands. "There's Dom!" He waves at his big brother, who just walked through the gym doors with his entire team behind him. "Over here!" Max yells.

Dom grins, waves back, and then makes his way over to us. Fist bumps for me, Max, Dad and Curtis, and kisses on the cheek for my mom, sister, and Belinda. Curtis and Belinda's daughters are here, too, but they're off doing cartwheels on the sidelines with a bunch of other kids. Next comes Dre, and then Oscar, and the rest of his team. They take up the entire row in front of us. Over the next few minutes, more and more people arrive, until the only room left in the gym is standing. I lean forward and ask Dom, "Is it always this packed?"

"No," he laughs, shaking his head.

Oscar turns to me, decked out in Phantom's gear. "He went up during assembly and threatened to throw state if the entire school didn't show up."

The moment I sit back, Max is right in my ear, whispering, "Did you bring the *thing*?"

I smile, whisper back. "We put it in your backpack before we left."

He's quick to unzip the side pocket of his backpack and reveal the beaded bracelet he'd spent all morning working on. Then he shoves Oscar and Dom forward and out of the way so he can squeeze past my legs and get to my sister on the other side of me. I scoot over so they can sit together. "I made you something," he tells her, hands behind his back.

Izzy gasps. "You did?"

He holds out his hands, palm up, then slowly unfurls his fingers.

"Maxy!" Izzy squeals. "I love it!" She takes the bracelet from him and slides it onto her wrist before hugging him. "Thank you!"

To say that Izzy and Max are *smitten* with each would be an under-statement, and yes, I'm incredibly jealous. Not that Izzy has found herself with a new little brother, but that I'm pretty sure Max likes her more than he likes me. Sad.

"I want one," Mom says, pouting.

"Me too," says Belinda.

"Me three," Dad tells him.

"I can make more!" Max exclaims and then music blares from the gym speakers—"Till I Collapse" by Eminem and Nate Dogg—and everyone's on their feet, cheering, and the cheers only get louder when the lights dim and the door to the locker rooms open. One by one, the players come out, dressed in Phantom's uniform—purple with black trim. Their names are announced, alongside their numbers, and I watch each one of them come through the doors, bouncing on my toes, and then swear, I could be standing next to a fighter jet and it wouldn't come close to the volume of the people around me when Olivia *Delgado* is announced. My girl runs onto the court as if she's done it a thousand times before. This is her first game in years, and she practically walked onto the team. Not because of her last name, but because she earned it.

After Dom dropped the idea of her and Oscar transferring to Philips, the seed was planted. Within days, Mom had made it happen, and when she gave Olivia her forms to sign, Olivia looked at her name and just... *hated* it. She hated that her last name linked her to someone who's had zero impact on her life, and so I told her she should change it. So she did.

Again, if you'd told me a year ago that I'd be sharing a bed with a Delgado, I would've *spat* in your face and told you to fuck yourself twice.

A lot can change in a year, or in my case, a few months.

"Let's go, Ollie!" Dom cheers, his hands cupped around his mouth. It's so loud that Liv hears it over the sound of everyone else, and her cheeks bloom pink as she shakes her head, then lifts her eyes just a tad to meet mine. Swear, my cheeks hurt with the force of my smile. "I love you," she mouths, and Oscar yells, "I love you, too, Ollie!"

The crowd settles while the opposing team comes out, and then a girl gets the microphone to sing the anthem. Before she can hand the mic back to the principal, Dom's rushing toward them, and the stands explode with just the sight of him.

"That's crazy," Izzy laughs.

"He's the James DeBron of the school!" Max tells her.

Dominic raises his hand, then slowly lowers it until the crowd goes quiet, and then it's just him, under the spotlight. He clears his throat, holding the microphone to his mouth. "There are two things in this world I'm sure of. Love and basketball," he says. "My sister, Ollie, introduced me to both."

The stadium fills with half *aaws* and half cheers, and I look over at Liv, expecting her to shy away from the attention, but she just stands there, her chin raised, hands by her side.

Dom adds, "Happy birthday, Ollie." And then he drops the mic, literally, and within minutes, I can't breathe. I thought the nerves and adrenaline *playing* were next level. It's nothing like watching my girl play. She's the shortest on the team, but she brings the type of fire and energy that's completely unmatched by any player on either team.

When she told me she wanted to try out, I told her I'd help train her, and I did, but *man*, I had no fucking clue how good she is... I mean, both she and Dom had mentioned it in the past, but I was not prepared. The girl's talents on the court are God-given, and I don't even believe in God. She'd told me she stopped playing to focus on her education, because she thought it would impress her *mother* more than basketball. It didn't. Also, did I mention I hate her mother, because I do.

Olivia gets checked from the side by a girl almost twice her size, and she drops to the floor, sliding across the hardwood, and swear, you've never seen grown-ass men get up so fast. Me, Dom, Dre, Oscar, Dad, Curtis... we're all on our feet, yelling and holding each other back. Olivia's slow to get up, dust herself off, and walk away, her eyes on her opponent the entire time. "Oh shit," Dom chuckles. "I know that look."

Liv scores the next twelve points, and after each one, she *winks* at her opponent.

"I think I'm in love," one of Dom's teammates says, holding a hand to his heart.

Dom laughs. "You'll have to get through Garrett first, then me..."

"Then me!" Max growls, thumping the guy on the back of the head.

"Fuck," he spits.

"Swear jar!" yells *everyone.*

69

Rhys

After the win, we celebrate Liv's birthday in a private room at Pino's. My family, her family, and all the extended family we've picked up along the way. My parents gift her with something I didn't even know they'd been working on—guardianship papers for Max and a check from her mother equaling the amount she'd stolen from Olivia all those years ago.

According to them, Dad hired a private investigator to find Liv's mother, and when they did, they threatened legal action for child abandonment unless she did exactly what they wanted—what Liv deserves. She folded, as anyone under the wrath of my mother would. The lawyers had drawn up different papers depending on how Liv and Dom wanted to go about his guardianship, and it's something they'll discuss later, in private. The money was great, Liv said, but it's nothing compared to the gift of not having to worry about Max's future anymore. She cried, as we all expected her to, and then everyone else joined in, because how could you not? After everything she'd been through and the fears she'd had to face, her family's stability was the greatest gift anyone could give her.

. . .

Now, it's just her and me, in my car, and she turns to me. "Do you need to get something from your parents' house?"

"No." My parents still own the house I grew up in, and it's fine. My mom and dad schedule who is where, when, making sure that at least one of them is with me or my sister most of the time. Izzy and her boyfriend fly down more often now, because—as she puts it—she loves "her new found family." She and Liv get along great, but she and Max— they can nerd out together for hours. Max has spent the night at the house a few times, mainly to build LEGOs with my dad and try out new cake recipes for my mom, and the boys and I go there often to use the gym and pool. I didn't realize when I told Dad I didn't want to live there that it had nothing to do with the house. I just didn't want to be away from Liv. And I haven't been.

I've spent every night with her, and Dom and Max don't seem to mind it. Granted, I've only been there just over a month. I do what I can around the house, and I'm now part of the dinner cooking—or in my case, *ordering*—schedule. And since I'm a lot more flexible with my time, I can hang out with Max and pick him up from school when Dom and Liv are busy. I even bought the safest car seat on the market, so we didn't have to keep transferring one over.

I'm working with my dad more, doing what I would've been doing had I moved to Colorado. But mainly, I'm focusing on the building I purchased. I have big plans for it, starting with giving Belinda an office she deserves. I can't wait to see it come to life.

"So, where are we going?" Liv asks, pulling me from my thoughts.

I shake my head, continue to drive. "You recognize this street?"

She groans. "You're never going to let me forget, are you?"

"Nope."

"I tapped you with the truck, Garrett."

"No, you crashed into me with a Boeing 747, causing my body to fly a million feet in the air! By the time I landed, I was dismembered from limb to limb. Torso. Two legs. One arm." I glance at her, smiling when I see her laughing silently. "I'm still looking for my other arm."

"And your head."

"Oh, yeah. That, too."

"Where are we going?" she almost squeals, and I chuckle.

"You'll see."

* * *

In under a minute I'm driving past my parents' house and entering a property two doors down, on the opposite side of the road. I pass the gates and make my way toward a house with a light brick facade and dark brown doors and shutters illuminated by ground lights. Liv sits higher in her seat to get a better look. "What's this?"

I stop at the end of the driveway, just outside the garage. "Remember how my parents were waiting for the perfect house for me to live in?"

Her gaze shifts to mine. "They bought this for you?"

"Yeah..." I watch her, gauging her reaction, my stomach dropping a little when she doesn't seem all that excited. "I mean, it's not as extravagant as theirs, I know, but wait till you see the view."

I get out of the car and wait for her to do the same. The brick driveway goes all the way to the front door, with only a few steps up to the house. Liv hesitates at the bottom of the stairs, her eyes narrowed. "You don't want to see it?"

She blinks, as if coming to. "Of course I do."

I open the door and wait for her to step inside. "It's a little outdated," I tell her. "So I want to do a few upgrades, but the layout is perfect, and bones are solid." The house has floorboards throughout, and it's empty, so my voice and our footsteps echo around us. I show her upstairs first, the bedrooms and bathrooms, the entire time watching her, waiting for a reaction. So far, *nothing*, and so I take her back down to the kitchen and living areas, and still... not even a smile or beat of excitement. "This is the best part," I say, flicking on the outdoor lights. The pool lights up, and I keep my eyes on her as she steps outside. I ask, confused and a little crestfallen, "What do you think?"

"It's nice," she says.

Nice. That's all I get? "Like I said, it's not as big or flashy as my parents' house, but none of the houses lakeside are."

"There's a lake?" she asks, her tone flat.

"Yeah." I sigh, then slip off my shoes. I sit at the edge of the pool, facing the lake that's currently invisible through the darkness. "I should've brought you here during the day so you could see it."

Liv slips off her shoes, and joins me, our legs knee-deep in the water. She hugs my arm to her chest, rests her head on it. "I'm sure it's beautiful, Rhys."

"Then what's wrong?" I ask, turning to her.

She looks up. "What do you mean?"

"I don't get it." I shake my head, my heart heavy, and try not to let my disappointment show when I add, "Dominic said you'd love the place."

"You showed him?"

"I brought him through yesterday... He thought you'd be excited, not... I don't know... You're acting like you hate it."

"I don't hate it," she's quick to say, holding my arm tighter. She goes back to looking over the pool and into the darkness. "I've just gotten so used to sleeping beside you every night. I don't know how I'm going to feel when you move out."

I pull away to glare at her, eyebrows drawn, because she can't be serious. "Liv..."

Her eyes meet mine. "What?"

"This is for *us* to live in."

She looks mad. "*What?*"

I backpedal. "Dominic said you didn't have any emotional attachment to your house—"

"Rhys!"

"Hear me out!" I'm almost shouting now. "You can keep the house, rent it out for additional income. And I know it's only a four-car garage, and we already have three cars—"

"Three?"

"Well, until Dom goes to Indiana!" I rush out, then add before she can say anything more, "But there's this massive storage room in my building that has roller door access, so I was thinking of converting that into a workshop for you—you'll easily fit all your tools and furniture —*if* you want to keep doing that. You don't have to. You can do whatever you want. And Max—I was thinking he can have the two rooms upstairs, you know, the adjoining ones with the Jack and Jill bathroom. He can have one for his bed and the other can be his little creator space with his LEGOs and stuff. And my parents are literally two houses over, so you know... they can come over to babysit, and oh! I forgot to mention—my dad and sister asked if they could take Max to NASA. I was thinking we could all go, and the boys and I could catch a Rockets game. You, too, of course. And I checked—it's the same distance from here to Philips as your house now, so it won't be inconvenient. And Dom, he can have the basement apartment. *Fuck.* I didn't even show you the basement. But he loved it when I showed him. And it doesn't have to be forever; it can just be for now. Or until Dominic gets that NBA contract. I know you're not sure what will happen then—if you'll move with him or stay here so Max can stay at Philips—but it's whatever. I'm flexible. I can work anywhere. Go wherever you go. And I know you're not thinking about college right now, but if you decide that's something you want to do, then... Why are you crying?"

She drops her face in her hands, her shoulders shaking with the force of her sobs.

I hold her to me. "I'm sorry," I tell her, my chest tight. "I should've asked first, but I thought the surprise would be better." I scoff at myself. "Happy birthday, I guess..."

She lifts her head just so she can glare at me. "Rhys!"

I cower an inch. "Sorry."

"Where is your phone?"

"What?"

She puts her hand out between us. "Phone."

I give her my phone and the PIN in case she'd forgotten it, and if she's pissed about something that might be in there, then I'm safe. I ain't got shit to hide. But she doesn't look at the phone. She just sets it beside her, next to hers, and the next thing I know she throws her arms around my neck, then... throws herself in the pool, taking me with her.

I'm so shocked by the move that I take longer to get my bearings than she does, and by the time I come up for air, she's been waiting for me, and she's laughing, and swear, every inch of tension that had been inside me dissipates with the sound. I grab her around the waist and let her wrap her legs around my middle, her arms around my neck.

"Is that a yes?" I ask, leading us back to the edge.

"Yes!" She kisses me, taking all my insecurities with her, and when she's done, she pulls away, saying, "Just so we're clear, this has nothing to do with the house."

"No?"

She shakes her head. "I'd be happy to live where we are now, but I've just... I've been wanting to ask you what your plans are, but I didn't want to come across as too needy."

"Needy? Have you met me, Cheeks?"

"I think you highly underestimate how many times you saved me, too, and sure, I may not have had a loaded gun, but... I didn't need it. I was barely surviving, let alone *living*."

I pout, then lead her out of the pool. "Wait here," I say once we're out, and I go into the house to retrieve the towels and spare clothes I'd prepared earlier. When I'm back out, I wrap the towel around her shivering body and hold her close. "I figured we'd end up in the pool one way or another, so I prepared."

"I love that about you," she says, sitting on the edge of the pool again.

I match her position. "What do you mean?"

"You take care of us."

"So do you," I say and then stay quiet while I gather my thoughts. Belinda says it's important to have the conversation *before* the commitment, though she was sure it would be okay. But still—the conversation was important. "Liv, I—" I clear the knot in my throat. "I don't want you to feel like moving in here means that you can't just up and leave for your own happiness. That's why I think it's important you keep that house." A deep ache forms in my chest at the thought of her leaving. It would be unbearable, sure, but it's also possible. Nothing about our relationship is fairytale. No happily ever after is guaranteed. "And as much as I'm working on me and I'm doing better, it doesn't mean that there won't be moments of darkness, or weakness, and when that comes, you need to promise me not to take it personally. And you need to promise that if it gets too much, you'll walk away."

"Rhys..." She wipes her eyes with the corner of the towel. "I promise not to take it personally, but I can't promise that I'll walk away..." She faces me, those muddy brown eyes right on mine. "You know what my favorite lines are from *The Count of Monte Cristo*?"

I smile to one side. "Tell me."

She giggles, getting to her feet and putting on a performance, using her towel as a cape. "*Life is a storm, young friend!*" she announces, then tugs on my arm until I'm standing with her. "And when that storm comes, my *love,* I will hold your hand..." She grins from ear to ear, then takes my hand in hers, guiding me to face the darkness. "... and we will face it together, and we'll yell..." She faces me. "Are you ready?"

I inhale a sharp breath, let it out slowly. "I'm ready."

She squares her shoulders, and I find myself doing the same. Then, because she's read the book almost as many times I have, she recites The Count word for word. "*Do your worst...*" she yells into the darkness, and then we face the symbolic storms ahead of us, hand in hand, and together we shout, "*for I will do mine!*"

EPILOGUE

Olivia

"What the hell are you doing?" Rhys murmurs, and I'm quick to lock my phone, hide it under my pillow.

Face smeared into his bicep, he chuckles. "If I didn't know exactly what you were doing on that phone, I'd assume you were cheating on me." He flips to his back. "What time is it?"

"Um..."

"Cheeks..."

"Three."

"Jesus," he sighs. "You've got to be up for school soon, and don't think I didn't see your coach yelling at you at practice earlier."

I grimace. "You saw that?"

"Yes, and she's right. You've been draggin' ass the past two weeks."

I gasp. "I have not."

He groans. "Alexa, sex lights."

A low glow fills the room. Just enough to see, but not enough that we'd cower when they turn on.

Rhys sits up, stretching his back, and have I mentioned how much I love his back... the way the muscles ripple when he moves. "Show me," he says, half turning to me, hand out between us.

"Show you what?" I ask, feigning innocence.

He rolls his eyes. "Your phone, Cheeks."

If squee was a sound, I just made it. I grab my phone from under my pillow and practically jump on his lap. He doesn't complain that I've woken him in the middle of the night. Isn't irritated by my excitement even though he's half asleep. He just sits there, one hand stroking my leg, while the other twirls a strand of my hair, and I show him picture after picture of the things I want to do in the new house.

It's been the same every night for the past two weeks, ever since he showed it to me. I try to sleep, but all I can think about are all the things I want to do with it, furniture, finishings, all of it. There were some immediate things he and his parents wanted to get done—like updating the security, the hardware, and the basement kitchen and bathroom, as well as redoing the dock to our part of *the lake*. Pinch me, because I'm dreaming, right?

Only I'm not.

And I know it's not technically *mine*, but Rhys is, so it's mine by association.

Anyway, because of the work in the house, we waited to move in until this weekend.

"So we're keeping the exposed beams?" he asks.

I look at him, disgusted that he would even think otherwise.

"Sorry," he chuckles, then lifts me up and off of him.

I watch him go into the bathroom, then I go back to scrolling on Pinterest, only looking up when the door opens again. I wait for him to get back into bed so I can bore him with more of my ramblings but, instead, he slips on some clothes and his shoes, then grabs his keys. One hand on the door to the garage, he asks, "Are you coming?"

With a heavy sigh, I climb out of bed, throw on one of his hoodies and slip my feet into slides. "One day," I tell him, "I'm going to actually say no when you ask me that."

. . .

I don't know where we're going, but then again, the destination hardly matters when it comes to Rhys. I'm just happy to be on the ride.

He drives us to the hospital.

The emergency room entrance to be exact.

After he finds a spot and puts his SUV in park, I tell him, "You don't have to admit me."

"What?"

"I'm not clinically insane," I answer, wide-eyed. "So maybe I'm a little obsessed with the house, but can you blame me?"

Rhys chuckles, a deep sound that forms in his gut, and I wish I could bottle it. He reaches up, pinches both my cheeks, and I shove his hands away. "Come on, my little nutjob."

He's holding my hand in the middle of the waiting room and pointing to an empty seat. "That's the one," he says.

I look up at him. "Maybe you need to be committed."

"That's the one," he repeats, motioning to the seat. "That's the exact one you were sitting in the first night we met in person."

I look from the chair, to him, a slow smile spreading across my lips. "It is," I say, releasing his hand so I can sit down. I look around the space. It's quieter now than it was back then, with hardly any patients waiting to be seen.

"Max was here," I murmur, pointing to the two chairs beside me. "And I remember you asked the nurses for a blanket for him and covered him up. I thought you were so sweet."

Rhys nods, still standing in front of me. "What else did you think about me that night?"

"That you were cocky as hell, but you kind of had every right to be, considering how hot you were. I mean, I'd seen you before," I say, lowering my gaze. Shame heats my cheeks, but I don't hold back. "I'd looked up pictures of you, seen you play against Dominic, and watched videos of you."

"So, technically, you stalked me first, huh?"

I shrug, laugh under my breath. "I guess."

He sits down beside me. "I sat here that night," he murmurs. "So many empty seats and I chose the one next to yours."

I smile, getting lost in the memories. "Your arm kept brushing against mine."

"A hundred percent on purpose," he says, and I face him, eyebrows raised in question. He simply nods. "That's why I sat so close. It happened once in the truck, and there was something about your touch. About our connection." He laughs, almost embarrassed. "That's why I asked you to hang out with me. I... couldn't get enough of you then, and I still can't now."

"I feel the same," I admit, "and I don't think that's ever changing."

Rhys nods, agreeing, and for a long moment, we sit in silence, lost in our thoughts. Our emotions. "If it wasn't in the contract with my mom—would you have wanted to meet me in person? Because I asked once, and you never acknowledged reading it."

I swallow my nerves. "Of course, I *wanted* to, but..."

"But what?"

"I don't know," I say shrugging. "I was scared."

"Of *me*?"

"No," I'm quick to say, facing him again. "I was scared that reality wouldn't live up to the fantasy, I guess."

"Like I wouldn't live up to the image you had of me in your head."

"You forget I knew who you were, Rhys. I knew who you were through that phone, and I knew who you were to the rest of the world. I knew how your mom saw you, and your peers, your teammates... your *enemies*. That wasn't the problem..."

Rhys inhales a sharp breath, lets it out in a sigh. "So, what was it?"

"Me," I admit, focusing on my lap. "I was scared that I didn't live up to your expectations of me. Of *Mercedes*."

"Babe..." he says, laughing once, but then he must notice my discomfort, my insecurities, because he puts his arm around me, pulling me closer. Finger to my chin, he guides my head up. He's a blur beyond my tears, and he waits until they fall before wiping them away.

"I was so guarded when you met me, for obvious reasons, but I was also a realist. I had come to terms with being alone. At least for a while. I mean, who would want to be with a girl in my position? At the minimum, I'm going to be sharing the responsibility of raising Max until he's eighteen, and that doesn't—"

"Matter," Rhys cuts in. "At least to me."

I sniff back my emotions. "I didn't know that then."

"But you know it now, right?"

I nod, certain. "I do."

He kisses me—the type that clears my mind, dries my eyes of the tears that had been living there. The type of kiss that steals my breath and renders me speechless.

His thumbs stroke my cheeks when he pulls away, and he smiles, his eyes bright against the overhead lights. The same lights that cast a shadow across his features, highlighting the tiny scars on his face. I press my mouth to the one on his lips. Just once. Just so he knows that I love every part of him—scars and all. "I love you," I tell him.

"I love you, too," he says, then releases me to sit all the way back in his chair, getting comfortable as he stares ahead.

I rest my head on his shoulder and let minutes of silence pass before my curiosity gets the best of me. "Rhys?"

"Yeah?"

"What are we doing here?"

He eyes me sideways, his smile restrained. "Check under your chair, Cheeks."

I hesitate a beat, confused, then do as he says.

Taped to the underside of my chair is a rectangle package wrapped in brown paper. It's obviously a book, but—

"You can unwrap it," he says, but I just hold it instead.

"How did you even—"

"Unwrap it, Cheeks."

Again, I do as he says.

It's a copy of *The Count of Monte Cristo*, but... it's not any of the ones I've seen on his shelf before. This one is a small format paperback, so worn that it may as well live in an under-funded public library. I run my fingers over the cover, then the spine—so faded from being open and closed too many times. There's a stain on the top, a dark brown, and my eyes immediately go to his. "Is this..."

Rhys nods. "It's the one Curtis gave me when I was in juvie," he confirms. "They let me take it with me when I left."

"Rhys..."

"Besides Curtis, it's the only thing that saved me while I was in there. And it's only fitting that you have it, considering you're the only thing that saved me once I was out."

Tears fill my eyes again, overflow and land on the book in my possession.

"It's bookmarked," he tells me, and I flip the book up to see where it's marked. Slowly, carefully, I open the pages, already expecting what quote he's marked.

I gasp.

Out loud.

My hand coming to my mouth.

Not because of the words highlighted on the page:

Wait and Hope.

But the words written beneath.

I'm done waiting and hoping...

And underneath that, sitting where the pages have been cut to create a hole just big enough... is a ring...

The ring.

"You asked me before what we were doing here," he says, and I force myself to take a breath before turning to him. He takes my trembling hands in his, kissing the tips of my fingers before sliding the ring where it belongs. "I wanted us to be exactly where we were when my life changed forever. We were right here when I asked you for your name, and you said it was Olivia... but all I heard was *Liv*... and every day since, that's all I've wanted to do... *Live.*"

The end

. . .

If this story was your first time meeting Rhys, you can read more of him
pre-Olivia in the Heartache Duet.

ALSO BY JAY MCLEAN

Sign up to Jay McLean's Newsletter

Visit Jay McLean's Website

See all Jay McLean books on Amazon & Kindle Unlimited

See Jay McLean on Goodreads

Jay McLean books on BookBub

ABOUT THE AUTHOR

 Jay McLean is an international best-selling author and full-time reader, writer of New Adult and Young Adult romance, and skilled procrastinator. When she's not doing any of those things, she can be found running after her three boys, investing way too much time on True Crime Documentaries and binge-watching reality TV.

She writes what she loves to read, which are books that can make her laugh, make her hurt and make her feel.

Jay lives in the suburbs of Melbourne, Australia, in her dream home where music is loud and laughter is louder.

Connect With Jay
www.jaymcleanauthor.com
jay@jaymcleanauthor.com

Made in the USA
Coppell, TX
12 April 2024

31147922R00208